John Vanbrugh

The Provok'd Wife

John Vanbrugh

The Provok'd Wife

ISBN/EAN: 9783743388987

Manufactured in Europe, USA, Canada, Australia, Japa

Cover: Foto ©Andreas Hilbeck / pixelio.de

Manufactured and distributed by brebook publishing software (www.brebook.com)

John Vanbrugh

The Provok'd Wife

THE
PROVOK'D WIFE.

A COMEDY,

As written by Sir JOHN VANBURGH.

DISTINGUISHING ALSO THE

VARIATIONS OF THE THEATRE,

AS PERFORMED AT THE

𝕿heatre-𝕽oyal in 𝕯rury-𝕷ane.

Regulated from the Prompt-Book,

By PERMISSION *of the* MANAGERS,

By Mr. HOPKINS, Prompter.

LONDON:

Printed for JOHN BELL, near *Exeter-Exchange*, in the *Strand*.

MDCCLXXVII.

PROLOGUE.

SINCE 'tis th' intent and bufinefs of the ftage,
   To copy out the follies of the age ;
To hold to ev'ry man a faithful glafs,
And fhew him of what fpecies he's an afs,
I hope the next that teaches in the fchool,
Will fhew our author he's a fcribbling fool :
And that the fatire may be fure to bite,
Kind Heav'n, infpire fome venom'd prieft to write, }
And grant fome ugly lady may indite ;
For I would have him lafh'd, by Heav'n, I would,
Till his prefumption fwam away in blood.
Three plays at once proclaim a face of brafs ;
No matter what they are, that's not the cafe, }
To write three plays, e'en that's to be an afs.
But what I leaft forgive, he knows it too ;
For to his coft he lately has known you.
Experience fhews, to many a writer's fmart,
You hold a court where mercy ne'er had part ;
So much of the old ferpent's fting you have,
You love to damn, as Heav'n delights to fave.
In foreign parts, let a bold volunteer,
For public good, upon the ftage appear, }
He meets ten thoufand fmiles to diffipate his fear.
All tickle on th' adventuring young beginner,
And only fcourge the incorrigible finner ;
They touch indeed his faults, but with a hand
So gentle, that his merits ftill may ftand ;
Kindly they bury the follies of his pen,
That he may fhun them when he writes again.
But 'tis not fo in this good-natur'd town ;
All's one, an ox, a poet, or a crown ; }
Old England's play, was always knocking down.

A 2

DRA-

DRAMATIS PERSONÆ.

MEN.

	Drury-Lane.	*Covent-Garden.*
Conſtant,	Mr. Brereton.	Mr. Wroughton.
Heartfree,	Mr. Benſley.	Mr. Smith.
Sir John Brute,	Mr. Garrick.	Mr. Macklin.
Lord Rake, a companion to *Sir John,*	Mr. Davis.	Mr. Mahon.
Col. Bully, another,	Mr. Vernon.	Mr. Mattocks.
Razor, Valet de Chambre to *Sir John,*	Mr. Baddeley.	Mr. Quick.
Juſtice of the Peace,	Mr. Branſby.	Mr. Thompſon.

WOMEN.

	Drury-Lane.	*Covent-Garden.*
Lady Brute,	Miſs Younge.	Mrs. Bulkely.
Belinda,	Mrs. Greville.	Miſs Leeſon.
Lady Fancyful,	Mrs. Abington.	Mrs. Mattocks.
Mademoiſelle,	Mrs. Bradſhaw.	Mrs. Green.
Cornet, Servant to *Lady Fancyful,*		

Conſtable and Watch.

THE
PROVOK'D WIFE.

⁎ *The lines diſtinguiſhed by inverted commas, ' thus,' are omitted in the representation.*

ACT I.

SCENE, Sir John Brute's *Houſe*.

Enter Sir John.

Sir John.

WHAT cloying meat is love, when matrimony's the ſauce to it!—Two years marriage has debauch'd my five ſenſes. Every thing I ſee, every thing I hear, every thing I feel, every thing I ſmell, and every thing I taſte, methinks, has wife in't. No boy was ever ſo weary of his tutor, no girl of her bib, no nun of doing penance, or old maid of being chaſte, as I am of being married. Sure there's a ſecret curſe entailed upon the very name of wife. My lady is a young lady, a fine lady, a witty lady, a virtuous lady——and yet I hate her. There is but one thing on earth I loath beyond her, and that's fighting. Would my courage come up to a fourth part of my ill-nature, I'd ſtand buff to her relations, and thruſt her out of doors. But marriage has ſunk me down to ſuch an ebb of reſolution, I dare not draw my ſword, tho' even to get rid of my wife. But here ſhe comes.

Enter Lady Brute.

Lady Brute. Do you dine at home to-day, Sir John?

Sir John. Why, do you expect I ſhould tell you what I don't know myſelf?

Lady Brute. I thought there was no harm in aſking you.

Sir John. If thinking wrong were an excuſe for imper-

A 3

tinence,

tinence, women might be juſtified in moſt things they ſay or do.

Lady Brute. I'm ſorry I have ſaid any thing to diſpleaſe you.

Sir John. Sorry for things paſt, is of as little importance to me, as my dining at home or abroad ought to be to you.

Lady Brute. My enquiry was only that I might have provided what you liked.

Sir John. Six to four you had been in the wrong there again ; for what I liked yeſterday I don't like to-day, and what I like to-day, 'tis odds I mayn't like to-morrow.

Lady Brute. But if I had aſked you what you liked—

Sir John. Why, then there would be more aſking about it than the thing is worth.

Lady Brute. I wiſh I did but know how I might pleaſe you.

Sir John. Aye ; but that ſort of knowledge is not a wife's talent.

Lady Brute. Whate'er my talent is, I'm ſure my will has ever been to make you eaſy.

Sir John. If women were to have their wills, the world would be finely govern'd.

Lady Brute. What reaſon have I given you to uſe me as you do of late ? It once was otherwiſe : you married me for love.

Sir John. And you me for money : ſo you have your reward, and I have mine.

Lady Brute. What is it that diſturbs you ?

Sir John. A parſon.

Lady Brute. Why, what has he done to you ?

Sir John. He has married me, and be damn'd to him.

[Exit.

Lady Brute. The devil's in the fellow, I think——I was told before I married him, that thus 'twould be ; but I thought I had charms enough to govern him ; and that where there was an eſtate, a woman muſt needs be happy : ſo my vanity has deceived me, and my ambition has made me uneaſy. But there's ſome comfort ſtill ; if one would be revenged of him, theſe are good times ; a woman may have a gallant, and a ſeparate maintenance too——The ſurly puppy !——Yet he's a fool for it ; for hitherto he

has

has been no monster : but who knows how far he may provoke me ? I never loved him, yet I have been ever true to him ; and that, in spite of all the attacks of art and nature upon a poor weak woman's heart, in favour of a tempting lover. Methinks, so noble a defence as I have made, should be rewarded with a better usage——Or who can tell——Perhaps a good part of what I suffer from my husband, may be a judgment upon me for my cruelty to my lover——But hold—let me go no further—I think I have a right to alarm this surly brute of mine ; but if I know my heart, it will never let me go so far as to injure him.

Enter Belinda.

Lady Brute. Good-morrow, dear cousin.

Bel. Good-morrow, Madam. You look pleased this morning.

Lady Brute. I am so.

Bel. With what, pray ?

Lady Brute. With my husband.

Bel. Drown husbands ! for yours is a provoking fellow. As he went out just now, I prayed him to tell me what time of day 'twas ; and he asked me if I took him for the church-clock, that was obliged to tell all the parish.

Lady Brute. He has been saying some good obliging things to me too. In short, Belinda, he has used me so barbarously of late, that I could almost resolve to play the downright wife—and cuckold him.

Bel. That would be downright, indeed.

Lady Brute. Why, after all, there is more to be said for it than you'd imagine, child. He is the first aggressor, not I.

Bel. Ah, but you know we must return good for evil.

Lady Brute. That may be a mistake in the translation. Pr'ythee, be of my opinion, Belinda ; for I'm positive I'm in the right ; and if you'll keep up the prerogative of a woman, you'll likewise be positive you are in the right, whenever you do any thing you have a mind to. But I shall play the fool, and jest on, till I make you begin to think I'm in earnest.

Bel. I shan't take the liberty, Madam, to think of any thing that you desire to keep a secret from me.

Lady

Lady Brute. Alas, my dear, I have no secrets! My heart could never yet confine my tongue.

Bel. Your eyes, you mean; for I am sure I have seen them gadding, when your tongue has been locked up safe enough.

Lady Brute. My eyes gadding! Pr'ythee, after whom, child?

Bel. Why, after one that thinks you hate him as much as I know you love him.

Lady Brute. Constant, you mean.

Bel. I do so.

Lady Brute. Lord, what should put such a thing into your head?

Bel. That which puts things into most people's heads, observation.

Lady Brute. Why, what have you observed, in the name of wonder?

Bel. I have observed you blush when you met him; force yourself away from him; and then be out of humour with every thing about you. In a word, never was a poor creature so spurred on by desire, or so reined in with fear!

Lady Brute. How strong is fancy!

Bel. How weak is woman!

Lady Brute. Pr'ythee, niece, have a better opinion of your aunt's inclination.

Bel. Dear aunt, have a better opinion of your niece's understanding.

Lady Brute. You'll make me angry.

Bel. You'll make me laugh.

Lady Brute. Then you are resolved to persist?

Bel. Positively.

Lady Brute. And all I can say——

Bel. Will signify nothing.

Lady Brute. Tho' I should swear 'twere false——

Bel. I should think it true.

Lady Brute. Then let us forgive; [*Kissing her.*] for we have both offended: I, in making a secret; you, in discovering it.

Bel. Good-nature may do much: but you have more reason to forgive one, than I have to pardon t'other.

Lady Brute. 'Tis true, Belinda, you have given me so

many

many proofs of your friendſhip, that my reſerve has been indeed a crime. ' But, that you may more eaſily forgive ' me, remember, child, that when our nature prompts ' us to a thing our honour and religion have forbid us, ' we would (wer't poſſible) conceal, even from the ſoul ' itſelf, the knowledge of the body's weakneſs.

' *Bel.* Well, I hope, to make your friend amends, ' you'll hide nothing from her for the future, tho' the ' body ſhould ſtill grow weaker and weaker.

' *Lady Brute.* No, from this moment I have no more ' reſerve;' and as a proof of my repentance, I own, Belinda, I'm in danger. ' Merit and wit aſſault me from ' without, nature and love ſolicit me within; my huſ- ' band's barbarous uſage piques me to revenge; and Sa- ' tan, catching the fair occaſion, throws in my way that ' vengeance, which of all vengeance, pleaſes woman beſt.

' *Bel.* 'Tis well Conſtant don't know the weakneſs of ' the fortification; for, o' my conſcience, he'd ſoon ' come on to the aſſault.

' *Lady Brute.* Ay, and I'm afraid, carry the town too.' But whatever you may have obſerved, I have diſſembled ſo well as to keep him ignorant. So you ſee I'm no co- quet, Belinda; ' and if you follow my advice, you'll ne- ' ver be one neither. 'Tis true, coquetry is one of the ' main ingredients in the natural compoſition of a woman; ' and I, as well as others, could be well enough pleaſed ' to ſee a crowd of young fellows ogling, and glancing, ' and watching all occaſions to do forty fooliſh officious ' things; nay, ſhould ſome of them puſh on even to ' hanging or drowning—why—faith—if I ſhould let ' pure woman alone, I ſhould e'en be but too well pleaſed ' with it.

' *Bel.* I'll ſwear 'twould tickle me ſtrangely.

' *Lady Brute.* But after all, 'tis a vicious practice in ' us to give the leaſt encouragement, but where we deſign ' to come to a concluſion:' for 'tis an unreaſonable thing to engage a man in a diſeaſe, which we before-hand re- ſolve we will never apply a cure to.

Bel. 'Tis true; but then a woman muſt abandon one of the ſupreme bleſſings of her life. For I am fully con- vinced, no man has half that pleaſure in gallanting a miſtreſs, as a woman has in jilting a gallant.

Lady

Lady Brute. The happiest woman then on earth must be our neighbour.

Bel. Oh, the impertinent composition! She has vanity and affectation enough to make her a ridiculous original, and in spite of all that art and nature ever furnished to any of her sex before her.

Lady Brute. She concludes all men her captives; and whatever course they take, it serves to confirm her in that opinion.

Bel. If they shun her, she thinks 'tis modesty, and takes it for a proof of their passion.

Lady Brute. And if they are rude to her, 'tis conduct, and done to prevent town-talk.

' *Bel.* When her folly makes them laugh, she thinks
' they are pleased with her wit.

' *Lady Brute.* And when her impertinence makes them
' dull, concludes they are jealous of her favours.'

Bel. All their actions and their words, she takes for granted, aim at her.

Lady Brute. And pities all other women, because she thinks they envy her.

Bel. Pray, out of pity to ourselves, let us find a better subject, for I'm weary of this. Do you think your husband inclined to jealousy?

Lady Brute. Oh, no; he does not love me well enough for that. Lord, how wrong men's maxims are! They are seldom jealous of their wives, unless they are very fond of them; whereas, they ought to consider the women's inclinations, for there depends their fate. Well, men may talk; but they are not so wise as we——that's certain.

Bel. At least in our affairs.

Lady Brute. Nay, I believe we should out-do them in the business of the state too; for, methinks, they do and undo, and make but bad work on't.

Bel. Why then don't we get into the intrigues of government as well as they?

Lady Brute. Because we have intrigues of our own, that make us more sport, child. And so let's in and consider of them.   [*Exeunt.*

SCENE,

SCENE, *a Dressing-room.*

Enter Lady Fanciful, Mademoiselle, *and* Cornet.

Lady Fan. How do I look this morning?

Cor. Your Ladyship looks very ill, truly.

Lady Fan. Lard, how ill-natured thou art, Cornet! to tell me so, tho' the thing should be true. Don't you know that I have humility enough to be but too easily out of conceit with myself?—Hold the glass; I dare swear that will have more manners than you have——Mademoiselle, let me have your opinion too.

Mad. My opinion pe, Matam, dat your Ladyship never look so well in your life.

Lady Fan. Well, the French are the prettiest, obliging people: they say the most acceptable, well-mannered things——and never flatter.

Mad. Your Ladyship say great justice inteed.

Lady Fan. Nay, every thing's just in my house but Cornet. The very looking-glass gives her the *dementi.* But I'm almost afraid it flatters me, it makes me look so very engaging.   [*Looking affectedly in the glass.*

Mad. Inteed, Matam, your face pe handsomer than all de looking-glass in de world, *croyez moy.*

Lady Fan. But is it possible my eyes can be so languishing——and so very full of fire?

Mad. Matam, if de glass was burning-glass, I believe your eyes set de fire in de house.

Lady Fan. You may take that nightgown, Mademoisell—Get out of the room, Cornet; I can't endure you. This wench, methinks, does look so insufferably ugly.

Mad. Every ting look ugly, Matam, dat stand by your Ladyship.

Lady Fan. No, really, Mademoiselle, methinks you look mighty pretty.

Mad. Ah, Matam, de moon have no *eclat,* ven de sun appear.

Lady Fan. Oh, pretty expression! Have you ever been in love, Mademoiselle?

Mad. Ouy, Matam.   [*Sighing.*

Lady Fan. And were you beloved again?

Mad. No, Matam.   [*Sighing.*
Lady

4

Lady Fan. Oh, ye gods, what an unfortunate creature should I be in such a case! But nature has made me nice for my own defence—I'm nice, strangely nice, Mademoiselle. I believe, were the merit of whole mankind bestowed upon one single person, I should still think the fellow wanted something to make it worth my while to take notice of him—And yet I could love, nay, fondly love, were it possible to have a thing made on purpose for me: for I'm not cruel, Mademoiselle; I'm only nice.

Mad. Ah, Matam! I wish I was fine gentleman for your sake. I do all de ting in de world, to get a little way into your heart. I make song, I make verse, I give you de serenade, I give great many present to Mademoiselle; I no eat, I no sleep, I be lean, I be mad, I hang myself, I drown myself—*Ah, ma chere dame, que je vous aimerois!*
                                        [*Embracing her.*

Lady Fan. Well, the French have strange obliging ways with them; you may take those two pair of gloves, Mademoiselle.

Mad. Me humbly tank my sweet lady.
                    Enter Servant with a letter.

Ser. Madam, here's a letter for your Ladyship. [*Exit.*

Lady Fan. 'Tis thus I am importun'd every morning, Mademoiselle—Pray, how do the French ladies, when they are thus *acablées?*

Mad. Matam, dey never complain.——Au contraire, when one Frense lady have got a hundred lover, den she do all she can—to get a hundred more.

Lady Fan. Well let me die, they have *le goût bon.* For 'tis an unutterable pleasure to be adored by all the men, and envied by all the women—Yet, I'll swear, I'm concerned at the torture I give them. Lard! why was I formed to make the whole creation uneasy?—But let me read my letter—[*Reads.*]—" If you have a mind to hear of your faults, instead of being praised for your virtues, take the pains to walk in the Green-walk in St. James's Park, with your woman, an hour hence. You'll there meet one, who hates you for some things, as he could love you for others: and therefore is willing to endeavour your reformation——If you come to the place I mention, you'll know who I am; if you don't, you never shall: so take your choice."——This is strangely familiar,
                                        Mademoiselle!

Mademoiſelle! Now have I a provoking fancy to know who this impudent fellow is.

Mad. Den take your ſcarf and your maſk, and go to de rendezvous. De Frenſe laty do juſtement comme ça.

Lady Fan. Rendezvous! What, rendezvous with a man, Mademoiſelle?

Mad. Eh, pourquoy non?

Lady Fan. What, and a man perhaps I never ſaw in my life!

Mad. Tant mieux: c'eſt donc quelque choſe de nouveau.

Lady Fan. Why, how do I know what deſigns he may have? He may intend to raviſh me, for aught I know.

Mad. Raviſh!—Bagatelle. I would fain ſee one impudent rogue raviſh Mademoiſelle. Oui, je le voudrois.

Lady Fan. Oh, but my reputation, Mademoiſelle, my reputation; ah, ma chere reputation!

Mad. Matam——Quand on l'a une fois perdus——on n'en eſt plus embarraſſée.

Lady Fan. Fie, Mademoiſelle, fie; reputation is a jewel.

Mad. Qui coute bien chere, Matam.

Lady Fan. Why ſure you would not ſacrifice your honour to your pleaſure!

Mad. Je ſuis philoſophe.

Lady Fan. Bleſs me, how you talk! Why, what if honour be a burden, Madememoiſelle, muſt it not be borne?

Mad. Chaqu'un à ſa façon——Quand quelque choſe m'incommode, moi——je m'en defais, vite.

Lady Fan. Get you gone, you little naughty Frenchwoman you: I vow and ſwear I muſt turn you out of doors, if you talk thus.

Mad. Turn me out of doors!——turn yourſelf out of doors, and go ſee what de gentleman have to ſay to you —Tenez. Voilà [*Giving her her things haſtily.*] votre eſharp, voilà votre coife, voilà votre maſque, voilà tout. Hey, Mercure, coquin: call one chair for Matam, and one oder [*Calling within.*] for me. Va-t'en, vite. [*Turning to her lady, and helping her on haſtily with her things.*] Allons, Matam; depechez vous donc. Mon dieu, quelles ſcruples!

B

Lady

Lady Fan. Well, for once, Mademoiselle, I'll follow your advice, out of the intemperate defire I have to know who this ill-bred fellow is. But I have too much delica-teffe to make a practice on't.

Mad. Belle chofe vraiment que la delicateffe, lors qu'il s'agit de divertir——à ça—Vous voilà équipée, partons.—Hé bien !—qu'avez vous donc?

Lady Fan. J'ai peur.

Mad. Je n'en ai point moï.

Lady Fan. I dare not go.

Mad. Demeurez donc.

Lady Fan. Je fuis poltronne.

Mad. Tant pis pour vous.

Lady Fan. Curiofity's a wicked devil.

Mad. C'eft une charmante fainte.

Lady Fan. It ruin'd our firft parents.

Mad. Elle a bien diverti leurs enfans.

Lady Fan. L'honneur eft contre.

Mad. Le plaifir eft pour.

Lady Fan. Muft I then go?

Mad. Muft you go?——muft you eat, muft you drink, muft you fleep, muft you live? De nature bid you do one, de nature bid you do toder. Vous me ferez enrager.

Lady Fan. But when reafon corrects nature, Mademoifelle.

Mad. Elle eft donc bien infolente, c'eft fa fœur ainée.

Lady Fan. Do you then prefer your nature to your reafon, Mademoifelle?

Mad. Oui da.

Lady Fan. Pourquoi?

Mad. Becaufe my nature make me merry, my reafon make me mad.

Lady Fan. Ah, la méchante Françoife !

Mad. Ah, la belle Angloife ! [*Forcing her lady off.*

END of the FIRST ACT.

ACT

A C T II.

SCENE, *St. James's Park*.

Enter Lady Fancyful *and* Mademoiselle.

LADY FANCYFUL.

WELL, I vow, Mademoiselle, I'm strangely impatient to know who this confident fellow is.

Enter Heartfree.

Look, there's Heartfree. But sure it can't be him: he's a professed woman-hater. Yet who knows what my wicked eyes may have done?

Mad. Il nous approche, Matam.

Lady Fan. Yes, 'tis he: now will he be most intolerably cavalier, though he should be in love with me.

Heart. Madam, I'm your humble servant; I perceive you have more humility and good-nature than I thought you had.

Lady Fan. What you attribute to humility and good-nature, Sir, may perhaps be only due to curiosity. I had a mind to know who 'twas had ill manners enough to write that letter.   [*Throwing him his letter.*

Heart. Well, and now I hope you are satisfied.

Lady Fan. I am so, Sir; good-by t'ye.

Heart. Nay, hold there; though you have done your business, I han't done mine: by your Ladyship's leave, we must have one moment's prattle together. Have you a mind to be the prettiest woman about town, or not? How she stares upon me! What! this passes for an impertinent question with you now, because you think you are so already.

Lady Fan. Pray, Sir, let me ask you a question in my turn: by what right do you pretend to examine me?

Heart. By the same right that the strong govern the weak, because I have you in my power; for you cannot get so quickly to your coach, but I shall have time enough to make you hear every thing I have to say to you.

Lady Fan. These are strange liberties you take, Mr. Heartfree.

Heart. They are so, Madam, but there's no help for it; for know that I have a design upon you.

                    Lady

Lady Fan. Upon me, Sir!

Heart. Yes; and one that will turn to your glory, and my comfort, if you will but be a little wiser than you use to be.

Lady Fan. Very well, Sir.

Heart. Let me see—Your vanity, Madam, I take to be about some eight degrees higher than any woman's in the town, let t'other be who she will; and my indifference is naturally about the same pitch. Now could you find the way to turn this indifference into fire and flame, me-thinks your vanity ought to be satisfied; and this, perhaps, you might bring about upon pretty reasonable terms.

Lady Fan. And pray at what rate would this indiffe-rence be bought off, if one should have so depraved an appetite to desire it?

Heart. Why, Madam, to drive a quaker's bargain, and make but one word with you, if I do part with it—you must lay down—your affectation.

Lady Fan. My affectation, Sir!

Heart. Why I ask you nothing but what you may very well spare.

Lady Fan. You grow rude, Sir. Come, Mademoiselle, it is high time to be gone.

Mad. Allons, allons, allons.

Heart. [*Stopping them.*] Nay, you may as well stand still; for hear me you shall, walk which way you please.

Lady Fan. What mean you, Sir?

Heart. I mean to tell you, that you are the most un-grateful woman upon earth.

Lady Fan. Ungrateful! to whom?

Heart. To nature.

Lady Fan. Why, what has nature done for me?

Heart. What you have undone by art! It made you handsome; it gave you beauty to a miracle, a shape without a fault, wit enough to make them relish, and so turned you loose to your own discretion; which has made such work with you, that you are become the pity of our sex, and the jest of your own. There is not a feature in your face, but you have found the way to teach it some affected convulsion; your feet, your hands, your very fingers' ends are directed never to move without some
ridi-

ridiculous air or other; and your language is a suitable trumpet, to draw people's eyes upon the raree-show.

Mad. [*Aside.*] Eſt-ce qu'on fait l'amour en Angleterre comme ça?

Lady Fan. [*Aside.*] Now could I cry for madneſs, but that I know he'd laugh at me for it.

Heart. Now do you hate me for telling you the truth, but that's becauſe you don't believe 'tis ſo; for were you once convinced of that, you'd reform, for your own ſake.

Lady Fan. Every circumſtance of nice breeding muſt needs appear ridiculous, to one who has ſo natural an antipathy to good-manners.

Heart. But ſuppoſe I could find the means to convince you, that the whole world is of my opinion.

Lady Fan. Sir, though you, and all the world you talk of, ſhould be ſo impertinently officious, as to think to perſuade me I don't know-how to behave myſelf; I ſhould ſtill have charity enough for my own underſtanding, to believe myſelf in the right, and all you in the wrong.

Mad. Le voilà mort.

[*Exeunt Lady* Fancyful *and* Mademoiſelle.

Heart. [*Gazing after her.*] There her ſingle clapper has publiſhed the ſenſe of the whole ſex. Well, this once I have endeavoured to waſh the black-moor white, but henceforward I'll ſooner undertake to teach ſincerity to a courtier, generoſity to an uſurer, honeſty to a lawyer, than diſcretion to a woman I ſee has once ſet her heart upon playing the fool.

Enter Conſtant.

Morrow, Conſtant.

Conſt. Good-morrow, Jack. What are you doing here this morning?

Heart. Doing! Gueſs, if you can.——Why I have been endeavouring to perſuade my Lady Fancyful, that ſhe's the moſt fooliſh woman about town.

Conſt. A pretty endeavour truly.

Heart. I have told her in as plain Engliſh as I could ſpeak, both what the town ſays of her, and what I think of her. In ſhort, I have uſed her as an abſolute king would do Magna Charta.

B 3

Conſt.

Conft. And how does she take it ?

Heart. As children do pills; bite them, but can't swallow them.

Conft. But, pr'ythee, what has put it into your head, of all mankind, to turn reformer ?

Heart. Why, one thing was, the morning hung upon my hands, I did not know what to do with myfelf: and another was, that as little as I care for women, I could not fee with patience one that Heaven had taken fuch wonderous pains about, be fo very induftrious to make herfelf the jack-pudding of the creation.

Conft. Well, now could I almoft wish to fee my cruel miftrefs make the felf-fame ufe of what Heaven has done for her, that fo I might be cured of the fame difeafe that makes me fo very uneafy; for love, love is the devil, Heartfree.

Heart. And why do you let the devil govern you ?

Conft. Becaufe I have more flefh and blood than grace and felf-denial. My dear, dear miftrefs, 'fdeath ! that fo genteel a woman fhould be a faint, when religion's out of fafhion.

Heart. Nay, she's much in the wrong truly ; but who knows how far time and good example may prevail ?

Conft. Oh ! they have played their parts in vain already: 'tis now two years fince the fellow her hufband invited me to his wedding ; and there was the firft time I faw that charming woman, whom I have loved ever fince; but she is cold, my friend, ftill cold as the northern ftar.

Heart. So are all women by nature, which makes them fo willing to be warmed.

Conft. Oh, don't profane the fex ; pr'ythee think them all angels for her fake; for she's virtuous even to a fault.

Heart. A lover's head is a good accountable thing truly ; he adores his miftrefs for being virtuous, and yet is very angry with her becaufe she won't be kind.

Conft. Well, the only relief I expect in my mifery is to fee thee fome day or other as deeply engaged as myfelf, which will force me to be merry in the midft of all my misfortunes.

Heart. That day will never come, be affured, Ned: ' not but that I can pafs a night with a woman, and for ' the time, perhaps, make myfelf as good fport as you
' can

' can do. Nay, I can court a woman too, call her nymph,
' angel, goddeſs, what you pleaſe: but here's the diffe-
' rence between you and I; I perſuade a woman ſhe's an
' angel, and ſhe perſuades you ſhe's one.' But, pr'y-
thee, let me tell you how I avoid falling in love; that
which ſerves me for prevention, may chance to ſerve you
for a cure.

Conſt. Well, uſe the ladies moderately then, and I'll
hear you.

Heart. That uſing them moderately undoes us all: but
I'll uſe them juſtly, and that you ought to be ſatisfied
with. I always conſider a woman, not as the taylor, the
ſhoemaker, the tire-woman, the ſemptreſs, and (which is
more than all that) the poet makes her; but I conſider
her as pure nature has contrived her, and that more ſtrictly
than I ſhould have done our old grandmother Eve, had
I ſeen her naked in the garden; for I conſider her turned
inſide out. Her heart well examined, I find there pride,
vanity, covetouſneſs, indiſcretion; but above all things,
malice: plots eternally forging to deſtroy one another's
reputations, and as honeſtly to charge the levity of men's
tongues with the ſcandal; hourly debates how to make
poor gentlemen in love with them, with no other intent
but to uſe them like dogs when they have done; a conſtant deſire of doing more miſchief, and an everlaſting
war waged againſt truth and good-nature.

Conſt. Very well, Sir; an admirable compoſition truly!

Heart. Then for her outſide, I conſider it meerly as an
outſide; ſhe has a thin tiffany covering, juſt over ſuch
ſtuff as you and I are made on. As for her motion, her
mien, her airs, and all thoſe tricks, I know they affect
you mightily. If you ſhould ſee your miſtreſs at a coronation, dragging her peacock's train, with all her ſtate
and inſolence about her, 'twould ſtrike you with all the
awful thoughts that Heaven itſelf could pretend to from
you: whereas I turn the whole matter into a jeſt, and
ſuppoſe her ſtrutting in the ſelf ſame ſtately manner,
with nothing on her but her ſtays, and her ſcanty quilted
under petticoat.

Conſt. Hold thy profane tongue; for I'll hear no more.

Heart. What, you'll love on then?

Conſt. Yes.

Heart.

Heart. Yet have no hopes at all.

Conſt. None.

Heart. Nay, the reſolution may be diſcreet enough; perhaps you have found out ſome new philoſophy, that love, like virtue, is its own reward: ſo you and your miſtreſs will be as well content at a diſtance, as others that have leſs learning are in coming together.

Conſt. No; but if ſhe ſhould prove kind at laſt, my dear Heartfree. *[Embracing him.*

Heart. Nay, pr'ythee don't take me for your miſtreſs; for lovers are very troubleſome.

Conſt. Well, who knows what time may do?

Heart. And juſt now he was ſure time could do nothing.

Conſt. Yet not one kind glance in two years, is ſomewhat ſtrange.

Heart. Not ſtrange at all; ſhe don't like you, that's all the buſineſs.

Conſt. Pt'ythee don't diſtract me.

Heart. Nay, you are a good handſome young fellow, ſhe might uſe you better. Come, will you go ſee her? Perhaps ſhe may have changed her mind; there's ſome hopes, as long as ſhe's a woman.

Conſt. Oh, 'tis in vain to viſit her! Sometimes, to get a ſight of her, I viſit that beaſt her huſband, but ſhe certainly finds ſome pretence to quit the room as ſoon as I enter.

Heart. It's much ſhe don't tell him you have made love to her too; for that's another good-natured thing uſual amongſt women, in which they have ſeveral ends. Sometimes 'tis to recommend their virtue, that they may be kind with the greater ſecurity. Sometimes 'tis to make their huſbands fight, in hopes they may be killed, when their affairs require it ſhould be ſo: but moſt commonly 'tis to engage two men in a quarrel, that they may have the credit of being fought for; and if the lover's killed in the buſineſs, they cry, Poor fellow, he had ill luck—— and ſo they go to cards.

Conſt. Thy injuries to women are not to be forgiven. Look to't, if ever you fall into their hands——

Heart. They can't uſe me worſe than they do you, that peak well of them. Oh, ho! here comes the knight.

Enter

Enter Sir John Brute.

Heart. Your humble servant, Sir John.

Sir John. Servant, Sir.

Heart. How does all your family?

Sir John. Pox o' my family.

Conft. How does your Lady? I han't seen her abroad a good while.

Sir John. Do! I don't know how she does, not I; she was well enough yesterday; I han't been at home to-night.

Conft. What, were you out of town?

Sir John. Out of town! No, I was drinking.

Conft. You are a true Englishman; don't know your own happiness. If I were married to such a woman, I would not be from her a night, for all the wine in France.

Sir John. Not from her!—'Oons—what a time should a man have of that!

Heart. Why, there's no division, I hope.

Sir John. No; but there's a conjunction, and that's worse; a pox of the parson—Why the plague don't you two marry? I fancy I look like the devil to you.

Heart. Why, you don't think you have horns, do you?

Sir John. No; I believe my wife's religion will keep her honest.

Heart. And what will make her keep her religion?

Sir John. Persecution; and therefore she shall have it.

Heart. Have a care, knight, women are tender things.

Sir John. And yet, methinks, 'tis a hard matter to break their hearts.

Conft. Fy, fy! you have one of the best wives in the world, and yet you seem the most uneasy husband.

Sir John. Best wives!—the woman's well enough; she has no vice that I know of; but she's a wife, and—damn a wife; if I were married to a hogshead of claret, matrimony would make me hate it.

Heart. Why did you marry then? You were old enough to know your own mind.

Sir John. Why did I marry! I married because I had a mind to lay with her, and she would not let me.

Heart. Why did you not ravish her?

Sir John. Yes, and so have hedged myself into forty quarrels with her relations, besides buying my pardon:

but

but more than all that, you muſt know I was afraid of being damned in thoſe days: for I kept ſneaking cowardly company, fellows that went to church, ſaid grace to their meat, and had not the leaſt tincture of quality about them.

Heart. But I think you are got into a better gang now.

Sir John. Zoons, Sir, my Lord Rake and I are hand and glove: I believe we may get our bones broke together to-night. Have you a mind to ſhare a frolic?

Conſt. Not I, truly; my talent lies in ſofter exerciſes.

Sir John. What, a down-bed and a ſtrumpet? A pox of venery, I ſay. Will you come and drink with me this afternoon?

Conſt. I can't drink to-day; but we'll come and ſit an hour with you if you will.

Sir John. Pough, pox, ſit an hour! Why can't you drink?

Conſt. Becauſe I'm to ſee my miſtreſs.

Sir John. Who's that?

Conſt. Why do you uſe to tell?

Sir John. Yes.

Conſt. So won't I.

Sir John. Why?

Conſt. Becauſe it is a ſecret.

Sir John. Would my wife knew it, 'twould be no ſecret long.

Conſt. Why, do you think ſhe can't keep a ſecret?

Sir John. No more than ſhe could keep Lent.

Heart. Pr'ythee, tell it her to try, Conſtant.

Sir John. No, pr'ythee don't, that I mayn't be plagued with it.

Conſt. I'll hold you a guinea you don't make her tell it you.

Sir John. I'll hold you a guinea I do.

Conſt. Which way?

Sir John. Why, I'll beg her not to tell it me.

Heart. Nay, if any thing does it, that will.

Conſt. But do you think, Sir——

Sir John. 'Oons, Sir, I think a woman and a ſecret are the two impertinenteſt themes in the univerſe; therefore pray let's hear no more of my wife nor your miſtreſs. Damn them both with all my heart and every thing elſe.

that

that daggles a petticoat, except four generous whores who
are drunk with my Lord Rake and I ten times in a fortnight.   [*Exit Sir* John.

Conſt. Here's a dainty fellow for you! and the verieſt
coward too. But his uſage of his wife makes me ready
to ſtab the villain.

Heart. Lovers are ſhort-ſighted: all their ſenſes run
into that of feeling. This proceeding of his is the only
thing on earth can make you fortunate. If any thing can
prevail with her to accept a gallant, 'tis his uſage of her.
Pr'ythee, take heart, I have great hopes for you; and
ſince I can't bring you quite off her, I'll endeavour to
bring you quite on; for a whining lover is the damneſt
companion upon earth.

Conſt. My dear friend, flatter me a little more with
theſe hopes; for whilſt they prevail, I have Elyſium
within me, and could melt with joy.

Heart. Pray no melting yet; ' let things go farther
' firſt.' This afternoon perhaps we ſhall make ſome advance. In the mean while, let's go dine at Locket's, and
let hope get you a ſtomach.   [*Exeunt.*

SCENE, *Lady* Fancyful's *Houſe.*

Enter Lady Fancyful, *and* Mademoiſelle.

Lady Fan. Did you ever ſee any thing ſo importune,
Mademoiſelle?

Mad. Inteed, Matam, to ſay de trute, he want leetel
good-breeding.

Lady Fan. Good-breeding! He wants to be caned,
Mademoiſelle. An inſolent fellow! and yet, let me ex-
poſe my weakneſs, 'tis the only man on earth I could re-
ſolve to diſpenſe my favours on, were he but a fine gentleman. Well, did men but know how deep an impreſſion
a fine gentleman makes in a lady's heart, they would re-
duce all their ſtudies to that of good-breeding alone.

Enter Servant.

Serv. Will your Ladyſhip pleaſe to dine yet?

Lady Fan. Yes, let them ſerve, [*Exit Servant.*] Sure
this Heartfree has bewitch'd me, Mademoiſelle. ' You
' can't imagine how oddly he mixed himſelf in my
' thoughts during my rapture e'en now.' I vow 'tis a
                                                    thouſand

houſand pities he is not more poliſhed ; don't you think ſo ?

Mad. Matam, I think it ſo great pity, that if I was in your Ladyſhip's place, I take him home in my houſe, I lock him up in my cloſet, and I never let him go, till I teach him every ting dat fine lady expect from fine gentleman.

Lady Fan. Why truly I believe, I ſhould ſoon ſubdue his brutality ; for, without doubt, he has a ſtrange penchant to grow fond of me, in ſpite of his averſion to the ſex, elſe he would ne'er have taken ſo much pains about me. Lord, how proud would ſome poor creatures be of ſuch a conqueſt ! But I, alas ! I dont know how to receive as a favour, what I take to be ſo infinitely my due. But what ſhall I do to new mould him, Mademoiſelle, for till then, he's my utter averſion ?

Mad. Matam, you muſt laugh at him in all de place dat you meet him, and turn into de riticule all he ſay, and all he do.

Lady Fan. Why truly ſatire has ever been of wond'rous uſe to reform ill-manners. Beſides, 'tis my particular talent to ridicule folks. I can be ſevere, ſtrangely ſevere, when I will, Mademoiſelle—Give me the pen and ink— I find myſelf whimſical—I'll write to him—Or I'll let it alone, and be ſevere upon him that way. [*Sitting down to write, riſing up again.*]—Yet active ſeverity is better than paſſive.—[*Sitting down.*]—'Tis as good to let it alone too ; for every laſh I give him, perhaps he'll take for a favour. —*Riſing.*] Yet 'tis a thouſand pities ſo much ſatire ſhould be loſt. [*Sitting.*]—But if it ſhould have a wrong effect upon him, 'twould diſtract me. [*Riſing.*]—Well, I muſt write though after all. [*Sitting.*]—Or I'll let it alone, which is the ſame thing. [*Riſing.*

Mad. La voilà determinée. [*Exeunt.*

End of the Second Act.

ACT

A C T III.

SCENE *opens.* *Sir* John, *Lady* Brute, *and* Belinda, *rising from the table.*

SIR JOHN.

HERE; take away the things: I expect company. But first bring me a pipe: I'll smoke.

[*To a Servant.*

Lady Brute. Lord, Sir John, I wonder you won't leave that nasty custom.

Sir John. Pr'ythee, don't be impertinent.

Bel. [*To Lady* Brute.] I wonder who those are he expects this afternoon.

Lady Brute. I'd give the world to know. Perhaps 'tis Constant, he comes here sometimes; if it does prove him, I'm resolved I'll share the visit.

Bel. We'll send for our work, and sit here.

Lady Brute. He'll choak us with his tobacco.

Bel. Nothing will choak us when we are doing what we have a mind to. Lovewel'.

Enter Lovewell.

Love. Madam.

Lady Brute. Here; bring my cousin's work and mine hither.   [*Exit Lov. and re-enters with their work.*

Sir John. Why, pox, can't you work somewhere else?

Lady Brute. We shall be careful not to disturb you, Sir.

Bel. Your pipe would make you too thoughtful, uncle, if you were left alone; our prittle prattle will cure your spleen.

Sir John. Will it so, Mrs. Pert! Now I believe it will so increase it, [*Sitting and smoking.*] I shall take my own house for a paper-mill.

Lady Brute. [*To Bel. aside.*] Don't let's mind him; let him say what he will.

Sir John. A woman's tongue a cure for the spleen— 'oons—[*Aside.*] If a man had got the head-ach, they'd be for applying the same remedy.

Lady Brute. You have done a great deal, Belinda, since yesterday.

C

Bel.

Bel. Yes, I have worked very hard; how do you like it?

Lady Brute. Oh! 'tis the prettiest fringe in the world. Well, cousin, you have the happiest fancy; pr'ythee advise me about altering my crimson petticoat.

Sir John. A pox o' your petticoat; here's such a prat'ng, a man can't digest his own thoughts for you.

Lady Brute. Don't answer him. [*Aside.*] Well, what do you advise me?

Bel. Why, really, I would not alter it at all. Methinks, 'tis very pretty as it is.

Lady Brute. Ay, that's true: but you know one grows weary of the prettiest things in the world when one has had them long.

Sir John. Yes, I have taught her that.

Bel. Shall we provoke him a little?

Lady Brute. With all my heart. Belinda, don't you long to be married?

Bel. Why, there are some things in it which I could like well enough.

Lady Brute. What do you think you should dislike?

Bel. My husband, a hundred to one else.

Lady Brute. Oh, ye wicked wretch! Sure you don't speak as you think?

Bel. Yes, I do: especially if he smoked tobacco.

[*Sir* John *looks earnestly at them.*

Lady Brute. Why, that many times takes off worse smells.

Bel. Then he must smell very ill indeed.

Lady Brute. So some men will, to keep their wives from coming near them.

Bel. Then those wives should cuckold them at a distance.

[*He rises in a fury, throws his pipe at them, and drives them out. As they run off,* Constant *and* Heartfree *enter.* Lady Brute *runs against* Constant.

Sir John. 'Oons, get you gone up stairs, you confederating strumpets you, or I'll cuckold you with a vengeance.

Lady Brute. Oh, lord, he'll beat us, he'll beat us. Dear, dear Mr. Constant, save us.   [*Exeunt.*

Sir John. I'll cuckold you, with a pox.

Const. Heav'n! Sir John, what's the matter!

Sir

Sir John. Sure if women had been ready crea ed, the devil, inftead of being kicked down into hell, had been married.

Heart. Why, what new plagues have you found now?

Sir John. Why thefe two gentlewomen did but hear me fay I expected you here this afternoon; upon which, they prefently refolved to take up the room, o' purpofe to plague me and my friends.

Conft. Was that all? Why we fhould have been glad of their company.

Sir John. Then I fhould have been weary of yours; for I can't relifh both together. They found fault with my fmoking tobacco too; and faid men ftunk. But I have a good mind—to fay fomething.

Conft. No, nothing againft the ladies, pray.

Sir John. Split the ladies. Come, will you fit down? Give us fome wine, fellow. You won't fmoke!

Conft. No, nor drink neither, at this time, I muft afk your pardon.

Sir John. What, this miftiefs of yours runs in your head! I'll warrant it's fome fuch fqueamifh minx as my wife, that's grown fo dainty of late, fhe finds fault even with a dirty fhirt.

Heart. That a woman may do, and not be very dainty neither.

Sir John. 'Pox o' the women, let's drink.' Come you fhall take one glafs, though I fend for a box of lozenges to fweeten your mouth after it.

Conft. Nay, if one glafs will fatisfy you, I'll drink it, without putting you to that expence.

Sir John. Why that's honeft. Fill fome wine, firrah. So here's to you, gentlemen—A wife's the devil. To your both being married.   *[They drink.*

Heart. Oh, your moft humble fervant, Sir.

Sir John. Well, how do you like my wine?

Conft. 'Tis very good, indeed.

Heart. 'Tis admirable.

Sir John. Then give us t'other glafs.

Conft. No, pray excufe us now: we'll come another time, and then we won't fpare it.

Sir John. This one glafs, and no more. Come, it fhall

be your miftrefs's health; and that's a great compliment from me, I affure you.

Conft. And 'tis a very obliging one to me: fo give us the glaffes.

Sir John. So—let her live.

[*Sir John coughs in the glafs.*

Heart. And be kind.

Conft. What's the matter? Does it go the wrong way?

Sir John. If I had love enough to be jealous, I fhould take this for an ill omen: for I never drank my wife's health in my life, but I puked in my glafs.

Conft. Oh, fhe's too virtuous to make any reafonable man jealous.

Sir John. Pox of her virtue. If I could catch her adulterating, I might be divorc'd from her by law.

Heart. And fo pay her a yearly penfion, to be a diftinguifhed cuckold.

Enter Servant.

Serv. Sir, there's my Lord Rake, Colonel Bully, and fome other gentlemen at the Blue Pofts, defire your company.

Sir John. Gad fo, we are to confult about playing the devil to-night.

Heart. Well, we won't hinder bufinefs.

Sir John. Methinks, I don't know how to leave you two; but for once I muft make bold. Or, look you; may be the conference mayn't laft long! So if you'll wait here half an hour, or an hour; if I don't come then —why then—I won't come at all.

Heart. [*To* Conft.] A good modeft propofition, truly.

[*Afide.*

Conft. But let's accept on't, however. Who knows what may happen.

Heart. Well, Sir, to fhew you how fond we are of your company, we'll expect your return as long as we can.

Sir John. Nay, may be I mayn't ftay at all; but bufinefs, you know, muft be done. So your fervant—Or, hark you, if you have a mind to take a frifk with us, I have an intereft with my Lord; I can eafily introduce you.

Conft.

Conſt. We are much beholden to you; but for my part, I'm engaged another way.

Sir John. What! to your miſtreſs, I'll warrant. Pr'ythee, leave your naſty punk to entertain herſelf with her own wicked thoughts, and make one with us to-night.

Conſt. Sir, 'tis buſineſs that is to employ me.

Heart. And me; and buſineſs muſt be done, you know.

Sir John. Ay, women's buſineſs, though the world were conſumed for it.   [*Exit Sir* John.

Conſt. Farewel, beaſt; and now, my dear friend, would my miſtreſs be but as complaiſant as ſome men's wives, who think it a piece of good-breeding to receive the viſits of their huſband's friends in his abſence.

Heart. Why, for your ſake, I could forgive her, ' tho' ' ſhe ſhould be ſo complaiſant to receive ſomething elſe ' in his abſence.' But what way ſhall we invent to ſee her?

Conſt. Oh, ne'er hope it: invention will prove as vain as wiſhes.

Enter Lady Brute *and* Belinda.

Heart. What do you think now, friend?

Conſt. I think I ſhall ſwoon.

Heart. I'll ſpeak firſt then, whilſt you fetch breath.

Lady Brute. We think ourſelves obliged, gentlemen, to come and return you thanks for your knight-errantry. We were juſt upon being devoured by the fiery dragon.

Bel. Did not his fumes almoſt knock you down, gentlemen?

Heart. Truly, ladies, we did undergo ſome hardſhips; and ſhould have done more, if ſome greater heroes than ourſelves, hard by, had not diverted him.

Conſt. Though I am glad of the ſervice you are pleaſed to ſay we have done you, yet I'm ſorry we could do it in no other way, than by making ourſelves privy to what you would perhaps have kept a ſecret.

Bel. For Sir John's part, I ſuppoſe he deſigned it no ſecret, ſince he made ſo much noiſe. And for myſelf, truly I'm not much concerned, ſince 'tis fallen only into this gentleman's hands and yours; who, I have many reaſons to believe, will neither interpret nor report any thing to my diſadvantage.

C 3

Conſt.

Conſt. Your good opinion, Madam, was what I feared
I never could have merited.

Lady Brute. Your fears were vain then, Sir; for I'm
juſt to every body.

Heart. Pr'ythee, Conſtant, what is't you do to get the
ladies' good opinions; for I'm a novice at it?

Bel. Sir, will you give me leave to inſtruct you?

Heart. Yes, that I will, with all my ſoul, Madam.

Bel. Why then, you muſt never be a ſloven; never be
out of humour, never ſmoke tobacco, nor drink but when
you are dry.

Heart. That's hard.

Conſt. Nay, if you take his bottle from him, you break
his heart, Madam.

Bel. Why, is it poſſible the gentleman can love drinking?

Heart. Only by way of antidote.

Bel. Againſt what, pray?

Heart. Againſt love, Madam.

Lady Brute. Are you afraid of being in love, Sir?

Heart. I ſhould, if there were any danger of it.

Lady Brute. Pray, why ſo?

Heart. Becauſe I always had an averſion to being uſed
like a dog.

Bel. Why, truly, men in love are ſeldom uſed better.

Lady Brute. But was you never in love, Sir?

Heart. No, I thank Heaven, Madam.

Bel. Pray, where got you your learning then?

Heart. From other people's expence.

Bel. That's being a ſpunger, Sir, which is ſcarce honeſt:
if you'd buy ſome experience with your own money, as
'twould be fairlier got, ſo 'twould ſtick longer by you.

Enter Footman.

Foot. Madam, here's my Lady Fancyful, to wait upon
your Ladyſhip.

Lady Brute. Shield me, kind Heaven! What an inundation of impertinence is here coming upon us!

Enter Lady Fancyful, who runs firſt to Lady Brute, then
to Belinda, kiſſing them.

Lady Fan. My dear Lady Brute, and ſweet Belinda,
methinks, 'tis an age ſince I ſaw you.

Lady

Lady Brute. Yet 'tis but three days; sure you have passed your time very ill, it seems so long to you.

Lady Fan. Why really, to confess the truth to you, I am so everlastingly fatigued with the addresses of unfortunate gentlemen, that, were it not for the extravagancy of the example, I should e'en tear out these wicked eyes with my own fingers, to make both myself and mankind easy. What think you on't, Mr. Heartfree? for I take you to be my faithful adviser.

Heart. Why, truly, Madam,—I think—every project that is for the good of mankind, ought to be encouraged.

Lady Fan. Then I have your consent, Sir?

Heart. To do whatever you please, Madam.

Lady Fan. You had a much more limited complaisance this morning, Sir. Would you believe it, ladies? the gentleman has been so exceeding generous, to tell me of above fifty faults, in less time than it was well possible for me to commit two of them.

Const. Why truly, Madam, my friend there is apt to be something familiar with the ladies.

Lady Fan. He is indeed, Sir; but he's wonderous charitable with it: he has had the goodness to design a reformation, e'en down to my fingers' ends.— 'Twas thus, I think, Sir, [*Opening her fingers in an awkward manner.*] you'd have them stand—My eyes too he did not like: how was't you would have directed them? Thus I think. [*Staring at him.*]—Then there was something amiss in my gait too: I don't know well how 'twas! but as I take it, he would have me walk like him. Pray, Sir, do me the favour, to take a turn or two about the room, that the company may see you—He's sullen, ladies, and won't. But, to make short, and give you as true an idea as I can of the matter, I think 'twas much about this figure in general, he would have moulded me to: but I was an obstinate woman, and could not resolve to make myself mistress of his heart, by growing as aukward as his fancy.

   [*She walks aukwardly about, staring and looking un-*
      gainly, then changes on a sudden to the extremity
      of her usual affectation.

Heart. Just thus women do, when they think we are in love with them, or when they are so with us.

   [*Here* Constant *and Lady* Brute *talk together apart.*
                             Lady

Lady Fan. 'Twould, however, be less vanity for me to conclude the former, than you the latter, Sir.

Heart. Madam, all I shall presume to conclude, is, that if I were in love, you'd find the means to make me soon weary on't.

Lady Fan. Not by over-fondness, upon my word, Sir. But, pr'ythee, let's stop here; for you are so much governed by instinct, I know you'll grow brutish at last.

Bel. [*Aside.*] Now am I sure she's fond of him. I'll I'll try to make her jealous. Well, for my part, I should be glad to find somebody would be so free with me, that I might know my faults, and mend them.

Lady Fan. Then, pray, let me recommend this gentleman to you: I have known him some time, and will be surety for him, that upon a very limited encouragement on your side, you shall find an extended impudence on his.

Heart. I thank you, Madam, for your recommendation: but, hating idleness, I'm unwilling to enter into a place where I believe there would be nothing to do. I was fond of serving your Ladyship, because I knew you would find me constant employment.

Lady Fan. I told you he'd be rude, Belinda.

Bel. Oh, a little bluntness is a sign of honesty, which makes me always ready to pardon it. So, Sir, if you have no other objections to my service, but the fear of being idle in it, you may venture to list yourself: I shall find you work, I warrant you.

Heart. Upon those terms I engage, Madam; and this, with your leave, I take for earnest.

[Offering to kiss her hand.

Bel. Hold there, Sir; I'm none of your earnest givers. But if I'm well served, I give good wages, and pay punctually.

[Heart. *and* Bel. *seem to continue talking familiarly.*

Lady Fan. [*Aside.*] I don't like this jesting between them. Methinks the fool begins to look as if he were in earnest—but then he must be a fool indeed. Lard, what a difference there is between me and her! [*Looking at* Bel. *scornfully.*] How I should despise such a thing, if I were a man!——What a nose she has—What a chin— What a neck—Then her eyes—And the worst kissing lips

in

in the univerfe——No, no, he never can like her, that's
pofitive——Yet I can't fuffer them together, any longer.
Mr. Heartfree, do you know, that you and I muft have
no quarrel, for all this ? I can't forbear being a little fevere now and then; but women, you know, may be allowed any thing.

Heart. Up to a certain age, Madam.

Lady Fan. Which I'm not yet paft, I hope.

Heart. [*Afide.*] Nor never will, I dare fwear.

Lady Fan. [*To* Lady Brute.] Come, Madam, will your
Ladyfhip be witnefs to our reconciliation ?

Lady Brute. You are agreed then at laft.

Heart. [*Slightingly.*] We forgive.

Lady Fan. [*Afide.*] That was a cold, ill-natured reply.

Lady Brute. Then there's no challenges fent between
you ?

Heart. Not from me, I promife. [*Afide to* Conft.]
But that's more than I'll do for her ; for I know fhe can
as well be hanged as forbear writing to me.

Conft. That I believe. But I think we had beft be going, left fhe fhould fufpect fomething, and be malicious.

Heart. With all my heart.

Conft. Ladies, we are your humble fervants. I fee Sir
John is quite engaged ; 'twould be in vain to expect him.
Come, Heartfree.   [*Exit.*

Heart. Ladies, your fervant. [*To* Belinda.] I hope,
Madam, you won't forget our bargain ; I'm to fay what
I pleafe to you.

Bel. Liberty of fpeech entire, Sir.   [*Exit* Heart.

Lady Fan. [*Afide.*] Very pretty, truly !——But how
the blockhead went out languifhing at her, and not a look
towards me. Well, people may talk, but miracles are
not ceafed : for 'tis more than natural, fuch a rude fellow
as he, and fuch a little impertinent as fhe, fhould be capable of making a woman of my fphere uneafy. But I can
bear her fight no longer. Methinks fhe's grown ten times
uglier than Cornet. I muft home, and ftudy revenge.
[*To* Lady Brute.] Madam, your humble fervant ; I muft
take my leave.

Lady Brute. What, going already, Madam ?

Lady Fan. I muft beg you'll excufe me this once ; for
really, I have eighteen vifits to return this afternoon——

So,

So, you fee I'm importuned by the women, as well as the men.

Bel. [*Aside.*] And fhe's quits with them both.

Lady Fan. [*Going.*] Nay, you fhan't go one ftep out of the room.

Lady Brute. Indeed I'll wait upon you down.

Lady Fan. No, fweet Lady Brute; you know I fwoon at ceremony.

Lady Brute. Pray, give me leave.

Lady Fan. You know I won't.

Lady Brute. Indeed I muft.

Lady Fan. Indeed you fhan't.

Lady Brute. Indeed I will.

Lady Fan. Indeed you fhan't.

Lady Brute. Indeed I will.

Lady Fan. Indeed you fhan't. Indeed, indeed, indeed you fhan't.   [*Exit* Lady Fan. *running; they follow.*

Re-enter Lady Brute.

Lady Brute. This impertinent woman has put me out of humour for a fortnight. What an agreeable moment has her foolifh vifit interrupted! Lord, what a pleafure there is in doing what we fhould not do!

Re-enter Conftant.

Ha! here again!

Conft. Tho' the renewing my vifit may feem a little irregular, I hope I fhall obtain your pardon for it, Madam, when you know I only left the room, left the lady who was here fhould have been as malicious in her remarks, as fhe is foolifh in her conduct.

Lady Brute. He who has difcretion enough to be tender of a woman's reputation, carries a virtue about him that may atone for a great many faults.

Conft. If it has a title to atone for any, its pretenfions muft needs be ftrongeft, where the crime is love. ' I ' therefore hope I fhall be forgiven the attempt I have ' made upon your heart, fince the enterprife has been a ' fecret to all the world but yourfelf.

' *Lady Brute.* Secrecy, indeed, in fins of this kind, is ' an argument of weight to leffen the punifhment; but ' nothing's a plea for a pardon entire, without a fincere ' repentance.

' *Conft.* If fincerity in repentance confifts in forrow for
' offending,

' offending, no cloister ever inclosed so true a penitent as
' I should be.   But I hope it can't be reckoned an offence
' to love, where it is a duty to adore.'

Lady Brute. 'Tis an offence, a great one, where it
would rob a woman of all she ought to be adored for, her
virtue.

Const. Virtue! that phantom of honour, which men
in every age have so condemned; they have thrown it
amongst the women to scramble for.

Lady Brute. If it be a thing of so very little value,
why do you so earnestly recommend it to your wives and
daughters?

Const. We recommend it to our wives, Madam, because
we would keep them to ourselves; and to our daughters,
because we would dispose of them to others.

Lady Brute. 'Tis then of some importance, it seems,
since you can't dispose of them without it.

' *Const.* That importance, Madam, lies in the humour
' of the country, not in the nature of the thing.   Pray,
' what does your Ladyship think of a powdered coat for
' deep mourning?

' *Lady Brute.* I think, Sir, your sophistry has all the
' effect that you can reasonably expect it should have;
' it puzzles, but don't convince.

' *Const.* I'm sorry for it.

' *Lady Brute.* I'm sorry to hear you say so.

' *Const.* Pray, why?

' *Lady Brute.* Because if you expected more from it,
' you have a worse opinion of my understanding than I
' desire you should have.

' *Const.* [*Aside.*] I comprehend her: she would have
' me set a value upon her chastity, that I might think
' myself the more obliged to her, when she makes me a
' present of it.' [*To her.*] I beg you will believe I did
but railly, Madam: ' I know you judge too well of right
' and wrong, to be deceived by arguments like those.'
And I hope you will have so favourable an opinion of my
understanding too, to believe the thing called virtue has
worth enough with me, to pass for an eternal obligation
where'er 'tis sacrificed.

Lady Brute. It is, I think, so great a one, as nothing
can repay.

Const.

Conſt. Yes; the making the man you love your ever-laſting debtor.

Lady Brute. When debtors once have borrowed all we have to lend, they are very apt to grow ſhy of their creditor's company.

Conſt. That, Madam, is only when they are forced to borrow of uſurers, and not of a generous friend. Let us chuſe our creditors, and we are ſeldom ſo ungrateful as to ſhun them.

Lady Brute. What think you of Sir John, Sir? I was his free choice.

Conſt. I think he's married, Madam.

Lady Brute. Does marriage then exclude men from your rule of conſtancy?

Conſt. It does. Conſtancy's a brave, free, haughty, generous agent, that cannot buckle to the chains of wed-lock.

' *Lady Brute.* Have you no exceptions to this general
' rule, as well as to t'other?

' *Conſt.* Yes, I would, after all, be an exception to
' it myſelf, if you were free in power and will to make
' me ſo.

' *Lady Brute.* Compliments are well placed, where 'tis
' impoſſible to lay hold on them.

' *Conſt.* I would to Heaven 'twere poſſible for you to
' lay hold on mine, that you might ſee 'tis no compli-
' ment at all. But ſince you are already diſpoſed of, be-
' yond redemption, to one who does not know the value
' of the jewel you have put into his hands, I hope you
' would not think him greatly wronged, tho' it ſhould
' ſometimes be looked on by a friend, who knows how to
' eſteem it as he ought.

' *Lady Brute.* If looking on't alone would-ſerve his
' turn, the wrong, perhaps, might not be very great.

' *Conſt.* Why, what if he ſhould wear it now and then
' a day, ſo he gave good ſecurity to bring it home again
' at night?

' *Lady Brute.* Small ſecurity, I fancy, might ſerve for
' that. One might venture to take his word.

' *Conſt.* Then where's the injury to the owner?

' *Lady Brute.* 'Tis an injury to him, if he thinks it
' one.

‘ one.   For if happiness be seated in the mind, unhappi-
‘ ness must be so too.

‘ *Const.* Here I close with you, Madam, and draw my
‘ conclusive argument from your own position. If the
‘ injury lie in the fancy, there needs nothing but secrecy
‘ to prevent the wrong.

‘ *Lady Brute.* [*Going.*] A surer way to prevent it, is to
‘ hear no more arguments in its behalf.

‘ *Const.* [*Following her.*]’ But, Madam——

Lady Brute. But, Sir, 'tis my turn to be discreet now,
and not suffer too long a visit.

Const. [*Catching her hand.*] By Heaven, you shall not
stir, till you give me hopes that I shall see you again, at
some more convenient time and place.

Lady Brute. I give you just hopes enough—[*Breaking
from him.*] to get loose from you; and that's all I can afford you at this time.   [*Exit running.*

Const. Now, by all that's great and good, she's a charming woman! In what ecstacy of joy she has left me!
for she gave me hope. Did she not say she gave me hope?
Hope! ay; what hope?—Enough to make me let her
go—Why, that's enough in conscience. Or—no matter
how 'twas spoke; hope was the word, it came from her,
and it was said to me.

Enter Heartfree.

Ha, Heartfree! Thou hast done me noble service in
prattling to the young gentlewoman without there——
Come to my arms, thou venerable bawd, and let me
squeeze thee [*Embracing him eagerly.*] as a new pair of
stays does a fat country girl, when she's carried to court,
to stand for a maid of honour.

Heart. Why, what the devil's all this rapture for?

Const. Rapture! There's ground for rapture, man;
there's hopes, my Heartfree; hopes, my friend.

Heart. Hopes! Of what?

Const. Why, hopes, that my Lady and I together, (for
'tis more than one body's work) should make Sir John a
cuckold.

Heartf. Pr'ythee, what did she say to thee?

Const. Say! What did she not say? She said that—
says she—she said—Zoons! I don't know what she said;
but she looked as if she said every thing I'd have her; and

so, if thou'lt go to the tavern, I'll treat thee with any thing that gold can buy; I'll give all my silver among the drawers, make a bonfire before the door, ; swear that the Pope's turned proteſtant, and that all the politicians in England are of one mind. [*Exeunt.*

S C E N E *opens.* Lord Rake, Sir John, *&c. at a table, drinking.*

All. Huzza!

Lord Rake. Come, boys, charge again—So—Confuſion to all order. Here's liberty of conſcience.

All. Huzza!

Lord Rake. Come, ſing the ſong I made this morning, to this purpoſe.

Sir John. 'Tis wicked, I hope.

Lord Rake. Don't I tell you that I made it?

Sir John. My Lord, I beg your pardon, for ſuſpecting you of any virtue. Come, begin.

S O N G, *by* Col. BULLY.

I.

We're gayly yet, we're gayly yet,
And we're not very fu', but we're gayly yet.
Then ſit ye a while, and tipple a bit,
For we's not very fu', but we're gayly yet.
   And we're gayly yet, *&c. &c.*

II.

There was a lad, and they ca'd him Dicky;
He ga' me a kiſs, and I bit his lippy,
Then under my apron he ſhew'd me a trick:
And we's not very fu', but we're gayly yet.
   And we're gayly yet, *&c. &c.*

III.

There were three lads, and they were clad;
There were three laſſes, and them they had.
Three trees in the orchard are newly ſprung,
And we's a' get geer enough, we're but young.
   And we're gayly yet, *&c. &c.*

IV. Then

IV.

Then up went Ailey, Ailey, up went Ailey now:
Then up went Ailey, quo' Crumma, we's a' get roar-
    ing fu'.
And one was kifs'd in the barn, another was kifs'd on
    the green,
And t'other behind the peafe-ftack, till the mow flew up
    to her eyn.
    Then up went Ailey, Ailey, &c. &c.

V.

Now, fie, John Thompfon, run,
Gin ever ye run in your life,
Deel get ye; but hye, my dear Jack,
There's a mon got to bed with your wife.
    Then up went Ailey, Ailey, &c. &c.

VI.

Then away John Thompfon ran,
And, 'egad, he ran with fpeed;
But before he had run his length,
The falfe loon had done the deed.
    Then up went Ailey, Ailey, &c. &e.

' *Lord Rake.* Well, how do you like it, gentlemen?
' *All.* Oh, admirable!
' *Sir John.* I would not give a fig for a fong that is not
' full of fin and impudence.
' *Lord Rake.* Then my mufe is to your tafte. But
' drink away; the night fteals upon us; we fhall want
' time to be lewd in.' Hey, page! fally out, firrah,
and fee what's doing in the camp; we'll beat up their
quarters prefently.

    Page. I'll bring your Lordfhip an exact account.

                        [*Exit* Page.

    Lord Rake. ' Now let the fpirit of Clary go round.
' Here's to our forlorn hope.' Courage, Knight! Victory attends you.

    Sir John. And laurels fhall crown me. Drink away,
and be damn'd.

Lord Rake. Again, boys; t'other glaſs, and no morality.

Sir John. [*Drunk.*] Ay, no morality—and damn the watch, and let the conſtable be married.

All. Huzza!

Re-enter Page.

Lord Rake. How are the ſtreets inhabited, ſirrah?

Page. My Lord, it's Sunday night, they are full of drunken citizens.

Lord Rake. Along, then, boys; we ſhall have a feaſt.

Col. Bully. Along, noble Knight.

Sir John. Ay, along, Bully; and he that ſays Sir John Brute is not as drunk and as religious as the drunkeneſt citizen of them all——is a liar, and the ſon of a whore.

Col. Bully. Why, that was bravely ſpoke, and like a free-born Engliſhman.

Sir John. What's that to you, Sir, whether I am an Engliſhman or a Frenchman?

Col. Bully. Zoons! you are not angry, Sir?

Sir John. Zoons! I am angry, Sir—for if I am a free-born Engliſhman, what have you to do, even to talk of my privileges?

Lord Rake. Why, pr'ythee, Knight, don't quarrel here: leave private animoſities to be decided by day-light; let the night be employed againſt the public enemy.

Sir John. My Lord, I reſpect you, becauſe you are a man of quality. But I'll make that fellow know, I am within a hair's breadth as abſolute by my privileges, as the King of France is by his prerogative. He, by his prerogative, takes money where it is not his due; I, by my privilege, refuſe paying it where I owe it. Liberty and property, and old England. Huzza!

All. Huzza! [*Exit* Sir John, *reeling, all following him.*

END of the THIRD ACT.

ACT

A C T   IV.

SCENE, *a Bed-chamber.*

Enter Lady Brute *and* Belinda.

LADY BRUTE.

SURE it's late, Belinda; I begin to be sleepy.

Bel. Yes, 'tis near twelve. Will you go to bed?

Lady Brute. To bed, my dear! And by that time I am fallen into a sweet sleep, (or perhaps a sweet dream, which is better and better) Sir John will come home roaring drunk, and be overjoyed he finds me in a condition to be disturbed.

Bel. Oh, you need not fear him! he's in for all night. The servants say he's gone to drink with my Lord Rake.

Lady Brute. Nay, 'tis not very likely, indeed, such suitable company should part presently. What hogs men are, Belinda, when they grow weary of women!

Bel. And what owls they are, whilst they are fond of them!

Lady Brute. But that we may forgive well enough, because they are so upon our accounts. But, pr'ythee, one word of poor Constant ' before we go to bed, if it be but ' to furnish matter for dreams.' I dare swear he's talking of me now, or thinking of me at least.

' *Bel.* So he ought, I think; for you were pleased to ' make him a good round advance to-day, Madam.

' *Lady Brute.* Why, I have e'en plagu'd him enough ' to satisfy any reasonable woman. He has besieged me ' these two years, to no purpose.

' *Bel.* And if he besieged you two years more, he'd ' be well enough paid, so he had the plundering of you ' at last.

' *Lady Brute.* That may be; but I'm afraid the town ' won't be able to hold out much longer: for, to confess ' the truth to you, Belinda, the garrison begins to grow ' mutinous.

' *Bel.* Then the sooner you capitulate, the better.

' *Lady Brute.* Yet, methinks, I would fain stay a little ' longer, to see you fixed too, that we might start toge- ' ther, and see who could love longest.' What think you, if Mr. Heartfree should have a month's mind to you.

Bel.

Bel. Why, I could almost be in love with him, for despising that foolish, affected Lady Fancyful. ' But I'm ' afraid he's too cold, ever to warm himself by my fire.

' *Lady Brute.* Then he deserves to be frozen to death. ' Would I were a man for your sake, dear rogue !

[*Kissing her.*

' *Bel.* You'd wish yourself a woman for your own, or ' men are mistaken. But if I could make a conquest of ' this son of Bacchus, and rival his bottle, what should I ' do with him ? He has no fortune; I can't marry him ; ' and sure you would not have me do I don't know what ' with him.

' *Lady Brute.* Why, if you did, child, 'twould be but ' a good friendly part, if 'twere only to keep me in coun- ' tenance, whilst I play the fool with Constant.

' *Bel.* Well, if I can't resolve to serve you that way, I ' may, perhaps, some other, as much to your satisfaction.' But, pray, how shall we contrive to see these blades again quickly ?

Lady Brute. We must e'en have recourse to the old way ; make them an appointment 'twixt jest and earnest : 'twill look like a frolic, and that, you know, is a very good thing to save a woman's blushes.

Bel. You advise well. But where shall it be ?

Lady Brute. In Spring-garden. But they shan't know their women, till they pull off their masks ; for a surprise is the most agreeable thing in the world : ' and I find my- ' self in a very good humour, ready to do them any good ' turn I can think on.'

Bel. Then, pray, write them the necessary billet with- out farther delay.

Lady Brute. Let's go into your chamber, then ; and whilst you undress I'll do it, child. [*Exeunt.*

S C E N E, *Covent-Garden.*

Enter Lord Rake, Sir John, *&c. with swords drawn.*

Lord Rake. Is the dog dead ?

Col. Bully. No, damn him, I heard him wheeze.

Lord Rake. How the witch his wife howled !

Col. Bully. Ay ; she'll alarm the watch presently.

Lord Rake. Appear, Knight, then. Come, you have a good cause to fight for ; there's a man murdered.

Sir

Sir John. Is there? Then let his ghost be satisfied; for I'll sacrifice a constable to it presently, and burn his body upon his wooden chair.

Enter a Taylor, with a bundle under his arm.

Col. Bully. How now? What have we got here? A thief?

Tay. No, an't please you, I'm no thief.

Lord Rake. That we'll see presently. Here, let the General examine him.

Sir John. Ay, ay, let me examine him, and I'll lay a hundred pounds I find him guilty in spite of his teeth—for he looks like a—sneaking rascal. Come, sirrah, without equivocation or mental reservation, tell me of what opinion you are, and what calling; for by them I shall guess at your morals.

Tay. An't please you, I'm a dissenting journeyman woman's taylor.

Sir John. Then, sirrah, you love lying by your religion, and theft by your trade: and so, that your punishments may be suitable to your crimes, I'll have you first gagged—and then hanged.

Tay. Pray, good, worthy gentlemen, don't abuse me. Indeed I'm an honest man, and a good workman, tho' I say it, that should not say it.

Sir John. No words, sirrah; but attend your fate.

Lord Rake. Let me see what's in that bundle.

Tay. An't please you, it's my Lady's short cloak and wrapping gown.

Sir John. What Lady, you reptile you?

Tay. My Lady Brute, an't please your honour.

Sir John. My Lady Brute! my wife! the robe of my wife!—With reverence let me approach it. The dear angel is always taking care of me in danger, and has sent me this suit of armour to protect me in this day of battle. On they go.

All. Oh, brave Knight!

Lord Rake. Live, Don Quixote the second!

Sir John. Sancho, my 'squire, help me on with my armour.

Tay. Oh, dear gentlemen! I shall be quite undone, if you take the sack.

Sir

Sir John. Retire, firrah; and fince you carry off your fkin, go home, and be happy. So, how d'ye like my fhapes now?

Lord Rake. To a miracle! He looks like a Queen of the Amazons. But, to your arms, gentlemen——The enemy's upon the march—here's the watch——

Sir John. Oons! if it were Alexander the Great, at the head of his army, I would drive him into a horfe-pond.

All. Huzza! Oh, brave Knight!

Enter Watchmen.

Sir John. See, here he comes, with all his Greeks about him. Follow me, boys.

Watch. Hey-day! Who have we got here? Stand.

Sir John. May-hap not.

Watch. What are you all doing here in the ftreets, at this time o' night? And who are you, Madam, that feems to be at the head of this noble crew?

Sir John. Sirrah, I am Bonduca, Queen of the Welch-men; and with a leek as long as my pedigree, I will de-ftroy your Roman legions in an inftant. Britons, ftrike home.

[*Snatches a Watchman's ftaff, ftrikes at the Watch, and falls down; his party drove off.*

Watch. So; we have got the Queen, however. We'll make her pay well for her ranfom——Come, Madam, will your Majefty pleafe to walk before the conftable?

Sir John. The conftable's a rafcal, and you are a fon of a whore.

Watch. A moft noble reply, truly! If this be her roy-al ftile, I'll warrant her maids of honour prattle prettily. But we'll teach you fome of our court dialect, before we part with you, Princefs. Away with her to the round-houfe.

Sir John. Hands off, you ruffians! My honour's dear-er to me than my life. I hope you won't be uncivil.

Watch. Away with her. [*Exeunt.*

S C E N E, *a Bed-chamber.*

Enter Heartfree.

Heart. What the plague ails me?——Love! No, I thank you for that; my heart's rock ftill—Yet 'tis Belin-

da

da that diſturbs me, that's poſitive——Well, what of all that? Muſt I love her for being troubleſome? At that rate I might love all the women I meet, 'egad. But hold; tho' I don't love her for diſturbing me, yet ſhe may diſturb me, becauſe I love her—Ay, that may be, faith—I have dreamt of her, that's certain—Well, ſo I have of my mother: therefore, what's that to the purpoſe?—Ay, but Belinda runs in my mind waking; and ſo does many a damn'd thing, that I don't care a farthing for——Methinks, tho', I would fain be talking to her; and yet I have no buſineſs—Well, am I the firſt man that has had a mind to do an impertinent thing?

Enter Conſtant.

Conſt. How now, Heartfree? What makes you up and dreſs'd ſo ſoon? I thought none but lovers quarrelled with their beds. I expected to have found you ſnoring, as I uſed to do.

Heart. Why, faith, friend, 'tis the care I have of your affairs, that makes me ſo thoughtful: I have been ſtudying all night how to bring your matter about with Belinda.

Conſt. With Belinda!

Heart. With my Lady, I mean: and faith I have mighty hopes on't. Sure you muſt be very well ſatisfied with her behaviour to you yeſterday.

Conſt. So well, that nothing but a lover's fears can make me doubt of ſucceſs. But what can this ſudden change proceed from?

Heart. Why, you ſaw her huſband beat her, did you not?

Conſt. That's true: a huſband is ſcarce to be borne upon any terms, much leſs when he fights with his wife. Methinks ſhe ſhould e'en have cuckolded him upon the ſpot, to ſhew that after the battle ſhe was maſter of the field.

Heart. A council of war of women would infallibly have adviſed her to it. But, I confeſs, ſo agreeable a woman as Belinda deſerves better uſage.

Conſt. Belinda again!

Heart. My Lady, I mean. What a pox makes me blunder ſo to-day? [*Aſide.*] A plague of this treacherous tongue!

Conſt. Pr'ythee, look upon me ſeriouſly, Heartfree—

Now,

Now, anfwer me directly: is it my Lady, or Belinda, employs your careful thoughts thus?

Heart. My, Lady, or Belinda!

Conft. In love, by this light; in love.

Heart. In love!

Conft. Nay, ne'er deny it; for thou'lt do it fo awkwardly, 'twill but make the jeft fit heavier about thee. My dear friend, I give you much joy.

Heart. Why, pr'ythee, you won't perfuade me to it, will you?

Conft. That fhe's miftrefs of your tongue, that's plain; and I know you are fo honeft a fellow, your tongue and heart always go together. But how—but how the devil—Pha, ha, ha, ha, ha, ha!

Heart. Hey-day! Why, fure you don't believe it in earneft?

Conft. Yes, I do; becaufe I fee you deny it in jeft.

Heart. Nay, but look you, Ned—a—deny in jeft—a—gadzooks, you know I fay—a—when a man denies a thing in jeft—a——

Conft. Pha, ha, ha, ha, ha, ha!

Heart. Nay, then we fhall have it. What, becaufe a man ftumbles at a word—Did you never make a blunder?

Conft. Yes; for I am in love, I own it.

Heart. Then fo am I——Now laugh, till thy foul's glutted with mirth. [*Embracing him.*] But, dear Conftant, don't tell the town on't.

Conft. Nay, then, 'twere almoft pity to laugh at thee, after fo honeft a confeffion. ' But, tell us a little, Jack, ' by what new-invented arms has this mighty ftroke been ' given?

' *Heart.* E'en by that unaccountable weapon called ' *je-ne-fçai-quoi:* for every thing that can come within ' the verge of beauty, I have feen it with indifference.

' *Conft.* So, in few words, then, the *je-ne-fçai-quoi* has ' been too hard for the quilted petticoat.

' *Heart.* 'Egad, I think the *je-ne-fçai-quoi* is in the ' quilted petticoat; at leaft, 'tis certain I never think on't ' without a *je-ne-fçai-quoi* in every part about me.

' *Conft.* Well, but have all your remedies loft their ' virtue? Have you turned her infide out yet?

' *Heart.* I dare not fo much as think on't.

' *Conft.*

' *Conſt.* But don't the two years fatigue I have ha d
' diſcourage you ?

' *Heart.* Yes; I dread what I foreſee ; yet cannot
' quit the enterpriſe : like ſome ſoldiers, whoſe courage
' dwells more in their honour than their nature, on they
' go, tho' the body trembles at what the ſoul makes it un-
' dertake.

' *Conſt.* Nay, if you expect your miſtreſs will uſe you
' as your profanations againſt her ſex deſerve, you tremble
' juſtly. But how do you intend to proceed, friend ?

' *Heart.* Thou know'ſt I am but a novice ; be friend-
' ly, and adviſe me.

' *Conſt.* Why, look you then ; I'd have you ſerenade
' and a—write a ſong—Go to church ; look like a fool ;
' be very officious ; ogle, write, and lead out : and who
' knows, but, in a year or two's time, you may be called
' a——troubleſome puppy, and ſent about your buſineſs.

' *Heart.* That's hard.

' *Conſt.* Yet thus it oft falls out with lovers, Sir.

' *Hear.* Pox on me, for making one of the number.

' *Conſt.* Have a care ; ſay no ſaucy things ; 'twill but
' augment your crime ; and if your miſtreſs hears on't,
' increaſe your puniſhment.

' *Heart.* Pr'ythee, ſay ſomething then, to encourage
' me ; you know I helped you in your diſtreſs.

' *Conſt.* Why then, to encourage you to perſeverance,
' that you may be thoroughly ill uſed for your offences,
' I'll put you in mind, that even the coyeſt ladies of them
' all are made up of deſires, as well as we ; and tho' they
' do hold out a long time, they will capitulate at laſt :
' for that thundering engineer, nature, does make ſuch
' havock in the town, they muſt ſurrender at long run,
' or periſh in their own flames.'

Enter Footman.

Foot. Sir, there's a porter without with a letter ; he deſires to give it into your own hands.

Conſt. Call him in.

Enter Porter.

What, Joe ! Is it thee ?

Port. An't pleaſe you, Sir, I was ordered to deliver
this into your own hands, by two well-ſhaped ladies, at
the

the New-Exchange. I was at your honour's lodgings, and your servants sent me hither.

Conft. 'Tis well, are you to carry any anfwer?

Porter. No, my noble mafter. They gave me my orders, and, whip, they were gone, ' like a maidenhead at ' fifteen.'

Conft. Very well; there.　　　　　[*Gives him money.*

Port. God blefs your honour.　　　　　[*Exit.*

Conft. Now let's fee what honeft, trufty Joe has brought us. [*Reads.*] " If you and your play-fellow can fpare time from your bufinefs and devotions, don't fail to be at Spring-garden about eight in the evening. You'll find nothing there but women, fo you need bring no other arms than what you ufually carry about you."——So, play-fellow; here's fomething to flay your ftomach, till your miftrefs's difh is ready for you.

Heart. Some of our old battered acquaintance. I won't go, not I.

Conft. Nay, that you can't avoid; there's honour in the cafe; 'tis a challenge, and I want a fecond.

Heart. I doubt I fhall be but a very ufelefs one to you; for I'm fo difheartened by this wound Belinda has given me, I don't think I fhall have courage enough to draw my fword.

Conft. Oh, if that be all, come along; I'll warrant you'll find fword enough for fuch enemies as we have to deal withal.　　　　　[*Exeunt.*

S C E N E, *a Street.*

Enter Conftable and Watchmen with Sir John.

Conft. Come, forfooth, come along, if you pleafe. I once, in compaffion, thought to have feen you fafe home this morning; but you have been fo rampant and abufive all night, I fhall fee what the Juftice of Peace will fay to you.

Sir John. And you fhall fee what I'll fay to the Juftice of Peace, firrah.　　　　　[*Watchman knocks at the door.*

Enter Servant.

Conft. Is Mr. Juftice at home?

Serv. Yes.

Conft. Pray, acquaint his worfhip we have got an unruly woman here, and defire to know what he'll pleafe to have done with her.

I　　　　　　　　　　　　　　　　　　　*Serv.*

Serv. I'll acquaint my master.   [*Exit.*

Sir John. Hark you, Constable; what cuckoldy Justice is this?

Conf. One that knows how to deal with such romps as you are, I'll warrant you.

Enter Justice.

Juſt. Well, Mr. Conſtable, what is the matter there?

Conſt. An't pleaſe your worſhip, this here comical ſort of a gentlewoman has committed great outrages to-night. She has been frolicking with my Lord Rake and his gang; they attacked the watch, and I hear there has been a man killed: I believe 'tis they have done it.

Sir John. Sir, there may have been murder, for ought I know; and there may have been a rape too—that fellow would have raviſhed me.

2d Watch. Raviſh! raviſh! Oh, lud! Oh, lud! Oh, lud! raviſh her! Why, pleaſe your worſhip, I heard Mr. Conſtable ſay, he believed ſhe was little better than a maphrodite.

Juſt. Why, truly, ſhe does ſeem a little maſculine about the mouth.

2d Watch. Yes, and about the hands too, an't pleaſe your worſhip. I did but offer, in mere civility, to help her up the ſtairs into our apartment, and with her gripen fiſt, thus——   [Sir John *knocks him down.*

Sir John. Ay, juſt ſo, Sir, I felled him to the ground like an ox.

Juſt. Out upon this boiſterous woman! out upon her!

Sir John. Mr. Juſtice, he would have been uncivil: it was in defence of my honour, and I demand ſatisfaction.

2d Watch. I hope your worſhip will ſatisfy her honour in Bridewell. That fiſt of hers will make an admirable hemp-beater.

Sir John. Sir, I hope you will protect me againſt that libidinous raſcal. I am a woman of quality, and virtue too, for all I am in an undreſs this morning.

Juſt. Why, ſhe really has the air of a ſort of a woman, a little ſomethingiſh out of the common. Madam, if you expect I ſhould be favourable to you, I deſire I may know who you are.

Sir John. Sir, I am any body, at your ſervice.

Juſt. Lady, I deſire to know your name.

E   *Sir*

Sir John. Sir, my name's Mary.

Just. Ay, but your surname, Madam.

Sir John. Sir, my surname's the very same with my husband's.

Just. A strange woman this! Who is your husband, pray?

Sir John. Sir John——

Just. Sir John who?

Sir John. Sir John Brute.

Just. Is it possible, Madam, you can be my Lady Brute?

Sir John. That happy woman, Sir, am I; only a little in my merriment to-night.

Just. I am concerned for Sir John.

Sir John. Truly, so am I.

Just. I have heard he's an honest gentleman.

Sir John. As ever drank.

Just. Good lack! Indeed, Lady, I'm sorry he has such a wife.

Sir John. I am sorry he has any wife at all.

Just. And so perhaps may he—I doubt you have not given him a very good taste of matrimony.

Sir John. Taste, Sir! Sir, I have scorned to stint him to a taste, I have given him a full meal of it.

Just. Indeed, I believe so! But pray, fair Lady, may he have given you any occasion for this extraordinary conduct—Does he not use you well?

Sir John. A little upon the rough sometimes.

Just. Ay, any man may be out of humour now and then.

Sir John. Sir, I love peace and quiet, and when a woman don't find that at home, she's apt sometimes to comfort herself wih a few innocent diversions abroad.

Just. I doubt he uses you but too well. Pray how does he as to that weighty thing, money? Does he allow you what is proper of that?

Sir John. Sir, I have generally enough to pay the reckoning, if this son of a whore of a drawer would but bring his bill.

Just. A strange woman this—Does he spend a reasonable portion of his time at home, to the comfort of his wife and children?

Sir

Sir John. He never gave his wife cause to repine at his being abroad in his life.

Juſt. Pray, Madam, how may he be in the grand matrimonial point.—Is he true to your bed?

Sir John. Chaſte! 'Oons! This fellow aſks ſo many impertinent queſtions! 'Egad, I believe it is the Juſtice's wife, in the Juſtice's clothes.

Juſt. 'Tis great pity he ſhould have been thus diſpoſed of. Pray, Madam, (and then I've done) what may be your Ladyſhip's common method of life? If I may preſume ſo far.

Sir John. Why, Sir, much that of a woman of quality.

Juſt. Pray how may you generally paſs your time, Madam? Your morning, for example.

Sir John. Sir, like a woman of quality:——I wake about two o'clock in the afternoon—I ſtretch—and make a ſign for my chocolate—When I have drank three cups—I ſlide down again upon my back, with my arms over my head, while my two maids put on my ſtockings—Then hanging upon their ſhoulders, I am trailed to my great chair, where I ſit—and yawn—for my breakfaſt—If it don't come preſently, I lie down upon my couch to ſay my prayers, while my maid reads me the play-bills.

Juſt. Very well, Madam.

Sir John. When the tea is brought in, I drink twelve regular diſhes, with eight ſlices of bread and butter—And half an hour after, I ſend to the cook, to know if the dinner is almoſt ready.

Juſt. So, Madam!

Sir John. By that time my head is half dreſt, I hear my huſband ſwearing himſelf into a ſtate of perdition, that the meat's all cold upon the table; to amend which, I come down in an hour more, and have it ſent back to the kitchen, to be all dreſt over again.

Juſt. Poor man!

Sir John. When I have dined, and my idle ſervants are preſumptuouſly ſet down at their eaſe, to do ſo too, I call for my coach, to go viſit fifty dear friends, of whom I hope I never ſhall find one at home, while I ſhall live.

Juſt. So! there's the morning and afternoon pretty

well difpofed of——Pray now, Madam, how do you pafs your evenings?

Sir John. Like a woman of fpirit; a great fpirit. Give me a box and dice—Seven's the main Oons! Sir, I fet you a hundred pound! Why, do you think women are married now a-days, to fit at home and mend napkins? Oh, the lord help your head!

Juſt. Mercy upon us, Mr. Conſtable! what will this age come to?

Conſt. What will it come to, indeed, if fuch women as thefe are not fet in the ſtocks!

Sir John. Sir, I have a little urgent bufinefs calls upon me; and therefore I defire the favour of you to bring matters to a conclufion.

Juſt. Madam, if I were fure that bufinefs were not to commit more diforders, I would releafe you.

Sir John. None——By my virtue.

Juſt. Then, Mr. Conſtable, you may difcharge her.

Sir John. Sir, your very humble fervant. If you pleafe to accept of a bottle——

Juſt. I thank you kindly, Madam; but I never drink in a morning. Good-by-t'ye, Madam, good-by-t'ye.

Sir John. Good-by-t'ye, good Sir. [*Exit Juſtice.*] So—now, Mr. Conſtable, fhall you and I go pick up a whore together?

Conſt. No, thank you, Madam; my wife's enough to fatisfy any reafonable man.

Sir John. [*Aſide.*] He, he, he, he, he—the fool is married then. Well, you won't go!

Conſt. Not I, truly.

Sir John. Then I'll go by myfelf; and you and your wife may go to the devil. [*Exit Sir* John.

Conſt. [*Gazing after her.*] Why, God-a-mercy, Lady. [*Exeunt.*

SCENE, Spring-Garden.

Conſtant *and* Heartfree *crofs the Stage. As they go off, enter Lady* Fancyful *and* Mademoifelle *maſked, and dogging them.*

Conſt. So; I think we are about the time appointed. Let us walk up this way. [*Exeunt.*

Lady Fan. Good: thus far I have dogged them without

out being difcovered. 'Tis infallibly fome intrigue that brings them to Spring-Garden.. How my poor heart is torn and wrecked with fear and jealoufy! Yet let it be any thing but that flirt Belinda, and I'll try to bear it. But if it proves her, all that's woman in me fhall be employed to deftroy her.

[*Exit after* Conftant *and* Heartfree.

Re-enter Conftant *and* Heartfree. *Lady* Fancyful *and* Mademoifelle, *ftill following at a diftance.*

Conft. I fee no females yet, that have any thing to fay to us. I'm afraid we are bantered.

Heart. I wifh we were; for I'm in no humour to make either them or myfelf merry.

Conft. Nay, I'm fure you'll make them merry enough, if I tell them why you are dull. But, pr'ythee, why fo heavy and fad before you begin to be ill-ufed?

' *Heart.* For the fame reafon, perhaps, that you are ' fo brifk and well-pleafed; becaufe both pains and plea-
' fures are generally more confiderable in profpect, than ' when they come to pafs.'

Enter Lady Brute *and* Belinda, *mafked, and poorly dreffed.*

Conft. How now! who are are thefe? Not our game, I hope.

Heart. If they are, we are e'en well enough ferved, to come a hunting here, when we had fo much better game in chafe elfewhere.

Lady Fan. [*To Mademoifelle.*] So, thofe are their ladies, without doubt. But I'm afraid that Doily ftuff is not worne for want of better clothes. They are the very fhape and fize of Belinda and her aunt.

Mad. So dey be inteed, Madam.

Lady Fan. We'll flip into this clofe arbour, where we may hear all they fay.

[*Exeunt Lady* Fancyful *and* Mademoifelle.

Lady Brute. What, are you afraid of us, gentlemen?

Heart. Why, truly, I think we may, if appearance don't lie.

Bel. Do you always find women what they appear to be, Sir?

E 3

Heart.

Heart. No, forsooth; but I seldom find them better than they appear to be.

Bel. Then the outside's best, you think?

Heart. 'Tis the honestest.

Conft. Have a care, Heartfree; you are relapsing again.

Lady Brute. Why, does the gentleman use to rail at women?

Conft. He has done formerly.

Lel. I suppose he had very good call for't. They did not use you so well, as you thought you deserved, Sir?

Lady Brute. They made themselves merry, at your expence, Sir?

Bel. Laughed when you sighed?

Lady Brute. Slept while you were waking?

Bel. Had your porter beat?

Lady Brute. And threw your billet-doux in the fire?

Heart. Hey-day, I shall do more than rail, presently.

Bel. Why, you won't beat us, will you?

Heart. I don't know but I may.

Conft. What the devil's coming here? Sir John—and drunk, i'faith.

Enter Sir John.

Sir John. What a pox——here's Conftant, Heartfree —and two whores 'egad—Oh, you covetous rogues!— what have you never a spare punk for your friend?— But I'll share with you.

Heart. Why what the plague have you been doing, knight?   [*He seizes both the women.*

Sir John. Why, I have been beating the watch, and scandalizing the women of quality.

Heart. A very good account, truly.

Sir John. And what do you think I'll do next?

Conft. Nay, that no man can guess.

Sir John. Why, if you'll let me sup with you, I'll treat both your strumpets.

Lady Brute. [*Afide.*] Oh, lord! we're undone.

Heart. No, we can't sup together, because we have some affairs elsewhere. But if you'll accept of these two ladies, we'll be so complaisant to you, to resign our right to them.

Bel. [*Afide.*] Lord, what shall we do?'

Sir

Sir John. Let me fee, their cloaths are fuch damned clothes, they won't pawn for the reckoning.

Heart. Sir John, your fervant.   Raptures attend you.

Conft. Adieu, ladies, make much of the gentleman.

Lady Brute. Why fure you won't leave us in the hands of a drunken fellow to abufe us.

Sir John. Who do you call a drunken fellow, you flut you? I'm a man of quality; the king has made me a knight.

Heart. Aye, aye, you are in good hands; adieu, adieu.

[Heartfree *runs off.*

Lady Brute. The devil's hands! Let me go, or I'll— For Heaven's fake, protect us!

[She breaks from him, runs to Conftant, twitching off her mafk, and clapping it on again.

Sir John. I'll devil you, you jade you. I'll demolifh your ugly face.

Re-enter Heartfree. Belinda *runs to him, and fhews her face.*

Heart. Hold, thou mighty man! Look ye, Sir, we did but jeft with you. Thefe are ladies of our acquaintance that we had a mind to frighten a little, but now you muft leave us.

Sir John. 'Oons, I won't leave you, not I.

Heart. Nay, but you muft though; and therefore make no words on't.

Sir John. Then you are a couple of damned uncivil fellows. And I hope your punks will give you fauce to your mutton.   [*Exit Sir* John.

Lady Brute. Oh, I fhall never come to myfelf again, I'm fo frightened!

Conft. 'Tis a narrow efcape, indeed.

Bel. Women muft have frolicks, you fee, whatever they coft them.

Heart. This might have proved a dear one though.

Lady Brute. You are the more obliged to us for the rifk we run upon your accounts.

Conft. And I hope you'll acknowledge fomething due to our knight-errantry, ladies. This is the fecond time we have delivered you.

Lady Brute. 'Tis true; and fince we fee fate has de-

fign'd

signed you for our guardians, 'twill make us the more willing to truſt ourſelves in your hands. But you muſt not have the worſe opinion of us for our innocent frolick.

Heart. Ladies, you may command our opinions in every thing that is to your advantage.

Bel. Then, Sir, I command you to be of opinion, that women are ſometimes better than they appear to be.

[*Lady* Brute *and* Conſtant *talk apart.*

Heart. Madam, you have made a convert of me in every thing. I'm grown a fool. I could be fond of a woman.

Bel. I thank you, Sir, in the name of the whole ſex;

Heart. Which ſex nothing but yourſelf could ever have atoned for.

Bel. Now has my vanity a deviliſh itch to know in what my merit conſiſts.

Heart. In your humility, Madam, that keeps you ignorant it conſiſts at all.

Bel. One other compliment, with that ſerious face, and I hate you for ever after.

Heart. Some women love to be abuſed; is that it you would be at?

Bel. No, not that neither: but I'd have men talk plainly what's fit for women to hear, without putting them either to a real or an affected bluſh.

Heart. Why then, in as plain terms as I can find to expreſs myſelf, I could love you even to matrimony itſelf almoſt, 'egad.

Bel. Juſt as Sir John did her Ladyſhip there—' What
' think you? Don't you believe one month's time might
' bring you down to the ſame indifference, only clad in
' a little better manners, perhaps? ' Well, you men are
' unaccountable things, mad till you have your miſtreſſes,
' and then ſtark mad till you are rid of them again. Tell
' me honeſtly, is not your patience put to a much ſeverer
' trial after poſſeſſion than before?

' *Heart.* With a great many, I muſt confeſs it is, to
' our eternal ſcandal; but I'—dear creature, do but try
me.

Bel. That's the ſureſt way, indeed, to know, but not the ſafeſt. [*To Lady* Brute.] Madam, are not you for

taking

taking a turn in the great walk? It's almost dark, nobody will know us.

Lady Brute. Really I find myself something idle, Belinda: besides I doat upon this little odd private corner. But don't let my lazy fancy confine you.

Const. [*Aside.*] So, she would be left alone with me; that's well.

Bel. Well, we'll take one turn, and come to you again. [*To* Heartfree.] Come, Sir, shall we go pry into the secrets of the garden? Who knows what discoveries we may make.

Heart. Madam, I am at your service.

Const. [*To* Heartf. *aside.*] Don't make too much haste back; for, d'ye hear——' I may be busy.'

Heart. Enough.   [*Exeunt* Belinda *and* Heartfree.

Lady Brute. Sure you think me scandalously free, Mr. Constant, I'm afraid I shall lose your good opinion of me.

Const. My good opinion, Madam, is like your cruelty, never to be removed.

Lady Brute. Indeed, I doubt you much; why, suppose you had a wife, and she should entertain a gallant?

Const. If I gave her just cause, how should I justly condemn her?

Lady Brute. Ah, but you differ widely about just causes.

Const. But blows can bear no dispute.

Lady Brute. Nor ill manners much, truly.

Const. Then no woman upon earth has so just a cause as you have.

' *Lady Brute.* But can a husband's faults release my
' duty?

' *Const.* In equity, without doubt. And where laws
' dispense with equity, equity should dispense with laws.

' *Lady Brute.* Pray let us leave this dispute; for you
' men have as much witchcraft in your arguments, as
' women have in their eyes.

' *Const.* But whilst you attack me with your charms,
' 'tis but reasonable I assault you with mine.

' *Lady Brute.* The case is not the same. What mis-
' chief we do we can't help, and therefore are to be for-
' given.

' *Const.* Beauty soon obtains pardon for the pain that
' it gives, when it applies the balm of compassion to the
' wound: but a fine face and a hard heart is almost as bad

' as an ugly face and a foft one; both very troublefome
' to many a poorgentleman.

' *Lady Brute.* Yes, and to many a poor gentlewoman
' too, I can affure you. But pray which of them is it
' that moft afflicts you?

' *Conft.* Your glafs and confcience will inform you,
' Madam.' But for Heaven's fake, (for now I muft be
ferious) if pity, or if gratitude can move you; [*Taking
her hand.*] if conftancy and truth have power to tempt
you; if love, if adoration can affect you, give me at leaft
fome hopes, that time may do, what you perhaps mean
never to perform; 'twill eafe my fufferings, though not
quench my flame.

Lady Brute. Your fufferings eafed, your flame would
foon abate; and that I would preferve, not quench it,
Sir.

Conft. Would you preferve it, nourifh it with favours;
for that's the food it naturally requires.

Lady Brute. Yet on that natural food, 'twould furfeit
foon, fhould I refolve to grant all you would afk.

Conft. And in refufing all, you ftarve it. Forgive me
therefore, fince my hunger rages, if I at laft grow wild,
and in my frenzy force at leaft this from you. [*Kiffing
her hand.*] Or if you'd have my flame foar higher ftill,
then grant me this, and this, and thoufands more; [*Kiffing firft her hand and then her neck.*] for now's the time
fhe melts into compaffion.   [*Afide.*

Lady Brute. Oh, heavens! Let me go.

Conft. Ay, go, ay: where fhall we go, my charming
angel——into this private arbour——Nay, let's lofe no
time——moments are precious——

Lady Brute. And lovers wild. Pray let us ftop here;
at leaft for this time.

Conft. 'Tis impoffible; he that has power over you,
can have none over himfelf.

> [*As he is forcing her into the arbour,* Lady Fancyful
> *and* Mademoifelle *bolt upon them, and run over the
> ftage.*

Lady Brute. Ah! I'm loft.

Lady Fan. Fe, fe, fe, fe, fe.

Mad. Fe, fe, fe, fe, fe.

Conft. Death and furies, who are thefe?

Lady

Lady Brute. Oh, heavens! I'm out of my wits; if they know me, I am ruined.

Conſt. Don't be frightened: ten thouſand to one they are ſtrangers to you.

Lady Brute. Whatever they are, I won't ſtay here a moment longer.

Conſt. Whither will you go?

Lady Brute. Home, as if the devil were in me. Lord, where's this Belinda now?

Enter Belinda *and* Heartfree.

Oh! 'tis well you are cóme; I'm ſo frightened, ' my ' hair ſtands an end.' Let's begone, for Heaven's ſake.

Bel. Lord, what's the matter?

Lady Brute. The devil's the matter; here's a couple of women have done the moſt impertinent thing. Away, away, away, away, away.   [*Exeunt running.*

END of the FOURTH ACT.

A C T · V.

SCENE, *Lady* Fancyful's *Houſe.*

Enter Lady Fancyful *and* Mademoiſelle.

LADY FANCYFUL.

WELL, Mademoiſelle; did you dodge the filthy things?

Mad. Oh, qu' oui, Madame.

Lady Fan. And where are they?

Mad. Au logis.

Lady Fan. What, men and all?

Mad. Tous enſemble.

Lady Fan. Oh, confidence! What, carry their fellows to their own houſe!

Mad. C'eſt que le mari n'y eſt pas.

Lady Fan. No, ſo I believe, truly. But he ſhall be there, and quickly too, if I can find him out. Well, 'tis a prodigious thing, to ſee when men and women get together, how they fortify one another in their impudence. But if that drunken fool, her huſband, be to be found in e'er a tavern in town, I'll ſend him amongſt them; I'll ſpoil their ſport.

Mad.

Mad. En vérité, Madame, ce seroit domage.

Lady Fan. 'Tis in vain to oppose it, Mademoiselle; therefore never go about it: for I am the steadiest creature in the world——when I have determined to do mischief. So come along. [*Exeunt.*

SCENE, *Sir* John Brute's *House.*

Enter Constant, Heartfree, *Lady* Brute, Belinda, *and* Lovewell.

Lady Brute. But you are sure you don't mistake, Lovewell?

Love. Madam, I saw them all go into the tavern together, and my master so drunk he could scarce stand. [*Exit.*

Lady Brute. Then, gentlemen, I believe we may venture to let you stay, and play at cards with us an hour or two: for they'll scarce part till morning.

Bel. I think, 'tis pity they should ever part——

Const. The company that's here, Madam.

Lady Brute. Then, Sir, the company that's here must remember to part itself in time.

Const. Madam, we don't intend to forfeit your future favours, by an indiscreet usage of this. The moment you give us the signal, we shan't fail to make our retreat.

Lady Brute. Upon those conditions then let us sit down to cards.

Enter Lovewell.

Love. Oh, lord, Madam! here's my master just staggering in upon you: he has been quarrelsome yonder, and they have kicked him out of the company.

Lady Brute. Into the closet, gent'emen, for Heaven's sake; I'll wheedle him to-bed, if possible.

[Const. *and* Heartf. *run into the closet.*
Enter Sir John, *all dirt and bloody.*

Lady Brute. Ah ——Ah —— he's all over blood.

Sir John. What the plague does the woman squall for? Did you never see a man in a pickle before?

Lady Brute. Lord, where have you been?

Sir John. I have been at——cuffs.

Lady Brute. I fear that is not all. I hope you are not wounded.

Sir John. Sound as a roach, wife.

Lady

Lady Brute. I'm mighty glad to hear it.

Sir John. You know—I think you lie.

Lady Brute. You do me wrong to think so. For Heaven's my witness, I had rather see my own blood trickle down, than yours.

Sir John. Then will I be sacrificed.

Lady Brute. 'Tis a hard fate I should not be believed.

Sir John. 'Tis a damned atheistical age, wife.

Lady Brute. I am sure I have given you a thousand tender proofs how great my care is of you. But, spite' of all your cruel thoughts, I'll still persist, and at this moment, if I can, persuade you to lie down and sleep a little.

Sir John. Why—do you think I am drunk—you slut, you?

Lady Brute. Heaven forbid I should: but I'm afraid you are feverish. Pray, let me feel your pulse.

Sir John. Stand off, and be damned.

Lady Brute. Why, I see your distemper in your very eyes. You are all on fire. Pray, go to bed; let me intreat you.

Sir John.——Come, kiss me, then.

Lady Brute. [*Kissing him.*] There: now go. [*Aside.*] He stinks like poison.

Sir John. I see it goes damnably against your stomach.—and therefore—kiss me again.

Lady Brute. Nay, now you fool me.

Sir John. Do't, I say.

Lady Brute. [*Aside.*] Ah, lord have mercy upon me. Well; there: now will you go?

Sir John. Now, wife, you shall see my gratitude. You gave me two kisses—I'll give you—two hundred.

[*Kisses and tumbles her.*

Lady Brute. Oh, lord! pray, Sir John, be quiet. Heavens, what a pickle am I in!

' *Bel.* [*Aside.*] If I were in her pickle, I'd call my
' gallant out of the closet, and he should cudgel him
' soundly.'

Sir John. So, now you being as dirty and as nasty as myself, we may go pig together. But first I must have a cup of your cold tea, wife.   [*Going to the closet.*

F

Lady

L. B. Oh, I'm ruin'd! There's none there, my dear.

Sir John. I'll warrant you, I'll find some, my dear.

Lady Brute. You can't open the door, the lock's fpoiled; I have been turning and turning the key this half hour to no purpofe. I'll fend for the fmith to-morrow.

Sir John. There's ne'er a fmith in Europe can open a door with more expedition than I can do—As for example—Pou. [*He burfts ofen the door with his foot.*]—How now! What the devil have we got here?—Conftant—Heartfree—and two whores again, 'egad—This is the worft cold tea—that ever I met with in my life——

Enter Conftant *and* Heartfree.

Lady Brute. [*Afide.*] Oh, lord, what will become of us?

Sir John. Gentlemen—I am your very humble fervant—I give you many thanks—I fee you take care of my family—I fhall do all I can to return the obligation.

Conft. Sir, how oddly foever this bufinefs may appear to you, you'd have no caufe to be uneafy, if you knew the truth of all things? Your Lady is the moft virtuous woman in the world, and nothing has paft, but an innocent frolick.

Heart. Nothing elfe, upon my honour, Sir.

Sir John. You are both very civil gentlemen—And my wife there, is a very civil gentlewoman; therefore I don't doubt but many civil things have paft between you. Your very humble fervant.

Lady Brute. [*Afide to* Conft.] Pray begone: he's fo drunk, he can't hurt us to-night, and to-morrow morning you fhall hear from us.

Conft. I'll obey you, Madam. Sir, when you are cool, you'll underftand reafon better. So then I fhall take the pains to inform you. If not—I wear a fword, Sir, and fo good-by-t'ye. Come along, Heartfree.   [*Exeunt.*

Sir John. Wear a fword, Sir—And what of all that, Sir? He comes to my houfe; eats my mea; lies with my wife; difhonours my family; gets a baftard to inherit my eftate—And when I afk a civil account of all this—Sir, fays he, I wear a fword.—Wear a fword, Sir? Yes, Sir, fays he, I wear a fword.—It may be a good anfwer at crofs purpofes; but 'tis a damned one to a man in my whimfical circumftances—Sir, fays he, I wear a

fword!

word! [*To Lady* Brute.] And what do you wear now? Ha! tell me, [*Sitting down in a great chair.*] What you are modest, and can't—Why then I'll tell you, you slut you. You wear—an impudent lewd face—a damned, designing heart—and a tail—and a tail full of ——

[*He falls fast asleep snoring.*

Lady Brute. So, thanks to kind Heaven, he's fast for some hours.

Bel. 'Tis well he is so, that we may have time to lay our story handsomely; for we must lie like the devil, to bring ourselves off.

Lady Brute. What shall we say, Belinda?

Bel. [*Musing.*]—I'll tell you: it must all light upon Hearttree and I. We'll say he has courted me some time, but for reasons unknown to us, has ever been very earnest the thing might be kept from Sir John. That therefore hearing him upon the stairs, he run into the closet, tho' against our will, and Constant with him, to prevent jealousy. And to give this a good impudent face of truth, (that I may deliver you from the trouble you are in) I'll e'en, if he pleases, marry him.

Lady Brute. I'm beholden to you, cousin; but that would be carrying the jest a little too far, for your own sake: you know he's a younger brother, and has nothing.

Bel. 'Tis true: but I like him, and have fortune enough to keep above extremity: I can't say I would live with him in a cell, upon love and bread and butter: but I'd rather have the man I love, and a middle state of life, that that gentleman in the chair there, and twice your Ladyship's splendor.

Lady Brute. In truth, niece, you are in the right on't; but 'tis late: let's end our discourse for to-night, and out of an excess of charity, take a small care of that nasty drunken thing there—do but look at him, Belinda.

Bel. Ah—'tis a savoury dish.

Lady Brute. As savoury as 'tis, I'm cloyed with it. Pr'ythee call the butler to take away.

Bel. Call the butler?—Call the scavenger! [*To a servant within.*] Who's there? Call Rasor! Let him take away his master, scour him clean with a little soap and sand, and so put him to bed.

Lady Brute. Come, Belinda, I'll e'en lie with you to-

night;

night; and in the morning we'll fend for our gentlemen to fet this matter even.

Bel. With all my heart.

Lady Brute. Good-night, my dear.

[*Making a low curtefy to Sir* John.

Beth. Ha, ha, ha.   [*Exeunt.*

Enter Rafor.

Raf. My Lady there's a wag—My mafter there's a a cuckold. Marriage is a flippery thing—Women have depraved appetites—My Lady's a wag; I have heard all; I have feen all; I underftand all; and I'll tell all; for my little Frenchwoman loves news dearly. This ftory will gain her heart, or nothing will. [*To his mafter.*] Come, Sir, your head's too full of fumes at prefent, to make room for your jealoufy; but I reckon we fhall have rare work with you, when your pate's empty. Come to your kennel, you cuckoldy, drunken fot, you.

[*Carries him on his back.*

My mafter's afleep, in his chair, and a fnoring,
My Lady's abroad, and—Oh, rare matrimony!

SCENE, *Lady* Fancyful's *Houfe.*

Enter Lady Fancyful *and* Mademoifelle.

Lady Fan. But, why did not you tell me before, Mademoifelle, that Rafor and you were fond?

Mad. De modefty hinder me, Matam.

Lady Fan. Why, truly modefty does often hinder us from doing things we have an extravagant mind to. But does he love you well enough yet, to do any thing you bid him? Do you think, to oblige you, he would fpeak fcandal?

Mad. Matam, to oblige your Ladyfhip, he fhall fpeak any thing.

Lady Fan. Why then, Mademoifelle, I'll tell you what you fhall do. You fhall engage him to tell his mafter, all that paft at Spring Garden: I have a mind he fhould know what a wife and a niece he has got.

Mad. Il le fera, Madame.

Enter a Footman, who fpeaks to Mademoifelle *apart.*

Foot. Mademoifelle, yonder's Mr. Rafor defires to fpeak with you.

Mad.

Mad. Tell him, I come prefently. [*Exit Footman.*
Rafor be dere, Madame.

Lady Fan. That's fortunate : well, I'll leave you together.   And if you find him ftubborn, Mademoifelle ——
hark you—don't refufe him a few reafonable little liberties, to put him in humour.

Mad. Laiffez moi faire.   [*Exit Lady* Fan.

   [Rafor *peeps in* ; *and feeing Lady* Fancyful *gone, turns
         to* Mademoifelle, *takes her about the neck, and
         kiffes her.*

Mad. How now, confidence !

Raf. How now, modefty !

Mad. Who make you fo familiar, firrah ?

Raf. My impudence, huffy.

Mad. Stand off, rogue-face.

Raf. Ah—Mademoifelle—great news at our houfe.

Mad. Why, vat be de matter ?

Raf. The matter ?—Why uptails all's the matter.

Mad. Tu te mocque de moi.

Raf. Now do you long to know the particulars : the
time when ; the place where ; the manner how.   But I
won't tell you a word more.

Mad. Nay, den dou kill me, Rafor.

Raf. Come, kifs me, then.

Mad. Nay, pridee tell me.
                              [*Clapping his hands behind.*

Raf. Good-by-t'ye.   [*Going.*

Mad. Hold, hold ; I will kifs dee.   [*Kiffing him.*

Raf. So, that's civil : why now, my pretty Poll ; my
goldfinch ; my little waterwagtail—you muft know, that
——Come, kifs me again.

Mad. I won't kifs de no more.

Raf. Good-by-t'ye.   [*Going.*

Mad. Doucement ; dere ; es tu content ? [*Kiffing him.*

Raf. So ; now I'll tell thee all. Why the news is, that
cuckoldom in folio is newly printed ; and matrimony in
quarto, is juft going into the prefs.   Will you buy any
books, Mademoifelle ?

Mad. Tu parles comme un libraire ; de devil, no underftand dee.

Raf. Why then, that I may make myfelf intelligible to

a waiting-woman, I'll fpeak like a valet de chambre. My Lady has cuckolded my mafter.

Mad. Bon.

Raf. Which we take very ill from her hands, I can tell her that. We can't yet prove matter of fact upon her.

Mad. N'importe.

Raf. But we can prove that matter of fact had like to have been upon her.

Mad. Oui-da.

Raf. For we have fuch terrible circumftances——

Mad. Sans doute.

Raf. That any man of parts may draw tickling conclufions from them.

Mad. Fort bien.

Raf. We found a couple of tight well-built gentlemen, ftuffed into her Ladyfhip's clofet.

Mad. Le diable !

Raf. And I, in my particular perfon, have difcovered a ' moft damnable' plot, how to perfuade my poor mafter, that all this hide and feek, this Will in the Wifp, has no other meaning than a Chriftian marriage for fweet Mrs. Belinda.

Mad. Une marriage ? Ah, les droleffes !

Raf. Don't you interrupt me, huffy ; 'tis agreed, I fay ; and my innocent Lady, to wriggle herfelf out at the back-door of the bufinefs, turns marriage-bawd to her niece, and refolves to deliver up her fair body to be tumbled and mumbled, by that young liquorifh whipfter, Heartfree. Now are you fatisfied ?

Mad. No.

Raf. Right woman ; always gaping for more.

Mad. Dis be all den, dat you know ?

Raf. All ! Ay, and a great deal too, I think.

Mad. Dou be fool, dou know nothing.—Ecoute, mon pauvre, Rafor. Dou fees des two eyes ?—Des two eyes have fee de devil.

Raf. The woman's mad.

Mad. In Spring Garden, dat rogue Conftant meet dy Lady.

Raf. Bon.

Mad.——I'll tell dee no more.

Mad.

Raf. Nay, pr'ythee, my fwan.

Mad. Come, kifs me den.

   [*Clapping her hands behind her, as he did before.*

Raf. I won't kifs you, not I.

Mad. Adieu.   [*Going.*

Raf. Hold—Now proceed. [*Gives her a hearty kifs.*

Mad. A ça—I hide myfelf in one cunning place, where I hear all, and fee all. Firft dy drunken mafter come mal-à-propos ? But de fot no know his own dear wife, fo he leave her to her fport.—Den de game begin. De lover fay foft ting ; de lady look upon de ground. [*As fhe fpeaks,* Rafor *ftill acts the man, and fhe the woman.*] He take her by de hand ; fhe turn her head on oder way. Den he fqueeze very hard ; den fhe pull—very foftly. Den he take her in his arms ; den fhe give him little pat. ' Den he kifs her tettons. Den fhe fay—pifh, nay fie.' Den he tremble ; den fhe figh. Den he pull her into de arbor ; den fhe pinch him.

Raf. Ay, but not fo hard, you baggage you.

Mad. Den he grow bold ; fhe grow weake, he tro her down, il tombe deffus, le Diable affifte, il emporte tout ; [Rafor *ftruggles with her, as if he would throw her down.*] ftand off, firrah.

Raf. You have fet me a-fire, you jade, you.

Mad. Den go to de river and quench dyfelf.

Raf. What an unnatural harlot this !

Mad. Rafor.   [*Looking languifhingly on him.*

Raf. M. demoifelle.

Mad. Dou no love me ?

Raf. Not love thee !——More than a Frenchman does foup.

Mad. Den you will refufe nothing dat I bid dee ?

Raf. Don't bid me hang myfelf then.

Mad. No ; only tell dy mafter, all I have tell dee of dy lady.

Raf. Why, you little malicious ftrumpet, you ; fhould you like to be ferved fo ?

Mad. Dou difpute den ?——Adieu.

Raf. Hold—But why wilt thou make me be fuch a rogue, my dear ?

Mad. Voilà un vrai Anglois ! il eft amoureux, et cependant il veut raifonner. Va t'en au diable.

          Raf.

Raf. Hold once more: in hopes thou'lt give me up thy body, I'll make thee a prefent of my honefty..

Mad. Bon ; écoute donc ;—if dou fail me—I never fee dee more---if dou obey me---Je m'abandonne à toi à toi. [*She takes him about the neck, and gives him a fmacking kifs.*]
[*Exit* Mademoifelle.

Raf. [*Licking his lips.*] Not be a rogue !---*Amor vincit omnia.* [*Exit* Rafor.

Enter *Lady* Fancyful *and* Mademoifelle.
Lady Fan. Marry, fay ye ! Will the two things marry ?
Mad. On le va faire, Madame.
Lady Fan. Look you, Mademoifelle, in fhort I can't bear it---No; I find I can't---If once I fee them a-bed together, I fhall have ten thoufand thoughts in my head will make me run diftracted. Therefore run and call Rafor back immediately ; for fomething muft be done to ftop this impertinent wedding. If I can but defer it four and twenty hours, I'll make fuch work about town, with that little pert flut's reputation, he fhall as foon marry a witch.

Mad. [*Afide.*] La voilà bien intentionée. [*Exeunt..*

SCENE, Conftant's *Lodgings.*

Enter Conftant *and* Heartfree.
Conft. But what doft think will become of this bufi-nefs ?
Heart. 'Tis eafier to think what will not become on't..
Conft.. What's that ?
Heart. A challenge. I know the knight too well for that ; his dear body will always prevail upon his noble foul to be quiet.

Conft. But though he dare not challenge me, perhaps he may venture to challenge his wife.

Heart. Not if you whifper him in the ear, you won't have him do't, and there's no other way left that I fee : for as drunk as he was, he'll remember you and I were where we fhould not be ; and I don't think him quite blockhead enough yet to be perfuaded we were got into his wife's clofet only to peep into her prayer-book.

Enter a *Servant with a letter.*
Serv. Sir, here's a letter, a porter brought it.
Conft. Oh, ho, here's inftructions for us. [*Reads.*

" The

" The accident that has happened, has touched our invention to the quick. We would fain come off without your help; but find that's impoſſible. In a word, the whole buſineſs muſt be thrown upon a matrimonial intrigue between your friend and mine. But if the parties are not fond enough to go quite through with the matter, 'tis ſufficient for our turn, they own the deſign. We'll find pretences enough to break the match. Adieu."
——Well, women for invention! How long would my blockhead have been producing this!—Hey, Heartfree! What muſing, man! Pr'ythee be chearful: what ſayeſt thou, friend, to this matrimonial remedy?

Heart. Why, I ſay, it's worſe than the diſeaſe.

Conſt. Here's a fellow for you: there's beauty and money on her ſide; and love up to the ears on his; and yet——

Heart. And yet, I think, I may reaſonably be allowed to boggle at marrying the niece, in the very moment that you are deluding the aunt.

Conſt. Why, truly, there may be ſomething in that. But have not you a good opinion enough of your own parts, to believe you could keep a wife to yourſelf?

Heart. I ſhould have, if I had a good opinion enough of hers, to believe ſhe could do as much by me. But pr'ythee adviſe me in this good and evil, this life and death, this bleſſing and curſe, that is ſet before me: ' for ' to do them right, after all, the wife ſeldom rambles, ' till the huſband ſhews her the way.

' *Conſt.* 'Tis true, a man of real worth ſcarce ever is a ' cuckold, but by his own fault. Women are not na- ' turally lewd; there muſt be ſomething to urge them to ' it. They'll cuckold a churl, out of revenge; a fool, ' becauſe they deſpiſe him; a beaſt, becauſe they loath ' him: but when they make bold with a man they once ' had a well grounded value for, 'tis becauſe they firſt ' ſee themſelves neglected by him.'

Heart. Shall I marry or die a maid?

Conſt. Why faith, Heartfree, matrimony is like an army, going to engage. Love's the forlorn hope, which is ſoon cut off; the marriage knot is the main body, which may ſtand buff a long time; and repentance is

the

the rear-guard, which rarely gives ground, as long as the main body has a being.

Heart. Conclufion then; you advife me to rake on, as you do.

Conft. That's not concluded yet: for though marriage be a lottery, in which there are wonderous many blanks; yet there is one ineftiamable lot, in which the only heaven on earth is written. Would your kind fate but guide your hand to that, though I were wrapped in all that luxury itfelf could cloath me with, I ftill fhould envy you.

Heart. And juftly too; for to be capable of loving one, doubtlefs, is better than to poffefs a thoufand. But how far that capacity's in me, alas, I know not.

Conft. But you would know.

Heart. I would fo.

Conft. Matrimony will inform you. Come, one flight of refolution carries you to the land of experience; where in a very moderate time you'll know the capacity of your foul and your body both, or I'm miftaken. [*Exeunt.*

S C E N E, *Sir* John Brute's *Houfe.*

Enter Lady Brute *and* Belinda.

Bel. Well, Madam, what anfwer have you from them?

Lady Brute. That they'll be here this moment. I fancy 'twill end in a wedding; I'm fure he's a fool if it don't. Ten thoufand pounds, and fuch a lafs as you are, is no contemptible offer to a younger brother. ' But are not ' you under ftrange agitations? Pr'ythee, how does your ' pulfe beat?

' *Bel.* High and low; I have much a-do to be valiant: ' is it not very ftrange to go to bed with a man?

' *Lady Brute.* Um—it is a little odd at firft, but it will ' foon grow eafy to you.'

Enter Conftant *and* Heartfree.

Good-morrow, gentlemen: how have you flept after your adventure?

Heart. Some careful thoughts, ladies, on your accounts, have kept us waking.

Bel. And fome careful thoughts on your own, I believe, have hindered you from fleeping. Pray how does this matrimonial project relifh with you?

Heart.

Heart. Why, faith, e'en as storming towns does with soldiers, where the hopes of delicious plunder banishes the fear of being knocked on the head.

Bel. Is it then possible, after all, 'that you dare think of downright lawful wedlock?

Heart. Madam, you have made me so fool-hardy, I dare do any thing.

Bel. Then, Sir, I challenge you; and matrimony's the spot where I expect you.

Heart. 'Tis enough; I'll not fail. [*Aside.*] So, now I am in for Hobbe's voyage; a great leap in the dark.

Lady Brute. Well, gentlemen, this matter being concluded then, have you got your lessons ready? for Sir John is grown such an atheist of late, he'll believe nothing upon easy terms.

Const. We'll find means to extend his faith, Madam. But pray how do you find him this morning?

Lady Brute. Most lamentably morose, chewing the cud after last night's discovery, of which however he has but a confused notion e'en now: but I'm afraid the valet de chambre has told him all; for they are very busy together at this moment. When I told him of Belinda's marriage, I had no other answer but a grunt; from which, you may draw what conclusions you think fit. But to your notes, gentlemen, he's here.

Enter Sir John *and* Rasor.

Const. Good-morrow, Sir.

Heart. Good-morrow, Sir John; I'm very sorry my indiscretion should cause so much disorder in your family.

Sir John. Disorders generally come from indiscretion, Sir; 'tis no strange thing at all.

Lady Brute. I hope, my dear, you are satisfied there was no wrong intended you.

Sir John. None, my dove.

Bel. If not, I hope, my consent to marry Mr. Heartfree will convince you. For, as little as I know of amours, Sir, I can assure you, one intrigue is enough to bring four people together, without further mischief.

Sir John. And I know too, that intrigues tend to procreation of more kinds than one. One intrigue will beget another, as soon as beget a son or a daughter.

Const. I am very sorry, Sir, to see you still seem unsa-
tisfied

tisfied with a lady, whose more than common virtue, I am sure, were she my wife, should meet with better usage.

Sir John. Sir, if her conduct has put a trick upon her virtue, her virtue's the bubble, but her husband's the loser.

Const. Sir, you have received a sufficient answer already, to justify both her conduct and mine. You'll pardon me for meddling in your family-affairs; but I perceive I am the man you are jealous of, and therefore it concerns me.

Sir John. Would it did not concern me, and then I should not care who it concerned.

Const. Well, Sir, if truth and reason won't content you, I know but one way more, which, if you think fit, you may take.

Sir John. Lord, Sir, you are very hasty: if I had been found at prayers in your wife's closet, I should have allowed you twice as much time to come to yourself in.

Const. Nay, Sir, if time be all you want, we have no quarrel.

Heart. I told you how the sword would work upon him.   [*Sir* John *muses.*

Const. Let him muse; however, I'll lay fifty pounds our foreman brings us in, not guilty.

Sir John. [*Aside.*] 'Tis well—'tis very well—In spite of that young jade's matrimonial intrigue, I am a downright stinking cuckold—Here they are—Boo—[*Putting his hand to his forehead.*] Methinks, I could butt with a bull. What the plague did I marry her for? I knew she did not like me; if she had, she would have lain with me; for I would have done so, because I liked her; but that's past, and I have her. And now, what shall I do with her?—If I put my horns into my pocket, she'll grow insolent—if I don't, that goat there, that stall on, is ready to whip me through the guts—The debate then is reduced to this; shall I die a hero, or live a rascal?— Why, wiser men than I have long since concluded, that a living dog is better than a dead lion. [*To* Constant *and* Heartfree.] Gentlemen, now my wine and my passion are governable, I must own, I have never observed any thing in my wife's course of life, to back me in my jea-

loufy

loufy of her : but jealoufy's a mark of love; fo fhe need not trouble her head about it, as long as I make no more words on't.

Lady Fancyful *enters difguifed, and addreffes* Belinda *apart.*

Conft. I'm glad to fee your reafon rule at laft. Give me your hand : I hope you'll look upon me as you ufed to do.

Sir John. Your humble fervant. [*Afide.*] A wheedling fon of a whore !

Heart. And that I may be fure you are friends with me too, pray give me your confent to wed your niece.

Sir John. Sir, you have it, with all my heart; damn me if you han't. [*Afide.*] 'Tis time to get rid of her : a young pert pimp : fhe'll make an incomparable bawd in a little time.

. Enter a Servant, who gives Heartfree *a letter.*

Bel. Heartfree your hufband, fay you ? 'Tis impoffible !

Lady Fan. Would to kind Heaven it were; but 'tis too true ; and in the world there lives not fuch a wretch. I'm young : and either I have been flattered by my friends, as well as glafs, or nature has been kind and generous to me. I had a fortune too was greater far than he could ever hope for ; but with my heart I am robbed of all the reft. I am flighted and I'm beggared both at once ; I have fcarce a bare fubfiftence from the villain, yet dare complain to none ; for he has fworn, if ever 'tis known I am his wife, he'll murder me.   [*Weeping.*

Bel. The traitor !

Lady Fan. I accidentally was told he courted you : charity foon prevailed upon me to prevent your mifery ; and, as you fee, I'm ftill fo generous even to him, as not to fuffer he fhould do any thing, for which the law might take away his life.   [*Weeping.*

Bel. Poor creature ! how I pity her !

[*They continue talking afide.*

Heart. [*Afide.*] Death and the devil—Let me read it again. [*Reads.*] " Though I have a particular reafon not to let you know who I am till I fee you ; yet you'll eafily believe 'tis a faithful friend that gives you this advice. I have lain with Belinda;" Good ! " I have a child by her," Better and better ! " which is now out at nurfe;" Hea-

ven be praifed ! " and I think the foundation laid for another ;" Ha ! old True-penny ! " no rack could have tor-
tured this ftory from me ; but friendfhip has done it.   I
heard of your defign to marry her, and could not fee you
abufed.   Make ufe of my advice ; but keep my fecret
till I afk you for it again.   Adieu."

[*Exit* Lady Fancyful.

Conft. [*To* Bel.] Come, Madam, fhall we fend for the
parfon ? I doubt here's no bufinefs for the lawyers ;
younger brothers have nothing to fettle but their hearts,
and that I believe my friend here has done very faithfully.

Bel. [*Scornfully.*] Are you fure, Sir, there are no old
mortgages upon it ?

Heart. [*Coldly.*] If you think there are, Madam, it
may'n't be amifs to defer the marriage till you are fure
they are paid off.

Bel. We'll defer it as long as you pleafe, Sir.

Heart. The more time we take to confider on't, Madam,
the lefs apt we fhall be to commit overfights ; therefore,
if you pleafe, we'll put it off for juft nine months.

Bel. Guilty confciences make men cowards.

Heart. And they make women defperate.

Bel. I don't wonder you want time to refolve.

Heart. I don't wonder you are fo quickly determined.

Bel. What does the fellow mean ?

Heart. What does the lady mean ?

Sir John. Zoons ! what do you both mean ?

[Heart. *and* Bel. *walk chafing about.*

Raf. [*Afide.*] Here is fo much fport going to be fpoil'd,
it makes me ready to weep again.   A pox o' this impertinent Lady Fancyful, and her plots, and her Frenchwoman too ! ' fhe's a whimfical, ill-natured bitch ; and
' when I have got my bones broke in her fervice, 'tis ten
' to one but my recompenfe is a clap.'   I hear them tit-
tering without ftill !   I'cod, I'll e'en go lug them both in
by the ears, and difcover the plot, to fecure my pardon.

[*Exit* Rafor.

Conft. Pr'ythee, explain, Heartfree.

Heart. A fair deliverance ; thank my ftars and my
friend.

Bel. 'Tis well it went no farther—A bafe fellow !

Lady Brute. What can be the meaning of all this ?

Bel.

Bel. What's his meaning I don't know; but mine is, that if I had married him—I had had no husband.

Heart. And what's her meaning I don't know; but mine is, that if I had married her——I had had wife enough.

Sir John. Your people of wit have got such cramp ways of expressing themselves, they seldom comprehend one another. Pox take you both, will you speak that you may be understood?

Enter Rasor *in sackcloth, pulling in* Lady Fancyful *and* Mademoiselle.

Rasor. If they won't, here comes an interpreter.

Lady Brute. Heavens! What have we here?

Rasor. A villain——but a repenting villain.

All. Rasor!

Lady Brute. What means this?

Rasor. Nothing, without my pardon.

Lady Brute. What pardon do you want?

Rasor. Imprimis. Your Ladyship's; for a damnable lie made upon your spotless virtue, and set to the tune of Spring-garden. [*To* Sir John.] Next at my generous master's feet I bend, for interrupting his more noble thoughts with phantoms of disgraceful cuckoldom. [*To* Const.] Thirdly, I to this gentleman apply, for making him the hero of my romance. [*To* Heart.] Fourthly, your pardon, noble Sir, I ask, for clandestinely marrying you, without either bidding of banns, bishop's licence, friends consent—or your own knowledge. [*To* Bel.] And, lastly, to my good young lady's clemency I come, for pretending the corn was sow'd in the ground, before ever the plough had been in the field.

Sir John. So that, after all, 'tis a moot point whether I am a cuckold or not.

Bel. Well, Sir, upon condition you confess all, I'll pardon you myself, and try to obtain as much from the rest of the company. But I must know then, who 'tis has put you upon all this mischief.

Raf. Satan and his equipage; woman tempted me, vice weakened me—and so, the devil overcame me; as fell Adam, so fell I.

G 2

Bel.

4

Bel. Then, pray, Mr. Adam, will you make us ac-quainted with your Eve?

Raf. [*To* Mad.] Unmask, for the honour of France.

Mad. Mademoiselle!

Mad. Me ask ten toufand pardon of all de good com-pany.

Sir John. Why, this myftery thickens, inftead of clear-ing up. [*To* Rafor.] You fon of a whore you, put us out our pain.

Raf. One moment brings funshine. [*Shewing* Madem.] 'Tis true, this is the woman that tempted me, but this is the ferpent that tempted the woman; and if my prayers might be heard, her punifhment for fo doing fhould be like the ferpent's of old——[*Pulls off* Lady Fancyful's *mafk.*] fhe fhould lie upon her face all the days of her life.

All. Lady Fancyful!

Bel. Impertinent!

Lady Brute. Ridiculous!

All. Ha, ha, ha, ha, ha!

Bel. I hope your Ladyfhip will give me leave to wifh you joy, fince you have owned your marriage yourfelf—[*To* Heart.] I vow, 'twas ftrangely wicked in you to think of another wife, when you had one already fo charming as her Ladyfhip.

All. Ha, ha, ha, ha, ha!

Lady Fan. [*Afide.*] Confufion feize them, as it feizes me!

'*Mad.* Que le diable étouffe ce maraut de Rafor!'

Bel. Your Ladyfhip feems difordered; a breeding qualm, perhaps: Mr. Heartfree, your bottle of Hungary water to your Lady. Why, Madam, he ftands as uncon-cerned as if he were your hufband in earneft.

Lady Fan. Your mirth's as naufeous as yourfelf. Be-linda, you think you triumph over a rival now: helas! ma pauvre fille. Where'er I'm rival, there's no caufe for mirth. No, my poor wretch, 'tis from another principle I have acted. I knew that thing there would make fo per-verfe a hufband, and you fo impertinent a wife, that, left your mutual plagues fhould make you both run mad, I charitably would have broke the match, he, he, he, he!

[*Exit, laughing affectedly,* Mademoifelle *following her.*

Mad. He, he, he, he, he!

All.

All. Ha, ha, ha, ha, ha!

Sir John. [*Aside.*] Why now, this woman will be married to somebody too.

Bel. Poor creature! What a paſſion ſhe is in! But I forgive her.

Heart. Since you have ſo much goodneſs for her, I hope you'll pardon my offence too, Madam.

Bel. There will be no great difficulty in that, ſince I am guilty of an equal fault.

'*Heart.* So, Madam, now had the parſon but done
' his buſineſs————

' *Bel.* You'd be half weary of your bargain.

' *Heart.* No, ſure, I might diſpenſe with one night's
' lodging.

' *Bel.* I'm ready to try, Sir.'

Heart. Then let's to church;
And if it be our chance to diſagree————

Bel. Take heed——the ſurly huſband's fate you ſee.

Sir John. Surly I may be, ſtubborn I am not,
For I have both forgiven and forgot:
If ſo, be theſe our judges, Mrs. Pert,
'Tis more by my goodneſs, than your deſert.

[Exeunt.

END of the FIFTH ACT.

EPI-

EPILOGUE.

Spoken by LADY BRUTE and BELINDA.

L. B. *NO epilogue!*
Bel.   *I swear I know of none.*
L. B. *Lord! how shall we excuse it to the town?*
Bel. *Why, we must e'en say something of our own.*
L. B. *Our own! Ay, that must needs be precious stuff!*
Bel. *I'll lay my life they'll like it well enough.*
    Come, faith, begin————————
L. B. *Excuse me; after you.*
Bel. *Nay, pardon me for that; I know my cue.*
L. B. *Oh, for the world, I would not have precedence.*
Bel. *Oh, lo-d!*
L. B. *I swear————*
Bel. *Oh, fie!*
L. B. *I'm all obedience.*
    First then, know all, before the doom is fix'd,
    The third day is for us————
Bel. *Nay, and the sixth.*
L. B. *We speak not from the poet now, nor is it*
    His cause———— (I want a rhyme)
Bel. *That we solicit.*
L. B. *Then sure you can't have hearts to be severe,*
    And damn us————
Bel. *Damn us! let them, if they dare.*
L. B. *Why, if they should, what punishment remains?*
Bel. *Eternal exile from behind our scenes.*
L. B. *But if they're kind, that sentence we'll recall.*
    We can be grateful————
Bel. *And have wherewithal.*
L. B. *But as grand treaties hope not to be trusted,*
    Before preliminaries are adjusted:
Bel. *You know the time, and we appoint this place;*
    Where, if you please, we'll meet, and sign the peace.

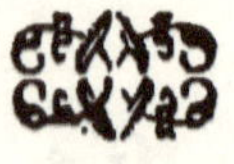

M.r *WOODWARD in the Character of* BOBADI[L]

"*I was planet-struck certainly.*"

Every Man in his Humour.

A COMEDY,

Written by *BEN JONSON*.

With Alterations and Additions,

By *D. GARRICK*.

AS PERFORMED AT THE

Theatre-Royal in Drury-Lane.

Regulated from the Prompt-Book,

By PERMISSION of the MANAGERS,

By Mr. HOPKINS, Prompter.

A NEW EDITION.

LONDON:

Printed for JOHN BELL, near *Exeter-Exchange*, in the *Strand*.

MDCCLXXVII.

[illegible]

PROLOGUE.

Spoken by Mr. GARRICK.

CRITICKS, your favour is our author's right—
The well-known scenes we shall present to-night
Are no weak efforts of a modern pen,
But the strong touches of immortal Ben;
A rough old bard, whose honest pride disdain'd
Applause itself, unless by merit gain'd——
And wou'd to-night your loudest praise disclaim,
Shou'd his great shade perceive the doubtful fame,
Not to his labours granted, but his name.
Boldly he wrote, and boldly told the age,
" He dar'd not prostitute the useful stage,
" Or purchase their delight at such a rate,
" As, for it, he himself must justly hate:
" But rather begg'd they wou'd be pleas'd to see
" From him, such plays as other plays shou'd be:
" Wou'd learn from him to scorn a motly scene,
" And leave their monsters, to be pleas'd with men."
Thus spoke the bard—And tho' the times are chang'd,
Since his free muse for fools the city rang'd
And satire had not then appear'd in state,
To lash the finer follies of the great.
Yet let not prejudice infect your mind,
Nor slight the gold, because not quite refin'd;
With no false niceness this performance view,
Nor damn for low, whate'er is just and true;
Sure to those scenes some honour shou'd be paid,
Which Cambden patroniz'd, and Shakespeare play'd:
Nature was Nature then, and still survives:
The garb may alter, but the substance lives.
Lives in this play——where each may find complete,
His pictur'd self——Then favour the deceit——
Kindly forget the hundred years between;
Become old Britons, and admire old Ben.

DRA-

DRAMATIS PERSONÆ.

MEN.

	Drury-Lane.	Covent-Garden.
Kitely, a Merchant,	Mr. Garrick.	Mr. Smith.
Captain *Bobadil*, -	Mr. King,	Mr. Woodward.
Kno'well, an old Gentleman, -	Mr. Hurſt.	Mr. Hull.
Ed. Kno'well, his Son	Mr. Aickin,	Mr. L. Lewes.
Brainworm, the Father's Man, -	Mr. Baddeley.	Mr. Dunſtall.
Mr. Stephen, a country Gull -	Mr. Dodd.	Mr. Shuter.
Downright, a plain Squire, -	Mr. Branſby.	Mr. Gardner.
Well-bred, his half Brother, -	Mr. Palmer.	Mr. Mattocks.
Juſtice *Clement*, an old merry Magiſtrate -	Mr. Parſons.	Mr. Kniveton.
Roger Formal, his Clerk -	Mr. Wright.	Mr. Baker.
Mr. Matthew, the town Gull, -	Mr. Burton.	Mr. Cuſhing.
Caſh, Kitely's Man	Mr. Brereton.	Mr. Thompſon.
Cob, a Water-bearer,	Mr. Moody.	Mr. Bates.

WOMEN.

	Drury-Lane.	Covent-Garden.
Dame *Kitely*,	Mrs. Greville.	Mrs. Bulkley.
Mrs. Bridget, ſiſter to *Kitely*, -	Mrs. Davies.	Mrs. Baker.
Tib, Wife to *Cob*,	Mrs. Bradſhaw.	Mrs. Pitt.

SCENE, *LONDON*.

EVERY

Every Man in his Humour.

⁎⁎⁎ *The lines distinguished by inverted commas, 'thus,' are omitted in the representation.*

A C T I.

SCENE, *A Court-yard before* KNO'WELL'*s House.*

Enter KNO'WELL *and* BRAINWORM.

KNO'WELL.

A GOODLY day toward, and a fresh morning. Brain-worm,
Call up young master. Bid him rise, Sir.
Tell him I have some business to employ him.

  Bra. I will, Sir, presently.

  Kno. But hear you, sirrah,
If he be at his book, disturb him not.

  Bra. Well, Sir.   [*Exit.*

  Kno. How happy, yet, should I esteem myself,
Could I, by any practice, wean the boy
From one vain course of study he affects.
He is a scholar, if a man may trust
'The liberal voice of Fame in her report,
Of good account in both our universities;
Either of which have favoured him with graces:
But their indulgence must not spring in me
A fond opinion, that he cannot err.
Myself was once a student; and, indeed,
Fed with the self-same humour he is now,
Dreaming on nought but idle poetry,
That fruitless and unprofitable art,
Good unto none, but least to the professors,
Which, then, I thought the mistress of all knowledge:

                               But

But fince, time and the truth have wak'd my judgment;
And reafon taught me better to diftinguifh
The vain from th' ufeful learnings——

Enter Mafter Stephen.

Coufin Stephen,
What news with you, that you are here fo early?

Step. Nothing, but e'en come to fee how you do, uncle.

Kno. That's kindly done, you are welcome, Coz.

Step. Ay, I know that, Sir, I would not ha' come elfe. How doth my coufin Edward, uncle?

Kno. Oh, well, Coz, go in and fee: I doubt he be fcarce ftirring yet.

Step. Uncle, afore I go in, can you tell me an' he have e'er a book of the fciences of hawking and hunting? I would fain borrow it.

Kno. Why, I hope you will not a hawking now, will you?

Step. No woffe, but I'll practife againft the next year, uncle. I have bought me a hawk, and a hood, and bells, and all; I lack nothing, but a book to keep it by.

Kno. Oh, moft ridiculous!

Step. Nay, look you now, you are angry, uncle. Why, you know, an' a man have not fkill in the hawking and hunting languages now-a-days, I'll not give a rufh for him. They are more ftudied than the Greek or the Latin. He is for no gallant's company without 'em. And by Gad's lid I fcorn it, I, fo I do, to be a confort for every hum-drum: hang 'em fcroyls, there's nothing in 'em, i' the world. What do you talk on it? Becaufe I dwell at Hogfden, I fhall keep company with with none but the archers of Finfbury! Or the citizent, that come a ducking to Iflington 'ponds! A fine jeft i' faith! Slid, a gentleman mun fhow himfelf like a gentleman. Uncle, I pray you be not angry; I know what I have to do, I trow, I am no novice.

Kno. You are a prodigal, abfurd coxcomb; go to!
Nay, never look at me, it's I that fpeak.
Take't as you will, Sir, I'll not flatter you.
Ha' you not yet found means enow, to wafte
That which your friends have left you, but you muft
Go caft away your money on a kite,
And know not how to keep it, when you've done?

Oh,

Oh, it's comely! This will make you a gentleman!
Well, coufin, well! I fee you are e'en paft hope
Of all reclaim. Ay, fo, now you're told on it,
You look another way.

   Step. What would you ha' me do?

   Kno. What would I have you do! I'll tell you, kinf-
Learn to be wife, and practife how to thirve;   [man;
That would I have thee do: and not to fpend
Your coin on every bawble that you fancy,
Or every foolifh brain that humours you.
' I would not have you to invade each place,
' Nor thruft yourfelf on all focieties,
' Till men's affections or your own defert,
' Should worthily invite you to your rank.
' He that is fo refpectlefs in his courfes,
' Oft fells his reputation at cheap market.
' Nor would I, you fhould melt away yourfelf
' In flafhing bravery, left while you affect
' To make a blaze of gentry to the world,
' A little puff of fcorn extinguifh it,
' And you be left, like an unfavory fnuff,
' Whofe property is only to offend.'
I'd ha' you fober and contain yourfelf:
Not that your fail be bigger than your boat;
But mod'rate your expences, now, (at firft)
As you may keep the fame proportion ftill;
Nor ftand fo much on your gentility,
Which is an airy, and mere borrow'd thing,
From dead men's duft and bones, and none of yours
Except you make or hold it. Who comes here?

Enter a Servant.

   Serv. Save you, gentlemen.

   Step. Nay, we do not ftand much on our gentility,
friend; yet, you are welcome; and I affure you, mine
uncle here is a man of a thoufand a year, Middlefex
land; he has but one fon in all the world, I am his
next heir at the common law, mafter Stephen, as fimple as I ftand here; if my coufin die, as there's hope
he will. I have a pretty living o' my own too, befide,
hard by here.

   Serv. In good time, Sir.

Step.

Step. In good time, Sir! Why? And in very good time, Sir. You do not flout, friend, do you?

Serv. Not I, Sir.

Step. Not you, Sir? You were not best, Sir: an' you should, here be them can perceive it, and that quickly too. Go to. And they can give it again soundly too, an' need be.

Serv. Why, Sir, let this satisfy you: good faith, I had no such intent.

Step. Sir, an' I thought you had, I would talk with you, and that presently.

Serv. Good master Stephen, so you may, Sir, at your pleasure.

Step. And so I would, Sir, good my saucy companion, an' you were out o' my uncle's ground, I can tell you; though I do not stand upon my gentility neither in't.

Kno. Cousin! cousin! Will this ne'er be left.

Step. Whorson base fellow! A mechanical serving man! By this cudgel, and 'twere not for shame, I would——

Kno. What would you do, you peremptory gull?
If you cannot be quiet, get you hence.
You see the honest man demeans himself
Modestly towards you, giving no reply
To your unseason'd, quarrelling, rude fashion:
And still you huff it, with a k nd of carriage,
As void of wit as of humanity.
Go get you in; 'fore heaven, I am asham'd
Thou hast a kinsman's interest in me.   [*Exit Step.*

Serv. I pray you, Sir, is this master Kno'well's house?

Kno. Yes, marry, is't, Sir.

Serv. I should enquire for a gentleman here, one Master Edward Kno'well: do you know any such, Sir, I pray you?

Kno. I should forget myself else, Sir.

Serv. Are you the gentleman: cry you mercy, Sir, I was required by a gentlemen i'the city, as I rode out at this end of the town, to deliver you this letter, Sir.

Kno. To me, Sir! [*Reads.*] " To his most selected friend, Master Edward Kno'well." What might the gentleman's name be, Sir; that sent it?

Serv.

Serv. One master Well-bred, Sir.

Kno. Master Well-bred! A young gentleman ? Is he not ?

Serv. The same, Sir ; Master Kitely married his sister: the rich merchant i'the Old Jewry.

Kno. You say very true. Brain-worm.

Enter Brain-worm.

Brain. Sir.

Kno. Make this honest friend drink here. Pray you go in.   [*Exeunt.* Brain *and servant.*
This letter is directed to my son:
Yet I am Edward Kno'well too, and may,
With the safe conscience of good-manners, use
The fellow's error to my satisfaction.
Well, I will break it ope, old men are curious,
Be it but for the stile's sake, and the phrase,
To see, if both do answer my son's praises,
Who is almost grown the idolator   [this ?
Of this young Well-bred : What have we here ? What's
                    [*The Letter.*]

" Why, Ned, I beseech thee, hast thou forsworn all thy friends i' th' Old Jewry ? or dost thou think us all Jews that inhabit there ? Leave thy vigilant father alone, to number over his green apricots, evening and morning, o' the north west wall : an' I had been his son, I had saved him the labour long since ; if, taking in all the young wenches that pass by, at the back door, and coddling every kernel of the fruit for 'em would ha' served. But pr'ythee, come over to me, quickly, this morning : I have such a present for thee, our Turkey company never sent the like to the Grand Signior. One is a rhimer, Sir, o' your own batch, your own leaven ; but doth think himself poet-major o' the town ; willing to be shewn, and worthy to be seen. The other—I will not venture his description with you till you come, because I would ha' you make hither with an appetite. If the worst of 'em be not worth your journey, draw your bill of charges, as unconscionable as any Guild-hall verdict will give it you, and you shall be allow'd your Viaticum.

                                    From the Wind-mill."
From the Burdello, it might come as well !
The Spittal ! Is this the man ?

                                          My

My son hath sung so, for the happiest wit,
The choicest brain, the times hath sent us forth?
1 know not what he may be, in the arts;
Nor what in schools: but surely, for his manners,
I judge him a profane and diffolute wretch:
Worfe, by proffeffion of fuch great good gifts,
Being the mafter of fo lofe a fpirit.
Why, what unhallowed ruffian would have writ
In fuch a fcurrilous manner, to a friend?
Why fhould he think I tell my apricots?
Or play th' Hefperian dragon with my fruit,
To watch it? Well, my fon, I 'ad thought
You'd had more judgment, 't have made election
Of your companions, ' than t'have ta'en on truft
' Such petulant, jeering gamefters, that can fpare
' No argument, or fubject from their jeft.'
But I perceive, affection makes a fool
Of any man, too much the father.   Brain-worm.
Enter Brain-worm.

Brain. Sir.
Kno. Is the fellow gone that brought this letter?
Brain. Yes, Sir, a pretty while fince.
Kno. And where's your young mafter?
Brain. In his chamber, Sir.
Kno. He fpake not with the fellow, did he?
Brain. No, Sir, he faw him not.
Kno. Take you this letter, feal it and deliver it my fon;
But with no notice that I have open'd it on your life.
Brain. O lord, Sir, that were a jeft, indeed!
Kno. I am refolv'd, I will not ftop his journey;
Nor practife any violent means to ftay
The unbridled courfe of youth in him: for that,
Reftrain'd, grows more impatient: ' and, in kind,
' Like to the eager, but the generous grey-hound,
' Who ne'er fo little from his game with-held,
' Turns head, and leaps up at his holder's throat.
There is a way of winning more by love,
And urging of the modefty, than fear:
Force works on fervile natures, not the free:
He, that's compell'd to goodnefs, may be good;
But, 'tis but for that fit: where others drawn
By foftnefs, and example, get a habit.

Ther

Then if they stray, but warn 'em : and, the same
They would for virtue do, they'll do for shame.

SCENE, *Young* Kno'well's *study.*

Enter Edward Kno'well *and* Brain-worm.

E. Kno. Did he open it, say'st thou ?

Brain. Yes, o'my word, Sir, and read the contents.

E. Kno. That's bad. What countenance, pray thee,
made he i' the reading of it ? Was he angry, or pleas'd ?

Brain. Nay, Sir, I saw him not read it, nor open it,
assure your worship.

E. Kno. No ! How know'st thou then, that he did either ?

Brain. Marry, Sir, because he charged me, on my
life, to tell nobody that he open'd it : which unless he
had done, he would never fear to have it revealed.

E. Kno. That's true : well, I thank thee, Brain-worm.

Enter Master Stephen.

Step. O, Brain worm, didst thou not see a fellow here,
i' a what-sha'call-him doublet ? He brought mine uncle a letter e'en now.

Brain. Yes, Master Stephen, what of him ?

Step. O ! I ha' such a mind to beat him—where is he ?
canst thou tell ?

Brain. Faith, he is not of that mind : he is gone
Master Stephen.

Step. Gone ! which way ? When went he ? How long
since ?

Brain. He is rid hence. He took horse at the street door.

Step. And I staid i' the fields ! Whorson, Scanderbeg
rogue ; O that I had but a horse to fetch him back again.

Brain. Why, you may ha' my master's gelding to save
your longing, Sir.

Step. But I have no boots, that's the spite on't.

Brain. Why, a fine whisp of hay, roll'd hard, Master
Stephen.

Step. No, faith, it's no boot to follow him now ; let
me e'en go and hang. Pr'ythee, help to truss me a little. He does so vex me——

Brain. You'll be worst vex'd, when you are trussed,
Master

I

Master Stephen. Best keep unbrac'd, and walk]
till you be cold, your choler may founder you els(

Step. By my faith, and so I will, now thou te
on't. How dost thou like my leg, Brain-worm?

Brain. A very good leg, Master Stephen ; l
woollen stocking does not commend it so well.

Step. Foh, the stockings be gocd enough, now]
is coming on, for the dust : I'll have a pair of silk
the winter, that I go to dwell i' the town. I th
leg would shew in a silk hose.

Brain. Believe me, Master Stephen, rarely we

Step. In sadness, I think it would ; I have a rea
good leg.

Brain. You have an excellent good leg, Mast
phen ; but I cannot stay to praise it longer now ;
very sorry for't.

Step. Another time will serve, Brain-worm. G
cy ; for this.

Enter Young Kno'well.

E. Kno. Ha, ha, ha !

Step. 'Slid ! I hope he laughs not at me ; an' h

E. Kno. Here was a letter, indeed, to be inte
by a man's father ! He cannot but think most vir
both of me and the sender, sure, that make the
coster-monger of him in our familiar epistles. I
knew the end of it, which now is doubtful, and
tens——What ! my wise cousin ! Nay, then I'll
our feast with one gull more tow'rd the mess. He
to me of a brace, and here's one, that's three ;
a fourth ! Fortune, if ever thou'lt use thine (
intreat thee——

Step. O, now I see who he laughs at. He la
somebody in that letter. By this good light, an'
laugh'd at me——

E. Kno. How now, cousin Stephen, melancho

Step. Yes, a little. I thought you had laugh'd
cousin.

E. Kno. Why, what an' I had, Coz, what wo
ha' done ?

Step. By this light, I would ha' told mine uncle.

E. Kno. Nay, if you would ha' told your uncle
laugh at you, Coz.

Step. Did you, indeed?

E. Kno. Yes, indeed.

Step. Why, then——

E. Kno. What then?

Step. I am satisfied; it is sufficient.

E. Kno. Why, be so, gentle Coz. And I pray you, let me intreat a courtesy of you. I am sent for, this morning, by a friend i' the Old Jewry, to come to him: it's but crossing over the fields to Moorgate? Will you bear me company? I protest, it is not to draw you into bond, or any plot against the state, Coz.

Step. Sir, that's all one, an 'twere; you shall command me twice so far as Moorgate to do you good, in such a matter. Do you think I would leave you? I protest——

E. Kno. No, no, you shall not protest, Coz.

Step. By my fackins, but I will, by your leave; I'll protest more to my friend than I'll speak of at this time.

E. Kno. You speak very well, Coz.

Step. Nay, not so, neither; you shall pardon me: but I speak to serve my turn.

E. Kno. Your turn, Coz! Do you know what you say? A gentleman of your sort, parts, carriage, and estimation, to talk o' your turn i' this company, and to me, alone, like a water-bearer at a conduit! ' Fie! A wight, that, ' hitherto, his every step hath left the stamp of a great ' foot behind him, at every word, the favour of a strong ' spirit; and he! this man, so graced, so gilded, or, as ' I may say, so tinfoil'd by nature.'—Come, come, wrong not the quality of your desert, with looking downward, Coz; but hold up your head, so; and let the idea of what you are, be portray'd i' your face, that men may read i' your physiognomy: " here, within this place, is to be seen the true and accomplished monster, or miracle of nature," which is all one. What think you of this, Coz?

Step. Why, I do think of it; and I will be more proud, and melancholy, and gentleman-like, than I have been, I'll assure you.

E. Kno. Why, that's resolute, Master Stephen! Now, if I can but hold him up to his height, as it is happily begun, it will do well for a suburb-humour: we may hap

B

have

have a match with the city, and play him for forty pounds.
Come, Coz.

Step. I'll follow you.

E. Kno. Follow me; you muſt go before.

Step. Nay, an' I muſt, I will. Pray you, ſhew me,
good couſin.   [*Exeunt.*

SCENE, *the Street before* Cob's *Houſe.*

Enter Mr. Matthew.

Mat. I think this be the houſe.   What, hoa!

Enter Cob, *from the Houſe.*

Cob. Who's there ? O, Maſter Matthew ! gi' your worſhip good morrow.

Mat. What, Cob! How doſt thou, good Cob ? Doſt
thou inhabit here, Cob ?

Cob. Ay, Sir, I and my lineage ha' kept a poor houſe
here in our days.

Mat. Cob, canſt thou ſhew me of a gentleman, one
Captain Bobadil, where his lodging is ?

Cob. O, my gueſt, Sir, you mean !

Mat. Thy gueſt ! Alas ! ha, ha.

Cob. Why do you laugh, Sir ? Do you not mean Captain Bobadil ?

Mat. Cob, pray thee, adviſe thyſelf well : do not wrong
the gentleman and thyſelf too. I dare be ſworn he ſcorns
thy houſe.   He ! he lodge in ſuch a baſe, obſcure place
as thy houſe ! Tut, I know his diſpoſition ſo well, he
would not lie in thy bed, if thou'dſt gi' it him.

Cob. I will not give it him, though, Sir. Maſs, I
thought ſomewhat was in't we could not get him to bed,
all night ! Well, Sir, though he lie not o' my bed, he
lies o' my bench.   An't pleaſe you to go up, Sir, you
ſhall find him with two cuſhions under his head, and his
cloak wrapped about him, as though he had neither won
nor loſt ; and yet, I warrant, he ne'er caſt better in his
life, than he has done to-night.

Mat. Why, was he drunk ?

Cob. Drunk, Sir ! you hear not me ſay ſo. Perhaps
he ſwallowed a tavern-token, or ſome ſuch device, Sir.: I
have nothing to do withall.   I deal with water, and not
with wine.   Gi' me my bucket there, hoa.   God b'wi'
                                                        you

you, Sir, it's fix o'clock : I fhould ha'carried two turns by this. What hoa! my ftopple! come.

Mat. Lie in a water-bearer's houfe! A gentleman of his havings! Well, I'll tell him my mind.

Cob. What, Tib, fhew this gentleman up to the Captain. [*Tib fhews Mafter Mat. into the houfe.*] You fhould ha' fome now, would take this Mr. Matthew to be a gentleman at the leaft. His father is an honeft man, a worfhipful fifhmonger, and fo forth; and now does he creep, and wriggle into acquaintance with all the brave gallants about the town, fuch as my gueft is. O, my gueft is a fine man! he does fwear the legibleft of any man chriftened : by St. George—the foot of Pharoah,—the body of me,—as I am a gentleman and a foldier; fuch dainty oaths! and withal, he does this fame filthy roguifh tobacco, the fineft and cleanlieft! it would do a man good to fee the fume come forth out at's tonnels! Well, he owes me forty fhillings, my wife lent him out of her purfe by fix-pence a time, befides his lodging; I would I had it. I fhall ha' it he fays, the next action. Helter fkelter, hang forrow, care'll kill a cat, up-tails all; and a loufe for the hang-man   [*Exit.*

SCENE, a room in Cob's Houfe.

Bobadil *difcovered upon a Bench.*   Tib *enters to him.*
Bob. Hoftefs, hoftefs!
Tib. What fay you, Sir?
Bob. A cup o' thy fmall-beer, fweet hoftefs.
Tib. Sir, there's a gentleman below, would fpeak with you.
Bob. A gentleman! 'Ods fo, I am not within.
Tib. My hufband told him you were, Sir.
Bob. What a plague——what meant he ?
Mat. [*within.*] Captain Bobadil!
Bob. Who's there !—Take away the bafon, good hoftefs. Come up, Sir.
Tib. He would defire you to come up, Sir. You come into a cleanly houfe here.

Enter Mr. Matthew.

Mat. 'Save you, Sir; 'fave you, Captain.
Bob. Gentle Mafter Matthew ! Is it you, Sir? Pleaf you fit down.

B 2

Mat.

Mat. Thank you, good Captain; you may see I am somewhat audacious.

Bob. Not so, Sir. I was requested to supper, last night, by a sort of gallants, where you were wish'd for, and drank to, I assure you.

Mat. Vouchsafe me by whom, good Captain.

Bob. Marry, by young Well-bred, and others. Why, hostess! a stool here for this gentleman.

Mat. No haste, Sir, 'tis very well.

Bob. Body of me! It was so late ere we parted last night, I can scarce open my eyes yet: I was but new risen, as you came. How passes the day abroad, Sir? you can tell.

Mat. Faith, some half hour to seven. Now, trust me, you have an exceeding fine lodging here, very neat, and private!

Bob. Ay, Sir: sit down. I pray you, Master Matthew, in any case, possess no gentleman of our acquaintance with notice of my lodging.

Mat. Who? I, Sir? No.

Bob. Not that I need to care who know it, for the cabin is convenient; but in regard I would not be too popular and generally visited, as some are.

Mat. True, Captain, I conceive you.

Bob. For, do you see, Sir, by the heart of valour in me, except it be to some peculiar and choice spirits, to whom I am extraordinarily engaged; as yourself, or so, I could not extend thus far.

Mat. O lord, Sir, I resolve so.

[Pulls out a paper, and reads.

Bob. I confess, I love a cleanly and quiet privacy, above all the tumult and roar of fortune. What new piece ha' you there? Read it.

Mat. [*Reads.*] To thee, the purest object of my sense,
The most refined essence Heaven covers,
Send I these lines, wherein I do commence
The happy state of turtle-billing lovers.

Bob. 'Tis good; proceed, proceed. Where's this?

Mat. This, Sir? a toy o' mine own, in my nonage: the infancy of my muses. But, when will you come and see my study? Good faith, I can shew you some

very

very good things I have done of late——That boot becomes your leg, paffing well, Captain, methinks.

Bob. So, fo: it's the fashion gentlemen now ufe.

Mat. Troth, Captain, and now you fpeak o' the fashion, Mafter Well-bred's elder brother and I are fallen out exceedingly: this other day, I happen'd to enter into fome difcourfe of a hanger, which I affure you, both for fashion and workmanfhip, was moft peremptory-beautiful and gentleman-like; yet he condemn'd, and cry'd it down, for the moft pied and ridiculous that ever he faw.

Bob. 'Squire Downright, the half-brother, was't not?

Mat. Ay, Sir, George Downright.

Bob. Hang him, rook! He! Why, he has no more judgment than a malt-horfe. By St. George, I wonder you'd lofe a thought upon fuch an animal! The moft peremptory abfurd clown of Chriftendom, this day, he is holden. I proteft to you, as I am a gentleman and a foldier, I ne'er chang'd words with his like. By his difcourfe, he fhould eat nothing but hay. He was born for the manger, pannier, or pack-faddle! He has not fo much as a good phrafe in his belly, but all old iron and rufty proverbs! A good commodity for fome fmith to make hob-nails of.

Mat. Ay, and he thinks to carry it away with his manhood ftill, where he comes. He brags he will gi' me the baftinado, as I hear.

Bob. How! He the baftinado! How came he by that word, trow?

Mat. Nay, indeed, he faid cudgel me; I term'd it fo, for my more grace.

Bob. That may be: for I was fure it was none of his word. But when? When faid he fo.

Mat. Faith, yefterday, they fay: a young gallant, friend of mine, told me fo,

Bob. By the foot of Pharoah, an' 'twere my cafe now, I fhould fend him a challenge, prefently. The baftinado! A moft proper and fufficient dependence, warranted by the great Caranza. Come hither, you fhall challenge him. I'll fhow you a trick or two, you fhall kill him with, at pleafure: the firft ftoccata, if you will, by this air.

B 3

Mat.

Mat. Indeed, you have abfolute knowledge i' the myftery, I have heard, Sir.

Bob. Of whom? Of whom ha' you heard it, I befeech you?

Mat. 'Troth, I have heard it fpoken of by divers, that you have very rare and un-in-one-breath-utterable fkill, Sir.

Bob. By heaven, no, not I; no fkill i'the earth: fome fmall rudiments i' the fcience, as to know my time, diftance, or fo. I have profeft it more for noblemen and gentlemen's ufe than mine own practice, I affure you. I'll give you a leffon. Look you, Sir. Exalt not your point above this ftate, at any hand; fo, Sir. Come on! Oh, twine your body more about, that you may fall to a more fweet, comely, gentleman-like, guard. So, indifferent. Hollow your body more, Sir, thus. Now, ftand faft o' your left leg; note your diftance; keep your due proportion of time—Oh, you diforder your point moft irregularly! Come, put on your cloak, and we'll go to fome private place, where you are acquainted, fome tavern, or fo—and have a bit——What money ha' you about you, Mr. Matthew?

Mat. Faith, I ha' not paft a two fhillings, or fo.

Bob. 'Tis fomewhat with the leaft: but come, we will have a bunch of raddifhes, and falt, to tafte our wine: and a pipe of tobacco, to clofe the orifice of the ftomach: and then we'll call upon young Well-bred. Perhaps we fhall meet the Corydon, his brother, there, and put him to the queftion. Come along, Mr. Matthew.   [*Exeunt.*

END OF THE FIRST ACT.

ACT II.

SCENE, *a Warehoufe, belonging to* Kitely.

Enter Kitely, Cafh, *and* Downright.

KITELY.

THOMAS, come hither.
There lies a note within, upon my defk,

Here

Here take my key——It is no matter, neither.
Where is the boy ?

   Cash. Within, Sir, i'the warehouse.

   Kite. Let him tell over straight that Spanish gold,
And weigh it, with the pieces of eight. Do you
See the delivery of those silver stuffs
To Mr. Lucar. Tell him, if he will,
He shall ha' the grograns at the rate I told him,
And I will meet him, on the Exchange, anon.

   Cash. Good, Sir.   [*Exit.*

   Kite. Do you see that fellow, brother Downright ?

   Down. I, what of him ?

   Kite. He is a jewel, brother,——
I took him of a child, up, at my door,
And christened him ; gave him my own name, Thomas :
Since bred him at the hospital ; where proving
A toward imp, I call'd him home, and taught him
So much, as I have made him my cashier,
And find him, in his place, so full of faith,
That I durst trust my life into his hands.

   Down. So would not I, in any bastard's brother,
As it is like, he is, although I knew
Myself his father. But you said you'd somewhat
To tell me, gentle brother. What is't ? What is't ?

   Kite. Faith, I am very loth to utter it,
As fearing it may hurt your patience :
But that I know your judgment is of strength,
Against the nearness of affection——

   Down. What need this circumstance ? Pray you be
direct.

   ' *Kite.* I will not say how much I do ascribe
' Unto your friendship ; nor, in what regard
' I hold your love : but let my past behaviour,
' And usage of your sister, but confirm
' How well I've been affected to your——

   Down. ' You are too tedious,' come to the matter,
the matter.

   Kite. Then, without further ceremony, thus.
My brother Well-bred, Sir, I know not how,
Of late, is much declin'd in what he was,
And greatly alter'd in his disposition.
When he came first to lodge here in my house,

Ne'er

Ne'er truſt me, if I were not proud of him :
' Methought he bare himſelf in ſuch a faſhion,
' So full of man, and ſweetneſs in his carriage,
' And, what was chief, it ſhew'd not borrow'd in him,
' But all he did became him as his own,
' And ſeem'd as perfect, proper, and poſſeſt,
' As breath with life, or colour with the blood : '
But now his courſe is ſo irregular,
So looſe, affected, and depriv'd of grace ;
'. And he himſelf withal ſo far fall'n off
' From that firſt place, as ſcarce no note remains,
' To tell men's judgments where he lately ſtood.
' He's grown a ſtranger to all due reſpect ;
' Forgetful of his friends, and not content
' To ſtale himſelf in all ſocieties, '
He makes my houſe here, common, as a mart,
A theatre, a public receptacle
For giddy humour, and diſeaſed riot ;
And here, as in a tavern or a ſtew,
He and his wild aſſociates ſpend their hours
In repetition of laſcivious jeſts :
Swear, leap, drink, dance, and revel night by night,
Controul my ſervants ; and indeed what not.

Down. 'Sdains, I know not what I ſhould ſay to him
i' the whole world ! He values me at a crack'd three-
farthings, for ought I ſee. It will never out o' the fleſh
that's bred i' the bone ! I have told him enough, one
would think, if that would ſerve. Well ! He knows
what to truſt to, for George. Let him ſpend and ſpend,
and domineer, till his heart ake ; an' he think to be re-
lieved by me, when he is got into one o' your city-
pounds, the counters ; he has the wrong ſow by the
ear, i' faith, and claps his diſh at a wrong man's door.
I'll lay my hand on my halfpenny, ere I part with't, to
fetch him out, I'll aſſure him.

Kite. Nay, good brother, let it not trouble you, thus.

Down. S'death, he made me—I could eat my very
ſpur-leathers, for anger ! But, why are you ſo tame ?
Why do not you ſpeak to him, and tell him how he diſ-
quiets your houſe ?

Kite. Oh, there are divers reaſons to diſſuade, brother ;
But, would yourſelf vouchſafe to travail in it,

Though

Though but with plain and eafy circumftance,
It would both come much better to his fenfe,
And favour lefs of ftomach, or of paffion.
You are his elder brother, and that title
Both gives and warrants you authority :
Whereas, if I fhould intimate the leaft,
It would but add contempt to his negleft ;
Heap worfe on ill, make a pile of hatred,
That, in the rearing, would come tott'ring down,
And, in the ruin, bury all our love.
Nay, more than this, brother; if I fhould fpeak,
He would be ready, from his heat of humour,
And over-flowing of the vapour in him,
To blow the ears of his familiars
With the falfe breath of telling what difgraces
And low difparagements I had put on him :
Whilft they, Sir, to relieve him in the fable,
Make their loofe comments upon ev'ry word,
Gefture, or look, I ufe ; mock me all o'er ;
And, out of their impetuous rioting phant'fies,
Beget fome flander, that fhall dwell with me.
And what would that be, think you ? Marry, this ;
They would give out, becaufe my wife is fair,
Myfelf but newly married, and my fifter
Here fojourning a virgin in my houfe,
That I were jealous ! Nay, as fure as death,
That they would fay.   And how that I had quarrell'd
My brother purpofely, thereby to find
An apt pretext to banifh them my houfe.

   Dow. Mafs, perhaps fo : they're like enough to do it,
   Kite. Brother, they would, believe it : fo fhould I,
Like one of thefe penurious quack-falvers,
But fet the bills up to mine own difgrace.
And try experiments upon myfelf :
Lend fcorn and envy, opportunity
To ftab my reputation and good name.——
          Enter Matthew *and* Bobadil.
   Mat. I will fpeak to him——
   Bob. Speak to him ! Away ! by the foot of Pharaoh,
you fhall not; you fhall not do him that grace.
   Kite. What's the matter, Sirs ?

Bob.

Bob. The time of day, to you, gentlemen o' the houfe:
Is Mr. Well-bred ftirring ?

Dow. How then ? what fhould he do ?

Bob. Gentleman of the houfe, it is you : is he within,
Sir ?

Kite. He came not to his lodging to-night, Sir, I affure you.

Dow. Why, do you hear ? you !

Bob. The gentleman-citizen hath fatisfy'd me, I'll talk
to no fcavenger.   [*Exeunt* Bob. *and* Mat.

Dow. How, fcavenger ! ftay, Sir, ftay !

Kite. Nay, brother Downright.

Dow. 'Heart ! ftand you away, an' you love me.

Kite. You fhall not follow him now, I pray you; brother ; good faith you fhall not : I will over-rule you.

Dow. Ha ! fcavenger ! Well, go to, I fay little :
but by this good day (God forgive me I fhould fwear) if
I put it up fo, fay I am the - rankeft coward ever lived.
'Sdains, an' I fwallow this, I'll ne'er draw my fword in the
fight of Fleet Street again, while I live ; I'll fet in a barn
with Madge howlet, and catch mice firft. Scavenger !

Kite. Oh, do not fret youfelf thus, never think on't.

Dow. Thefe are my brother's conforts, thefe ! thefe
are his comrades, his walking mates ! he's a gallant, a
cavaliero too, right, hangman cut ! Let me not live, an'
I could not find in my heart to fwinge the whole gang of
'em, one after another, and begin with him firft. I am
griev'd it fhould be faid he is my brother, and take thefe
courfes. Well, as he brews fo he fhall drink, for George,
again. Yet, he fhall hear on't, and that rightly too, an'
I live, i' faith.

Kite. But, brother, let your reprehenfion then
Run in an eafy current, not o'er-high
Carried with rafhnefs, or devouring choler ;
But rather ufe the foft perfuading way,
More winning than enforcing the confent.

Dow. Ay, ay, let me alone for that, I warrant you.
                              [*Bell rings.*

Kite. How now ! Oh, the bell rings to breakfaft.
Brother, I pray you, go in, and bear my wife
Company till I come ; I'll but give order
For fome difpatch of bufinefs to my fervant——

                                        Dow.

Dow. I will—Scavenger! scavenger!— [*Exit Dow.*

Kite. Well, tho' my troubled spirit's somewhat eas'd,
It's not repos'd in that security
As I could; wish but I must be content,
Howe'er I set a face on't to the world!
Would I had lost this finger, at a venture,
So Well-bred had ne'er lodg'd within my house.
Why't cannot be, where there is such resort
Of wanton gallants, and young revellers,
That any woman should be honest long.
Is't like, that factious beauty will preserve
The public weal of chastity unshaken,
When such strong motives muster and make head
Against her single peace? No, no.   Beware,
When mutual appetite doth meet to treat,
And spirits of one kind and quality
Come once to parly, in the pride of blood,
It is no slow conspiracy that follows.
Well, to be plain, if I but thought the time
Had answer'd their affections, all the world
Should not persuade me but I were a cuckold!
Marry, I hope they ha' not got that start;
For opportunity hath baulk'd 'em yet,
And shall do still, while I have eyes and ears
To attend the impositions of my heart.
My presence shall be as an iron-bar,
'Twixt the conspiring motions of desire:
Yea, every look or glance mine eye ejects,
Shall check occasion, as one doth his slave,
When he forgets the limits of prescripton.

Enter Dame Kitely.

Dame. Sister Bridget, pray you fetch down the rose-water above in the closet.   Sweetheart, will you come in to breakfast?

Kite. An' she overheard me now!

Dame. I pray thee, good Muss, we stay for you.

Kite. By heav'n, I wou'd not for a thousand angels.

Dame. What ail you, sweetheart? are you not well? Speak, good Muss.

Kite. Troth, my head akes extremely, on a sudden.

Dame. Oh, the lord!

Kite. How now! what!

Dame

Dame. Alas, how it burns ! Muſs, keep you warm, good truth it is this new diſeaſe there's a number are troubled withal ! For loves ſake, ſweetheart, come in, out of the air.

Kite. How ſimple, and how ſubtle are her anſwers ! A new diſeaſe, and many troubled with it ! Why, true ! ſhe heard me, all the world to nothing.

Dame. I pray thee, good ſweetheart, come in ; the air will do you harm in troth.

Kite. I'll come to you preſently ; 'twill away, I hope.

Dame. Pray Heav'n it do.   [*Exit Dame.*

Kite. A new diſeaſe ! I know not, new or old,
But it may well be call'd poor mortals' plague :
For like a peſtilence, it doth infect
The houſes of the brain. Firſt, it begins
Solely to work upon the phantaſy,
Filling her ſeat with ſuch peſtiferous air
As ſoon corrupts the judgment, and from thence
Sends like contagion to the memory ;
Still each to other giving the infection,
Which, as a ſubtle vapour, ſpreads itſelf
Confuſedly through every ſenſive part,
Till not a thought, or motion in the mind,
Be free from the black poiſon of ſuſpect.
Ah, but what miſery it is to know this !
Or, knowing it, to want the mind's direction,
In ſuch extremes ! Well, I will once more ſtrive,
In ſpite of this black cloud, myſelf to be,
And ſhake the fever off, that thus ſhakes me.   [*Exit.*

SCENE, *Moor-Fields.*

Enter Brain-worm, *diſguis'd like a Soldier.*

Brain. 'Slid, I cannot chooſe but laugh to ſee myſelf tranſlated thus. Now muſt I create an intolerable ſort of lies, or my preſent profeſſion loſes the grace ; and yet the lie to a man of my coat, is a ominous a fruit as the Fico. O, Sir, it holds for good polity ever, to have that outwardly in vileſt eſtimation that inwardly is moſt dear to us. So much for my borrowed ſhape. Well, the truth is, my old maſter intends to follow my young, dry foot, over Moor-fields to London this morning : now I, knowing of this hunting match, or rather conſpiracy, and to
inſinuate

.infinuate with my young mafter, for fo muft we that are
blue waiters and men of hope and fervice do, have got
me afore in this difguife, determining here to lie in am-
bufcade, and intercept him in the mid-way. If I can but
get his cloak, his purfe, his hat, nay any thing to cut
him off, that is, to ftay his journey—*Veni, vidi, vici*, I
may fay with captain Cæfar; I am made for ever, I faith.
Well, now muft I practife to get the true garb of one of
thofe lance-knights, my arm here, and my—Young mafter, and his coufin, Mr. Stephen, as I am a true counterfeit man of war, and no foldier!   [*Retires.*

　　　Enter Ed. Kno'well *and Mafter* Stephen.

E. Kno. So, Sir, and how then, Coz?

Step. S'foot, I have loft my purfe, I think.

E. Kno. How! loft your purfe! Where? When had
you it?

Step. I cannot tell: ftay.

Brain. 'Slid. I am afraid they will know me, would I
could get by them!

E. Kno. What! ha' you it?

Step. No, I think I was bewitched, I——

E. Kno. Nay, do not weep the lofs, hang it, let it go.

Step. Oh, it's here—No, an' it had been loft, I had
not car'd, but for a jet ring Miftrefs Mary fent me.

E. Kno. A jet ring! Oh, the pofey, the pofey!

Step. Fine, i'faith!—Though fancy fleep, my love is
deep.—Meaning that though I did not fancy her, yet fhe
loved me dearly.

E. Kno. Moft excellent!

Step. And then I fent her another, and my poefy was:
The deeper the fweeter, I'll be judg'd by St. Peter.

E. Kno. How by St. Peter? I do not conceive that.

Step. Marry, St. Peter, to make up the metre.

E. Kno. Well, there the faint was your good patron;
he help'd you at your need: thank him, thank him.

Brain. I cannot take leave of 'em fo; I will venture,
come what will. Gentlemen, pleafe you change a few
crowns, for a very excellent good blade, here? I am a
poor gentleman, a foldier, that, in the better ftate of my fortunes, fcorn'd fo mean a refuge, but now it is the humour
of neceffity to have it fo. You feem to be gentlemen,
well affected to martial men, elfe I fhould rather die with
　　　　　　　　C   filence

filence than live with fhame: however, vouchfafe to remember, it is my want fpeaks, not myfelf. This condition agrees not with my fpirit.——

E. Kno Where haft thou ferved ?

Brain. May it pleafe you, Sir, in all the late wars of
Bohemia, Hungaria, Dalamatia, Poland ; where not,
Sir ? I have been a poor fervitor by fea and land, any
time this fourteen years, and followed the fortunes of the
beft commanders in Chriftendom. I was twice fhot at the
taken of Aleppo ; once at the relief of Vienna. I have
been at Marfeilles, Naples, and the Adriatick gulf; a
gentleman flave in the galleys thrice, where I was moft
dangeroufly fhot in the head, through both thighs, and
yet, being thus maimed, I am void of maintenance ; nothing left me but my fcars, the noted marks of my refolution.

Step. How will you fell this rapier, friend ?

Brain. Generous Sir, I refer it to your own judgment ;
you are a gentleman, give me what you pleafe.

Step. True, I am a gentleman, I know that, friend :
but what though ? I pray you fay, what would you afk ?

Brain. I affure you the blade may become the fide or
thigh of the beft prince in Europe.

E. Kno. Ay, with a velvet fcabbard.

Step. Nay, and't be mine, it fhall have a velvet fcabbard, Coz, that's flat : I'd not wear it as 'tis, an' you
would give me an angel.

Brain. At your worfhip's pleafure, Sir ; nay, 'tis a
moft pure Toledo.

Step. I had rather it were a Spaniard ; but tell me,
what I fhall give you for it ? An' it had a filver hilt—

E. Kno. Come, come, you fhall not buy it ; hold,
there's a fhilling, fellow, take thy rapier.

Step. Why, but I will buy it now, becaufe you fay fo :
and there's another fhilling, fellow ; I fcorn to be out-
bidden. What, fhall I walk with a cudgel, like a higgin-
bottom, and may have a rapier for money ?

E. Kno. You may buy one in the city.

Step. Tut, I'll buy this i' the field, fo I will ; I have a
mind to't becaufe 'tis a field rapier. Tell me your loweft
price.

E. Kno.

E. Kno. You shall not buy it, I say.

Step. By this money but I will, though I give more than 'tis worth.

E. Kno. Come away, you are a fool.

Step. Friend, I am a fool, that's granted : but I'll have it for that word's sake.   Follow me for your money.

Brain. At your service, Sir.   [*Exeunt.*

Enter Kno'well.

Kno. I cannot lose the thought yet of this letter
Sent to my son; nor leave to admire the change
Of manners, and the breeding of our youth
Within the kingdom, since myself was one.
When I was young, he liv'd not in the stews
Durst have conceived a scorn, and utter'd it,
On a grey head : age was authority
Against a buffoon ; and a man had then
A certain reverence paid unto his years
That had none due unto his life.
But now we are fall'n ; youth from their fear,
And age from that which bred it, good example.
Nay, would ourselves were not the first, even parents,
That did destroy the hopes in our own children ;
' Or they not learn'd our vices in their cradles,
' And suck'd in our ill customs with their milk :
' Ere all their teeth be born, or they can speak,
' We make their palates cunning !' The first words
We form their tongues with, are licenteous jests.
Can it call whore ? cry bastard ? O, then kiss it,
A witty child ! Can't swear ? The father's darling !
Give it two plumbs.   Nay, rather than't shall learn
No bawdy song, the mother herself will teach it !
But this is in the infancy :
When it puts on the breeches,
It will put off all this.   Ay, it is like ;
When it is gone into the bone already !
No, no : this die goes deeper than the coat,
Or shirt, or skin ; it stains unto the liver
And heart, is some : and rather than it should not,
Note what we fathers do ; look how we live ;
What mistresses we keep ; at what expence ;
And teach them all bad ways to buy affliction !
Well, I thank Heav'n, I never yet was he

C 2

That

That travell'd with my fon before fixteen,
To fhew him the Venetian courtezans,
Nor read the grammar of cheating, I had made
To my fharp boy at twelve; repeating ftill
The rule, get money, ftill get money, boy,
No matter by what means.
Thefe are the trades of fathers, now. However,
My fon, I hope, hath met within my threfhold,
None of thefe houfhold precedents; which are ftrong
And fwift, to rape youth to their precipice.
But let the houfe at home be ne'er fo clean
Swept, or kept fweet from filth,
If he will live abroad with his companions,
In riot and mifrule, it is worth a fear.
' Nor is the danger of converfing lefs
' Than all that I have mention'd of example.'

Enter Brain-worm.

Brain. My mafter! Nay, faith have at you; I am
fleth'd now, I have fped fo well; though I muft attack
you in different way. Worfhipful Sir, I befeech you, refpect the ftate of a poor foldier! I am afham'd of this
bafe courfe of life (God's my comfort) but extremity
provokes me to't: what remedy?

Kno. I have not for you now.

Brain. By the faith I bear unto truth, gentleman, it is
no ordinary cuftom in me, but only to preferve manhood.
I proteft to you, a man I have been, a man I may be, by
your fweet bounty.

Kno. Pr'ythee, good friend, be fatisfied.

Brain. Good, Sir, by that hand, you may do the part
of a kind gentleman, in lending a poor foldier the price
of two cans of beer, a matter of fmall value; the King
of Heav'n fhall pay you, and I fhall reft thankful: fweet
worfhip——

Kno. Nay, an' you be fo importunate——

Brain. Oh, tender Sir, need will have his courfe: I
was not made to this vile ufe! Well the edge of the
enemy could not have abated me fo much. [*He weeps.*]
It's hard, when a man has ferved in his prince's caufe, and
be thus——Honourable worfhip, let me derive a fmall piece
of filver from you, it fhall not be given in the courfe of
time.

time. By this good ground, I was fain to pawn my rapier laft night for a poor fupper; I had fuck'd the hilts long before, I am a pagan elfe: fweet honour.

Kno. Believe me, I am taken with fome wonder,
To think a fellow of that outward prefence,
Should, in the frame and fafhion of his mind,
Be fo degenerate and fordid-bafe!
Art thou not a man, and fham'ft thou not to beg?
To practife fuch a fervile kind of life?
Why, were thy education ne'er fo mean,
Having thy limbs, a thoufand fairer courfes
Offer themfelves to thy election.
Either the wars might ftill fupply thy wants,
Or fervice of fome virtuous gentleman,
Or honeft labour: nay, what can I name,
But would become thee better than to beg!
But men of thy condition feed on floth,
As doth the beetle on the dung fhe breeds in,
Not caring how the metal of your minds
Is eaten with the ruft of idlenefs.
Now, afore me, whate'er he be that fhould
Relieve a perfon of thy quality,
While thou infifts in this loofe defperate courfe,
I would efteem the fin not thine, but his.

Brain. Faith, Sir, I would gladly find fome other courfe,
if fo——

Kno. Ay, you'ld gladly find it, but you will not feek it.

Brain. Alas! Sir, were fhould a man feek? In the wars there's no afcent by defert in thefe days, but—and for fervice, would it were as foon purchafed as wifh'd for. (the air's my comfort) I know what I would fay—

Kno. What's thy name!

Brain. Pleafe you, Fitz-Sword, Sir.

Kno. Fitz-Sword,
Say that a man fhould entertain thee now,
Would'ft thou be honeft, humble, juft and true?

Brain. Sir, by the place and honour of a foldier—

Kno. Nay, nay, I like not thofe affected oaths!
Speak plainly, man: what think'ft thou of my words?

Brain. Nothing, Sir. but wifh my fortunes were as happy as my fervice fhould be honeft.

C 3

Kno.

Kno. Well, follow me; I'll prove thee, if thy deeds
will carry a proportion to thy words.   [*Exit.*

Brain. Yes, Sir, straight: I'll but garter my hose.
Oh, that my belly were hoop'd now, for I am ready to
burst with laughing! Never was bottle or bagpipe fuller.
S'lid! was there ever seen a fox in years to betray himself thus? Now I shall be possessed of all his counsels!
and by that conduit my young master. Well, he is resolved to prove my honesty: faith, and I am resolved to
prove his patience. Oh, I shall abuse him intolerably!
This small piece of service will bring him clean out of
love with the soldier for ever. He will never come
within the sight of a red coat, or a musket-rest again. It's
no matter, let the world think me a bad counterfeit, if
I cannot give him the slip at an instant. Why, this is
better than to have staid his journey! Well, I'll follow
him. Oh, how I long to be employed!
With change of voice, these scars, and many an oath,
I'll follow son and sire, and serve 'em both.   [*Exit.*

End of the Second Act.

A C T   III.

SCENE, *Stocks-Market.*

Enter Matthew, Well-bred, *and* Bobadil.

MATTHEW.

YES, faith, Sir! We were at your lodging to see
you, too.

Well. Oh, I came not there to-night.

Bob. Your brother delivered us as much.

Well. Who? My brother, Downright?

Bob. He. Mr. Well-bred, I know not in what kind
you hold me; but let me say to you this: as sure as
honour, I esteem it so much out of the sunshine of reputation to throw the least beam of regard upon such
a——

Well. Sir, I must hear no ill words of my brother.

Bob. I protest to you, as I have a thing to be saved
about me, I never saw any gentleman-like part——

Well.

Well. Good Captain [*Faces about.*] to some other dif-
course.

Bob. With your leave, Sir, an' there were no more
men living upon the face of the earth, I should not fancy
him, by St. George.

Mat. Troth, nor I; he is of a rustical cut, I know
not how: he doth not carry himself like a gentleman of
fashion——

Well. Oh, Mr. Matthew, that's a grace peculiar but
to a few, ' *quos æquus amavit Jupiter.*

' *Mat.* I understand you, Sir.'

Enter Young Kno'well *and* Stephen.

Well. ' No question you do, or you do not, Sir?'
Ned Kno'well! By my soul, welcome! How dost thou,
sweet spirit, my genius? 'Slid, I shall love Apollo, and
the mad Thespian girls, the better while I live, for this,
my dear fury. Now I see there's some love in thee!
Sirrah, these be the two I writ to you of. Nay, what
a drowsy humour is this now? Why dost thou not speak?

E. Kno. Oh, you are a fine gallant; you sent me a
rare letter.

Well. Why, was't not rare?

E. Kno. Yes, I'll be sworn, I was never guilty of reading the like. Match it in all Pliny's epistles, and I'll
have my judgment burn'd in the ear for a rogue: make
much of thy vein, for it is inimitable. But I marvel
what camel it was that had the carriage of it; for doubt-
less he was no ordinary beast that brought it.

Well. Why?

E. Kno. Why, sayest thou? Why, dost thou think that
any reasonable creature, especially in the morning, the
sober time of the day too, could have mistaken my father
for me?

Well. 'Slid, you jest, I hope.

E. Kno. Indeed, the best use we can turn it to, is to
make a jest on't now; but I'll assure you, my father had
the full view o' your flourishing style, before I saw it.

Well. What a dull slave was this! But, sirrah, what
said he to it, i'faith?

E. Kno. Nay, I know not what he said: but I have a
shrewd guess what he thought.

Well. What, what?

E. Kno.

E. Kno. Marry, that thou art some strange, dissolute young fellow, and I not a grain or two better, for keeping thee company.

Well. Tut, that thought is like the moon in her last quarter, 'twill change shortly. But, sirrah, I pray thee be acquainted with my two hang-bys here ; thou wilt take exceeding pleasure in 'em, if thou hearest 'em once go : my wind-instruments. I'll wind 'em up——But what strange piece of silence is this ?. The sign of the dumb man.

E. Kno. Oh, Sir, a kinsman of mine, one that may make your musick the fuller, an' he please ; he has his humour, Sir.

Well. Oh, what is'r, what is't ?

E. Kno. Nay, I'll neither do your judgment, nor his folly, that wrong, as to prepare your apprehensions. I'll leave him to the mercy o' your search, if you can take him so.

Well. Well, Captain Bobadil, Mr. Matthew, I pray you know this gentleman here ; he is a friend of mine, and one that will deserve your affection. I know not your name, Sir, but shall be glad of any occasion to render me more familar to you.

Step. My name is Mr. Stephen, Sir; I am this gentleman's own cousin, Sir: his father is mine uncle, Sir ; I am somewhat melancholy, but you shall command me, Sir, in whatsoever is incident to a gentleman.

Bob. I must tell you this, I am no general man ; but for Mr. Well-bred's sake (you may embrace it at what height of favour you please) I do communicate with you ; and conceive you to be a gentleman of some parts. I love few words.

E. Kno. And I fewer, Sir. I have scarce enow to thank you.

Mat. But are you indeed, Sir, so given to it ?
[To Mr. Stephen.

Step. Ay, truly, Sir, I am mightily given to melancholy,.

Mat. Oh, it's your only fine humour, Sir ; your true melancholy breeds you perfect fine wit, Sir: I am melancholy myself divers times, Sir ; and then do I no more
but

4

but take a pen and paper prefently, and overflow you
half a fcore or a dozen of fonnets, at a fitting.

Step. Coufin, it is well; am I melancholy enough?

E. Kno. Oh, ay, excellent!

Well. Captain Bobadil, why mufe you fo?

E. Kno. He is melancholy too.

Bob. Faith, Sir, I was thinking of a moft honourable
piece of fervice was perform'd, to-morrow, being St.
Mark's day, fhall be fome ten years now.

E. Kno. In what place, Captain?

Bob. Why, at the beleag'ring of Strigonium, where,
in lefs than two hours, feven hundred refolute gentlemen,
as any were in Europe, loft their lives upon the breach.
I'll tell you, gentlemen, it was the firft, but the beft lea-
gure, that ever I beheld with thefe eyes, except the taking
of——what do you call it, laft year, by the Genoefe;
but that (of all others) was the moft fatal and dangerous
exploit that ever I was ranged in, fince I firft bore arms
before the face of the enemy, as I am a gentleman and a
foldier.

Step. 'So, I had a lief as an angel, I could fwear as well
as that gentleman.

E. Kno. Then you were a fervitor at both, it feems; at
Strigonium, and what do you call't?

Bob. Oh, lord, Sir! by St. George, I was the firft
man that enter'd the breach; had I not affected it with refolution, I had been flain, if I had had a million of lives.

E. Kno. 'Twas pity you had not ten; a cat's, and
your own, i' faith. But, was it poffible?

Mat. Pray you, mark this difcourfe, Sir.

Step. So I do.

Bob. I affure you, upon my reputation, 'tis true, and
yourfelf fhall confefs.

E. Kno. You muft bring me to the rack firft.

Bob. Obferve me judicially, fweet Sir: they had plan-
ted me three demi-culverins, juft in the mouth of the
breach: now, Sir, as we were to give on, their mafter
gunner (a man of no mean fkill and mark, you muft think)
confronts me with his linftock, ready to give fire: I, fpy-
ing his intendment, difcharg'd my petrionel in his bofom,
and with thefe fingle arms, my poor rapier, ran violently
upon

upon the Moors, that guarded the ordnance, and put them all pell-mell to the sword.

Well. To the sword! to the rapier, Captain!

E. Kno. Oh, it was a good figure obſerved, Sir! but did you all this, Captain, without hurting your blade?

Bob. Without any impeach o' the earth: you ſhall perceive, Sir. It is the moſt fortunate weapon, that ever rid on poor gentleman's thigh. Shall I tell you, Sir? You talk of Morglay, Excalibur, Durindina, or ſo? Tut, I lend no credit to that is fabled of 'em; I know the virtue of mine own, and therefore I dare the boldlier maintain it.

Step. I marvel whether it be a Toledo, or no.

Bob. A moſt perfect Toledo, I aſſure you, Sir.

Step. I have a countryman of his here.

Mat. Pray you, let's ſee, Sir. Yes, faith, it is!

Bob. This a Toledo! piſh.

Step. Why do you piſh, Captain?

Bob. A Fleming, by heaven! I'll buy them for a guilder a piece, an' I will have a thouſand of them.

E. Kno. How ſay you, couſin? I told you thus much.

Well. Where bought you it, Mr. Stephen?

Step. Of a ſcurvey rogue ſoldier (a hundred of lice go with him) he ſwore it was a Toledo.

Bob. A poor Provant rapier, no better.

Mat. Maſs, I think it be, indeed, now I look on't better.

E. Kno. Nay, the longer you look on't the worſe. Put it up, put it up!

Step. Well, I will put it up, but by—(I ha' forgot the Captain's oath, I thought to have ſworn by it) an' e'er I meet him——

Well. O, 'tis paſt help now, Sir; you muſt ha' patience.

Step. Whorſon coney-catching raſcal! I could eat the very hilts for anger.

E. Kno. A ſign of good digeſtion; you have an oſtrich ſtomach, couſin.

Step. A ſtomach! I would I had him here; you ſhould ſee an' I had a ſtomach.

Well. It's better as 'tis. Come, gentlemen, ſhall we go?

Enter

Enter Brain-worm.

E. Kno. A miracle! coufin! look here! look here!

Step. O, god'flid, by your leave, do you know me, Sir?

Brain. Ay, Sir, I know you by fight.

Step. You fold me a rapier, did you not!

Brain. Yes, marry, did I, Sir.

Step. You faid, it was a Toledo, ha?

Brain. True, I did fo.

Step. But it is none!

Brain. No, Sir, I confefs, it is none.

Step. Do you confefs it? Gentlemen, bear witnefs, he has confefs'd it. By God's will, an' you had not confefs'd it———

E. Kno. Oh, coufin, forbear, forbear.

Step. Nay, I have done, coufin.

Well. Why, you have done like a gentleman, he has confefs'd it, what would you more?

Step. Yet, by his leave, he is a rafcal under his favour, do you fee.

E. Kno. Ay, by his leave, he is, and under favour. Pretty piece of civility! Sirrah, how doft thou like him?

Well. Oh, it's a moft precious fool, make much on him. I can compare him to nothing more happily, than a drum; for every one may play upon him.

E. Kno. No, no, a child's whiftle were far the fitter.

Brain. Sir, fhall I intreat a word with you?

E. Kno. With me, Sir! You have not another Tole-do to fell, ha' you?

Brain. You are conceited, Sir; your name is Mr. Kno'well, as I take it?

E. Kno. You are i' the right. You mean not to pro-ceed in the catechifm, do you?

Brain. No, Sir, I am none of that coat.

E. Kno. Of as bare coat, though! Well, fay, Sir?

Brain. Faith, Sir, I am but a fervant to the drum extraordinary, and indeed, this fmoky varnifh being wafhed off, and three or four patches removed, I appear your worfhip's in reverfion, after the deceafe of your good father—Brain-worm.

E. Kno. Brain-worm! 'Slight, what breath of a con-jurer hath blown thee hither in this fhape?

Brain.

Brain. The breath o' your letter, Sir, this morning: the fame that blew you to the wind-mill, and your fa-ther after you.

E. Kno. My father!

Brain. Nay, never ftart: 'tis true; he has followed you over the fields by the foot, as you would do a hare i' the fnow.

E. Kno. Sirrah, Well-bred, what fhall we do, firrah? My father is come over after me.

Well. Thy father! Where is he?

Brain. At Juftice Clement's houfe, here, in Cole-man-Street, where he but ftays my return; and then—

Well. Who's this? Brain-worm?

Brain. The fame, Sir.

Well. Why, how, i' the name of wit, comeft thou tranfmuted thus?

Brain. Faith, a device! A device! Nay, for the love of reafon, gentlemen, and avoiding the danger, ftand not here: withdraw, and I'll tell you all.

E. Kno. Come, coufin.   [*Exeunt.*

S C E N E, *the Warehoufe.*

Enter Kitely *and* Cafh.

Kite. What fays he, Thomas? Did you fpeak with him?

Cafh. He will expect you, Sir, within this half hour.

Kite. Has he the money ready, can you tell?

Cafh. Yes, Sir, the money was brought in laft night.

Kite. Oh, that's well: fetch me my cloak, my cloak.
Stay, let me fee, an hour to go and come;
Ay, that will be the leaft; and then 'twill be
An hour before I can difpatch him,
Or very near: well, I will fay two hours.
Two hours! Ha! Things, never dream't of yet,
May be contriv'd, ay, and effected too,
In two hours abfence. Well, I will not go.
Two hours; no, fleering opportunity,
I will not give your fubtlety that fcope.
Who will not judge him worthy to be robb'd,
That fets his doors wide open to a thief,
And fhews the felon where his treafure lies?
Again, what earthly fpirit but will attempt
To tafte the fruit of beauty's golden tree,

                                        When

When leaden sleep seals up the dragon's eyes?
I will not go.   Business, go by, for once.
No, beauty, no; you are too, too precious
To be left so, without a guard, or open!
You then must be kept up close, and well watch'd!
For, give you opportunity, no quick-sand
Devours or swallows swifter! He that leads
His wife, if she be fair, or, time or place,
Compels her to be false.   I will not go.
The dangers are too many.   I am resolv'd for that.
Carry in my cloak again.   Yet, stay.   Yet do, too.
I will defer going on all occasions.
   Cash. Sir, Snare, your scrivner, will be there with
the bonds.
   Kite. That's true! Fool on me! I had clean forgot
it! I must go.   What's o'clock?
   Cash. Exchange time, Sir,
   Kite. 'Heart, then will Well-bred presently be here
With one or other of his loose consorts.   [too,
I am a knave, if I know what to say,
What course to take, or which way to resolve.
My brain, methinks, is like an hour-glass,
Wherein my imagination runs; like sands,
Filling up time; but then are turn'd and turn'd;
So that I know not what to stay upon,
And less to put in act: It shall be so.
Nay, I dare build upon his secrecy,
He knows not to deceive me.   Thomas!
   Cash. Sir.
   Kite. Yet now, I have bethought too, I will not—
Thomas, is Cob within?
   Cash. I think he be, Sir.
   Kite. But he'll prate too, there's no speech of him.
No, there were no man o' the earth to Thomas,
If I durst trust him; there is all the doubt.
But should he have a chink in him, I were gone,
Lost i' my fame for ever; talk for th' exchange.
The manner he hath stood with, 'till this present,
Doth promise no such change! What should I fear then?
Well, come what will, I'll tempt my fortune once.
Thomas—you may deceive me, but I hope—
Your love to me is more——
                    *   D   *Cash.*

Cash. Sir, if a servant's
Duty, with faith, may be call'd love, you are
More than in hope, you are possess'd of it.
   Kite. I thank you heartily, Thomas; gi' me your
      hand.
With all my heart, good Thomas. I have, Thomas,
A secret to impart to you—but
When once you have it, I must seal your lips up.
So far I tell you, Thomas.
   Cash. Sir, for that——
   Kite. Nay, hear me out. Think, I esteem you,
      Thomas,
When I will let you in, thus to my private.
It is a thing fits nearer to my crest,
Than thou 'rt aware of, Thomas. If thou shouldst,
Reveal it, but——
   Cash. How! I reveal it!
   Kite. Nay,
I do not think thou wouldst; but if thou shouldst,
'Twere a great weakness.
   Cash. A great treachery.
Give it no other name.
   Kite. Thou wilt not do't then?
   Cash. Sir, if I do, mankind disclaim me ever.
   Kite. He will not swear; he has some reservation,
Some conceal'd purpose, and close meaning, sure.
Else, being urg'd so much, how should he choose,
But lend an oath to all this protestation?
He's no fanatic, I have heard him swear.
What should I think of it? Urge him again,
And by some other way? I will do so.
Well, Thomas, thou hast sworn not to disclose;
Yes, you did swear.
   Cash. Not yet, Sir, but I will,
Please you——
   Kite. No, Thomas, I dare take thy word,
But if thou wilt swear, do, as thou think'st good;
I am resolv'd without it; at thy pleasure.
   Cash. By my soul's safety then, Sir, I protest
My tongue shall ne'er take knowledge of a word,
Deliver'd me in nature of your trust.

4

Kite.

Kite. It's too much ; thefe ceremonies need not ;
I know thy faith to be as firm as rock.
Thomas, come hither, near ; we cannot be
Too private in this bufinefs.   So it is.
Now he has fworn, I dare the fafelier venture :
I have of late, by divers obfervations—
But whether his oath can bind him, there it is.
I will bethink me e'er I do proceed.
Thomas, it will be now too long to ftay,
I'll fpy fome fitter time foon, or to-morrow.
    Cafh. Sir, at your pleafure.
    Kite. I will think.   Give me my cloak.   And, Tho-
I pray you fearch the books 'gainft my return,   [mas,
For the receipts 'twixt me and Traps.
    Cafh. I will, Sir.
    Kite. And, hear you, if your miftrefs' brother,   Well-
Chance to bring hither any gentlemen,   [bred,
Ere I come back, let one ftraight bring me word.
    Cafh. Very well, Sir.
    Kite. To the exchange ; do you hear ?
Or here in Coleman-Street, to Juftice Clement's.
Forget it not, nor be out of the way.
    Cafh. I will not, Sir.
    Kite. I pray you have a care on't.
Or whether he come or no, if any other
Stranger, or elfe, fail not to fend me word.
    Cafh. I fhall not, Sir.
    Kite. Be't your fpecial bufinefs
Now to remember it.
    Cafh. Sir, I warrant you.
    Kite. But, Thomas, this is not the fecret, Thomas,
I told you of.
    Cafh. No, Sir.   I do fuppofe it.
    Kite. Believe me, it is not.
    Cafh. Sir, I do believe you.
    Kite. By heaven, it is not ! That's enough.   But,
        Thomas,
I would not you fhould utter it, do you fee,
To any creature living ; yet I care not.
Well, I muft hence.   Thomas, conceive thus much ;
It was a trial of you, when I meant
So deep a fecret to you : I meant not this,

D 2

But

But that I have to tell you.   This is nothing, this.
But, Thomas, keep this from my wife, I charge you.
Lock'd up in filence, midnight, buried here,
No greater hell than to be flave to fear.   [*Exit.*

Cafh. Lock'd up in filence, midnight, buried here.
Whence fhould this flood of paffion, trow, take head?
Beft dream no longer of this running humour,   [Ha!
For fear I fink! The violence of the ftream
Already hath tranfported me fo far,
That I can feel no ground at all! But foft,
Here is company; now muft I————

Enter Well-bred, Edw. Kno'well, Brainworm, Bobadil,
                and Stephen.

Well. Befhrew me, but it was an abfolute good jeft,
and exceedingly well carried.

E. Kno. Ay, and our ignorance maintained it as well,
did it not?

Well. Yes, faith! But was't poffible thou fhouldft not
know him? I forgive Mr. Stephen, for he is ftupidity
itfelf.

E. Kno. 'Fore heav'n, not I. 'He had fo written
' himfelf into the habit of one of your poor infantry,
' your decayed, ruinous, worm-eaten gentlemen of the
' round.'

Well. Why, Brain-worm, who would have thought
thou hadft been fuch an artificer?

E. Kno. An artificer! An architect! Except a man
had ftudied begging all his life-time, and been a weaver
of language from his infancy, for the clothing of it! I
never faw his rival.

Well. Where got'ft thou this coat, I marvel?

Brain. Of a Houndfditch man, Sir, one of the devil's
near kinfmen, a broker.

Enter Cafh.

Cafh. Francis! Martin! Ne'er a one to be found
now? What a fpite's this?

Well. How now, Thomas, is my brotherly Kitely
within?

Cafh. No, Sir; my mafter went forth e'en now; but
mafter Downright is within. Cob! What, Cob! Is he
gone too?

Well.

Well. Whither went your master, Thomas, can'st thou tell?

Cash. I know not; to Justice Clement's, I think, Sir. Cob!   *[Exit Cash.*

E. Kno. Justice Clement's! What's he?

Well. Why, dost thou not know him? He is a city magistrate, a justice here; an excellent good lawyer, and a great scholar: but the only mad and merry old fellow in Europe! I shewed you him the other day.

E. Kno. Oh, is that he? I remember him now. Good faith! and he has a very strange presence, methinks; it shews as if he stood out of the rank from other men. I have heard many of his jests i' the university. They say, he will commit a man for taking the wall of his horse.

Well. Ay, or wearing his cloak on one shoulder, or serving of God. Any thing indeed, if it come in the way of his humour.

Enter Cash.

Cash. Gasper, Martin, Cob! 'Heart! where should they be, trow?

Bob. Master Kitely's man, pr'ythee vouchsafe us the lighting of this match.

Cash. Fire on your match! no time but now to vouchsafe? Francis! Cob!

Bob. Body of me! Here's the remainder of seven pound since yesterday was seven-night. 'Tis your right Trinidado! Did you never take any, master Stephen?

Step. No, truly, Sir! but I'll learn to take it now, since you commend it so.

Bob. Sir, believe me, upon my relation, for what I tell you the world shall not reprove. I have been in the Indies, where this herb grows, where neither myself, nor a dozen gentlemen more, of my knowledge, have received the taste of any other nutriment in the world for the space of one and twenty weeks, but the fume of this simple only. Therefore it cannot be but 'tis most divine, especially your Trinidado. Your Nicotian is good too. I do hold it, and will affirm it before any prince in Europe, to be the most sovereign and precious weed that ever the earth tendered to the use of man.

E. Kno. This speech would have done decently in a tobacco-trader's mouth.

D 3   *Enter*

Enter Cash *and* Cob.

Cash. At justice Clement's he is, in the middle of Cole-man-street.

Cob. O, ho!

Bob. Where's the match I gave thee, master Kitely's man?

Cash. Here it is, Sir.

Cob. By God's-me! I marvel what pleasure or felicity they have in taking this roguish tobacco! it's good for nothing but to choak a man, and fill him full of smoak and embers.

[*Bob. beats him with a cudgle,* Mat. *runs away.*

All. Oh, good Captain! hold, hold!

Bob. You base scullion, you.

Cash. Come, thou must need be talking too; thou'rt well enough serv'd.

Cob. Well, it shall be a dear beating, an I live! I will have justice for this.

Bob. Do you prate? Do you murmur?

[*Bob. beats him off.*

E. Kno. Nay, good Captain, will you regard the humour of a fool?

Bob. A whoreson filthy slave, a dung-worm, an excrement! Body o' Cæsar, but that I scorn to let forth so mean a spirit, I'd have stabb'd him to the earth.

Well. Marry, the law forbid, Sir.

Bob. By Pharaoh's foot, I would have done it. [*Exit.*

Step. Oh, he swears admirably! By Pharaoh's foot, body of Cæsar; I shall never do it, sure; upon mine honour, and by St. George; no I han't the right grace.

Well. But soft, where's Mr. Matthew; gone?

Brain. No, Sir; they went in here.

Well. O, let's follow them: Master Matthew is gone to salute his mistress in verse. We shall have the happiness to hear some of his poetry now. He never comes unfurnish'd. Brain-worm!

Step. Brain-worm! Where? Is this Brain-worm?

E. Kno. Ay, cousin, no words of it, upon your gentility.

Step. Not I, body of me! by this air, St. George, and the foot of Pharaoh!

Well.

Well. Rare! your cousin's discourse is simply drawn out with oaths.

E. Kno. 'Tis larded with 'em. A kind of French dressing, if you love it. Come, let's in. Come, cousin.

[Exeunt.

SCENE, *a Hall in Justice* Clement's *House.*

Enter Kitely *and* Cob.

Kite. Ha! How many are there, say'st thou?

Cob. Marry, Sir, your brother, Master Well-bred—

Kite. Tut, beside him: what strangers are there, man?

Cob. Strangers! let me see; one, two; mass, I know not well, there are so many.

Kite. How, so many?

Cob. Ay, there's some five or six of them, at the most.

Kite. A swarm, a swarm!
Spite of the devil, how they sting my head
With forked stings, thus wide and large! But, Cob,
How long hast thou been coming hither, Cob?

Cob. A little while, Sir.

Kite. Didst thou come running?

Cob. No, Sir.

Kite. Nay, then I am familiar with thy haste!
Bane to my fortunes. What meant I to marry?
I, that before was rank'd in such content,
My mind at rest too in so soft a peace,
Being free master of my own free thoughts,
And now become a slave? What, never sigh!
Be of good cheer, man, for thou art a cuckold.
'Tis done, 'tis done! Nay, when such flowing store,
Plenty itself falls into my wife's lap,
The Cornucopia will be mine, I know. But, Cob,
What entertainment had they? I am sure
My sister and my wife would bid them welcome! Ha!

Cob. Like enough, Sir; yet I heard not a word of it.

Kite. No; their lips were seal'd with kisses, and the
voice,
Drown'd in a flood of joy at their arrival,
Had lost her motion, state and faculty.
Cob, which of them was't that first kiss'd my wife?
My sister, I should say: my wife, alas!
I fear not her. Ha! Who was it, say'st thou?

Cob.

Cob. By my troth, Sir, will you have the truth of it?

Kite. Ay, good Cob, I pray thee heartily.

Cob. Then I am a vagabond, and fitter for Bridewell than your worship's company, if I saw any body to be kiss'd, unless they wou'd have kiss'd the post in the middle of the warehouse; for there I left them all, at their to-bacco, with a pox!

Kite. How! were they not gone in then, ere thou cam'st?

Cob. O, no, Sir!

Kite. Spite o' the devil? What do I stay here then! Cob, follow me.   [*Exit.*

' *Cob.* Nay, soft and fair, I have eggs on the spit.
' Now am I for some five and fifty reasons hammering,
' hammering revenge! Nay, an' he had not lain in my
' house, 'twould never have grieved me; but, being my
' guest, one that I'll be sworn I loved and trusted; and he
' to turn monster of ingratitude, and strike his lawful
' host! Well, I hope to raise up an host of fury for't.
' I'll to justice Clement for a warrant. Strike his lawful
' host!   [*Exit.*

END of the THIRD ACT.

ACT IV.

SCENE, *a room in* Kitely's *House.*

Enter Downright *and Dame* Kitely.

DOWNRIGHT.

WELL, sister, I tell you true; and you'll find it so, in the end.

Dame. Alas, brother, what would you have me to do? I cannot help it. You see my brother brings 'em in here, they are his friends.

Down. His friends! his friends! 'Slud they do no-thing but haunt him up and down, like a sort of unlucky spirits, and tempt him to all manner of villainy, that can be thought of. Well, by this light, a little thing wou'd make me play the devil with some of 'em. And 'twere not more for your husband's sake, than any thing else, I'd make the house too hot for the best on 'em. They should say,

say, and swear, hell were broken loose ere they went hence. But, by God's will, 'tis nobody's fault but your's; for an' you had done as you might have done, they should have been parboil'd and bak'd too, every mother's son, ere they should ha' come in e'er a one of 'em.

Dame. God's my life! did you ever hear the like? What a strange man is this? Could I keep out all them, think you? I should put myself against half a dozen men, should I? Good faith, you'd mad the patient'st body in the world to hear you talk so without any sense or reason!

Enter Mrs. Bridget, *Mr.* Matthew, Well-bred, Stephen, Edward Kno'well, Bobadil, *and* Cash.

Bridg. Servant, in troth, you are too prodigal
Of your wit's treasure, thus to pour it forth
Upon so mean a subject as my worth.

Mat. You say well, mistress; and I mean as well.

Down. Hey-day, here is stuff!

Well. O, now stand close. Pray Heav'n she can get him to read; he should do it of his own natural impudence.

Bridg. Servant, what is this same, I pray you?

Mat. Marry, an elegy! an elegy! an odd toy—I'll read it, if you please.

Bridg. Pray you do, servant.

Down. O, here's no foppery! Death! I can endure the stocks better.

E. Kno. What ails thy brother? Can he not bear the reading of a ballad?

Well. O, no; a rhime to him is worse than cheese, or a bagpipe. But, mark, you lose the protestation.

Bob. Master Matthew, you abuse the expectation of your dear mistress, and her fair sister. Fie, while you live, avoid this prolixity.

Mat. I shall, Sir.

Rare creature, let me speak without offence,
Would Heav'n my rude words had the influence
To rule thy thoughts, as thy fair looks do mine,
Then should'st thou be his prisoner, who is thine.

[*Master* Stephen *answers with shaking his head.*]

E. Kno. 'Slight, he shakes his head like a bottle, to feel an' there be any brain in it!

Well.

Well. Sifter, what ha' you here? Verfes? Pray you, let's fee. Who made thefe verfes? They are excellent good.

Mat. O, Mafter Well-bred, 'tis your difpofition to fay fo, Sir. They were good i' the morning; I made 'em extempore this morning.

Well. How, extempore!

Mat. I fhould I might be hang'd elfe; afk Captain Bobadil. He faw me write them at the——(pox on it) the Star yonder.

Step. Coufin, how do you like this gentleman's verfes?

E. Kno. O, admirable! the beft that ever I heard Coz!

Step. Body o' Cæfar! they are admirable! The beft that ever I heard, as I am a foldier.

Down. I am vext, I can hold ne'er a bone of me ftill! Heart, I think they mean to build and breed here.

Well. Sifter Kitely, I marvel you get you not a fervant that can rhime, and do tricks too.

Down. O, monfter! Impudence itfelf! Tricks! Come, you might practife your ruffian tricks fome where elfe, and not here, I wufs. This is no tavern, nor drinking-fchool, to vent your exploits in.

Well. How now! Whofe cow has calv'd?

Down. Marry, that has mine, Sir. Nay, boy, never look afkance at me for the matter; I'll tell you of it; aye, Sir, you and your companions; mend yourfelves, when I ha' done?

Well. My companions!

Down. Yes, Sir, your companions, fo I fay;—I am not afraid of you nor them neither, your hang-bys here. You muft have your poets, and your potlings, your foldados and foolados, to follow you up and down the city, and here they muft come to domineer and fwagger. Sirrah, you ballad-finger; and, flops, your fellow there, get you out; get you home; or, by this fteel, I'll cut off your ears, and that prefently.

Well. 'Slight, ftay, and let's fee what he dare do. Cut off his ears! Cut a whetftone. You are an afs, do you fee; touch any man here, and by this hand, I'll run my rapier to the hilts in you.

Down.

Down. Yea, that would I fain fee, boy,

[*They all draw, and they of the houfe make out to part them.*]

Dame. Oh, Jefu! Murder! Thomas, Gafper!

Bridge. Help, help, Thomas.

E. Kno. Gentlemen, forbear, I pray you.

Bob. Well, firrah! You Holofernes! by my hand, I will pink your flefh full of holes with my rapier, for this: I will, by this good Heav'n. Nay, let him come, gentlemen, by the body of St. George, I'll not kill him.

[*They offer to fight again, and are parted.*]

Cafh. Hold, hold, good gentlemen.

Down. You whorfon, bragging coiftril.

Enter Kitely.

Kite. Why, how now, what's the matter? What's the ftir here?

Put up your weapons, and put off this rage.

My wife and fifter, they're the caufe of this.

What, Thomas, where is the knave?

Cafh. Here, Sir.

Well. Come, let's go; this is one of my brother's an-cient humours, this.   [*Exit.*

Step. I am glad nobody was hurt by his antient hu-mour.   [*Exit.*

Kite. Why, how now, brother, who inforc'd this brawl?

Down. A fort of lewd rake-hells, that care neither for God nor the devil. And they muft come here to read ballads, and roguery, and trafh! I'll mar the knot of 'em ere I fleep, perhaps; efpecially Bob there, he that's all manner of fhapes; and fongs and fonnets, his fellow. But I'll follow 'em.   [*Exit.*

Bridge. Brother, indeed you are too violent,

Too fudden in your humour.

There was one a civil gentleman,

And very worthily demean'd himfelf.

Kite. Oh, that was fome love of yours, fifter.

Bridge. A love of mine! I would it were no worfe, brother! You'd pay my portion fooner than you think for.   [*Exit.*

Dame. Indeed, he feem'd to be a gentleman of ex-ceeding

ceeding fair difpofition, and of very excellent good
parts. What a coil and ſtir is here !   [*Exit.*

Kite. Her love, by Heav'n ! my wife's minion !
Death; theſe phrafes are intolerable !
Well, well, well, well, well, well !
It is too plain, too clear. Thomas, come hither,
What, are they gone?

Caſh. Ay, Sir, they went in.
My miſtreſs, and your ſiſter——

Kite. Are any of the gallants within ?

Caſh. No, Sir, they are all gone.

Kite. Art thou ſure of it ?

Caſh. I can aſſure you, Sir.

Kite. What gentleman was it that they prais'd ſo,
Thomas ?

Caſh. One, they call him Maſter Kno'well, a handſome young gentleman, Sir.

Kite. Ay, I thought ſo. My mind gave me as much.
I'll die, but they have hid him in the houſe
Somewhere ; I'll go and ſearch. Go with me, Thomas.
Be true to me, and thou ſhalt find me a maſter.
                                                    [*Exeunt.*

S C E N E, *Moor-fields.*

Enter Edw. Kno'well, Well-bred, *and* Brain-worm.

E. Kno. Well, Brain-worm, perform this buſineſs
happily, and thou makeſt a purchaſe of my love for
ever.

Well. I'faith, now let thy ſpirits uſe their beſt facul-
ties ; but at my hand, remember the meſſage to my brother : for there's no other means to ſtart him out of
his houſe.

Brain. I warrant you, Sir, fear nothing. I have a
nimble ſoul has waked all forces of my phant'ſy by this
time, and put 'em in true motion. What you have
poſſeſſed me withal, I'll diſcharge it amp'y, Sir. Make
it no queſtion.   [*Exit.*

Well. Forth, and proſper, Brainworm. Faith, Ned,
how doſt thou approve of my abilities in this device ?

E. Kno. Troth, well, howſoever : but it will come
excellent, if it take.
                                                    Well.

Well. Take, man! Why, it cannot chuse but take, if the circumstances miscarry not. But tell me ingenuously, dost thou affect my sister Bridget, as thou pretend'st.

E. Kno. Friend, am I worth belief?

Well. Come, do not protest. In faith, she is a maid of good ornament, and much modesty; and, except I conceiv'd very worthily of her, thou shouldst not have her.

E. Kno. Nay, that I'm afraid will be a question yet, whether I shall have her or no.

Well. 'Slid, thou shalt have her; by this light thou shalt.

E. Kno. Nay, do not swear.

Well. By this hand, thou shalt have her. I'll go fetch her presently. 'Point but where to meet, and as I am an honest man, I'll bring her.

E. Kno. Hold, hold, be temperate.

Well. Why, by——what shall I swear by? Thou shalt have her, as I am——

E. Kno. Pray thee be at peace, I am satisfied; and do believe thou wilt omit no offered occasion, to make my desires complete.

Well. Thou shalt see and know I will not.   [*Exeunt.*

Enter Formal *and* Kno'well.

Form. Was your man a soldier, Sir?

Kno. Aye, a knave, I took him begging o' the way, This morning, as I came over Moorfields.

Enter Brainworm.

Oh, here he is! You have made fair speed, believe me. Where i' the name of sloth could you be thus——

Brain. Marry, peace be my comfort, where I thought I should have had little comfort of your worship's service.

Kno. How so?

Brain. Oh, Sir! Your coming to the city, your entertainment of me, and your sending me to watch—— indeed, all the circumstances either of your charge, or my employment, are as open to your son as to yourself.

Kno. How should that be! Unless that villain, Brainworm,

                          *   E   Have

Have told him of the letter, and difcovered
All that I ftrictly charg'd him to conceal! 'Tis fo!
Brain. I am partly o' that faith, 'tis fo indeed.
Kno. But how fhould he know you to be my man?
Brain. Nay, Sir, I cannot tell; unlefs it be by the
black art! Is not your fon a fcholar, Sir?
Kno. Yes, but I hope his foul is not allied
Unto fuch hellifh practice: if it were,
I had juft caufe to weep my part in him,
And curfe the time of his creation.
But where didft thou find them, Fitz-Sword?
Brain. You fhould rather afk, where they found me,
Sir; for I'll be fworn I was going along in the ftreet,
thinking nothing, when (of a fudden) a voice calls, Mr.
Kno'well's man; another cries, Soldier: and thus, half
a dozen of 'em, 'till they had called me within a houfe,
where I no fooner came, but out flew all their rapiers at
my bofom, with fome three or fourfcore oaths to accom-
pany 'em, and all to tell me, I was a dead man, if I did
not confefs where you were, and how I was employed,
and about what; which, when they could not get out of
me (as I proteft they muft have diffected me, and made
an anatomy of me firft, and fo I told 'em) they locked me
up into a room i' the top of a high houfe, whence, by
great miracle, having a light heart, I flid down by a bottom of packthread into the ftreet, and fo 'fcaped. But,
Sir, thus much I can affure you; for I heard it while I
was lock'd up; there were a great many rich merchants'
and brave citizens' wives with 'em at a feaft, and your fon,
Mr. Edward, withdrew with one of 'em, and has 'pointed to meet her anon, at one Cob's houfe, a water-bearer,
that dwells by the wall. Now, there your worfhip
fhall be fure to take him, for there he preys, and fail he
will not.
Kno. Nor will I fail, to break his match I doubt not.
Go thou along with juftice Clement's man,
And ftay there for me. At one Cob's houfe, fay'ft thou?
Brain. Aye, Sir, there you fhall have him. [*Exit.*
Kno'well.] Yes! Invifible! Much wench, or much fon!
'Slight, when he has ftaid there three or four hours, tra-
vailing with the expectation of wonders, and at length be
delivered of air! O, the fport that I fhould then take to
look

look on him, if I durſt! But now I mean to appear no more before him in this ſhape. I have another trick to act yet. Sir, I make you ſtay ſomewhat long.

Form. Not a whit, Sir. You have been lately in the wars, Sir, it ſeems.

Brain. Marry have I, Sir, to my loſs, and expence of all, almoſt——

Form. Troth, Sir, I would be glad to beſtow a bottle o' you, if it pleaſe you to accept it——

Brain. O, Sir——

Form. But to hear the manner of your ſervices and your devices in the wars; they ſay they be very ſtrange, and not like thoſe a man reads in the Roman hiſtories, or ſees at Mile-End.

Brain. No, I aſſure you, Sir; why at any time when it pleaſe you, I ſhall be ready to diſcourſe with you all I know; and more too, ſomewhat.

Form. No better time than now, Sir. We'll go to the Windmill, there we ſhall have a cup of neat griſt, as we call it. I pray you, Sir, let me requeſt you to the Windmill.

Brain. I'll follow you, Sir, and make griſt o' you, if I have good luck.   [*Exeunt.*

Enter Matthew, Ed. Kno'well, Bobadil, *and* Stephen.

Mat. Sir, did your eyes ever taſte the like clown of him, where we were to-day, Mr. Well-bred's half brother? I think the whole earth cannot ſhew his parallel, by this day-light.

E. Kno. We are now ſpeaking of him. Captain Bobadil tells me, he is fallen foul o' you too.

Mat. O, aye, Sir! he threaten'd me with the baſtinado.

Bob. Aye, but I think I taught you prevention this morning for that——You ſhall kill him, beyond queſtion, if you be ſo generouſly minded.

Mat. Indeed, it is a moſt excellent trick!

Bob. O, you do not give ſpirit enough to your motion, you are too tardy, too heavy! O, it muſt be done like lightning; hey!   [*He practiſes at a poſt.*

Mat. Rare Captain!

Bob. Tut, 'tis nothing, an't be not done in a——punto!

E. Kno. Captain, did you ever prove yourself upon any of our masters of defence here?

Mat. O, good Sir! yes, I hope he has.

Bob. I will tell you, Sir. They have assaulted me some three, four, five, six of them together, as I have walked alone in divers skirts o' the town, where I have driven them before me the whole length of a street, in the open view of all our gallants, pitying to hurt them, believe me. Yet all this lenity will not overcome their spleen; they will be doing with the pismire, raising a hill, a man may spurn abroad with his foot at pleasure. By myself I could have slain them all, but I delight not in murder. I am loth to bear any other than this bastinado for 'em; yet I hold it good policy not to go disarmed, for though I be skilful, I may be oppressed with multitudes.

E. Kno. Aye, believe me, may you, Sir; and, in my conceit, our whole nation should sustain the loss by it, if it were so.

Bob. Alas, no! What's a peculiar man to a nation? Not seen.

E. Kno. O, but your skill, Sir!

Bob. Indeed, that might be some loss; but who respects it? I will tell you, Sir, by the way of private, and under seal, I am a gentleman, and live here obscure, and to myself: but were I known to his majesty, and the lords, observe me, I would undertake, upon this poor head and life, for the public benefit of the state, not only to spare the entire lives of his subjects in general, but to save the one half, nay, three parts of his yearly charge in holding war, and against what enemy soever. And how would I do it, think you?

E. Kno. Nay, I know not, nor can I conceive.

Bob. Why thus, Sir. I would select nineteen more to myself, throughout the land; gentlemen they should be, of a good spirit, strong, and able constitution; I would choose them by an instinct, a character that I have; and I would teach these nineteen the special rules, as your Punto, your Reverso, your Stoccata, your Imbroccata, your Passada, your Montonto; till they could all play very near, or altogether, as well as myself. This done, say the enemy were forty thousand strong, we twenty would come into the field the tenth of March, or there-
abouts;

abouts; and we would challenge twenty of the enemy; they could not, in their honour, refuse us! Well, we would kill them; challenge twenty more, kill them; twenty more, kill them; twenty more, kill them too; and thus would we kill every man his twenty a day, that's twenty score; twenty score, that's two hundred; two hundred a day five days a thousand: forty thousand; forty times five, five times forty, two hundred days kills them all up by computation. And this I will venture my poor gentleman-like carcase to perform, provided there be no treason practised upon us, by fair and discreet manhood, that is, civilly by the sword.

E. Kno. Why are you so sure of your hand, Captain, at all times?

Bob. Tut, never miss thrust, upon my reputation with you.

E. Kno. I would not stand in Downright's state then, an' you meet him, for the wealth of any one street in London.

Bob. Why, Sir, you mistake! If he were here now, by this welkin I would not draw my weapon on him! Let this gentleman do his mind: but I will bastinado him, by the bright sun, where ever I meet him.

Mat. Faith, and I'll have a fling at him, at my distance.

Enter Downright, *walking over the Stage.*

E. Kno. God's so! Look ye where he is; yonder he goes.

Down. What peevish luck have I, I cannot meet with these bragging rascals!

Bob. It's not he, is it?

E. Kno. Yes, faith, it is he!

Mat. I'll be hang'd then, if that were he.

E. Kno. I assure you that was he.

Step. Upon my reputation, it was he.

Bob. Had I thought it had been he, he must not have gone so: but I can hardly be induced to believe it was he yet.

E. Kno. That I think, Sir. But see, he is come again!

Down. Oh, Pharoah's foot! have I found you?
Come,

Come, draw; to your tools. Draw, gipfey, or I'll thresh you.

Bob. Gentleman of valour, I do believe in thee, hear me——

Down. Draw your weapon, then.

Bob. Tall man, I never thought on't till now; body of me! I had a warrant of the peace ferved on me even now, as I came along, by a water-bearer; this gentleman faw it, Mr. Matthew.

[*He beats him and difarms him.* Matthew, *runs away.*

Down. 'Sdeath, you will not draw, then?

Bob. Hold, hold, under thy favour, forbear.

Down. Prate again, as you like this, you whorfon foift, you. You'll controul the point, you! Your confort is gone; had he ftaid, he had fhared with you, Sir.

[*Exit* Downright.

E. Kno. Twenty, and kill 'em; twenty more, kill them too. Ha! Ha!

Bob. Well, gentlemen, bear witnefs, I was bound to the peace, by this good day.

E. Kno. No, faith, it's an ill day, Captain, never reckon it other: but fay you were bound to the peace, the law allows you to defend yourfelf; that will prove but a poor excufe.

Bob. I cannot tell, Sir. I defire good conftruction, in fair fort. I never fuftained the like difgrace, by heaven. Sure I was ftruck with a planet thence, for I had no power to touch my weapon.

E. Kno. Aye, like enough, I have heard of many that have been beaten under a planet. Go, get you to a furgeon. 'Slid, and thefe be your tricks, your paffado's and your montanto's, I'll none of them.

Bob. I was planet-ftruck certainly.   [*Exit.*

E. Kno. Oh, manners! That this age fhould bring forth fuch creatures! That nature fhould be at leifure to make 'em! Come, Coz.

Step. Mafs, I'll have this cloak.

E. Kno. God's will, 'tis Downright's.

Step. Nay, it's mine now; another might have ta'en it up as well as I. I'll wear it, fo I will.

E. Kno. How, an' he fee it? He'll challenge it, affure yourfelf.

Step.

Step. Aye, but he shall not ha't; I'll say, I bought it.

E. Kno. Take heed you buy it not too dear, Coz.

[*Exit.*

SCENE, *a Chamber in* Kitely's *House.*

Enter Kitely *and* Cash.

Kite. Art thou sure, Thomas, we have pry'd into all
and every part throughout the house? Is there no by-
place, or dark corner, has escaped our searches?

Cash. Indeed, Sir, none; there's not a hole or nook
unsearched by us, from the upper loft unto the cellar.

Kite. They have convey'd him then away, or hid him
in some privacy of their own——Whilst we were searching of the dark closet by my sister's chamber, didst
thou not think thou heard'st a rustling on the other side,
and a soft tread of feet?

Cash. Upon my truth, I did not, Sir; or if you did,
it might be only the vermine in the wainscot; the
house is old, and over-run with 'em.

Kite. It is, indeed, Thomas—we should bane these
rats—Dost thou understand me—we will—they shall not
harbour here; I'll cleanse my house from 'em, if fire
or poison can effect it—I will not be tormented thus—
They gnaw my brain, and burrow in my heart——I
cannot bear it.

Cash. I do not understand you, Sir! Good now, what
is't disturbs you thus? Pray be composed; these starts of
passion have some cause, I fear, that touches you more
nearly.

Kite. Sorely, sorely, Thomas—it cleaves too close
to me—Oh, me—[*Sighs.*] Lend me thy arm—so, good
Cash.

Cash. You tremble and look pale! Let me call assistance.

Kite. Not for ten thousand worlds—Alas! Alas!
'Tis not in medicine to give me ease——here, here it
lies.

Cash. What, Sir?

Kite. Why——nothing, nothing—I am not sick, yet
more than dead; I have a burning fever in my mind,
and long for that, which having, would destroy me.

Cash.

Cafh. Believe me, 'tis your fancy's impofition. Shut up your generous mind from fuch intruders—I'll hazard all my growing favour with you; I'll ftake my prefent, my future welfare, that fome bafe whifpering knave, nay, pardon me, Sir, hath in the beft and richeft foil, fown feeds of rank and evil nature! Oh, My mafter, fhould they take root——   [*Laughing within.*

Kite. Hark! Hark! Doft thou not hear! What think'ft thou now? Are they not laughing at me? They are, they are. They have deceived the wittol, and thus they triumph in their infamy—This aggravation is not to be borne. [*Laughing again.*] Hark, again! —Cafh, do thou unfeen fteal in upon 'em, and liften to their wanton conference.

Cafh. I fhall obey you, though againft my will.

[*Exit.*

Kite. Againft his will! Ha! It may be fo—He's young, and may be bribed for them—they've various means to draw the unwary in; if it be fo, I'm loft, deceived, betrayed, and my bofom, my full-fraught bofom, is unlocked and opened to mockery and laughter! Heaven forbid! He cannot be that viper; fting the hand that raifed and cherifh'd him! Was this ftroke added, I fhould be curfed—But it cannot be—no, it cannot be.

Enter Cafh.

Cafh. You are mufing, Sir.

Kite. I afk your pardon, Cafh—afk me not why— I have wronged you, and am forry—'tis gone.

Cafh. If you fufpect my faith——

Kite. I do not—fay no more—and for my fake let it die and be forgotton——Have you feen your miftrefs, and heard—whence was that noife?

Cafh. Your brother, Mafter Well-bred, is with 'em, and I found 'em throwing out their mirth on a very truly ridiculous-fubject: it is one Formal, as he ftiles himfelf, and he appertains, fo he phrafes it, to Juftice Clement, and wou'd fpeak with you.

Kite. With me! Art thou fure it is the Juftice's clerk? Where is he?

Enter Brain-worm, *as Formal.*

Who are you, friend?

Brain.

Brain. An appendix to Juſtice Clement, vulgarly called his clerk.

Kite. What are your wants with me ?

Brain. None.

Kite. Do you not want to ſpeak with me ?

Brain. No, but my maſter does.

Kite. What are the Juſtice's commands ?

Brain. He doth not command, but intreats Maſter Kitely to be with him directly, having matters of ſome moment to communicate unto him.

Kite. What can it be ! Say, I'll be with him inſtantly, and if your legs, friend, go not faſter than your tongue, I ſhall be there before you.

Brain. I will.   Vale.   [*Exit.*

Kite. 'Tis a precious fool, indeed !—I muſt go forth —But firſt, come hither, Thomas—I have admitted thee into the cloſe receſſes of my heart, and ſhewed thee all my frailties, paſſions, every thing.——
Be careful of thy promiſe, keep good watch.
Wilt thou be true, my Thomas ?

Caſh. As truth's ſelf, Sir——
But be aſſured you're heaping care and trouble
Upon a ſandy baſe; ill plac'd ſuſpicion
Recoils upon yourſelf—She's chaſte as comely !
Believe't ſhe is—Let her not note your humour;
Diſperſe the gloom upon your brow, and be
As clear as her unſullied honour.

Kite. I will then, Caſh—thou comfort'ſt me—I'll
        drive theſe
Fiend-like fancies from me, and be myſelf again.
Think'ſt thou ſhe has perceived my folly ? 'Twere
Happy, if ſhe had not—She has not——
They who know no evil will ſuſpect none.

Caſh. True, Sir ! Nor has your mind a blemiſh now.
This change has gladdened me—Here's my miſtreſs,
And the reſt; ſettle your reaſon to accoſt 'em.

Kite. I will, Caſh, I will——

   Enter Well-bred, *Dame* Kitely, *and* Bridget:
Well. What are you a plotting, brother Kitely,
That thus of late you muſe alone, and bear
Such weighty care upon your penſive brow ?   [*Laughs.*

Kite. My care is all for you, good ſneering brother,
                                                      And

And well I wish you'd take some wholesome counsel,
And curb your headstrong humours; trust me, brother,
You were to blame to raise commotions here,
And hurt the peace and order of my house.

   Well. No harm done, brother, I warrant you.
Since there is no harm done, anger costs
A man nothing, and a brave man is never
His own man 'till he be angry—To keep
His valour in obscurity, is to keep himself,
As it were, in a cloak-bag. What's a brave
Musician unless he play?
What's a brave man unless he fight?

   Dame. Aye, but what harm might have come of it,
brother?

   Well. What, school'd on both sides! Pr'ythee, Bridget, save me from the rod and lecture.

[Bridg. and Well. retire.

   Kite. With what a decent modesty she rates him!
My heart's at ease, and she shall see it is——
How art thou, wife! Thou look'st both gay and comely,
In troth, thou dost—I'm sent for out, my dear,
But I shall soon return—Indeed, my life,
Business that forces me abroad grows irksome,
I cou'd content me with less gain and 'vantage,
To have the more at home, indeed I cou'd.

   Dame. Your doubts, as well as love, may breed these
thoughts.

   Kite. That jar untunes me.   *[Aside.*
What dost thou say? Doubt thee?
I should as soon suspect myself—No, no,
My confidence is rooted in thy merit,
So fixt and settled, that, wert thou inclin'd
To masks, to sports, and balls, where lusty youth
Leads up the wanton dance, and the rais'd pulse
Beats quicker measures, yet I could with joy,
With heart's ease and security—not but
I had rather thou should'st prefer thy home,
And me, to toys and such like vanities.

   Dame. But sure, my dear,
A wife may moderately use these pleasures,
Which numbers and the time give sanction to,
Without the smallest blemish on her name.

Kite.

Kite. And so she may—And I'll go with thee, child,
I will indeed—I'll lead thee there myself,
And be the foremost reveller.——I'll silence
The sneers of envy, stop the tongue of slander;
Nor will I more be pointed at, as one
Disturb'd with jealousy——

Dame. Why, were you ever so?

Kite. What!—Ha! never—ha, ha, ha!
She stabs me home. [*Aside.*] Jealous of thee!
No, do not believe it—Speak low, my love,
Thy brother will overhear us—No, no, my dear,
It cou'd not be, it cou'd not be—for—for—
What is the time now?—I shall be too late—
No, no, thou may'st be satisfied
There's not the smallest spark remaining—
Remaining! What do I say? There never was
Nor can, nor never shall be—so be satisfied—
Is Cob within there? Give me a kiss,
My dear; there, there, now we are reconcil'd—
I'll be back immediately—Good-bye, good-bye—
Ha! ha! jealous, I shall burst my sides with laughing.
Ha, ha! Cob, where are you, Cob? Ha, ha.—

[Exit.

[Well-bred and Bridget come forward.

Well. What have you done to make your husband part
so merry from you? He has of late been little given to
laughter.

Dame. He laughed indeed, but seemingly without
mirth. His behaviour is new and strange. He is much
agitated, and has some whimsy in his head, that puzzles
mine to read it.

Well. 'Tis jealousy, good sister, and writ so largely,
that the blind may read it; have you not perceived it yet?

Dame. If I have, 'tis not always prudent that my
tongue should betray my eyes, so far my wisdom tends,
good brother, and little more I boast—But what makes
him ever calling for Cob so? I wonder how he can employ him.

Well. Indeed, sister, to ask how he employs Cob, is a
necessary question for you, that are his wife, and a thing
not very easy for you to be satisfied in—But this I'll assure
you, Cob's wife is an excellent bawd, sister, and often-

times

times your hufband haunts her houfe; marry to what end, I cannot altogether accufe him. Imagine you what you think convenient. But I have known fair hides have foul hearts ere now, fifter.

Dame. Never faid you truer than that, brother; fo much I can tell you for your learning. /O, ho! is this the fruits of 's jealoufy? I thought fome game was in the wind, he acted fo much tendernefs but now; but I'll be quit with him.—Thomas! /

Enter Cafh.

Fetch your hat, and go with me; I'll get my hood, and out the backward-way. I would to fortune I could take him there, I'd return him his own, I warrant him!/I'd fit him for his jealoufy! [*Exit.*

Well. Ha, ha! fo e'en let 'em go; this may make fport anon—What, Brain-worm?

Enter Brain-worm.

Brain. I faw the merchant turn the corner, and come back to fell you, all goes well; wind and tide, my mafter.

Well. But how got'ft thou this apparel of the juftice's man?

Brain. Marry, Sir, my proper fine penman would needs beftow the grift o' me at the Wind-mill, to hear fome martial difcourfe, where I fo marfhalled him, that I made him drunk with admiration; and becaufe too much heat was the caufe of his diftemper, I ftript him ftark naked, as he lay along afleep, and borrowed his fuit to deliver this counterfeit meffage in, leaving a rufty armour, and an old brown bill, to watch him 'till my return; which fhall be, when I have pawned his apparel, and fpent the better part of the money, perhaps.

Well. Well, thou art a fuccefsful merry knave, Brain-worm; his abfence will be fubject for more mirth. I pray thee, return to thy young mafter, and will him to meet me and my fifter Bridget at the Tower inftantly; for here, tell him, the houfe is fo ftored with jealoufy, there is no room for love to ftand upright in. We muft get our fortunes committed to fome large prifon, fay: and then the Tower, I know no better air, nor where the liberty of the houfe may do us more prefent fervice. Away. [*Exit* Brain.

Bridg. What, is this the engine that you told me of? What farther meaning have you in the plot?

Well.

Well. That you may know, fair fister-in-law, how, happy a thing it is to be fair and beautiful.

Bridg. That touches not me, brother.

Well. That's true; that's even the fault of it; for indeed, beauty ftands a woman in no ftead, unlefs it procure her touching — Well, there's a dear and well refpected friend of mine, fifter, ftands very ftrongly and worthily affected towards you, and hath vowed to inflame whole bonfires of zeal at his heart, in honour of your perfections. I have already engaged my promife to bring you where you fhall hear him confirm much more. Ned Kno'well is the man, fifter. There's no exception againft the party; you are ripe for a hufband, and a minute's lofs to fuch an occafion, is a great trefpafs in a wife beauty. What fay you, fifter? On my foul, he loves you; will you give him the meeting?

Bridg. Faith, I had very little confidence in my own conftancy, brother, if I dúrft not meet a man; but this motion of yours favours of an old knight adventurer's fervant, a little too much, methinks.

Well. What's that, fifter?

Bridg. Marry; of the go-between.

Well. No matter if it did; I would be fuch a one for my friend. But fee, who is returned to hinder us.

Enter Kitely.

Kite. What villainy is this? Called out on a falfe meffage! This was fome plot. I was not fent for. Bridget, where's your fifter?

Bridg. I think fhe be gone forth, Sir.

Kite. How! is my wife gone forth? Whither, for Heaven's fake.

Bridg. She's gone abroad with Thomas.

Kite. Abroad with Thomas! Oh, that villain cheats me!
He hath difcover'd all unto my wife;
Beaft that I was to truft him. Whither, I pray
You, went fhe?

Bridg. I know not, Sir.

Well. I'll tell you, brother, whither I fufpect fhe's gone.

Bite. Whither, good brother?

*   F   *Well.*

Well. To Cob's houfe, I believe; but keep my counfel.

Kite. I will, I will. To Cob's houfe! Does fhe haunt
        there?
She's gone on purpofe now to cuckold me,
With that lewd rafcal, who, to win her favour,
Hath told her all—Why wou'd you let her go?

Well. Becaufe fhe's not my wife; if fhe were, I'd keep
her to her tether.

Kno. So, fo; now 'tis plain. I fhall go mad
With my misfortunes, now they pour in torrents.
I'm bruted by my wife, betray'd by my fervant,
Mock'd at by my relations, pointed at by my neighbours,
Defpis'd by myfelf.—There is nothing left now
But to revenge myfelf firft, next hang myfelf;
And then—all my cares will be over.   [*Exit.*

Bridg. He ftorms moft loudly; fure you have gone too
far in this.

Well. 'Twill all end right, depend upon't.—But let
us lofe no time; the coaft is clear; away, away; the affair is worth it, and cries hafte.

Bridg. I truft me to your guidance, brother, and fo
fortune for us.   [*Exeunt.*

END of the FOURTH ACT.

A C T V.

SCENE, *Stocks-Market.*

Enter Matthew *and* Bobadil.

MATTHEW.

I WONDER, Captain, what they will fay of my going away? ha!

Bob. Why, what fhould they fay? but as of a difcreet
gentleman; quick, wary, refpectful of nature's fair li-
neaments, and that's all.

Mat. Why fo! but what can they fay of your beating?

Bob. A rude part, a touch with foft wood, a kind of
grofs battery ufed, lain on ftrongly, borne moft patient-
ly, and that's all. But wherefore do I wake their remembrance? I was fafcinated, by Jupiter! fafcinated;
but I will be unwitched, and revenged by law.

Mat.

Mat. Do you hear? Is't not beſt to get a warrant, and have him arreſted, and brought before Juſtice Clement?

Bob. It were not amiſs; would we had it!

Mat. Why, here comes his man, let's ſpeak to him.

Bob. Agreed, Do you ſpeak.

Enter Brain-worm *as* Formal.

Mat. Save you, Sir.

Brain. With all my heart, Sir!

Mat. Sir, there is one Downright hath abuſed this gentleman and myſelf, and we determine to make our ſelves amends by law; now, if you would do us the favour to procure a warrant to bring him before your maſter, you ſhall be well conſidered of, I aſſure you, Sir.

Brain. Sir, you know my ſervice is my living; ſuch favours as theſe, gotten of my maſter, is his only preferment, and therefore you muſt conſider me, as I may make benefit of my place.

Mat. How is that, Sir?

Brain. Faith, Sir, the thing is extraordinary, and the gentleman may be of great account. Yet, be what he will, if you will lay me down a brace of angels in my hand, you ſhall have it, otherwiſe not.

Mat. How ſhall we do, Captain? He aſks a brace of angels, you have no money.

Bob. Not a croſs, by fortune.

Mat. Nor I, as I am a gentleman, but two-pence left of my two ſhillings in the morning for wine and raddiſh. Let's find him ſome pawn:

Bob. Pawn! We have none to the value of his demand.

Mat. O, yes, I can pawn my ring here.

Bob. And heark'e, he ſhall have my truſty Toledo too; I believe I ſhall have no ſervice for it to-day.

Mat. Do you hear, Sir? We have no ſtore of money at this time, but you ſhall have good pawns; look you, Sir, I will pledge this ring, and that gentleman his Toledo, becauſe we would have it diſpatch'd,

Brain. I am content, Sir; I will get you the warrant preſently. What's his name, ſay you? Downright?

Mat. Aye, aye, George Downright.

Brain. Well, gentlemen, I'll procure you the warrant preſently; but who will you have to ſerve it?

Mat. That's true, Captain, that muft be confidered.

Bob. Body o' me, I know not! 'Tis fervice of danger!

Brain. Why, you were beft get one of the varlets o' the city, a ferjeant; I'll appoint you one, if you pleafe.

Mat. Will you, Sir? Why we can wifh no better.

Bob. We'll leave it to you, Sir.

[*Exeunt* Bob. *and* Mat.

Brain. This is rare! Now will I go pawn this cloak of the juftice's man's, at the broker's, for a varlet's fuit, and be the varlet myfelf, and fo get money <u>on all fides</u>.

[*Exit.*

SCENE, *the Street before* Cob's Houfe.

Enter Kno'well.

Kno. O, here it is; I have found it now—Hoa, who is within here?   [Tib *appears at the window.*

Tib. I am within, Sir, what is your pleafure?

Kno. To know who is within befides yourfelf.

Tib. Why, Sir, you are no conftable, I hope?

Kno. O, fear you the conftable? then I doubt not you have fome guefts within deferve that fear—I'll fetch him ftraight.

Tib. For heaven's fake, Sir—

Kno. Go to! Come tell me, is not young Kno'well here?

Tib. Young Kno'well! I know none fuch, Sir, o' my honefty.

Kno. Your honefty, dame! It flies too lightly from you. There is no way but fetch the conftable.

Tib. The conftable! the man is mad, I think.

Enter Cafh *and Dame* Kitely.

Cafh. Hoa! who keeps houfe here?

Kno. O, this is the female copefmate of my fon. Now fhall I meet him ftraight.   [*Afide.*

Dame. Knock, Thomas, hard.

Cafh. Hoa! good wife.

Tib. Why, what's the matter with you?

Dame. Why, woman, grieves it you to ope the door? Belike, you get fomething to keep it fhut.

Tib. What mean thefe queftions, pray you?

Dame. So ftrange you make it! Is not my hufband here?

Kno.

Kno. Her hufband !   [*Afide.*
Dame. My tried and faithful hufband, mafter Kitely.
Tib. I hope he needs not to be tried here.
Dame. Come hither, Cafh—I fee my turtle coming
to his haunts ; let us retire.   [*They retire.*
Kno. This muft be fome device to mock me withal.
Soft—who is this ?—Oh !. 'tis my fon difguis'd.
I'll watch him and furprize him.
                Enter Kitely *muffled in a Cloak.*
Kite. 'Tis truth, I fee : there fhe fkulks.
But I will fetch her from her hold—I will—
I tremble fo, I fcarce have power to do the juftice
Her infamy demands.
         [*As* Kitely *goes forward,* Dame Kitely *and* Kno'well
            lay hold of him.
Kno. Have I trapped you, youth ? You cannot 'fcape
me now.
  Dame. O, Sir ! have I foreftalled your honeft mar-
            ket ?
Found your clofe walks ! You ftand amazed
Now, do you ? Ah, hide, hide your face for fhame !
I'faith, I am glad I've found you out at laft.
What is your jewel, trow ? In : come let's fee her ; fetch
Forth the wanton dame—If fhe be fairer
In any honeft judgment, than myfelf,
I'll be content with it : but fhe is change ;
She feeds you fat, fhe fooths your appetite,
And you are well. Your wife, an honeft woman,
Is meat twice fod to you, Sir. O, you treacher !
  Kno. What mean you, woman ? Let go your hold.
I fee the counterfeit—I am his father, and claim him as
            my own.
  Kite. [*Difcovering himfelf.*] I am your cuckold, and
claim my vengeance.
  Dame. What, do you wrong me, and infult me too ?
Thou faithlefs man !
  Kite. Out on thy more than ftrumpet's impudence !
Steal'ft thou thus to thy haunts ? And have I taken
Thy bawd and thee, and thy companion,
This hoary-headed letcher, this old goat,
Clofe at your villainy, and would'ft thou 'fcufe it
With this ftale harlot's jeft, accufing me ?
            F 3   O, old

O, old incontinent, doſt thou not ſhame,
To have a mind ſo hot ; and to entice,
And feed the enticement of a luſtful woman ?
   Dame. Out ! 1 defy thee, thou diſſembling wretch !
   Kite. Defy me, ſtrumpet ! Aſk thy pander here,
Can he deny it, or that wicked elder ?
   Kno. Why, hear you, Sir———
   Caſb. Maſter, 'tis in vain to reaſon while theſe paſ-
ſions blind you—I'm griev'd to ſee you thus.
   Kite. Tut, tut, never ſpeak, I ſee thro' ev'ry
Veil you caſt upon your treachery : but I have
Done with you, and root you from my heart for ever.
For you, Sir, thus I demand my honour's due ;
Reſolv'd to cool your luſt, or end my ſhame.　　[*Draws.*
   Kno. What lunacy is this ? Put up your ſword, and
undeceive yourſelf—No arm that e'er pois'd weapon can
affright me.　But I pity folly, nor cope with madneſs.
   Kite. I will have proofs—I will---ſo you, good wife-
bawd, Cob's wife ; and you, that make your huſband
ſuch a monſter ; and you, young pander, an old cuc-
kold-maker, I'll ha' you every one before the juſtice---
Nay, you ſhall anſwer it ; I charge you go. Come forth,
thou bawd.　　　　[*Goes into the houſe and brings out* Tib.
   Kno. Marry, with all my heart, Sir ; I go willingly.
Tho' I do taſte this as a trick put on me,
To puniſh my impertinent ſearch ; and juſtly ;
And half forgive my ſon for the device.
   Kite. Come, will you go ?
   Dame. Go, to thy ſhame believe it.
   Kite. 'Tho' ſhame and ſorrow both my heart betide,
Come on---I muſt and will be ſatisfy'd.　　　[*Exeunt.*

SCENE, Stocks-Market.

Enter Brain-worm.

   Brain. Well, of all my diſguiſes yet, now am I moſt
like myſelf ; being in this ſerjeant's gown. A man of
my preſent profeſſion never counterfeits, till he lays hold
upon a debtor, and ſays, he 'reſts him ; for then he
brings him to all manner of unreſt.. A kind of little
kings we are, bearing the diminutive of a mace, made
like a young artichoke, that always carries pepper and
ſalt

falt in itfelf.   Well, 1 know not what danger I undergo
by this exploit ; pray Heaven I come well off !

Enter Bobadil and Mr. Matthew.

Mat. See, I think, yonder is the varlet, by his gown.
'Save you, friend : are not you here by appointment of
Juftice Clement's man ?

Brain. Yes, an' pleafe you, Sir, he told me two gentleman had willed him to procure a warrant from his mafter, which I have about me, to be ferved on one Downright.

Mat. It is honeftly done of you both ; and fee where
the party comes, you muft arreft.   Serve it upon him
quickly, before he be aware——

Enter Mr. Stephen in Downright's Cloak.

Bob. Bear back, Mafter Matthew.

Brain. Mafter Downright, I arreft you i'the queen's
name, and muft carry you before a juftice, by virtue of
this warrant.

Step. Me, friend, I am no Downright, I.   I am Mafter Stephen ; you do not well to arreft me, I tell you
truly.   I am in nobody's bonds or books, I would you
fhould know it.   A plague on you heartily, for making
me thus afraid before my time.

Brain. Why, now you are deceived, gentlemen ?

Bob. He wears fuch a cloak, and that deceived us :
But fee, here he comes indeed ! This is he, officer.

Enter Downright.

Down. Why, how now, fignor Gull ! Are you turned
filcher of late ? Come, deliver my cloak.

Step. Your cloak, Sir ! I bought it even now in open
market.

Brain. Mafter Downright, I have a warrant I muft
ferve upon you, procured by thefe two gentlemen.

Down. Thefe gentlemen ! Thefe rafcals !

Brain. Keep the peace, I charge you in her majefty's
name.

Down. I obey thee.   What muft I do, officer?

Brain. Go before mafter Juftice Clement, to anfwer
what they can object againft you, Sir.   I will ufe you
kindly, Sir.

Mat. Come, let's before, and make the Juftice, Captain——   [*Exit.*
                                                  Bob.

Bob. The varlet's a tall man, before heaven!

                                            [Exit.

Down. Gull, you'll gi' me my cloak?

Step. Sir, I bought it, and I'll keep it.

Down. You will?

Step. Aye, that I will.

Down. Officer, there's thy fee, arreſt him.

Brain. Maſter Stephen, I muſt arreſt you.

Step. Arreſt me, I ſcorn it; there, take your cloak, I'll none on't.

Down. Nay, that ſhall not ſerve your turn, now, Sir. Officer, I'll go with thee to the Juſtice's. Bring him along.

Step. Why, is not here your cloak, what would you have?

Down. I'll ha' you anſwer it.

Brain. Sir, I'll take your word, and this gentleman's too, for his appearance.

Down. I'll ha' no words taken. Bring him along.

Brain. So, ſo, I have made a fair maſh on't.

Step. Muſt I go?

Brain. I know no remedy, Maſter Stephen.

Down. Come along before me here. I do not love your hanging look behind.

Step. Why, Sir, I hope you cannot hang me for it. Can he, fellow?

Brain. I think not, Sir. It is but a whipping matter, ſure!

Step. Why, then let him do his worſt, I am reſolute.

                                            [Exit.

SCENE,   *a Hall in Juſtice* Clement's *Houſe.*

Enter Clement, Kno'well, Kitely, *Dame* Kitely, Tib, Caſh, Cob, *and Servants.*

Clem. Nay, but ſtay, ſtay, give me leave. My chair, ſirrah. You, Maſter Kno'well, ſay you went thither to meet your ſon?

Kno. Aye, Sir.

Clem. But who directed you thither?

Kno. That did mine own man, Sir.

Clem. Where is he?

                                            [Kno.

Kno. Nay, I know not, now; I left him with your clerk; and appointed him to stay for me.

Clem. My clerk! About what time was this?

Kno. Marry, between one and two, as I take it.

Clem. And what time came my man with the false mesſage to you, Maſter Kitely.

Kite. After two, Sir.

Clem. Very good: but, Mrs. Kitely, how chance it that you were at Cob's? Ha!

Dame. An' pleaſe you, Sir, I'll tell you. My brother Well-bred told me, that Cob's houſe was a ſuſpected place——

Clem. So it appears, methinks: but on.

Dame. And that my huſband uſed thither daily.

Clem. No matter, ſo he us'd himſelf well, Miſtreſs.

Dame. True, Sir; but you know what grows by ſuch haunts, oftentimes.

Clem. I ſee rank fruits of a jealous brain, Miſtreſs Kitely. But did you find your huſband there, in that eaſe, as you ſuſpected?

Kit. I found her there, Sir.

Clem. Did you ſo? That alters the caſe. Who gave you knowledge of your wife's being there?

Kite. Marry, that did my brother Well-bred.

Clem. How! Well-bred, firſt tell her, then tell you after! Where is Well-bred?

Kite. Gone with my ſiſter, Sir, I know not whither.

Clem. Why, this is a mere trick, a device; you are gulled in this moſt groſly, all! Alas, poor wench! wert thou ſuſpected for this?

Tib. Yes, and't pleaſe you.

Clem. I ſmell miſchief here, plot and contrivance, Maſter Kitely. However, if you will ſtep into the next room with your wife, and think coolly of matters, you'll find ſome trick has been played you——I fear there have been jealouſies on both parts, and the wags have been merry with you.

Kite. I begin to feel it——I'll take your counſel—— Will you go in, Dame?

Dame. I will have juſtice, Mr. Kitely.

[Exeunt Kite. and Dame.
Clem.

Clem. You will be a woman, Mrs. Kitely, that I see ———How now, what's the matter?

Enter a Servant.

Serv. Sir, there's a gentleman i' the court without, defires to fpeak with your worfhip.

Clem. A gentleman! What's he?

Serv. A foldier, Sir, he fays.

Clem. A foldier! My fword, quickly. A foldier fpeak with me! Stand by, I will end your matters anon ———Let the foldier enter. Now, Sir, what ha' you to fay to me?

Enter Bobadil *and* Matthew.

Bob. By your worfhip's favour———

Clem. Nay, keep out, Sir, I know not your pretence; you fend me word, Sir, you are a foldier? Why, Sir, you fhall be anfwered here; here be them have been among foldiers. Sir, your pleafure?

Bob. Faith, Sir, fo it is, this gentleman and myfelf, have been moft uncivilly wronged and beaten by one Downright, a coarfe fellow about the town here; and, for my own part, I proteft, being a man in no fort given to this filthy humour of quarrelling, he hath affaulted me in the way of my peace; defpoiled me of mine honour; difarmed me of my weapons; and rudely laid me along in the open ftreets, when I not fo much as once offered to refift him.

Clem. Oh, God's precious! Is this the foldier? Lie there, my fword, 'twill make him fwoon, I fear; he is not fit to look on't, that will put up a blow.

Mat. An't, pleafe your worfhip, he was bound to the peace.

Clem. Why, an' he were, Sir, his hands were not bound, were they?

Serv. There's one of the varlets of the city, Sir, has brought two gentlemen here, one upon your worfhip's warrant!

Clem. My warrant.

Serv. Yes, Sir, the officer fays, procured by thefe two.

Clem. Bid him come in. Set by this picture. What, Mr. Downright! are you brought at Mr. Frefhwater's fuit here?

Enter

Enter Downright, Stephen, *and* Brainworm.

Down. I'faith, Sir. And here's another, brought at my suit.

Clem. What are you, Sir?

Step. A gentleman, Sir? Oh, Uncle!

Clem. Uncle! Who, Master Kno'well?

Kno. Aye, Sir, this is a wise kinsman of mine.

Step. God's my witness, uncle, I am wronged here monstrously, he charges me with stealing of his cloak, and would I might never stir, if I did not find it in the street by chance.

Down. Oh, did you find it, now? You said you bought it ere-while.

Step. And you said I stole it. Nay, now my uncle is here, I'll do well enough with you.

Clem. Well, let this breathe a-while. You that have cause to complain there, stand forth. Had you my warrant for this gentleman's apprehension?

Bob. Aye, an't please your worship.

Clem. Nay, do not speak in passion so. Where had you it.

Bob. Of your clerk, Sir.

Clem. That's well, an' my clerk can make warrants, and my hand not at 'em! Where is the warrant? Officer, have you it?

Brain. No, Sir, your worship's man, Master Formal, bid me do it for these gentlemen, and he would be my discharge.

Clem. Why, Master Downright, are you such a novice to be served, and never see the warrant!

Down. Sir, he did not serve it on me.

Clem. No, how then?

Down. Marry, Sir, he came to me, and said he must serve it, and he would use me kindly, and so—

Clem. O, God's pity, was it so, Sir? He must serve it? Give me a warrant, I must serve one too—you knave, you slave, you rogue, do you say you must, sirrah? Away with him to the gaol. I'll teach you a trick for your *must*, Sir.

Brain. Good Sir, I beseech you be good to me.

Clem.

Clem. Tell him, he shall to the gaol : away with him,
I say.

Brain. Aye, Sir, if you will commit me, it shall be
for committing more than this. I will not lose by my
travail any grain of my fame certain.

[*Throws off his disguise.*

Clem. How is this !

Kno. My man Brain-worm !

Step. O, yes, uncle, Brain-worm has been with my
cousin Edward and I, all this day.

Clem. I told you all there was some device.

Brain. Nay, excellent Justice, since I have laid myself thus open to you, now stand strong for me, both with
your sword and your balance.

Clem. Body o' me, a merry knave ! Give me a bowl
of sack. If he belongs to you, Master Kno'well, I bespeak your patience.

Brain. That is it I have most need of. Sir, if you'll
pardon me only, I'll glory in all the rest of my exploits.

Kno. Sir, you know I love not to have my favours
come hard from me. You have your pardon ; though I
suspect you shrewdly for being of counsel with my son
against me.

Brain. Yes, faith, I have Sir ; though you retained
me doubly this morning for yourself ; first, as Brain-
worm, after, as Fitz-Sword. I was your reformed soldier. 'Twas I sent you to Cob's upon the errand without end.

Kno. Is it possible ! Or that thou shouldst disguise thyself so as I should not know thee ?

Brain. O, Sir ! this has been the day of my meta-
morphosis ; it is not that shape alone that I have run
through to-day. I brought Master Kitely a message too,
in the form of Master Justice's man here, to draw him
out o' the way, as well as your worship ; while Master
Well-bred might make a conveyance of mistress Bridget
to my young master.

Kno. My son is not married, I hope.

Brain. Faith, Sir, they are both, as sure as love, a
priest, and three thousand pounds, which is her portion,
can make 'em ; and by this time are ready to bespeak
their

their wedding fupper at the Wind-mill, except fome friend here prevent 'em, and invite 'em home.

Clem. Marry, that will I, I thank thee for putting me in mind on't. Sirrah, go you and fetch them hither upon my warrant. Neither's friends have caufe to be forry, if I know the young couple aright. But I pray thee, what haft thou done with my man Formal?

Brain. Faith, Sir, after fome ceremony paft, as making him drunk, firft with ftory, and then with wine, but all in kindnefs, and ftripping him to his fhirt; I left him in that cool vein, departed, fold your worfhip's warrant to thefe two, pawned his livery for that varlet's gown to ferve it in; and thus have brought myfelf, by my activity, to your worfhip's confideration.

Clem. And I will confider thee in a cup of fack. Here's to thee, which having drank off, this is my fentence, pledge me. Thou haft done, or affifted to nothing, in my judgment, but deferves to be pardoned for the wit o' the offence. Go into the next room; let Mafter Kitely into this whimfical bufinefs, and if he does not forgive thee, he has lefs mirth in him, than an honeft man ought to have. How now, who are thefe?

Enter Ed. Kno'well, Well-bred, *and* Bridget.

O, the young company. Welcome, welcome. Give you joy. Nay, Mrs. Bridget, blufh not, you are not fo frefh a bride, but the news of it is come hither before you. Mafter Bridegroom, I have made your peace, give me your hand. So will I for the reft, ere you forfake my roof.

All. We are the more bound to your humanity, Sir.

Clem. Only thefe two have fo little of man in 'em, they are no part of my care.

Step. And what fhall I do?

Clem. O! I had loft a fleep, an' he had not bleated. Why, Sir, you fhall give Mr. Downright his cloak; and I will intreat him to take it. A trencher and a napkin you fhall have in the butterry, and keep Cob and his wife company here; whom I will intreat firft to be reconciled; and you to endeavour with your wit to keep 'em fo.

Step. I'll do my beft.

G

Clem.

Clem. Call Mafter Kitely and his wife, there.

　　Enter Mr. Kitely *and Dame* Kitely.

Did not I tell you there was a plot againft you ? Did I not fmell it out, as a wife magiftrate ought? Have not you traced, have not you found it ? E h, Mafter Kitely?

Kite. I have—I confefs my folly, and own I have deferved what I have fuffer'd for it. The trial has been fevere, but it is paft. All I have to afk now, is, that as my folly is cured, and my perfecutors forgiven, my fhame may be forgotten.

Clem. That will depend upon yourfelf, Mafter Kitely ; do not yourfelf create the food for mifchief, and the mifchievous will not prey upon you. But come, let a general reconcilation go round, and let all difcontents be laid afide. You, Mr. Downright, put off your anger. You, Mafter Kno'well, your cares. And do you, Mafter Kitely, and your wife, put off your jealoufies.

Kite. Sir, thus they go from me : kifs me, my wife.
See, what a drove of horns fly in the air,
Wing'd with my cleanfed and my credulous breath ;
Watch 'em, fufpicious eyes, watch where they fall,
See, fee, on heads, that think they've none at all.
O, what a plenteous world of this will come,
When air rains horns, all may be fure of fome.

　‘ *Clem.* 'Tis well, 'tis well, This night we'll dedicate
‘ to friendfhip, love and laughter. Mafter bridegroom,
‘ take your bride, and lead, every one a fellow. Here
‘ is my miftrefs, Brain-worm ! to whom all my addreffes of courtfhip fhall have their reference : whofe adventures this day, when our grand children fhall hear to
‘ be made a fable, I doubt not but it fhall find both fpectators and applaufe.’

END of the FIFTH ACT.

Mr. SMITH in the Character of ARCHER.

My lady Howd'ye, the last Mistress I serv'd call'd me up one ...
& told me, Martin, go to my lady all night, with my humble Se ...

BELL'S EDITION.

THE
BEAUX STRATAGEM.

A COMEDY,

As written by Mr. FARQUHAR.

AS PERFORMED AT THE

Theatre-Royal in Drury-Lane.

Regulated from the Prompt-Book,

By PERMISSION of the MANAGERS,

By Mr. HOPKINS, Prompter.

A NEW EDITION.

LONDON:

Printed for JOHN BELL, near *Exeter-Exchange,* in the *Strand.*

MDCCLXXVIII.

PROLOGUE.

WHEN strife disturbs, or sloth corrupts an age,
Keen satire is the business of the stage.
When the Plain Dealer writ, he lash'd those crimes
Which then infested most——the modish times.
But now, when faction sleeps, and sloth is fled,
And all our youth in active fields are bred ;
When thro' Great Britain's fair extensive round,
The trumps of Fame the notes of Union sound ;
When Anna's sceptre points the laws their course,
And her example gives her precepts force ;
There scarce is room for satire ; all our lays
Must be, or songs of triumph or of praise.
But as in grounds best cultivated, tares
And poppies rise among the golden ears ;
Our product so, fit for the field or school,
Must mix with nature's favourite plant——a fool,
A weed that has to twenty summers ran,
Shoots up in stalk, and vegetates to man.
Simpling our author goes from field to field,
And culls such fools as may diversion yield.
And, thanks to nature, there's no want of those,
For rain or shine the thriving coxcomb grows.
Follies to-night we shew ne'er lash'd before,
Yet such as nature shews you every hour :
Nor can the picture give a just offence,
For fools are made for jests to men of sense.

DRAMATIS PERSONÆ.

MEN.

		Drury-Lane.	Covent-Garden.
Aimwell, *Archer,*	Two gentlemen of broken fortunes,	Mr. Packer. Mr. Garrick.	Mr. Wroughton. Mr. Lewis.
Sullen, a country blockhead		Mr. Hurſt,	Mr. Clarke.
Sir *Charles Freeman,* a gentleman from London - - -		Mr. Brereton.	Mr. Young.
Foigard, a French prieſt, - - -		Mr. Moody.	Mr. Fox,
Gibbet, a highwayman, - - -		Mr. Branſby.	Mr. Mahon.
Hounſlow & *Bagſhot* his companions.			
Boniface, landlord of the inn - - -		Mr. Uſher.	Mr. Dunſtall.
Scrub, Servant to Mr. Sullen		Mr. Yates.	Mr. Woodward.

WOMEN.

	Drury-Lane.	Covent-Garden.
Lady *Bountiful,* an old civil country gentlewoman, that cures all diſtempers, -	Mrs. Croſs.	Mrs. Pitt.
Dorinda, lady Bountiful's daughter, -	Miſs Sherry.	Mrs. Leſſingham.
Mrs. *Sullen,* her daughter-in-law, -	Mrs. Abington.	Mrs. Bulkley.
Gipſey, maid to the ladies - - -	Mrs. Davis.	Mrs. Willems.
Cherry, Boniface's daughter - - -	Miſs Jarratt.	Miſs Brown.

SCENE, *Litchfield.*

THE

THE
BEAUX STRATAGEM.

*** *The lines distinguished by inverted commas, ‘ thus,’ are omitted in the representation.*

ACT I.

SCENE, *An Inn,*

Enter Boniface *running.*

[*Bar-bell rings.*

BONIFACE.

CHamberlain! Maid! Cherry! daughter Cherry! all asleep, all dead?

Enter Cherry, *running.*

Cher. Here, here. Why d’ye bawl so, father? D’ye think we have no ears?

Bon. You deserve to have none, you young minx—the company of the Warrington coach have stood in the hall this hour, and nobody to shew them to their chambers.

Cher. And let ’em wait, father; there’s neither red coat in the coach, nor footman behind it.

Bon. But they threaten to go to another inn to-night.

Cher. That they dare not, for fear the coachman should overturn them to-morrow [*Ringing.*] Coming, coming: here’s the London coach arrived.

Enter several people with trunks, band-boxes, and other luggage, and cross the stage.

Bon. Welcome, ladies.

Cher. Very welcome, gentlemen.——Chamberlain, shew the Lion and the Rose. [*Exit with the company.*

A 3

Enter

Enter Aimwell *in a riding habit;* Archer, *as footman carrying a portmanteau.*

Bon. This way, this way, gentlemen.

Aim. Set down the things; go to the stable, and see my horses well rubbed.

Arch. I shall, Sir.

Aim. You're my landlord, I suppose?

Bon. Yes, Sir, I'm old Will Boniface, pretty well known upon this road, as the saying is.

Aim. O, Mr. Boniface, your servant.

Bon. O, Sir——What will your honour please to drink, as the saying is?

Aim. I have heard your town of Litchfield much fam'd for ale: I think I'll taste that.

Bon. Sir, I have now in my cellar ten tun of the best ale in Staffordshire: 'tis smooth as oil, sweet as milk, clear as amber, and strong as brandy, and will be just fourteen years old the fifth day of next March, old style.

Aim. You're very exact, I find, in the age of your ale.

Bon. As punctual, Sir, as I am in the age of my children; I'll shew you such ale.——Here, tapster, broach number 1706, as the saying is.—Sir, you shall taste my Anno Domini—I have lived in Litchfield, man and boy, above eight-and-fifty years, and, I believe, have not consumed eight-and-fifty ounces of meat.

Aim. At a meal, you mean, if one may guess your sense by your bulk.

Bon. Not in my life, Sir: I have fed purely upon ale: I have eat my ale, drank my ale, and I always sleep upon ale.

Enter Tapster *with a Tankard.*

Now, Sir, you shall see. [*Filling it out.*] You rworship's health. Ha! delicious, delicious——fancy it Burgundy, only fancy it, and 'tis worth ten shillings a quart.

Aim. [*Drinks.*] 'Tis confounded strong.

Bon. Strong! It must be so, or how would we be strong that drink it?

Aim. And have you lived so long upon this ale, land-lord?

Bon. Eight-and-fifty years, upon my credit, Sir; but it kill'd my wife, poor woman! as the saying is.

Aim.

Aim. How came that to pafs?

Bon. I don't know how, Sir; fhe would not let the ale take its natural courfe, Sir; fhe was for qualifying it every now and then with a dram, as the faying is; and an honeft gentleman that came this way from Ireland, made her a prefent of a dozen bottles of ufquebaugh—but the poor woman was never well after; but, however, I was obliged to the gentleman, you know.

Aim. Why, was it the ufquebaugh that killed her?

Bon. My lady Bountiful faid fo——fhe, good lady, did what could be done; fhe cur'd her of three tympanies, but the fourth carried her off; but fhe's happy, and I'm contented, as the faying is.

Aim. Who's that lady Bountiful, you mentioned?

Bon. Ods my life, Sir, we'll drink her health. [*Drinks.*] My lady Bouutiful is one of the beft of women: her laft hufband, Sir Charles Bountiful, left her worth a thoufand pounds a year; and, I believe, fhe lays out one half on't in charitable ufes for the good of her neighbours; fhe cures rheumatifms, ruptures, and broken fhins in men: ' green ficknefs, obftructions, and fits of the mo- ' ther in women;' the king's evil, chin-cough, and chilblains in children; in fhort, fhe has cured more people in and about Litchfield within ten years, than the doctors have killed in twenty, and that's a bold word.

Aim. Has the lady been any other way ufeful in her generation?

Bon. Yes, Sir, fhe has a daughter by Sir Charles, the fineft woman in all our country, and the greateft fortune; fhe has a fon too, by her firft hufband, 'fquire Sullen, who married a fine lady from London t'other day; if you pleafe, Sir, we'll drink his health.

Aim. What fort of a man is he?

Bon. Why Sir, the man's well enough; fays little, thinks lefs, and does——nothing at all, faith; but he's a man of great eftate, and values nobody.

Aim. A fportfman, I fuppofe?

Bon. Yes, Sir, he's a man of pleafure; he plays at whift, and fmoaks his pipe eight-and-forty hours together fometimes.

Aim. A fine fportfman, truly! and marry'd you fay?

Bon.

Bon. Ay, and to a curious woman, Sir—But he's a —he wants it here Sir.   [*Pointing to his forehead.*

Aim. He has it there, you mean.

Bon. That's none of my busineſs, he's my landlord, and ſo a man, you know, would not——But I cod, he's no better than——Sir, my humble ſervice to you. [*Drinks.*] Tho' I value not a farthing what he can do to me; I pay him his rent at quarter-day; I have a good running trade; I have but one daughter, and I can give her——but no matter for that.

Aim. You're very happy, Mr. Boniface; pray, what other company have you in town?

Bon. A power of fine ladies; and then we have the French officers.

Aim. O that's right, you have a good many of thoſe gentlemen: pray, how do you like their company?

Bon. So well, as the ſaying is, that I could wiſh we had as many more of 'em; they're full of money, and pay double for every thing they have; they know, Sir, that we paid good round taxes for the taking of 'em, and ſo we are willing to reimburſe us a little: one of 'em lodges in my houſe.

Enter Archer.

Arch. Landlord, there are ſome French gentlemen below that aſk for you.

Bon. I'll wait on 'em——Does your maſter ſtay long in town, as the ſaying is?   [*To Archer.*

Arch. I can't tell, as the ſaying is.

Bon. Come from London?

Arch. No.

Bon. Going to London, may hap?

Arch. No.

Bon. An odd fellow this! [*Bar bell rings.*] I beg your worſhip's pardon, I'll wait on you in half a minute.

[*Exit.*

Aim. The coaſt's clear, I ſee——Now, my dear Archer, welcome to Litchfield.

Arch. I thank thee, my dear brother in iniquity.

Aim. Iniquity! pr'ythee, leave canting; you need not change your ſtile with your dreſs.

Arch. Don't miſtake me, Aimwell, for 'tis ſtill my maxim, that there's no ſcandal like rags, nor any crime

ſo

so shameful as poverty. Men must not be poor; idleness is the root of all evil : the world's wide enough, let 'em bustle : Fortune has taken the weak under her protection, but men of sense are left to their industry.

Aim. Upon which topic we proceed, and, I think, luckily hitherto. Would not any man swear now that I am a man of quality, and you my servant, when, if our intrisic value were known———

Arch. Come, come, we are the men of intrisic value, who can strike our fortunes out of ourselves, whose worth is independent of accidents in life, or revolutions in government : we have heads to get money, and hearts to spend it.

Aim. As to our hearts, I grant ye they are as willing tits as any within twenty degrees; but I can have no great opinion of our heads, from the service they have done us hitherto, unless it be that they brought us from London hither to Litchfield, made me a lord, and you my servant.

Arch. That's more than you could expect already.—— But what money have we left ?

Aim. But two hundred pounds.

Arch. And our horses, cloaths, rings, &c. Why, we have very good fortunes now for moderate people ; and let me tell you, that this two hundred pounds, with the experience that we are now masters of, is a better estate than the ten thousand we have spent--Our friends, indeed, began to suspect that our pockets were low ; but we came off with flying coulours, shewed no signs of want either in word or deed.

Aim. Ay, and our going to Brussels was a good pretence enough for our sudden disappearing ; and, I warrant you, our friends imagine that we are gone a volunteering.

Arch. Why 'faith if this project fails, it must e'en come to that. I am for venturing one of the hundreds, if you will, upon this knight errantry ; but in case it should fail, we'll reserve the other to carry us to some counterscarp, where we may die as we liv'd, in a blaze.

Aim. With all my heart ; and we have liv'd justly, Archer ; we can't say that we have spent our fortunes, but that we have enjoy'd 'em.

Arch.

Arch. Right; so much pleasure for so much money; we have had our penny-worths; and had I millions I would go to the same market again. O London, London! Well, we have had our share, and let us be thankful: past pleasures, for ought I know, are best, such as we are sure of: those to come may disappoint us. But you command for the day, and so I submit---At Nottingham, you know, I am to be master.

Aim. And at Lincoln I again.

Arch. Then, at Norwich I mount, which, I think, shall be our last stage; for if we fail there, we'll embark for Holland, bid adieu to .Venus, and welcome Mars.

Aim. A match! [*Enter* Boniface.] Mum.

Bon. What will your worship please to have for supper?

Aim. What have you got?

Bon. Sir, we have a delicate piece of beef in the pot, and a pig at the fire.

Aim. Good supper-meat, I must confess——I can't eat beef, landlord.

Arch. And I hate pig.

Aim. Hold your prating, sirrah! Do you know who you are? [*Aside.*

Bon. Please to bespeak something else; I have every thing in the house.

Aim. Have you any veal?

Bon. Veal! Sir, we had a delicate loin of veal on Wednesday last.

Aim. Have you got any fish, or wild fowl?

Bon. As for fish, truly, Sir, we are an inland town, and indifferently provided with fish, that's the truth on't; but then for wild fowl!——We have a delicate couple of rabbets.

Aim. Get me the rabbets fricasseed.

Bon. Fricasseed! Lard, Sir, they'll eat much better smother'd with onions.

Arch. Pshaw! Rot your onions.

Aim. Again, sirrah!——Well, landlord, what you please; but hold, I have a small charge of money, and your house is so full of strangers, that I believe it may be safer in your custody than mine; for when this fellow,

low of mine gets drunk, he minds nothing——Here, firrah, reach me the ftrong box.

Arch. Yes, Sir——This will give us reputation.

[*Afide. Brings the box.*

Aim. Here, landlord, the locks are fealed down, both for your fecurity and mine; it holds fomewhat above two hundred pounds: if you doubt it, I'll count them to you after fupper; but be fure you lay it where I may have it at a minute's warning; for my affairs are a little dubious at prefent; perhaps I may be gone in half an hour; perhaps I may be your gueft till the beft part of that be fpent; and pray order your hoftler to keep my horfes ready faddled: but one thing above the reft, I muft beg that you will let this fellow have none of your Anno Domini, as you call it;——for he's the moft infufferable fot——Here, firrah, light me to my chamber.

Arch. Yes, Sir. [*Exit, lighted by* Archer.

Bon. Cherry, daughter Cherry!

Enter Cherry.

Cher. D'ye call, father.

Bon. Ay, child, you muft lay by this box for the gentleman, 'tis full of money.

Cher. Money! Is all that money! Why fure, father, the gentleman comes to be chofen parliament-man. Who is he?

Bon. I don't know what to make of him; he talks of keeping his horfes ready faddled, and of going perhaps at a minute's warning, or of ftaying perhaps till the beft part of this be fpent.

Cher. Ay! Ten to one, father, he's a highwayman.

Bon. A highwayman! Upon my life, girl, you have hit it; and this box is fome new purchafed booty.——Now, could we find him out, the money were ours.

Cher. He don't belong to our gang.

Bon. What horfes have they?

Cher. The mafter rides upon a black.

Bon. A black! Ten to one the man upon the black mare; and fince he don't belong to our fraternity, we may betray him with a fafe confcience. I don't think it lawful to harbour any rogues but my own. Look ye,

child,

child, as the faying is, we muſt go cunningly to work; proofs we muſt have; the gentleman's ſervant loves drink, I'll ply him that way; and ten to one he loves a wench; you muſt work him t'other way.

Cher. Father, would you have me give my ſecret for his?

Bon. Confider, child, there's two hundred pounds to boot. [*Ringing without.*] Coming, coming———— Child, mind your buſineſs.　　　　　　[*Exit* Bon.

Cher. What a rogue is my father!——My father! I deny it————My mother was a good, generous, free-hearted woman, and I can't tell how far her good-nature might have extended for the good of her children. This landlord of mine, for I think I can call him no more, would betray his gueſt and debauch his daughter into the bargain———— by a footman too!

Enter Archer.

Arch. What footman, pray, miſtreſs, is ſo happy as to be the ſubject of your contemplation?

Cher. Whoever he is, friend, he'll be but little the better for't.

Arch. I hope ſo, for I'm ſure you did not think of me.

Cher. Suppoſe I had!

Arch. Why then you're but even with me: for the minute I came in, I was conſidering in what manner I ſhould make love to you.

Cher. Love to me, friend!

Arch. Yes, child.

Cher. Child! Manners! If you kept a little more di-ſtance, friend, it would become you much better.

Arch. Diſtance! Good night, ſauce-box.　　.[*Going.*

Cher. A pretty fellow! I like his pride—Sir; pray, Sir; you ſee, Sir; [Archer *returns.*] I have the creꞇit to be truſted with your maſter's fortune here, which ſets me a degree above his footman. I hope, Sir, you an't affronted?

Arch. Let me look you full in the face, and I'll tell you whether you can affront me or no.————'Sdeath, child, you have a pair of delicate eyes, and you don't know what to do with 'em.

Cher. Why, Sir, don't I ſee every body?

Arch.

Arch. Ay, but if some women had 'em, they would kill every body,——Pr'ythee instruct me; I would fain make love to you, but I don't know what to say.

Cher. Why, did you never make love to any body before?

Arch. Never to a person of your figure, I can assure you, Madam; my addresses have always been confined to persons within my own sphere; I never aspir'd so high before.

S O N G.

But you look so bright,
And are dress'd so tight,
That a man would swear you're right
As arm was e'er laid over.
Such an air
You freely wear
To ensnare,
As makes each guest a lover:
Since then, my dear, I'm your guest.
Pr'ythee give me of the best
Of what is ready dress.
Since then my dear, &c.

Cher. ' What can I think of this man?' [*Aside.*] Will you give me that song, Sir?

Arch. Ay, my dear, take it while it is warm. [*Kisses her.*] Death and Fire! Her lips are honey-combs.

Cher. And I wish there had been a swarm of bees too, to have stung you for your impudence.

Arch. There's a swarm of Cupids, my little Venus, that has done the business much better.

Cher. This fellow is misbegotten as well as I. [*Aside.*] What's your name, Sir?

Arch. Name! 'egad, I have forgot it. [*Aside.*] Oh, Martin.

Cher. Where was you born?

Arch. In St. Martin's parish.

Cher. What was your father?

Arch. Of——of——St. Martin's parish.

Cher. Then, friend, good night.

Arch. I hope not.

* B

Cher.

Cher. You may depend upon't.

Arch. Upon what?

Cher. That you are very impudent.

Arch. That you are very handsome.

Cher. That you're a footman.

Arch. That you're an angel.

Cher. I shall be rude.

Arch. So shall I.

Cher. Let go my hand.

Arch. Give me a kiss.   [*Kisses her*

Boniface *calls without*, Cherry, Cherry.

Cher. I'm———My father calls, you plaguy devil, how durst you stop my breath so?—Offer to follow me one step, if you dare.   [*Exit*

Arch. A fair challenge, by this light; this is a pretty fair opening of an adventure; but we are knight-errants, and so fortune be our guide.   [*Exit*

END of the FIRST ACT.

ACT II.

SCENE, *a gallery in Lady* Bountiful's *house.*

Mrs. Sullen *and* Dorinda *meeting.*

DORINDA.

MORROW, my dear sister; are you for church this morning?

Mrs. Sul. Any where to pray; for heaven alone can help me: but I think, Dorinda, there's no form of prayer in the liturgy against bad husbands.

Dor. But there's a form of law at Doctors Commons, and I swear, sister Sullen, rather than see you thus continually discontented, I would advise you to apply to that: for besides the part that I bear in your vexatious broils, as being sister to the husband, and friend to the wife, your examples give me such an impression of matrimony, that I shall be apt to condemn my person to a long vacation all its life. But supposing, Madam, that you brought it to a case of separation, what can you urge against your husband? My brother is, first, the most constant man alive.

Mrs. Su

Mrs. Sul. The moſt conſtant huſband, I grant you.

Dor. He never ſleeps from you.

Mrs. Sul. No, he always ſleeps with me.

Dor. He allows you a maintenance ſuitable to your quality.

Mrs. Sul. A maintenance! Do you take me, Madam, for an hoſpital child, that I muſt ſit down and bleſs my benefactors for meat, drink, and clothes? As I take it, Madam, I brought your brother ten thouſand pounds, out of which I might expect ſome pretty things called pleaſures.

Dor. You ſhare in all the pleaſures the country affords.

Mrs. Sul. Country pleaſures! Racks and torments! Doſt think, child, that my limbs were made for leaping of ditches, and clambering over ſtiles. Or, that my parents, wiſely foreſeeing my future happineſs in country pleaſures, had early inſtructed me in rural accompliſhments, of drinking fat ale, playing at whiſt, and ſmoaking tobacco with my huſband; or of ſpreading of plaiſters, brewing of diet drinks, and ſtilling roſemary-water, with the good old gentlewoman, my mother-in law?

Dor. I'm ſorry, Madam, that it is not more in our power to divert you: I could wiſh, indeed, that our entertainments were a little more polite, or your taſte a little leſs refined; but pray, Madam, how came the poets and philoſophers, that laboured ſo much in hunting after pleaſure, to place it at laſt in a country life?

Mrs. Sul. Becauſe they wanted money, child, to find out the pleaſures of the town. Did you ever hear of a poet or philoſopher worth ten thouſand pounds? If you can ſhew me ſuch a man, I'll lay you fifty-pounds, you'll find him ſomewhere within the weekly bills. Not that I diſapprove rural pleaſures, as the poets have painted them in their landſcapes; every Phillis has her Corydon; every murmuring ſtream, and every flowery mead, gives freſh alarm to love. Beſides, you'll find, that their couples were never married. But yonder I ſee my Corydon, and a ſweet ſwain it is, heaven knows! Come, Dorinda, don't be angry, he's my

 huſband,

hufband, and your brother, and between both is he not a fad brute?

Dor. I have nothing to fay to your part of him, you're the beft judge.

Mrs. Sul. Oh, fifter, fifter! If ever you marry, beware of a fullen, filent fot, one that's always mufing, but never thinks.—There's fome diverfion in a talking blockhead; and fince a woman muft wear chains, I would have the pleafure of hearing 'em rattle a little. Now you fhall fee; but take this by the way; he came home this morning at his ufual hour of four, wakened me out of a fweet dream of fomething elfe, by tumbling over the tea-table, which he broke all to pieces. After his man and he had rolled about the room, like fick paffengers in a ftorm, he comes flounce into bed, dead as a falmon into a fifhmonger's bafket; his feet cold as ice; his breath hot as a furnace; and his hands and his face as greafy as his flannel night-cap———Oh, matrimony! matrimony!———He toffes up the clothes with a barbarous fwing over his fhoulders, diforders the whole œconomy of my bed, leaves me half-naked, and my whole night's comfort is the tuneable ferenade of that wakeful nightingale, his nofe.———Oh, the pleafure of counting the melancholy clock by a fnoring hufband!—But now, fifter, you fhall fee how handfomely, being a well-bred man, he will beg my pardon.

Enter Sullen.

Sul. My head achs confumedly.

Mrs. Sul. Will you be pleafed, my dear, to drink tea with us this morning; it may do your head good?

Sul. No.

Dor. Coffee, brother?

Sul. Pfhaw!

Mrs. Sul. Will you pleafe to drefs, and go to church with me? the air may help you.

Sul. Scrub!

Enter Scrub.

Scrub. Sir!

Sul. What day o'the week is this?

Scrub. Sunday, an't pleafe your worfhip.

Sul. Sunday! Bring me a dram; and d'ye hear, fet

out

out the venison-pasty and a tankard of strong beer, upon
the hall table, I'll go to breakfast.   [*Going.*

Dor. Stay, stay, brother, you shan't get off so; you
were very naughty last night, and must make your wife
reparation.   Come, come, brother, won't you ask pardon?

Sul. For what?

Dor. For being drunk last night,

Sul. I can afford it, can't I?

Mrs. Sul. But I can't, Sir.

Sul. Then you may let it alone.

Mrs. Sul. But I must tell you, Sir, that this is not to
be borne.

Sul. I'm glad on't.

Mrs. Sul. What is the reason, Sir, that you use me
thus inhumanly?

Sul. Scrub!

Scrub. Sir!

Sul. Get things ready to shave my head.   [*Exit.*

Mrs. Sul. Have a care of coming near his temples,
Scrub, for fear you meet something there that may turn
the edge of your razor. [*Exit* Scrub.] Inveterate stupidity! Did you ever know so hard, so obstinate a spleen
as his? Oh, sister, sister! I shall never have any
good of the beast till I get him to town; London,
dear London, is the place for managing and breaking
a husband.

Dor. And has not a husband the same opportunities
there for humbling a wife?

Mrs. Sul. No, no, child; 'tis a standing maxim in
conjugal discipline, that when a man would enslave his
wife, he hurries her into the country; and when a
lady would be arbitrary with her husband, she weedles
her booby up to town.——A man dare not play the
tyrant in London, because there are so many examples
to encourage the subject to rebel. Oh, Dorinda, Dorinda! A fine woman may do any thing in London.
O' my conscience, she may raise an army of forty thousand men.

Dor. I fancy, sister, you have a mind to be trying
your power that way here in Litchfield; you have drawn
the French Count to your colours already.

B 3

Mrs. Sul.

Mrs. Sul. The French are a people that can'
without their gallantries.

Dor. And some English that I know, sister, ai
averse to such amusements.

Mrs. Sul. Well, sister, since the truth must c
may do as well now as hereafter; I think one v
rouse my lethargic, sottish husband, is to give hin
val; security begets negligence in all people, an
must be alarmed to make 'em alert in their duty. W
are like pictures, of no value in the hands of a foo
he hears men of sense bid high for the purchase.

Dor. This might do, sister, if my brother's unde
ding were to be convinced into a passion for you; l
believe, there's a natural aversion on his side; and
cy, sister, that you don't come much behind him,
dealt fairly.

Mrs. Sul. I own it; we are united contradiction
and water. But I could be contented, with a grea
ny other wives, to humour the censorious vulga
give the world an appearance of living well wit
husband, could I bring him but to dissemble a little
ness to keep me in countenance.

Dor. But how do you know, sister, but that inst
rousing your husband by this artifice to a counterfeit
ness, he should awake in a real fury?

Mrs. Sul. Let him.——If I can't entice him t
one, I would provoke him to the other.

Dor. But how must I behave myself between yo

Mrs. Sul. You must assist me.

Dor. What, against my own brother?

Mrs. Sul. He's but half a brother, and I'm your
friend. If I go a step beyond the bounds of he
leave me; till then, I expect you shall go along wi
in every thing. The Count is to dine here to-day.

Dor. 'Tis a strange thing, sister, that I can't lik
man.

Mrs. Sul. You like nothing; your time is not
Love and death have their fatalities, and strike hon
time or other.—You'll pay for all one day, I warra
——But come, my lady's tea is ready, and 'tis
church-time.   [*E*

SC

SCENE, *the Inn.*

Enter Aimwell *dreſſed, and* Archer.

Aim. And was ſhe the daughter of the houſe?

Arch. The landlord is ſo blind as to think ſo; but I dare ſwear ſhe has better blood in her veins.

Aim. Why doſt think ſo?

Arch. Becauſe the baggage has a pert *je-ne-ſçais-quoi*; ſhe reads plays, keeps a monkey, and is troubled with vapours.

Aim. By which diſcoveries I gueſs that you know more of her.

Arch. Not yet, faith. The lady gives herſelf airs, forſooth: nothing under a gentleman.

Aim. Let me take her in hand.

Arch. Say one word more o'that, and I'll declare my-ſelf, ſpoil your ſport there, and every where elſe. Look ye, Aimwell, every man in his own ſphere.

Aim. Right, and therefore you muſt pimp for your maſter.

Arch. In the uſual forms, good Sir, after I have ſer-ved myſelf—but to our buſineſs. You are ſo well dreſs'd, Tom, and make ſo handſome a figure, that I fancy you may do execution in a country church; the exterior part ſtrikes firſt, and you're in the right to make that impreſ-ſion favourable.

Aim. There's ſomething in that which may turn to ad-vantage. The appearance of a ſtranger in a country church, draws as many gazers as a blazing ſtar; no ſooner he comes into the cathedral, but a train of whiſ-pers runs buzzing round the congregation in a moment. ——Who is he? Whence comes he? Do you know him!——Then I, Sir, tips me the verger half a crown; he pockets the ſimony, and inducts me into the beſt pew in the church; I pull out my ſnuff-box, turn myſelf round, bow to the biſhop, or the dean, if he be the com-manding officer, ſingle out a beauty, rivet both my eyes to hers, ſet my noſe a bleeding by the ſtrength of ima-gination, and ſhew the whole church my concern, by my endeavouring to hide it; after the ſermon, the whole town gives me to her for a lover, and by perſuading the

.lad_y

lady that I am dying for her, the tables are turned, and she in good earnest falls in love with me.

Arch. There's nothing in this, Tom, without a precedent; but instead of rivetting your eyes to a beauty, try to fix them upon a fortune; that's our business at present.

Aim. Pshaw! no woman can be a beauty without a fortune. Let me alone for a markfman.

Arch. Tom!

Aim. Aye!

Arch. When were you at church before, pray?

Aim. Um—I was there at the coronation.

Arch. And how can you expect a bleffing by going to church now?

Aim. Bleffing! Nay, Frank, I afk but for a wife.

[*Exit.*

Arch. Truly, the man is not very unreasonable in his demands. [*Exit at the oppofite door.*

Enter Boniface *and* Cherry.

Bon. Well, daughter, as the faying is, have you brought Martin to confefs?

Cher. Pray, father, don't put me upon getting any thing out of a man; I'm but young, you know, father, and don't underftand wheedling.

Bon. Young! why you jade, as the faying is, can any woman wheedle that is not young? Your mother was ufelefs at five and twenty. Would you make your mother a whore, and me a cuckold, as the faying is? I tell you, his filence confeffes it, and his mafter fpends his money fo freely, and is fo much a gentleman every manner of way, that he muft be a highwayman..

Enter Gibbet *in a cloak.*

Gib. Landlord, landlord, is the coaft clear?

Bon. O, Mr. Gibbet, what's the news?

Gib. No matter, afk no queftions, all's fair and honourable; here, my dear Cherry. [*Gives her a bag.*] two hundred fterling pounds, as good as ever hanged or faved a rogue; lay 'em by with the reft; and here ——three wedding —— or mourning rings, 'tis much the fame, you know——Here, two filver hilted fwords; I took thofe from fellows that never fhew any part of their fwords but the hilts. Here is a diamond neck-lace,

which

which the lady hid in the privateſt place in the coach, but I found it out. This gold watch I took from a pawn-broker's wife, it was left in her hands by a perſon of quality, there's the arms upon the caſe.

Cher. But who had you the money from?

Gib. Ah! poor woman! I pitied her;——from a poor lady juſt eloped from her huſband; ſhe had made up her cargo, and was bound for Ireland, as hard as ſhe could drive; ſhe told me of her huſband's barbarous uſage, and ſo faith, I left her half a crown. But I had almoſt forgot, my dear Cherry, I have a preſent for you.

Cher. What is't.

Gib. A pot of ceruſe, my child, that I took out of a lady's under-petticoat pocket.

Cher. What, Mr. Gibbet, do you think that I paint?

Gib. Why, you jade, your betters do; I'm ſure the lady that I took it from had a coronet upon her hand-kerchief.——Here, take my cloak, and go ſecure the premiſes.

Cher. I will ſecure 'em. [*Exit.*

Bon. But heark ye, where's Hounſlow and Bagſhot?

Gib. They'll be here to-night.

Bon. D'ye know of any other gentleman o' the pad on this road?

Gib. No.

Bon. I fancy that I have two that lodge in the houſe juſt now.

Gib. The devil! how d'ye ſmoak 'em?

Bon. Why, the one is gone to church.

Gib. To church! That's ſuſpicious, I muſt confeſs.

Bon. And the other is now in his maſter's chamber; he pretends to be a ſervant to the other; we'll call him out, and pump him a little.

Gib. With all my heart.

Bon. Mr. Martin! Mr. Martin!

Enter Archer, *combing a periwig, and ſinging.*

Gib. The roads are conſumed deep, I'm as dirty as Old Brentford at Chriſtmas.——A good pretty fellow that; whoſe ſervant are you, friend?

Arch. My maſter's.

Gib. Really?

Arch.

Arch. Really.

Gib. That's much.---That fellow has been at the bar by his evasions :----But pray, Sir, what is your master's name ?

Arch. Tall, all, dall.---[*Sings and combs the periwig.*] This is the most obstinate curl------

Gib. I ask you his name ?

Arch. Name, Sir---Tall, all, dall---I never asked him his name in my life---Tall, all, dall.

Bon. What think you now ?

Gib. Plain, plain; he talks now as if he were before a judge. But pray, friend, which way does your master travel ?

Arch. A horseback.

Gib. Very well again ; an old offender---Right---But I mean does he go upwards or downwards ?

Arch. Downwards, I fear, Sir---Tall, lall.

Gib. I'm afraid thy fate will be a contrary way.

Bon. Ha, ha, ha ! Mr. Martin, you're very arch. —This gentleman is only travelling towards Chester, and would be glad of your company, that's all.---Come, Captain, you'll stay to-night, I suppose; I'll shew you a chamber------Come, Captain.

Gib. Farewel, friend------ [*Exeunt.*

Arch. Captain, your servant.---Captain ! a pretty fellow ! 'Sdeath ! I wonder that the officers of the army don't conspire to beat all scoundrels in red but their own.

Enter Cherry.

Cher. Gone, and Martin here ! I hope he did not listen : I would have the merit of the discovery all my own, because I would oblige him to love me. [*Aside.*] Mr. Martin, who was that man with my father ?

Arch. Some recruiting serjeant, or whipp'd-out trooper, I suppose.

Cher. All's safe, I find. [*Aside.*

Arch. Come, my dear, have you conn'd over the catechism I taught you last night ?

Cher. Come, question me.

Arch. What is love ?

Cher. Love is I know not what, it comes I know not how, goes I know not when.

Arch.

Arch. Very well, an apt scholar. [*Chucks her under the chin.*] Where does love enter?

Cher. Into the eyes.

Arch. And where go out?

Cher. I won't tell you.

Arch. What are the objects of that paſſion!

Cher. Youth, beauty, and clean linen.

Arch. The reaſon.

Cher. The two firſt are faſhionable in nature, and the third at court.

Arch. That's my dear. What are the ſigns and tokens of that paſſion?

Cher. A ſtealing look, a ſtammering tongue, words improbable, deſigns impoſſible, and actions impracticable.

Arch. That's my good child; kiſs me —————— What muſt a lover do to obtain his miſtreſs?

Cher. He muſt adore the perſon that diſdains him, he muſt bribe the chambermaid that betrays him, and court the footman that laughs at him!---He muſt, he muſt——

Arch. Nay, child, I muſt whip you if you don't mind your leſſon? he muſt treat his—————

Cher. O! aye. He muſt treat his enemies with reſpect, his friends with indifference, and all the world with contempt; he muſt ſuffer much, and fear more; he muſt deſire much, and hope little; in ſhort, he muſt embrace his ruin, and throw himſelf away.

Arch. Had ever a man ſo hopeful a pupil as mine! my dear; why is love called a riddle?

Cher. Becauſe being blind, he leads thoſe that ſee; though a child, he governs a man.

Arch. Mighty well---And why is love pictured blind?

Cher. Becauſe the painters, out of their weakneſs, or the privilege of their art, choſe to hide thoſe eyes they could not draw.

Arch. That's my dear little ſcholar, kiſs me again--- And why ſhould love, that's a child, govern a man?

Cher. Becauſe that a child is the end of love.

Arch. And ſo ends love's catechiſm——And now, my dear, we'll go in and make my maſter's bed.

Cher. Hold, hold, Mr. Martin——you have taken a great deal of pains to inſtruct me, and what d'ye think I have learned by it?

Arch. What? *Cher.*

Cher. That your difcourfe and your habit are contra-
dictions, and it would be nonfenfe in me to believe you a
footman any longer.

Arch. 'Oons, what a witch it is!

Cher. Depend upon this, Sir, nothing in that garb fhall
ever tempt me : for though I was born to fervitude, I hate
it.——Own your condition, fwear you love me, and
then———

Arch. And then we fhall go make my mafter's bed ?

Cher. Yes.

Arch. You muft know then, that I am born a gentleman, my education was liberal: but I went to London,
a younger brother, fell into the hands of fharpers, who
ftript me of my money, my friends difowned me, and
now my neceffity brings me to what you fee.

Cher. Then take my hand——promife to marry me
before you fleep, and I'll make you mafter of two thoufand pounds.

Arch. How !

Cher. Two thoufand pounds that I have this minute in
my own cuftody ; fo throw off your livery this inftant,
and I'll go find a parfon.

Arch. What faid you ? a parfon !

Cher. What ! Do you fcruple ?

Arch. Scruple ! No ! no, but—two thoufand pounds
you fay ?

Cher. And better.

Arch. 'Sdeath, what fhall I do ?——But hea
what need you make me mafter of yourfelf,
when you may have the fame pleafure out of,
ftill keep your fortune in your own hands ?

Cher. Then you won't marry me ?

Arch. I would marry you, but———

Cher. O, fweet Sir, I'm your humble fervant, you're
fairly caught. Would you perfuade me that any gentleman who could bear the fcandal of wearing a livery,
wou'd refufe two thoufand pounds, let the condition be
what it wou'd---No, no, Sir---But I hope you'll pardon
the freedom I have taken, fince it was only to inform
myfelf of the refpect that I ought to pay to you. [*Going.*

Arch. Fairly bit, by Jupiter—Hold, hold ! and have
you actually two thoufand pounds ?

Cher.

Cher. Sir, I have my fecrets as well as you—when you pleafe to be more open, I fhall be more free; and be affured that I have difcoveries that will match yours, be they what they will.——In the mean while, be fatisfy'd, that no difcovery I make fhall hurt you; but beware of my father.—— [*Exit.*

Arch. So—we're like to have as many adventures in our inn, as Don Quixote had in his—Let me fee— two thoufand pounds! If the wench wou'd promife to die when the money were fpent, 'egad, one wou'd marry her; but the fortune may go off in a year or two, and the wife may live————Lord knows how long! Then an inn-keeper's daughter! Aye, that's the devil—there my pride brings me off:

For whatfoe'er the fages charge on pride,
The angels' fall, and twenty faults befide;
On earth, I'm fure, 'mong us of mortal calling,
Pride faves man oft, and woman too, from falling.
[*Exit.*

END of the SECOND ACT.

A C T III.

SCENE, *Lady* Bountiful's *Houfe.*

Enter Mrs. Sullen *and* Dorinda.

Mrs. SULLEN.

HA, ha, ha, my dear fifter! let me embrace thee: now we are friends indeed; for I fhall have a fecret of yours, as a pledge for mine——Now you'll be good for fomething, I fhall have you converfable in the fubjects of the fex.

Dor. But do you think that I am fo weak as to fall in love with a fellow at firft fight?

Mrs. Sul. Pfhaw! now you fpoil all; why fhou'd not we be as free in our friendfhips as the men? I warrant you, the gentleman has got to his confident already, has avowed his paffion, toafted your health, called you ten thoufand angels, has run over your lips, eyes, neck, fhape, air, and every thing, in a defcription that warms their mirth to a fecond enjoyment.

* C

Dor

Dor. Your hand, fister: I an't well.

Mrs. Sul. So—fhe's breeding already—Come, child, up with it—hem a little—fo—Now tell me, don't you like the gentleman that we faw at church juft now ?

Dor. The man's well enough.

Mrs. Sul. Well enough ! Is he not a demi-god, a Narciffus, a ftar, the man i' the moon ?

Dor. O, fifter, I'm extremely ill.

Mrs. Sul. Shall I fend to your mother, child, for a little cephalic plaifter to put to the foles of your feet ? Or fhall I fend to the gentleman for fomething for you ?——Come, unbofom yourfelf—the man is perfectly a pretty fellow; I faw him when he firft came into church.

Dor. I faw him too, fifter, and with an air that fhone, methought, like rays about his perfon.

Mrs. Sul. Well faid, up with it.

Dor. No forward coquet behaviour, no air to fet him off, no ftudy'd looks, nor artful pofture——but nature did it all————

Mrs. Sul. Better and better——one touch more—— come————

Dor. But then his looks—did you obferve his eyes ?

Mrs. Sul. Yes, yes, I did————his eyes; well, what of his eyes?

Dor. Sprightly, but not wandering; they feemed to view, but never gazed on any thing but me——and then his looks fo humble were, and yet fo noble, that they aimed to tell me, that he could with pride die at my feet, though he fcorn'd flavery any where elfe.

Mrs. Sul. The phyfic works purely.——How d'ye find yourfelf now, my dear ?

Dor. Hem ! Much better, my dear—Oh, here comes our Mercury !

Enter Scrub.

Dor. Well, Scrub, what news of the gentleman ?

Scrub. Madam, I have brought you a whole packet of news.

Dor. Open it quickly ; come.

Scrub. In the firft place, I enquired who the gentleman was ? They told me he was a ftranger. Secondly, I afked what the gentleman was ? They anfwered and faid, that they never faw him before. Thrdly, I enquired

quired what countryman he was ? They replied, 'twas more than they knew. Fourthly, I demanded whence he came ? Their anſwer was, they could not tell. And fiſtbly, I aſked whither he went ? and they replied, they knew nothing of the matter.——And this is all I could learn.

Mrs. Sul. But what do the people ſay ? Can't they gueſs'?

Scrub. Why ſome think he's a ſpy, ſome gueſs he's a mountebank, ſome ſay one thing, ſome another ; but for my own part, I believe he's a Jeſuit.

Dor. A Jeſuit ! why a Jeſuit ?

Scrub. Becauſe he keeps his horſes always ready ſad-dled, and his footman talks French.

Mrs. Sul. His footman !

Scrub. Ay, he and the count's footman were gabbering French like two intriguing ducks in a mill-pond ; and I believe they talked of me, for they laughed confumedly.

Dor. What ſort of livery has the footman ?

Scrub. Livery ! lord, Madam, I took him for a cap-tain, he's ſo bedizened with lace ; and then he has tops to his ſhoes, up to his mid-leg, a ſilver-headed cane dan-gling at his knuckles :——he caries his hands in his poc-kets, and walks juſt ſo [*Walks in a French air.*] and has a fine long periwig tied up in a bag——Lord, Madam, he's clear another ſort of a man than I.

Mrs. Sul. That may eaſily be——But what ſhall we do now, ſiſter ?

Dor. I have it——this fellow has a world of ſimplici-ty, and ſome cunning ; the firſt hides the latter by abun-dance.————Scrub.

Scrub. Madam.

Dor. We have a great mind to know who this gentle-man is, only for our ſatisfaction.

Scrub. Yes, Madam, it would be a ſatisfaction, no doubt.

Dor. You muſt go and get acquainted with his foot-man, and invite him hither to drink a bottle of your ale, becauſe you're butler to-day.

Scrub. Yes, Madam, I am butler every Sunday.

Mrs. Sul. O brave ſiſter ! o' my conſcience you under-ſtand the mathematics already.—'Tis the beſt plot in the world! your mother, you know, will be gone to church, my spouse will be got to the alehouse with his scoundrels, and the house will be our own——so we drop in by accident, and ask the fellow some questions ourselves. In the country, you know, any stranger is company, and we are glad to take up with the butler in a country dance, and happy if he'll do us the favour.

Scrub. Oh, Madam, you wrong me; I never refus'd your ladyship the favour in my life.

Enter Gipsey.

Gip. Ladies, dinner's upon table.

Dor. Scrub, we'll excuse your waiting——go where we order'd you.

Scrub. I shall.

S C E N E *changes to the Inn.*
Enter Aimwell *and* Archer.

Arch. Well, Tom, I find you're a marksman.

Aim. A marksman! who so blind could be as not discern a swan among the ravens?

Arch. Well, but heark'e, Aimwell.

Aim. Aimwell! call me Oroondates, Cesario, Amadis, all that romance can in a lover paint, and then I'll answer. Oh, Archer! I read her thousands in her looks; she looked like Ceres in her harvest; corn, wine, and oil, milk, honey, gardens, groves, and purling streams, played on her plenteous face.

Arch. Her face! her pocket, you mean! the corn, wine and oil lie there. In short, she has twenty thousand pounds, that's the English on't.

Aim. Her eyes——

Arch. Are demi-cannons, to be sure; so I won't stand their battery. [*Going.*

Aim. Pray, excuse me, my passion must have vent.

Arch. Passion! what a plague, d'ye think these romantic airs will do our business? Were my temper as extravagant as yours, my adventures have something more romantic by half.

Aim. Your adventures!

Arch. Yes.

'The nymph that with her twice ten hundred pounds,
With brazen engine hot, and coif clear starched,

Can

Can fire the guest in warming of the bed——

There's a touch of sublime Milton for you, and the subject but an inn-keeper's daughter. I can play with a girl
as an angler does with his fish; he keeps it at the end of
his line, runs it up the stream, and down the stream, till
at last he brings it to hand, tickles the trout, and so
whips it into his basket.

Enter Boniface.

Bon. Mr. Martin, as the saying is; yonder's an honest fellow below, my lady Bountiful's butler, who begs
the honour that you would go home with him and see
his cellar.

Arch. Do my *baisemains* to the gentleman, and tell
him, I will do myself the honour to wait on him immediately, as the saying is.

Bon. I shall do your worship's commands, as the saying is.   [*Exit, bowing obsequiously.*

Aim. What do I hear? Soft Orpheus play, and fair
Toftida sing!

Arch. Pshaw! Damn your raptures; I tell you here's
a pump going to be put into the vessel, and the ship
will get into harbour, my life on't. You say there's
another lady very handsome there.

Aim. Yes, faith.

Arch. I am in love with her already.

Aim. Can't you give me a bill upon Cherry in the
mean time?

Arch. No, no, friend, all her corn, wine, and oil
is ingross'd to my market——And once more I warn
you, to keep your anchorage clear of mine; for if
you fall foul of me, by this light, you shall go to the
bottom——What, make a prize of my little frigate,
while I am upon the cruize for you! You're a pretty
fellow indeed!   [*Exit.*

Enter Boniface.

Aim. Well, well, I won't——Landlord, have you
any tolerable company in the house? I don't care for
dining alone.

Bon. Yes, Sir, there's a Captain below, as the saying
is, that arriv'd about an hour ago.

Aim. Gentlemen of his coat are welcome every-
C 3   where;

where; will you make a compliment for me, and tell him I fhould be glad of his company, that's all?

Bon. Who fhall I tell him, Sir, wou'd——

Aim. Ha! That ftroke was well thrown in——I'm only a traveller, like himfelf, and would be glad of his company, that's all.

Bon. I obey your commands, as the faying is. [*Exit.*

Enter Archer.

Arch. 'Sdeath! I had forgot; what title will you give yourfelf?

Aim. My brother's, to be fure; he would never give me any thing elfe, fo I'll make bold with his honour this bout——You know the reft of your cue?

Arch. Ay, ay.   [*Exit.*

Enter Gibbet.

Gib. Sir, I'm yours.

Aim. 'Tis more than I deferve, Sir, for I don't know you.

Gib. I don't wonder at that, Sir, for you never faw me before—I hope.   [*Afide.*

Aim. And pray, Sir, how came I by the honour of feeing you now?

Gib. Sir, I fcorn to intrude upon any gentleman— but my landlord——

Aim. Oh, Sir, I afk your pardon, you are the Captain he told me of.

Gib. At your fervice, Sir.

Aim. What regiment, may I be fo bold?

Gib. A marching regiment, Sir; an old corps.

Aim. Very old, if your coat be regimental.   [*Afide.*] You have ferved abroad, Sir?

Gib. Yes, Sir, in the Plantations; 'twas my lot to be fent into the worft fervice; I would have quitted it indeed, but a man of honour, you know. Befides, 'twas for the good of my country that I fhou'd be abroad—Any thing for the good of one's country—I'm a Roman for that.

Aim. One of the firft, I'll lay my life. [*Afide.*] You found the Weft-Indies very hot, Sir?

Gib. Ay, Sir, too hot for me.

Aim.

Aim. Pray, Sir, han't I seen your face at Will's Coffee-house?

Gib. Yes, Sir, and at White's too.

Aim. And where's your company now, Captain?

Gib. They an't come yet.

Aim. Why, d'ye expect them here?

Gib. They'll be here to night, Sir.

Aim. Which way do they march?

Gib. Across the country.—The devil's in't if I han't said enough to encourage him to declare—But I'm afraid he's not right, I must tack about. [*Aside.*

Aim. Is your company to quarter at Litchfield?

Gib. In this house, Sir.

Aim. What, all?

Gib. My company is but thin, ha, ha, ha! We are but three, ha, ha, ha!

Aim. You are merry, Sir?

Gib. Ay, Sir, you must excuse me. Sir, I understand the world, especially the art of travelling. I don't care, Sir, for answering questions directly upon the road——for I generally ride with a charge about me.

Aim. Three or four, I believe. [*Aside.*

Gib. I am credibly inform'd that there are highway-men upon this quarter; not, Sir, that I could suspect a gentleman of your figure——But truly, Sir, I have got such a way of evasion upon the road, that I don't care for speaking truth to any man.

Aim. Your caution may be necessary——Then I presume you're no Captain.

Gib. Not I, Sir: Captain is a good travelling name, and so I take it; it stops a great many foolish enquiries that are generally made about gentlemen that travel: it gives a man an air of something, and makes the drawers obedient ——And thus far I am a Captain, and no farther.

Aim. And pray, Sir, what is your true profession?

Gib. Oh, Sir, you must excuse me—upon my word, Sir, I don't think it safe to tell you.

Aim. Ha, ha! Upon my word, I commend you.

Enter Boniface.

Well, Mr. Boniface, what's the news?

Bon.

Bon. There's another gentleman below, as the saying is, that hearing you were but two, would be glad, to make the third man, if you'd give him leave.

Aim. What is he?

Bon. A clergyman, as the saying is.

Aim. A clergyman! Is he really a clergyman? or is it only his travelling-name, as my friend the Captain has it?

Bon. Oh, Sir, he's a priest, and chaplain to the French officers in town.

Aim. Is he a Frenchman?

Bon. Yes, Sir, born at Bruffels.

Gib. A Frenchman, and a prieft! I won't be feen in his company, Sir; I have a value for my reputation, Sir.

Aim. Nay, but Captain, fince we are by ourfelves —Can he fpeak English, landlord?

Bon. Very well, Sir; you may know him, as the saying is, to be a foreigner by his accent, and that's all.

Aim. Then he has been in England before?

Bon. Never, Sir; but he's mafter of languages, as the saying is; he talks Latin; it does me good to hear him talk Latin.

Aim. Then you underftand Latin, Mr. Boniface?

Bon. Not I, Sir, as the saying is; but he talks it fo very faft, that I'm fure it muft be good.

Aim. Pray defire him to walk up.

Bon. Here he is, as the faying is.

Enter Foigard.

Foig. Save you, gentlemens bote.

Aim. A Frenchman! Sir, your moft humble fervant.

Foig. Och, dear joy, I am your moft faithful fhervant, and yours alfho.

Gib. Doctor, you talk very good English, but you have a mighty twang of the foreigner.

Foig. My English is very well, for the vords, but we foreigners, you know, cannot bring our tongues about the pronunciation fo foon.

Aim. A foreigner! A downright Teague, by this light. [*Afide.*] Were you born in France, Doctor?

Foig.

Foig. I was educated in France, but I was borned at Bruſſels: I am a ſubject of the king of Spain, joy.

Gib. What king of Spain, Sir? Speak.

Foig. Upon my ſhoul, joy, I cannot tell you as yet.

Aim. Nay, Captain, that was too hard upon the Doctor, he's a ſtranger.

Foig. Oh, let him alone, dear joy, I'm of a nation that is not eaſily put out of countenance.

Aim. Come, gentlemen, I'll end the diſpute—— Here, landlord, is dinner ready?

Bon. Upon the table, as the ſaying is.

Aim. Gentlemen——pray——that door.——

Foig. No, no, fait, the Captain muſt lead.

Aim. No, Doctor, the church is our guide.

Gib. Ay, ay, ſo it is—— [*Exit foremoſt, they follow.*

SCENE *changes to a gallery in Lady* Bountiful's *houſe.*

Enter Archer *and* Scrub *ſinging, and hugging one ano- ther;* Scrub *with a tankard in his hand,* Gipſey *liſtening at a diſtance.*

Scrub. Tall, all, dall——Come, my dear boy—— let us have that ſong once more.

Arch. No, no, we ſhall diſturb the family——but will you be ſure to keep the ſecret?

Scrub. Pho! Upon my honour, as I'm a gentleman.

Arch. 'Tis enough——You muſt know then, that my maſter is the lord viſcount Aimwell; he fought a duel t'other day in London, wounded his man, ſo dange- rouſly that he thinks fit to withdraw till he hears whether the gentleman's wounds be mortal or not: he never was in this part of England before, ſo he choſe to retire to this place, that's all.

Gip. And that's enough for me. [*Exit.*

Scrub. And where were you when your maſter fought?

Arch. We never know of our maſters' quarrels.

Scrub. No! If our maſters in the country here re- ceive a challenge, the firſt thing they do is to tell their wives; the wife tells the ſervants, the ſervants alarm the tenants, and in half an hour you ſhall have the whole country up in arms——

Arch.

Arch. To hinder two men from doing what they have no mind for——But if you fhould chance to talk, now, of this bufinefs?

Scrub. Talk! Ah, Sir, had I not learn'd the knack of holding my tongue, I had never liv'd fo long in a great family.

Arch. Ay, ay, to be fure, there are fecrets in all families.

Scrub. Secrets, O Lud!——but I'll fay no more. Come, fit down, we'll make an end of our tankard, here.

Arch. With all my heart: who knows but you and I may come to be better acquainted, eh? Here's your lady's health: you have three, I think; and to be fure there muft be fecrets among 'em.

Scrub. Secrets! Ah! Friend, friend!—I wifh I had a friend.

Arch. Am I not your friend? Come, you and I will be fworn brothers.

Scrub. Shall we?

Arch. From this minute——Give me a kifs. And now, brother Scrub.

Scrub. And now, brother Martin, I will tell you a fecret that will make your hair ftand an end. You muft know, that I am confumedly in love.

Arch. That's a terrible fecret, that's the truth on't.

Scrub. That jade, Gipfey, that was with us juft now in the cellar, is the erranteft whore that ever wore a petticoat, and I'm dying for love of her.

Arch. Ha, ha, ha!—Are you in love with her perfon, or her virtue, brother Scrub?

Scrub. I fhould like virtue beft, becaufe it's more durable than beauty; for virtue holds good with fome women, long and many a day after they have loft it.

Arch. In the country, I grant ye, where no woman's virtue is loft, till a baftard be found.

Scrub. Ay, cou'd I bring her to a baftard, I fhould have her all to myfelf; but I dare not put it upon that lay, for fear of being fent for a foldier—Pray, brother, how do you gentlemen in London like that fame prefsing act?

Arch. Very ill, brother Scrub——'Tis the worft that

ever

ever was made for us; formerly, I remember the good days when we could dun our masters for our wages, and if they refused to pay us, we could have a warrant to carry 'em before a Justice; but now, if we talk of eating, they have a warrant for us, and carry us before three Justices.

Scrub. And to be sure we go, if we talk of eating; for the Justices won't give their own servants a bad example Now this is my misfortune—I dare not speak in the house, while that jade, Gipsey, dings about like a fury. Once I had the better end of the staff.

Arch. And how comes the change now?

Scrub. Why, the mother of all this mischief is a priest.

Arch. A priest!

Scrub. Ay, a damn'd son of a whore of Babylon, that came over hither to say grace to the French officers, and eat up our provisions——There's not a day goes over his head without a dinner or supper in this house.

Arch. How came he so familiar in the family!

Scrub. Because he speaks English as if he had liv'd here all his life, and tells lies as if he had been a traveller from his cradle.

Arch. And this priest, I'm afraid, has converted the affections of your Gipsey.

Scrub. Converted! ay, and perverted, my dear friend ————for I'm afraid he has made her a whore and a papist—But this is not all; there's the French count and Mrs. Sullen, they're in the confederacy, and for some private end of their own too, to be sure.

Arch. A very hopeful family, yours, brother Scrub; I suppose the maiden lady has her lover too.

Scrub. Not that I know——She's the best on 'em, that's the truth on't: but they take care to prevent my curiosity, by giving me so much business that I am a perfect slave:—What d'ye think is my place in this family?

Arch. Butler, I suppose.

Scrub. Ah, Lord help your silly head—I'll tell you— Of a Monday I drive the coach; of a Tuesday I drive the plough; on Wednesday I follow the hounds; on Thursday I dun the tenants; on Friday I go to market;

on

on Saturday I draw warrants ; and on Sunday I draw beer.

Arch. Ha, ha, ha! if variety be a pleasure in life, you have enough on't, my dear brother—But what ladies are thofe ?

Scrub. Ours, ours ; that upon the right hand is Mrs. Sullen, and the other Mrs. Dorinda——Don't mind 'em, fit ftill, man——

Enter Mrs. Sullen *and* Dorinda.

Mrs. Sul. I have heard my brother talk of my lord Aimwell, but they fay that his brother is the finer gentleman.

Dor. That's impoffible, fifter.

Mrs. Sul. He's vaftly rich, and very clofe, they fay.

Dor. No matter for that ; if I can creep into his heart, I'll open his breaft, I warrant him : I have heard fay, that people may be guefs'd at by the behaviour of their fervants ; I cou'd wifh we might talk to that fellow.

Mrs. Sul. So do I ; for I think he's a very pretty fellow. Come this way ; I'll throw out a lure for him prefently.

[*They walk a turn to the oppofite fide of the ftage.* Mrs. Sullen *drops her fan,* Archer *runs, takes it up, and gives it to her.*

Arch. Corn, wine, and oil, indeed—But I think the wife has the greateft plenty of flefh and blood ; fhe fhould be my choice—Ay, ay, fay you fo—Madam——your ladyfhip's fan.

Mrs. Sul. O Sir, I thank you——What a handfome bow the fellow made !

Dor. Bow ! Why, I have known feveral footmen come down from London, fet up here for dancing-mafters, and carry off the beft fortunes in the country.

Arch. [*Afide.*] That projeçt, for aught I know, had been better than ours—Brother Scrub, why don't you introduce me ?

Scrub. Ladies, this is the ftrange gentleman's fervant that you faw at church-to-day ; I underftood he came from London, and fo I invited him to the cellar, that he might fhew me the neweft flourifh in whetting my knives.

Dor. And I hope you have made much of him ?

Arch. O yes, Madam; but the ftrength of your ladyfhip's

hip's liquor is a little too potent for the conſtitution of
our humble ſervant.

Mrs. Sul. What then you don't uſually drink ale.

Arch. No Madam, my conſtant drink is tea, or a little
vine and water! 'tis preſcribed me by the phyſician, for
. remedy againſt the ſpleen.

Scrub. O la! O la!—a footman have the ſpleen!

Mrs. Sul. I thought that diſtemper had been only pro-
er to people of quality.

Arch. Madam, like all other faſhions, it wears out,
nd ſo deſcends to their ſervants : tho' in a great many of
is, I believe, it proceeds from ſome melancholy particles
a the blood, oceaſioned by the ſtagnation of wages.

Dor. How affectedly the fellow talks !—How long,
ray, have you ſerv'd your preſent maſter ?

Arch. Not long ; my life has been moſtly ſpent in the
ervice of the ladies.

Mrs. Sul. And, pray, which ſervice do you like beſt ?

Arch. Madam, the ladies pay beſt ; the honour of ſer-
ing them is ſufficient wages : there is a charm in their
ooks that delivers a pleaſure with their commands, and
ives our duty the wings of inclination.

Mrs. Sul. That flight was above the pitch of a livery :
nd, Sir, wou'd not you be ſatisfy'd to ſerve a lady again ?

Arch. As groom of the chambers, Madam, but not as
footman.

Mrs. Sul. I ſuppoſe you ſerv'd as footman before.

Arch. For that reaſon I wou'd not ſerve in that poſt
gain ; for my memory is too weak for the load of meſ-
iges that the ladies lay upon their ſervants in London :
ly Lady How-d'ye, the laſt miſtreſs I ſerv'd, call'd me
p one morning, and told me, Martin, go to my Lady
llnight with my humble ſervice ; tell her I was to wait
n her ladyſhip yeſterday, and left word with Mrs. Re-
ecca, that the preliminaries of the affair ſhe knows of,
e ſlopt till we know the concurrence of the perſon that
know of, for which there are circumſtances wanting
hich we ſhall accommodate at the old place ; but that in
ie mean time there is a perſon about her ladyſhip, that
om ſeveral hints and ſurmiſes, was acceſſary at a certain
me to the diſappointments that naturally attend things,
nat to her knowledge are of more importance————

Mrs. Sul. and Dor. Ha, ha! where are you going Sir ?

Arch. Why, I ha'n't half done.

Scrub. I fhould not remember a quarter of it.

Arch. The whole how-d'ye, was about half an hour long ; fo I happened to mifplace two fyllables, and was turned off, and rendered incapable——

Dor. The pleafanteft fellow, fifter, I ever faw.—But, friend, if your mafter be married—I prefume you ftill ferve a lady ?

Arch. No, Madam, I take care never to come into a married family, the commands of the mafter and miftrefs are always fo contrary, that 'tis impoffible to pleafe both.

Dor. There's a main point gain'd.—My lord is not married, I find.   [*Afide.*

Mrs. Sul. But I wonder, friend, that in fo many good fervices, you had not a better provifion made for you !

Arch. I don't know how, Madam.——but I am very well as I am.

Mrs. Sul. Something for a pair of gloves.

[*Offering him money.*

Arch. I humbly beg leave to be excufed. My mafter, Madam, pays me ; nor dare I take money from any other hand, without injuring his honour, and difobeying his commands.   [*Exit.*

Scrub. Brother Martin, brother Martin.

Arch. What do you fay, brother Scrub ?

Scrub. Take the money, and give it to me.

[*Exeunt* Archer *and* Scrub.

Dor. This is furprifing. Did you ever fee fo pretty a well-bred fellow ?

Mrs. Sul. The devil take him for wearing the livery.

Dor. I fancy, fifter, he may be fome gentleman, a friend of my lord's, that his lordfhip has pitch'd upon for his courage, fidelity, and difcretion, to bear him company in this drefs, and who, ten to one, was his fecond.

Mrs. Sul. It is fo, it muft be fo, and it fhall be fo--- for I like him.

Dor. What ! better than the count !

Mrs. Sul. The count happened to be the moft agreeable man upon the place ; and fo I chofe him to ferve me in

my

ny defign upon my hufband——But I fhould like this
ellow better in a defign upon myfelf.

Dor. But now, fifter, for an interview with this lord,
ind this gentleman ; how fhall we bring that about ?

Mrs. Sul. Patience ! you country ladies give no quar-
er, ' if once you be entered.' ----Wou'd you prevent
heir defires, and give the fellows no wifhing time ?---
Look'e, Dorinda, if my Lord Aimwell loves you or deferves you, he'll find a way to fee you, and there we muft
eave it——My bufinefs comes now upon the tapis
——Have you prepared your brother ?

Dor. Yes, yes,

Mrs. Sul. And how did he relifh it ?

Dor. He faid little, mumbled fomething to himfelf
ind promifed to be guided by me—but here he comes---
Enter Sullen.

Sul. What finging was that I heard juft now ?

Mrs. Sul. The finging in your head, my dear ; you
omplained of it all day.

Sul. You're impertinent.

Mrs. Sul. I was ever fo, fince I became one flefh with
ou.

Sul. One flefh ! rather two carcafes joined unnatural-
y together.

Mrs. Sul. Or rather, a living foul coupled to a dead
ody.

Dor. So, this is fine encouragement for me !

Sul. Yes, my wife fhews you what you muft do.

Mrs. Sul. And my hufband fhews you what you muft
uffer.

Sul. 'Sdeath ! why can't you be filent ?

Mrs. Sul. 'Sdeath ! why can't I talk ?

Sul. Do you talk to any purpofe !

Mrs. Sul. Do you think to any purpofe ?

Sul. Sifter, heark'e---[*Whifpers.*] I fhan't be home till
: be late.   [*Exit.*

Mrs. Sul. What did he whifper to ye ?

Dor. That he would go round the back way, come into the clofet, and liften as I directed him. But let me
eg once more, dear fifter, to drop this project : for, as
told you before, inftead of awaking him to kindnefs,

D 2   you

you may provoke him to rage ; and then who knows how far his brutality may carry him ?

Mrs. Sul. I'm provided to receive him, I warrant you. Away. [*Exeunt.*

END of the THIRD ACT.

A C T.   IV.
S C E N E *continues.*

Enter Dorinda, *meeting Mrs.* Sullen *and Lady* Bountiful.

DORINDA.

NEWS, dear fifter, news, news!
Enter Archer *running.*

Arch. Where, where is my Lady Bountiful?---Pray which is the old lady of you three?

L. Boun. I am.

Arch. O, Madam, the fame of your ladyfhip's charity, goodnefs, benevolence, fkill, and ability, have drawn me hither to implore your ladyfhip's help in behalf of my unfortunate mafter, who is this moment breathing his laft.

Lady Boun. Your mafter! where is he?

Arch. At your gate, Madam: drawn by the appearance of your handfome houfe to view it nearer, and walking up the avenue, he was taken ill of a fudden, with a fort of I know not what: but down he fell, and there he lies.

L. Boun. Here, Scrub, Gipfey, all run, get my eafy chair down ftairs, put the gentleman in it, and bring him in quickly, quickly.

Arch. Heaven will reward your ladyfhip for this charitable act.

L. Boun. Is your mafter ufed to thefe fits?

Arch. O, yes, Madam, frequently.——I have known him have five or fix of a night.

L. Boun. What's his name?

Arch. Lord, Madam, he's a dying; a minute's care or neglect, may fave or deftroy his life.

L. Boun. Ah, poor gentleman! Come, friend fhew me the way; I'll fee him brought in myfelf.
[*Exit with* Archer.
Dor.

Dor. O, fister, my heart flutters about ftrangely, I can hardly forbear running to his affiftance.

Mrs. Sul. And I'll lay my life he deferves your affi-ftance more than he wants. Did not I tell you that my lord would find a way to come at you. Love's his diftem-per, and you muft be the phyfician; put on all your charms, fummon all your fire into your eyes, plant the whole artillery of your looks againft his breaft, and down with him.

Dor. O, fifter, I'm but a young gunner; I fhall be afraid to fhoot, for fear the piece fhould recoil, and hurt myfelf.

Mrs. Sul. Never fear; you fhall fee me fhoot before you, if you will.

Dor. No, no, dear fifter, you have mifs'd your mark fo unfortunately, that I fhan't care for being inftructed by you.

Enter Aimwell *in a chair carried by* Archer *and* Scrub. *Lady* Bountiful, Gipfey; Aimwell *counterfeiting a fwoon.*

L. Boun. Here, here, let's fee the hartfhorn drops —Gipfey, a glafs of fair water, his fit's very ftrong——Blefs me, how his hands are clench'd!

Arch. For fhame, ladies, what d'ye do? Why don't you help us?——Pray, Madam, [*To* Dorinda.] take his hand, and open it, if you can, whilft I hold his head.

[Dorinda *takes his hand.*

Dor. Poor gentleman——Oh---he has got my hand within his, and fqueezes it unmercifully——

L. Boun. 'Tis the violence of his convulfion, child.

Arch. O, Madam, he's perfectly poffefs'd in thefe ca-fes—He'll bite you, if you don't have a care.

Dor. Oh, my hand! my hand!

L. Boun. What's the matter with the foolifh girl! I have got this hand open, you fee, with a great deal of eafe.

Arch. Aye, but, Madam, your daughter's hand is fomewhat warmer than your ladyfhip's, and the heat of it draws the force of the fpirits that way.

Mrs. Sul. I find, friend, you are very learned in thefe fort of fits.

Arch. 'Tis no wonder, Madam, for I'm often trou

ble

bled with them myfelf; I find myfelf extremly ill at this minute.   [*Looking hard at Mrs.* Sullen.

Mrs. Sul. [*Afide.*] I fancy I cou'd find a way to cure you.

L. Boun. His fit holds him very long.

Arch. Longer than ufual, Madam.

L. Boun. Where did his illnefs take him firft, pray?

Arch. To-day, at church, Madam.

L. Boun. In what manner was he taken?

Arch. Very ftrangely, my lady. He was of a fudden touched with fomething in his eyes, which at the firft he only felt, but could not tell whether it was pain or pleafure.

L. Boun. Wind, nothing but wind. Your mafter fhould never go without a bottle to fmell to—Oh!— he recovers—the lavender water—fome feathers to burn under his nofe. Hungary water to rub his temples.— Oh, he comes to himfelf. Hem a little, Sir, hem,— Gipfey, bring the cordial water.

[*Aimwell feems to awake in amaze.*

Dor. How do you, Sir?

Aim. Where am I?   [*Rifing.*

Sure I have pafs'd the gulf of filent death,
And now am landed on th' Elyfian fhore—
Behold the goddefs of thofe happy plains,
Fair Proferpine—Let me adore thy bright divinity.

[*Kneels to* Dorinda, *and kiffes her hand.*

Mrs. Sul. So, fo, fo, I knew where the fit would end.

Aim. Eurydice perhaps————
How cou'd thy Orpheus keep his word,
And not look back on thee?
No treafure but thyfelf cou'd fure have brib'd him
To look one minute off thee.

L. Boun. Delirious, poor gentleman!

Arch. Very delirious, Madam, very delirious,

Aim. Martin's voice, I think.

Arch. Yes, my lord.———How does your lordfhip?

L. Boun. Lord! Did you mind that, girls?

Aim. Where am I?

Arch. In very good hands, Sir.—You were taken juft now with one of your old fits, under the trees, juft by this good lady's houfe; her ladyfhip had you taken

in,

in, and has miraculously brought you to yourself, as you see.

Aim. I am so confounded with shame, Madam, that I can now only beg pardon—and refer my acknowledgments for your ladyship's care, till an opportunity offers of making some amends. I dare to be no longer troublesome. Martin, give two guineas to the servants.

[*Going.*

Dor. Sir, you may catch cold by going so soon into the air; you don't look, Sir, as if you were perfectly recovered.

[*Here* Archer *talks to Lady* Bountiful *in dumb shew.*

Aim. That I shall never be, Madam; my present illness is so rooted, that I must expect to carry it to my grave.

L. Boun. Come, Sir, your servant has been telling me that you are apt to relapse, if you go into the air— Your good-manners sha'n't get the better of ours— You shall sit down again, Sir. Come, Sir, we don't mind ceremonies in the country. Here, Gipsey, bring the cordial water. Here, Sir, my service t'ye. You shall taste my water; 'tis a cordial, I can assure you, and of my own making. [Aimwell *drinks.*] Drink it off, Sir. And how d'ye find yourself now, Sir?

Aim. Somewhat better; though very faint still.

L. Boun. Ay, ay, people are always faint after those fits. Come, girls, you shall shew the gentleman the house: 'tis but an old family building, Sir; but you had better walk about and cool by degrees, than venture immediately into the air: but you'll find some tolerable pictures. Dorinda, shew the gentleman the way. [*Exit.*] I must go to the poor woman below.

Dor. This way, Sir.

Aim. Ladies, shall I beg leave for my servant to wait on you, for he understands pictures very well.

Mrs. Sul. Sir, we understand originals as well as he does pictures, so he may come along.

[*Exeunt* Dor. *Mrs.* Sul. Arch. Aim. *leads* Dor.
Enter Foigard.

Foig. Save you, Master Scrub.

Scrub. Sir, I won't be sav'd your way. I hate a priest, I abhor the French, and I defy the devil. Sir,

I am

I am a bold Briton, and will spill the last drop of my blood to keep out popery and slavery.

Foig. Master Scrub, you would put me down in politics, and so I wou'd be speaking with Mrs. Gipsey.

Scrub. Good Mr. Priest, you can't speak with her; she's sick, Sir; she's gone abroad, Sir; she's—dead two months ago, Sir.

Enter Gipsey.

Gip. How now, impudence! How dare you talk so saucily to the Doctor? Pray, Sir, don't take it ill; for the common people of England are not so civil to strangers, as——

Scrub. You lie, you lie! 'Tis the common people, such as you are, that are civilest to strangers.

Gip. Sirrah, I have a good mind to—Get you out, I say.

Scrub. I won't.

Gip. You won't, sauce-box. Pray, Doctor, what is the Captain's name that came to your inn last night?

Scrub. The Captain! Ah, the devil! There she hampers me again; the Captain has me on one side, and the priest on the other: so between the gown and sword I have a fine time on it. *[Going.*

Gip. What, sirrah, won't you march?

Scrub. No, my dear, I won't march: but I will walk: ——And I'll make bold to listen a little too.

[Goes behind the side-scene, and listens.

Gip. Indeed, Doctor, the Count has been babarously treated, that is the truth on it.

Foig. Ah, Mrs. Gipsey! upon my shoul, now gra, his complainings would mollify the marrow in your bones, and move the bowels of your commiseration; he weeps, and he dances, and he fistles, and he swears, and he laughs, and he stamps, and he sings; in conclusion, joy, he's afflicted, *à la François*, and a stranger would not know whider to cry or to laugh with him.

Gip. What wou'd you have me do, Doctor?

Foig. Noting, joy, but only hide the Count in Mrs. Sullen's closet, when it is dark.

Gip. Nothing! Is that nothing? It would be both a sin and a shame, Doctor.

Foig.

Foig. Here are twenty louidores, joy, for your shame; and I will give you an absolution for the shin.

Gip. But won't that money look like a bribe?

Foig. Dat is according as you shall tauk it. If you receive the money before-hand, 'twill be, logicè, a bribe; but if you stay till afterwards, 'twill be, only a gratification.

Gip. Well, Doctor, I'll take it logicè. But what must I do with my conscience, Sir?

Foig. Leave dat wid me, joy; I am your priest, gra; and your conscience is under my hands.

Gip. But should I put the count into the closet?

Foig. Vell, is dere any shin for a man's being in a closhet? One may go to prayers into a closhet.

Gip. But if the lady shou'd come into her chamber, and go to bed?

Foig. Vel, and is dere any shin in going to bed, joy?

Gip. Ay, but if the parties shou'd meet, Doctor?

Foig. Vel, den, the parties must be responsible. Do you begone, after putting the Count into the closet, and leave the shins wid themselves. I will come with the Count to instruct you in your chamber.

Gip. Well, Doctor, your religion is so pure; ' me- ' thinks I'm so easy after an absolution, and can sin afresh ' with so much security,' that I'm resolved to die a mar- tyr it to. Here's the key of the garden-door; come in the back way, when 'tis late; I'll be ready to receive you. But don't so much as whisper; only take hold of my hand; I'll lead you, and do you lead the Count, and follow me. [*Exeunt.*

Enter Scrub.

Scrub. What witchcraft now have these two imps of the devil been a hatching here? There's twenty lewi- dores; I heard that, and saw the purse: but I must give room to my betters.

Enter Mrs. Sullen *and* Archer.

Mrs. Sul. Pray, Sir, [*To* Archer.] How d'ye like that piece?

Arch. Oh! 'tis Leda. You find, Madam, how Jupi- ter came disguised to make love.

Mrs. Sul. Pray, Sir, what head is that in the corner there?

Arch.

Arch. Oh, Madam, 'tis poor Ovid in his exile.

Mrs. Sul. What was he banished for?

Arch. His ambitious love, Madam. [*Bowing.*] His misfortune touches me.

Mrs. Sul. Was he successful in his amours?

Arch. There he has left us in the dark. He was too much a gentleman to tell.

Mrs. Sul. If he were secret, I pity him.

Arch. If he were successful, I envy him.

Mrs. Sul. How d'ye like that Venus over the chimney?

Arch. Venus! I protest, Madam, I took it for your picture; but, now I look again, 'tis not handsome enough.

Mrs. Sul. Oh, what a charm is flattery! If you would see my picture, there it is, over the cabinet. How d'ye like it?

Arch. I must admire any thing, Madam, that has the least resemblance of you. But, methinks, Madam——— [*He looks at the picture and* Mrs. Sullen *three or four times by turns.*] Pray, Madam, who drew it?

Mrs. Sul. A famous hand, Sir.

[*Here* Aimwell *and* Dorinda *go off.*

Arch. A famous hand, Madam! Your eyes, indeed, are featured here; but where's the sparkling moisture, shining fluid, in which they swim? The picture, indeed, has your dimples; but where's the swarm of killing Cupids that should ambush there? The lips too are figured out; but where's the carnation dew, the pouting ripeness, that tempts the taste in the original?

Mrs. Sul. Had it been my lot to have matched with such a man! [*Aside.*

Arch. Your breasts too; presumptuous man! What! paint heaven! A-propos, Madam, in the very next picture is Salmonius, that was struck dead with lightning, for offering to imitate Jove's thunder; I hope you served the painter so, Madam.

Mrs. Sul. Had my eyes the power of thunder, they should employ their lightning better.

Arch. There's the finest bed in that room, Madam; I suppose 'tis your Ladyship's bed-chamber.

Mrs. Sul. And what then, Sir?

Arch. I think the quilt is the richest that I ever saw.
I can't,

I can't at this diftance, Madam, diftinguifh the figures of the embroidery, Will you give me leave, Madam ?

Mrs. Sul. The devil take his impudence---Sure, if I gave him an opportunity, he durft not be rude. I have a great mind to try.————[*Going, returns.*] 'Sdeath ! what am I doing !---And alone too !---Sifter, fifter !

Arch. I'll follow her clofe————
For where a Frenchman durft attempt to ftorm,
A Briton fure may well the work perform.   [*Going.*
Enter Scrub.

Scrub. Martin ! Brother Martin !

Arch. O brother Scrub, I beg your pardon, I was not a going : here's a guinea my mafter order'd you.

Scrub. A guinea ! hi, hi, hi, a guinea ! Eh————by this light it is a guinea ; but I fuppofe you expect twenty fhillings in change.

Arch. Not at all ; I have another for Gipfey.

Scrub. A guinea for her ! Fire and faggot for the witch ————Sir, give me that guinea ; and I'll difcover a plot.

Arch. A plot !

Scrub. Ay, Sir, a plot, a horrid plot—Firft, it muft be a plot, becaufe there's a woman in't : fecondly, it muft be a plot, becaufe there's a prieft in't : thirdly, it muft be a plot, becaufe there's French gold in't ; and fourthly, it muft be a plot becaufe I don't know what to make on't.

Arch. Nor any body elfe, I'm afraid, brother Scrub.

Scrub. Truly I'm afraid fo too ; for where there's a prieft and a woman, there's always a myftery, and a riddle. This I know, that here has been the doctor with a temptation in one hand, and an abfolution in the other, and Gipfey has fold herfelf to the devil : I faw the price paid down ; my eyes fhall take their oath on't.

Arch. And is all this buftle about Gipfey ?

Scrub. That's not all ; I could hear but a word here and there ; but I remember they mentioned a count, a clofet, a back-door, and a key.

Arch. The count ! did you hear nothing of Mrs. Sullen ?

Scrub. I did hear fome word that founded that way : but whether it was Sullen or Dorinda, I cou'd not diftinguifh.

Arch.

Arch. You have told this matter to nobody, brother?

Scrub. Told! No, Sir, I thank you for that; I'm re-solved never to speak one word, pro nor con, till we have a peace.

Arch. You're i' th' right, brother Scrub. Here's a trea-ty a-foot between the count and the lady.—The prieft and the chamber-maid are plenipotentiaries.—It ſhall go hard but I'll find a way to be include in the treaty. Where's the doctor now?

Scrub. He and Gipſey are this moment devouring my lady's marmalade in the cloſet.

Aim. [*From without.*] Martin, Martin!

Arch. I come, Sir, I come.

Scrub. But you forget the other guinea, brother Mar-tin.

Arch. Here, I give it with all my heart.

Scrub. And I take it with all my ſoul. [*Exeunt ſeve-rally.*] I cod, I'll ſpoil your plotting, Mrs. Gipſey: and if you ſhou'd ſet the captain on me, theſe two guineas wou'd buy me off.   [*Exit.*

Enter Mrs. Sullen *and* Dorinda, *meeting.*

Mrs. Sul. Well, ſiſter.

Dor. And well, ſiſter.

Mrs. Sul. What's become of my lord?

Dor. What's become of his ſervant?

Mrs. Sul. Servant! He's a prettier fellow, and a finer 'gentleman by fifty degrees, than his maſter.

Dor. O' my conſcience, I fancy you cou'd beg that fellow at the gallows' foot.

Mrs. Sul. O' my conſcience, I could, provided I could put a friend of yours in his room.

Dor. You defired me, ſiſter, to leave you, when you tranfgreſs'd the bounds of honour.

Mrs. Sul. Thou dear, cenforious country girl—what doſt mean? You can't think of the man without the bedfel-low, I find.

Dor. I don't find any thing unnatural in that thought; while the mind is converfant with fleſh and blood, it muſt conform to the humours of the company.

Mrs. Sul. How a little love and converſation improve a woman!

woman! Why, child, you begin to live.—You never spoke before.

Dor. Becaufe I was never fpcke to before; my lord has told me, that I have more wit and beauty than any of my fex; and truly I begin to think the man is fincere.

Mrs. Sul. You're in the right, Dorinda; pride is the life of a woman, and flattery is our daily bread.. But I'll lay you a guinea that I had finer things faid to me than you had.

Dor. Done.—What did your fellow fay to ye?

Mrs. Sul. My fellow took the picture of Venus for mine.

Dor. But my lover took me for Venus herfelf.

Mrs. Sul. Common cant! Had my fpark called me a Venus directly, I fhould have believed him to be a footman in good earneft.

Dor. But my lover was upon his knees to me.

Mrs. Sul. And mine was upon his tip-toes to me.

Dor. Mine vowed to die for me.

Mrs. Sul. Mine fwore to die with me.

Dor. Mine kifs'd my hand ten thoufand times.

Mrs. Sul. Mine has all that pleafure to come.

Dor. Mine fpoke the fofteft moving things.

Mrs. Sul. Mine had his moving things too.

Dor. Mine offered marriage.

Mrs. Sul. O Lard! D'ye call that a moving thing?

Dor. The fharpeft arrow in his quiver, my dear fifter: —Why, my twenty thoufand pounds may lie brooding here thefe feven years, and hatch nothing at laft but fome ill-natur'd clown like yours:—whereas, if I marry my Lord Aimwell, there will be title, place, and precedence, the park, the play, and the drawing-room, fplendor, equipage, noife and flambeaux—Hey, my Lady Aimwell's fervants there—Lights, lights to the ftairs—My Lady Aimwell's coach, put forward---Stand by; make room for her ladyfhip---Are not thefe things moving? What, melancholy of a fudden!

Mrs. Sul. Happy, happy, fifter! Your angel has been watchful for your happinefs, whilft mine has flept, regardlefs of his charge--- Long fmiling years of circling joys for you; but not one hour for me!   [*Weeps.*

* E

Dor.

Dor. Come, my dear, we'll talk on something else.

Mrs. Sul. O Dorinda, I own myself a woman, full of my sex, a gentle, generous soul,---' easy and yielding ' to soft desires ; a spacious heart, where Love and all his ' train might lodge :' and must the fair apartment of my breast be made a stable for a brute to lie in !

Dor. Meaning your husband, I suppose.

Mrs. Sul. Husband ! No---Even husband is too soft a name for him---But come, I expect my brother here to-night or to-morrow : he was abroad when my father marry'd me ; perhaps he'll find a way to make me easy.

Dor. Will you promise not to make yourself easy in the mean time with my lord's friend ?

Mrs. Sul. You mistake me, sister—It happens with us as among the men, the greatest talkers are the greatest cowards : and there's a reason for it ; those spirits evaporate in prattle, which might do more mischief if they took another course---Though, to confess the truth, I do love that fellow ;——and if I met him drest as he shou'd be, and I undrest as I shou'd be——Look'e sister, I have no supernatural gifts ;——I can't swear I cou'd resist the temptation——though I can safely promise to avoid it : and that's as much as the best of us can do.

[Exeunt.

Enter Aimwell and Archer laughing.

Arch. And the awkward kindness of the good motherly old gentlewoman,——

Aim. And the coming easiness of the young one.—'Sdeath, 'tis a pity to deceive her.

Arch. Nay, if you adhere to those principles, stop where you are.

Aim. I can't stop, for I love her to distraction.

Arch. 'Sdeath, if you love her a hair's breadth beyond discretion, you must go no farther.

Aim. Well, well, any thing to deliver us from sauntering away our idle evenings at White's, Tom's, or Will's ' and be stinted to bare looking at our old acquaintance, ' the cards, because our impotent pockets can't afford us ' a guinea for the mercenary drabs ; and ten thousand ' such rascally tricks——had we outliv'd our fortunes ' among our acquaintance.'——But now---

2

Arch.

Arch. Aye, now is the time to prevent all this.---
Strike while the iron is hot.---This priest is the luckiest
part of our adventure; he shall marry you, and pimp
for me.

' *Aim.* But I should not like a woman that can be so
' fond of a Frenchman.

' *Arch.* Alas, Sir! necessity has no law; the lady may
' be in distress.' But if the plot lies as I suspect---I must
put on the gentleman.——But here comes the doctor.   I
shall be ready.   [*Exit.*

Enter Foigard.

Foig. Save you, noble friend.

Aim. O Sir, your servant.   Pray, doctor, may I crave
your name?

Foig. Fat naam is upon me? My name is Foigard,
joy.

Aim. Foigard! a very good name for a clergyman.
Pray, doctor Foigard, were you ever in Ireland?

Foig. Ireland! no, joy. Fat sort of plaace is dat saam
Ireland? Dey say, de people are catch'd dere when dey
are young.

Aim. And some of 'em here, when they are old——
as for example---[*Takes* Foigard *by the shoulder.*] Sir I ar-
rest you as a traitor against the government; you're a subject of England, and this morning shewed me a commission, by which you served as chaplain in the French army.
This is death by our law, and your reverence must hang
for it.

Foig. Upon my shoul, noble friend, dis is strange news
you tell me; fader Foigard a subject of England! the
son of a burgomaster of Brussels a subject of England!
Ubooboo.——

Aim. The son of a bog-trottor in Ireland! Sir, your
tongue will condemn you before any bench in the kingdom.

Foig. And is my tongue all your evidensh, joy?

Aim. That's enough.

Foig. No, no, joy, for I will never speak English no
more.

Aim. Sir, I have other evidence.——Here, Martin,
you know this fellow.

Enter

Enter Archer.

Arch. [*In a brogue.*] Saave you, my dear cuffen, how does your health?

Foig. Ah! upon my fhoul, dere is my countryman, and his brogue will hang mine. [*Afide.*] Mynhere, Ick wit neat watt hey zackt, Ick Univerfton ewe neat, facrament.

Aim. Altering your language won't do, Sir; this fellow knows your perfon, and will fwear to your face.

Foig. Faafh! Fey, is dere brogue upon my faafh too?

Arch. Upon my foulvation dere is, joy——But, cuffen Mackfhane, vill you not put a remembrance upon me?

Foig. Mackfhane! by St. Patrick, dat is my naame fhure enough, [*Afide.*

Aim. I fancy, Archer, you have it.

Foig. The devil hang you, joy————By fat acquaintance are you my cuffen?

Arch. O, the devil hang yourfelf, joy; you know we were little boys togeder upon de fchool, and your fofter-moder's fon was matry'd upon my nurfe's fhifter, joy, and fo we are Irifh cuffens.

Foig. De devil take de relation! Vel, joy, and fat-fchool was it?

Arch. I think it vas---Aay---'twas Tipperary.

Foig. Now, upon my fhoul, joy, it was Kilkenny.

Arch. That's enough for us---Self confeffion———— Come, Sir, we muft deliver you into the hands of the next magiftrate.

Aim. He fends you to gaol, you're try'd next affizes, and away you go fwing into purgatory.

Foig. And is it fo wid you, cuffen?

Arch. It vill be fo vid you, cuffen; if you don't immediately confefs the fecret between you and Mrs. Gipfey————Look'e, Sir, the gallows or the fecret, take your choice.

Foig. The gallows! Upon my fhoul I hate that fhame gallows, for it is a difeafhe dat is fatal to our family—— Vel, den, there is noting, fhentlemens, but Mrs. Sullen wou'd fpeak wid de count in her chamber at midnight, and dere is no harm, joy, for I am to conduct the count to de plaafh myfelf.

Arch.

Arch. As I guefs'd——Have you communicated the matter to the count.

Foig. I have not fheen him fince.

Arch. Right agen; why then, doctor—you fhall conduct me to the lady inftead of the count.

Foig. Fat, my cufhen to the lady! Upon my fhoul, gra, dat's too much upon the brogue.

Arch. Come, come, doctor, confider we have got a rope about your neck, and if you offer to fpeak, we'll ftop your wind-pipe, moft certainly; we fhall have another job for you in a day or two, I hope.

Aim. Here's company coming this way; let's into my chamber, and there concert our affairs farther.

Arch. Come, my dear cuffen, come along.　　[*Exeunt.*

Foig. Arra, the devil take our relafhion.

Enter Boniface, Hounflow, *and* Bagfhot *at one door;* Gibbet *at the oppofite.*

Gib. Well, gentlemen, 'tis a fine night for our enterprize.

Hounf. Dark as hell.

Bag. And blows like the devil; our landlord here has fhew'd us the window where we muft break in, and tells us the plate ftands in the wainfcot cupboard in the parlour.

Bon. Ay, ay, Mr. Bagfhot, as the faying is, knives and forks, cups and cans, tumblers and tankards——There's one tankard, as the faying is, that's near upon as big as me; it was a prefent to the 'fquire from his godmother, and fmells of nutmeg and toaft like an Eaft-Inia fhip.

Hounf. Then you fay we muft divide at the ftair head.

Bon. Yes, Mr. Hounflow, as the faying is——At one end of the gallery lies my Lady Bonntiful and her daughter; and, at the other, Mrs. Sullen—As for the 'fquire—

Gib. He's fafe enough, I have fairly enter'd him, and he's more than half feas over already———But fuch a parcel of fcoundrels aregot about him there, that, 'e-gad, I was afhamed to be feen in their company.

Bon. 'Tis now twelve, as the faying is—Gentlemen, you muft fet out at one.

Gib. Hounflow, do you and Bagfhot fee our arms fix'd, and I'll come to you prefently.

E 3

Hounf.

Houns. and *Bag.* We will.   [*Exeunt.*

Gib. Well, my dear Bonny, you affure me that Scrub is a coward.

Bon. A chicken, as the faying is. You'll have no creature to deal with but the ladies.

Gib. And I can affure you, friend, there's a great deal of addrefs and good-manners in robbing a lady; I am the moft a gentleman that way that ever travelled the road—But, my dear Bonny, this prize will be a galleon, a Vigo bufinefs. I warrant you we fhall bring off three or four thoufand pound.

Bon. In plate, jewels, and money, as the faying is, you may.

Gib. Why then, Tyburn, I defy thee; I'll get up to town, fell off my horfe and arms, buy myfelf fome pretty employment in the law, and be as fnug and as honeft as e'er a long gown of them all.

Bon. And what think you then of my daughter Cherry for a wife?

Gib. Look'e, my dear Bonny: Cherry is the goddefs I adore, as the fong goes; but it is a maxim, that man and wife fhould never have it in their power to hang one another; for if they fhou'd, the Lord have mercy upon them both.   [*Exeunt.*

END of the FOURTH ACT.

A C T V.

SCENE *continues. Knocking without.*

Enter Boniface.

BONIFACE.

COMING, coming. A coach and fix foaming horfes at this time o'night! Some great man, as the faying is, for he fcorns to travel with other people.

Enter Sir Charles Freeman.

Sir Ch. What, fellow! a public houfe, and a-bed when other people fleep!

Bon. I an't a-bed, as the faying is.

Sir Ch. I fee that, as the faying is! Is Mr. Sullen's family a-bed, think'e?

Bon.

Bon. All but the 'squire himself, Sir, as the saying is; he's in the house.

Sir Ch. What company has he?

Bon. Why, Sir, there's the conftable, Mr. Gage the exciseman, the hunch-back'd barber, and two or three other gentlemen.

Sir Ch. I find my fister's letters gave me the true picture of her spouse.

Enter Sullen, *drunk.*

Bon. Sir, here's the 'squire.

Sul. The puppies left me asleep——Sir.

Sir. Ch. Well, Sir.

Sul. Sir, I am an unfortunate man—I have three thousand pounds a year, and I can't get a man to drink a cup of ale with me.

Sir Ch. That's very hard.

Sul. Ay, Sir—And unless you have pity upon me, and smoke one pipe with me, I must e'en go home to my wife, and I had rather go to the devil by half.

Sir Ch. But I presume, Sir, you won't see your wife to-night, she'll be gone to bed——you don't use to lie with your wife in that pickle?

Sul. What! Not lie with my wife! Why, Sir, do you take me for an athiest or a rake?

Sir Ch. If you hate her, Sir, I think you had better lie from her.

Sul. I think so too, friend. But I am a Justice of the peace, and must do nothing against the law.

Sir Ch. Law! As I take it, Mr. Justice, nobody observes law for law's sake, only for the good of those for whom it was made.

Sul. But if the law orders me to send you to gaol, you must lie there, my friend.

Sir Ch. Not unless I commit a crime to deserve it.

Sul. A crime! Oons, an't I marry'd?

Sir Ch. Nay, Sir, if you call marriage a crime, you must disown it for a law.

Sul. Eh!—I must be acquainted with you Sir. But, Sir, I should be very glad to know the truth of this matter.

Sir Ch. Truth, Sir, is a profound sea, and few there
be

be that dare wade deep enough to find the bottom on't. Befides, Sir, I am afraid the line of your underftanding may not be long enough.

Sul. Look'e, Sir, I have nothing to fay to your fea of truth, but if a good parcel of land can entitle a man to a little truth, I have as much as any he in the county.

Bon. I never heard your worfhip, as the faying is, talk fo much before.

Sul. Becaufe I never met with a man that I lik'd before.

Bon. Pray, Sir, as the faying is, let me afk you one queftion : are not man and wife one flefh ?

Sir Cb. You and your wife, Mr. Guts, may be one flefh, becaufe you are nothing elfe—But rational crea- tures have minds that muft be united.

Sul. Minds !

Sir Cb. Ay, minds, Sir. Don't you think that the mind takes place of the body ?

Sul. In fome people.

Sir Cb. Then the intereft of the mafter muft be con- fulted before that of the fervant.

Sul. Sir, you fhall dine with me to-morrow——Oons, I always thought that we were naturally one.

Sir Cb. Sir, I know that my two hands are naturally one, becaufe they love one another, ' kifs one ano- ther,' help one another in all actions of life ; but I cou'd not fay fo much if they were always at cuffs.

Sul. Then 'tis plain that we are two.

Sir Cb. Why don't you part with her, Sir ?

Sul. Will you take her, Sir ?

Sir Cb. With all my heart.

Sul. You fhall have her to-morrow morning, and a venifon pafty into the bargain,

Sir Cb. You'll let me have her fortune too ?

Sul. Fortune ! Why, Sir, I have no quarrel to her fortune——I hate only the woman, Sir, and none but the woman fhall go.

Sir Cb. But her fortune, Sir————

Sul. Can you play at whift, Sir ?

Sir Cb. No, truly, Sir.

Sul. Nor at all-fours ?

Sir Cb.

Sir Ch. Neither.

Sul. Oons! Where was this man bred. [*Aside.*] Burn me, Sir, I can't go home, 'tis but two o'clock.

Sir Ch. For half an hour, Sir, if you please—But you must consider it is late.

Sul. Late! That's the reason I can't go to bed—Come, Sir——— [*Exeunt.*

Enter Cherry, *runs across the stage, and knocks at Aim-well's chamber-door. Enter Aimwell, in his night-cap and gown.*

Aim. What's the matter? You tremble, child; you are frighted!

Cher. No wonder, Sir—But in short, Sir, this very minute a gang of rogues are gone to rob my Lady Bountiful's house.

Aim. How!

Cher. I dogg'd them to the very door, and left 'em breaking in.

Aim. Have you alarm'd any body else with the news?

Cher. No, no, Sir; I wanted to have discover'd the whole plot, and twenty other things, to your man Martin; but I have search'd the whole house, and can't find him: where is he?

Aim. No matter, child; will you guide me immediately to the house?

Cher. With all my heart, Sir; my Lady Bountiful is my godmother, and I love Mrs. Dorinda so well——

Aim. Dorinda! The name inspires me; the glory and the danger shall be all my own. Come, my life, let me but get my sword. [*Exeunt.*

SCENE *changes to the bed-chamber in Lady* Bountiful's *house.*

Enter Mrs. Sullen *and* Dorinda, *undress'd; a table and lights.*

Dor. 'Tis very late, sister; no news of your spouse yet?

Mrs. Sul. No, I am condemn'd to be alone till towards

wards four, and then, perhaps, I may be executed with his company.

Dor. Well, my dear, I'll leave you to your rest; you will go directly to bed, I suppose.

Mrs. Sul. I don't know what to do; heigh-ho!

Dor. That's a defiring figh, fifter.

Mrs. Sul. This is a languifhing hour, fifter.

Dor. And might prove a critical minute, if the pretty fellow were here.

Mrs. Sul. Here! What, in my bed-chamber, at two o'clock in the morning, I undrefs'd, the family afleep, my hated hufband abroad, and my lovely fellow at my feet. O gad, fifter.

Dor. Thoughts are free, fifter, and them I allow you. So, my dear, good night.   [*Exit.*

Mrs. Sul. A good reft to my dear Dorinda. Thoughts are free! Are they fo? Why then, fuppofe him here, drefs'd like a youthful, gay, and burning bridegroom, [*Here* Archer *fteals out of the clofet.*] with tongue enchanting, eyes bewitching, knees imploring. [*Turns a little on one fidt, and fees* Archer *in the pofture fhe defcribes.*] Ah! [*Shrieks, and runs to the other fide of the Stage.*] Have my thoughts rais'd a fpirit? What are you, Sir, a man or a devil?

Arch. A man, a man! Madam.   [*Rifing.*

Mrs. Sul. How fhall I be fure of it?

Arch. Madam, I'll give you demonftration this minute.   [*Takes her hand.*

Mrs. Sul. What, Sir! Do you intend to be rude?

Arch. Yes, Madam, if you pleafe.

Mrs. Sul. In the name of wonder, whence came you?

Arch. From the fkies, Madam—I am a Jupiter in love, and you fhall be my Alcmena.

Mrs. Sul. How came you in?

Arch. I flew in at the window, Madam; your coufin Cupid lent me his wings, and your fifter Venus open'd the cafement.

Mrs. Sul. I'm ftruck dumb with admiration.

Arch. And I with wonder. [*Looks paffionately at her.*] How beautiful fhe looks!——The teeming jolly fpring fmiles in her blooming face, and when fhe was conceiv'd her mother fmelt to rofes, look'd on lilies——

Lilies

Lilies unfold their white, their fragrant charms,
When the warm sun thus darts into their arms.
[*Runs to her.*

Mrs. Sul. Ah! [*Shricks.*]

Arch. Oons, Madam, what do you mean? You will raise the house.

Mrs. Sul. Sir, I'll wake the dead before I will bear this.——What! Approach me with the freedom of a keeper. I am glad on it. Your impudence has cur'd me.

Arch. If this be impudence, [*Kneels.*] I leave to your partial self; no panting pilgrim, after a tedious, painful voyage, ever bow'd before his faint with more devotion.

Mrs. Sul. Now, now, I am ruin'd, if he kneels. [*Afide.*] Rife, thou proftrate engineer, not all thy undermining kill fhall reach my heart. Rife, and know I am a woman without my fex; I can love to all the tender-nefs of wifhes, fighs and tears. But go no farther: Still to convince you that I am more than woman, I can fpeak my frailty, confefs my weaknefs, even for you. But——

Arch. For me! [*Going to lay hold on her.*

Mrs. Sul. Hold, Sir, build not upon that——for my moft mortal hatred follows, if you difobey what I command you now—Leave me this minute. If he denies, I am loft. [*Afide.*

Arch. Then you will promife——

Mrs Sul. Any thing another time.

Arch. When fhall I come?

Mrs. Sul. To-morrow; when you will.

Arch. Your lips muft feal the promife.

Mrs. Sul. Pfhaw!

Arch. They muft, they muft. [*Kiffes her.*] Raptures and Paradife! And why not now, my angel? The time, the place, filence and fecrefy all confpire. And now the confcious ftars have pre-ordained this moment for my happinefs. [*Takes her in his arms.*

Mrs. Sul. You will not, cannot, fure.

Arch. If the fun rides faft, and difappoints not mortals

tals of to-morrow's dawn, this night shall crown my joys.

Mrs. Sul. You shall kill me first.

Arch. I will die with you. [*Carrying her off.*

Mrs. Sul. Thieves, thieves, murder——

Enter Scrub, *in his breeches, and one shoe.*

Scrub. Thieves, thieves, murder, popery!

Arch. Ha! The very timorous stag will kill in rutting time. [*Draws and offers to stab* Scrub.

Scrub. [*Kneeling.*] O pray, Sir, spare all I have, and take my life.

Mrs. Sul. [*Holding* Archer's *hand.*] What does the fellow mean?

Scrub. O Madam, down upon your knees, your marrow-bones——He's one of them.

Mrs. Sul. Of whom?

Scrub. One of the rogues——I beg your pardon, one of the honest gentlemen that just now are broke into the house.

Arch. How!

Mrs. Sul. I hope you did not come to rob me?

Arch. Indeed I did, Madam; but I would have taken nothing but what you might very well have spared; but your crying thieves has waked this dreaming fool, and so he takes them for granted.

Scrub. Granted! 'Tis granted, Sir; take all we have.

Mrs. Sul. The fellow looks as if be were broke out of Bedlam.

Scrub. Oons, Madam, they are broke into the house with fire and sword; I saw them, heard them, they'll be here this minute.

Arch. What thieves?

Scrub. Under favour, Sir, I think so.

Mrs. Sul. What shall we do, Sir?

Arch. Madam, I wish your ladyship a good night.

Mrs. Sul. Will you leave me?

Arch. Leave you! Lord, Madam, did you not command me to be gone just now, upon pain of your immortal hatred?

Mrs. Sul. Nay, but pray, Sir—— [*Takes hold of him.*

Arch. Ha, ha, ha, now comes my turn to be ravish'd

You

You fee, Madam, you muſt uſe men one way or other; but take this by the way, good Madam, that none but a fool will give you the benefit of his courage, unleſs you will take his love along with it. How are they arm'd, friend?

Scrub. With ſword and piſtol, Sir.

Arch. Huſh! I ſee a dark lanthorn coming through the gallery. Madam, be aſſured I will protect you, or loſe my life.

Mrs. Sul. Your life! No, Sir, they can rob me of nothing that I value half ſo much; therefore, now, Sir, let me intreat you to be gone.

Arch. No, Madam, I will conſult my own ſafety for the ſake of yours; I'll work by ſtratagem. Have you courage enough to ſtand the appearance of them?

Mrs. Sul. Yes, yes, ſince I have eſcaped your hands I can face any thing.

Arch. Come hither, brother Scrub; don't you know me?

Scrub. Eh! My dear brother, let me kiſs thee.
[Kiſſes Archer.

Arch. This way——Here——
[Àrcher and Scrub hide behind the bed.

Eater Gibbet, *with a dark-lanthorn in one hand, and a piſtol in the other.*

Gib. Ay, ay, this is the chamber, and the lady alone.

Mrs. Sul. Who are you, Sir? What would you have? D'ye come to rob me?

Gib. Rob you! Alack-a-day, Madam, I am only a younger brother, Madam; and ſo, Madam, if you make a noiſe, I will ſhoot you through the head. But don't be afraid, Madam. [*Laying his lanthorn and piſtol upon the table.*] Theſe rings, Madam; don't be concerned, Madam; I have a profound reſpect for you, Madam; your keys, Madam; don't be frighted, Madam, I am the moſt of a gentleman——[*Searching her pockets.*] This necklace, Madam; I never was rude to any lady! I have a veneration—for this necklace——
[*Here Archer having come round, and ſeized the piſtol, takes Gibbet by the collar, trips up his heels, and claps the piſtol to his breaſt.*

*   F
Arch.

Arch. Hold, profane villain, and take the reward of thy facrilege.

Gib. Oh! pray, Sir, don't kill me I a'n't prepared.

Arch. How many are there of 'em, Scrub?

Scrub. Five and forty, Sir.

Arch. Then I muft kill the villain, to have him out of the way.

Gib. Hold, hold, Sir! we are but three, upon my honour.

Arch. Scrub, will you undertake to fecure him?

Scrub. Not I, Sir; kill him, kill him.

Arch. Run to Gipfey's chamber, there you'll find the doctor; bring him hither prefently.

[*Exit* Scrub *running.*

Come, rogue, if you have a fhort prayer, fay it.

Gib. Sir, I have no prayer at all; the government has provided a chaplain to fay prayers for us on thefe occafions.

Mrs. Sul. Pray, Sir, don't kill him——you fright me as much as him.

Arch. The dog fhall die, Madam, for being the oc-cafion of my difappointment—Sirrah, this moment is your laft.

Gib. Sir, I'll give you two hundred pounds to fpare my life.

Arch. Have you no more, rafcal?

Gib. Yes, Sir, I can command four hundred; but I muft referve two of 'em, to fave my life at the feffions.

Enter Scrub *and* Foigard.

Arch. Here, doctor; I fuppofe Scrub and you, be-tween you, may manage him—Lay hold on him.

[Foigard *lays hold of* Gibbet.

Gib. What! turn'd over to the prieft already—— Look'e, doctor, you come before your time; I a'n't con-demn'd yet, I thank ye.

Foig. Come, my dear joy, I vil fecure your body and your fhoul too; I vil make you a good catholic, and give you an abfolution.

Gib. Abfolution! Can you procure me a pardon, doc-tor?

Foig. No, joy——

Gib. Then you and your abfolution may go to the de-vil.

Arch.

Arch. Convey him into the cellar; there bind him:——take the piftol, and if he offers to refift, fhoot him thro' the head—and come back to us with all the fpeed you can.

Scrub. Ay, ay; come, doctor, do you hold him faft, and I'll guard him.   [*Exeunt.*

Mrs. Sul. But how came the doctor here?

Arch. In fhort, Madam——[*Shrieking without.*]—'Sdeath; the rogues are at work with the other ladies;---' I'm vex'd I parted with the piftol;' but I muft fly to their affiftance—Will you ftay here, Madam, or venture yourfelf with me?

Mrs. Sul. Oh, dear Sir, with you.
                 [*Takes him by the arm and exeunt.*

SCENE *changes to another apartment in the houfe.*

Enter Hounflow *dragging in Lady* Bountiful, *and* Bagfhot *hauling in* Dorinda; *the rogues with fwords drawn.*

Houn. Come, come, your jewels, miftrefs.

Bag. Your keys, your keys, old gentlewoman.
                 Enter Aimwell.

Aim. Turn this way, villains! I durft engage an army in fuch a caufe.   [*He engages them both.*

Enter Archer *and Mrs.* Sullen.

Arch. Hold, hold, my lord; every man his bird, pray.   [*They engage man to man: the rogues
                 are thrown down and difarmed.*

Arch. Shall we kill the rogues?

Aim. No, no, we'll bind them.

Arch. Ay, ay; here, Madam, lend me your garter.
                 [*To Mrs.* Sullen, *who ftands by him.*

Mrs. Sul. The devil's in this fellow; he fights, loves and banters, all in a breath. Here's a cord, that the rogues brought with them, I fuppofe.

Arch. Right, right, the rogue's deftiny, a rope to hang himfelf—Come, my lord---this is but a fcandalous fort of an office. [*Binding the rogues together.*] If our adventures fhould end in this fort of hangman work; but I hope there is fomething in profpect that—

                         Enter

Enter Scrub.

Well, Scrub, have you secured your Tartar?

Scrub. Yes, Sir, I left the priest and him disputing about religion.

Aim. And pray carry these gentlemen to reap the benefit of the controversy.

                [Delivers the prisoners to Scrub, *who leads them out.*

Mrs. Sul. Pray, sister, how came my lord here?

Dor. And pray, how came the gentleman here?

Mrs. Sul. I'll tell you the greatest piece of villainy.

                              [They talk apart.

Aim. I fancy, Archer, you have been more successful in your adventures than the house-breakers.

Arch. No matter for my adventure, yours is the principal---Press her this minute to marry you---now while she's hurried between the palpitation of her fear and the joy of her deliverance; now while the tide of her spirits is at high flood---throw yourself at her feet, speak some romantic nonsense or other---confound her senses, bear down her reason, and away with her---The priest is now in the cellar, and dares not refuse to do the work.

Aim. But how shall I get off without being observed?

Arch. You a lover! and not find a way to get off.— Let me see.

Aim. You bleed, Archer.

Arch. 'Sdeath, I'm glad on't; this wound will do the business. I'll amuse the old lady and Mrs. Sullen about dressing my wound, while you carry off Dorinda.

              Enter Lady Bountiful.

L. Boun. Gentlemen, could we understand how you would be gratified for the services ———

Arch. Come, come, my lady, this is no time for compliments; I'm wounded, Madam.

L. Boun. and Mrs. Sul. How, wounded!

Dor. I hope, Sir, you have received no hurt!

Aim. None but what you may cure---

                        [Makes love in dumb shew.

L. Boun. Let me see your arm, Sir—I must have some powder-sugar to stop the blood---O me! an ugly gash; upon my word, Sir, you must go to bed.

Arch. Ay, my lady, a bed would do very well---Madam,

                                    [To

[*To Mrs.* Sullen.] will you do me the favour to conduct me
o a chamber ?

L. Boun. Do, do, daughter---while I get the lint, and
the probs, and the plaifter ready.

[*Runs out one way,* Aim. *carries off* Dor. *another.*

Arch. Come, Madam, why don't you obey your mother's commands ?

Mrs. Sul. How can you, after what i thes paft, have
confidence to afk me ?

Arch. And, if you go to that, how can you, after
what is paft, have the confidence to deny me ?---Was not
this blood fhed in your defence, and my life expofed for
your protection ? Look'e, Madam, I'm none of your romantic fools, that fight giants and monfters for nothing ;
my valour is downright Swifs, I am a foldier of fortune,
and muft be paid.

Mrs. Sul. 'Tis ungenerous in you, Sir, to upbraid me
with your fervices.

Arch. 'Tis ungenerous in you, Madam, not to reward
'em.

Mrs. Sul. How ! at the expence of my honour ?

Arch. Honour ! Can honour confift with ingratitude ?
If you would deal like a woman of honour, do like a man
of honour. D'ye think I would deny you in fuch a cafe ?

Enter Gipfey.

Gip. Madam, my lady ordered me to tell you, that
your brother is below, at the gate.

Mrs. Sul. My brother ! Heavens be prais'd !---Sir, he
fhall thank you for your fervices, he has it in his power.

Arch. Who is your brother, Madam ?

Mrs. Sul. Sir Charles Freeman. You'll excufe me,
Sir, I muft go and receive him.

Arch. Sir Charles Freeman ! 'Sdeath and hell !---
my old acquaintance. Now, unlefs Aimwell has made
good ufe of his time, all our fair machine goes foufe into
the fea, like the Ediftone.   [*Exit.*

SCENE *changes to a gallery in the fame houfe.*

Enter Aimwell *and* Dorinda.

Dor. Well, well, my lord, you have conquered.
Your late generous action, will, I hope, plead for my

eafy

eafy yielding; though, I muſt own, your lordſhip had a friend in the fort before.

Aim. The ſweets of Hybla dwell upon her tongue.——Here, doctor————

Enter Foigard *with a book.*

Foig. Are you prepared, bote?

Dor. I'm ready: but firſt, my lord, one word—I have a frightful example of a haſty marriage in my own family; when I reflect upon't, it ſhocks me. Pray, my lord, conſider a little————————

Aim. Conſider! Do you doubt my honour, or my love?

Dor. Neither. I do believe you equally juſt as brave—And were your whole ſex drawn out for me to chuſe, I ſhou'd not caſt a look upon the multitude, if you were abſent—But, my lord, I'm a woman: colours, concealments, may hide a thouſand faults in me: therefore know me better firſt; I hardly dare affirm I know myſelf in any thing, except my love.

Aim. Such goodneſs who cou'd injure? I find myſelf unequal to the taſk of villain. She has gain'd my ſoul, and made it honeſt like her own---I cannot hurt her. [*Aſide.*] Doctor, retire. [*Exit* Foigard.] Madam, behold your lover and your proſelyte, and judge of my paſſion by my converſion.--I'm all a lie, nor dare I give a fiction to your arms; I'm all a counterfeit, except my paſſion.

Dor. Forbid it, heaven! A counterfeit!

Aim. I am no lord, but a poor needy man, come with a mean and ſcandalous deſign, to prey upon your fortune:————but the beauties of your mind and perſon have ſo won me from myſelf, that, like a truſty ſervant, I prefer the intereſt of my miſtreſs to my own.

' *Dor.* Sure I have had the dream of ſome poor ma-' riner; a ſleeping image of a welcome port, and wake in-' volv'd in ſtorms.'---Pray, Sir, who are you?

Aim. Brother to the man whoſe title I uſurped, but ſtranger to his honour or his fortune.

Dor. Matchleſs honeſty!---Once I was proud, Sir, of your wealth and title, but now am prouder you want it. Now I can ſhew my love was juſtly levelled, and had no aim but love. Doctor, come in.

Enter

Enter Foigard *at one door,* Gipfey *at another, who whifpers* Dorinda.

Dor. Your pardon, Sir ; we fha'n't want you now, Sir. You muft excufe me----I'll wait on you prefently.

[*Exit with* Gipfey.

Foig. Upon my fhoul, now dis is foolifh. [*Exit.*

Aim. Gone ! and bid the prieft depart—It has an ominous look.

Enter Archer.

Arch. Courage, Tom---Shall I wifh you joy ?

Aim. No.

Arch. Oons ! man, what ha' you been doing ?

Aim. O, Archer, my honefty, I fear, has ruined me.

Arch. How !

Aim. I have difcovered myfelf.

Arch. Difcovered ! and without my confent ? What ! Have I embark'd my fmall remains in the fame bottom with yours, and you difpofe of all without my partnerfhip ?

Aim. O, Archer, I own my fault,

Arch. After conviction---'Tis then too late for pardon ——You may remember, Mr. Aimwell, that you propofed this folly—As you begun, fo end it—Henceforth I'll hunt my fortune fingle-----So farewel.

Aim. Stay, my dear Archer, but a minute.

Arch. Stay ! What, to be defpis'd, expos'd, and laughed at !---No, I would fooner change conditions with the worft of the rogues we juft now bound, than bear one fcornful fmile from the proud knight that once I treated as my equal.

Aim. What knight ?

Arch. Sir Charles Freeman, brother to the lady that I had almoft——But no matter for that ; 'tis a curfed night's work, and fo I leave you to make the beft on't.

Aim. Freeman !——One word, Archer. Still I have hopes ; methought fhe received my confeffion with pleafure.

Arch. 'Sdeath, who doubts it ?

Aim. She confented after to the match ; and ftill I dare believe fhe will be juft.

Arch. To herfelf, I warrant her, as you fhou'd have been.

Aim.

Aim. By all my hopes she comes, and smiling comes.

Enter Dorinda, *mighty gay.*

Dor. Come, my dear lord—I fly with impatience to your arms——The minutes of my abfence were a tedious year. Where's this prieſt?

Enter Foigard.

Arch. Oons, a brave girl!

Dor. I ſuppoſe, my lord, this gentleman is privy to our affairs?

Arch. Yes, yes, Madam, I'm to be your father.

Dor. Come, prieſt, do your office.

Arch. Make haſte, make haſte, couple 'em any way. [*Takes* Aimwell's *hand.*] Come, Madam, I'm to give you —— ——

Dor. My mind's alter'd: I won't.

Arch. Eh ——— —

Aim. I'm confounded.

Foig. Upon my ſhoul, and ſo is my ſhelf.

Arch. What's the matter now, Madam?

Dor. Look'e, Sir, one generous action deſerves another. ——This gentleman's honour obliged him to hide nothing from me; my juſtice engages me to conceal nothing from him; in ſhort, Sir, you are the perſon that you thought you counterfeited; you are the true Lord Viſcount Aimwell, and I wiſh your lordſhip joy. Now, prieſt, you may begone; if my lord is now pleas'd with the match, let his lordſhip marry me in the face of the world.

Aim. Archer, what does ſhe mean?

Dor. Here's a witneſs for my truth.

Enter Sir Charles *and Mrs.* Sullen.

Sir Ch. My dear lord Aimwell, I wiſh you joy.

Aim. Of what?

Sir Ch. Of your honour and eſtate. Your brother died the day before I left London; and all your friends have writ after you to Bruſſels; among the reſt I did myſelf the honour,

Arch. Heark'e, Sir knight, don't you banter now?

Sir Ch. 'Tis truth, upon my honour.

Aim. Thanks to the pregnant ſtars that formed th is accident.

Arch. Thanks to the womb of time that brought it forth; away with it.

Aim.

Aim. Thanks to my guardian angel that led me to the prize————   [*Taking* Dorinda's *hand.*

Arch. And double thanks to the noble Sir Charles Freeman. My lord, I wish you joy. My lady, I wish you joy. 'Egad, Sir Freeman, you are the honestest fellow living. 'Sdeath, I am grown strangely airy upon this matter. My lord, how d'ye ?—A word, my lord. Don't you remember something of a previous agreement that intitles me to the moiety of this lady's fortune, which, I think, will amount to ten thousand pounds ?

Aim. Not a penny, Archer. You wou'd have cut my throat just now, because I wou'd not deceive this lady.

Arch. Ay, and I will cut your throat still, if you shou'd deceive her now.

Aim. That is what I expect; and to end the dispute, the lady's fortune is twenty thousand pounds ; we will divide stakes ; take the twenty thousand pounds, or the lady.

Dor. How ! Is your lordship so indifferent ?

Arch. No, no, no, Madam, his lordship knows very well that I will take the money ; I leave you to his lordship, and so we are both provided for.

Enter Foigard.

Foig. Arra fait, de people do say you be all robb'd, joy.

Aim. The ladies have been in some danger, Sir, as you saw.

Foig. Upon my shoul our inn be rob too.

Aim. Our inn ! By whom ?

Foig. Upon my shalvation, our landlord has robbed himself, and run away wid de money.

Arch. Robbed himself !

Foig. Ay fait ! And me too of a hundred pounds.

Arch. Robbed you of a hundred pounds !

Foig. Yes, fait honey, that I did owe to him.

Aim. Our money's gone, Frank.

Arch. Rot the money, my wench is gone——*Sçavez vous quelque chose de Mademoiselle* Cherry ?

Enter

Enter a Fellow with a strong box and letter.

Fell. Is there one Martin here?

Arch. Ay, ay,—who wants him?

Fell. I have a box here and a letter for him.

Arch. [*Taking the box.*] Ha, ha, ha, what's here? Legerdemain! By this light, my lord, our money again. But this unfolds the riddle. [*Opening the letter, reads.*] Hum, hum, hum——O, 'tis for the public good, and must be communicated to the company.

" Mr. Martin,

" My father, being afraid of an impeachment by the rogues that are taken to-night, is gone off; but if you can procure him a pardon, he will make great discoveries that may be useful to the country. Could I have met you instead of your master to-night, I would have delivered myself into your hands, with a sum that much exceeds that in your strong box, which I have sent you, with an assurance to my dear Martin, that I shall ever be his most faithful friend till death, . Cherry Boniface."

There's a billet-doux for you. As for the father, I think he ought to be encouraged; and for the daughter ——pray, my lord, persuade your bride to take her into her service instead of Gipsey.

Aim. I can assure you, Madam, your deliverance was owing to her discovery.

Dor. Your command, my lord, will do without the obligation. I will take care of her.

Sir Ch. This good company meets oppertunely in favour of a design I have in behalf of my unfortunate sister: I intend to part her from her husband—Gentlemen, will you assist me?

Arch. Assist you! 'Sdeath, who would not?

Foig. Ay, upon my shoul, we will all assist.

Enter Sullen.

Sul. What's all this? They tell me, spouse, that you had like to have been robbed.

Mrs. Sul. Truly, spouse, I was pretty near it——had not these two gentlemen interposed.

Sul. How came these gentlemen here?

Mrs. Sul. That is his way of returning thanks, you must know.

Foig.

Foig. Ay, but upon my fhoul de queftion be à-propos, for all dat.

Sir Ch. You promifed laft night, Sir, that you would deliver your lady to me this morning.

Sul. Humph.

Arch. Humph! What do you mean by Humph?—Sir, you fhall deliver her. In fhort, Sir, we have faved you and your family; and if you are not civil, we will unbind the rogues, join with them, and fet fire to your houfe——What does the man mean? not part with his wife!

Foig. Arra, not part wid your wife! Upon my fhoul, de man dofh not underftand common fhivility.

Mrs. Sul. Hold, gentlemen, all things here muft move by confent. Compulfion would fpoil us. Let my dear and I talk the matter over, and you fhall judge it between us.

Sul. Let me know firft, who are to be our judges.——Pray, Sir, who are you?

Sir Ch. I am Sir Charles Freeman, come to take away your wife.

Sul. And you, good Sir?

Aim. Thomas Vifcount Aimwell, come to take away your fifter.

Sul. And you, pray Sir?

Arch. Francis Archer efq. come——

Sul. To take away my mother, I hope——Gentlemen, you are heartily welcome. I never met with three more obliging people fince I was born. And now, my dear, if you pleafe, you fhall have the firft word.

Arch. And the laft, for five pounds.   [*Afide.*

Mrs. Sul. Spoufe.

Sul. Rib.

Mrs. Sul. How long have you been marry'd?

Sul. By the almanack, fourteen months;—but by my account, fourteen years.

Mrs. Sul. 'Tis thereabout by my reckoning.

Foig. Upon my confhience dere accounts vil agree.

Mrs. Sul. Pray, fpoufe, what did you marry for?

Sul. To get an heir to my eftate.

Sir Ch. And have you fuccceded?

I

Sul.

Sul. No.

Arch. The condition fails of his side—Pray, Madam, what did you marry for?

Mrs. Sul. To support the weaknefs of my fex by the ftrength of his, and to enjoy the pleafures of an agreeable fociety.

Sir Ch. Are your expectations anfwered?

Mrs. Sul. No.

Foig. Arra honeys, a clear caafe, a clear caafe!

Sir Ch. What are the bars to your mutual contentment?

Mrs. Sul. In the firft place, I cannot drink ale with him.

Sul. Nor can I drink tea with her.

Mrs. Sul. I cannot hunt with you.

Sul. Nor can I dance with you.

Mrs. Sul. I hate cocking and racing.

Sul. I abhor ombre and picquet.

Mrs. Sul. Your filence is intolerable.

Sul. Your prating is worfe.

' *Mrs. Sul.* Have we not been a perpetual offence to
' each other—a gnawing vulture at the heart?

' *Sul.* A frightful goblin to the fight?

' *Mrs. Sul.* A porcupine to the feeling?

' *Sul.* Perpetual wormwood to the tafte?'

Mrs. Sul. Is there on earth a thing we can agree in?

Sul. Yes—to part.

Mrs. Sul. With all my heart.

Sul. Your hand.

Mrs. Sul. Here.

Sul. Thefe hands joined us, thefe fhall part us——Away——

Mrs. Sul. Eaft.

Sul. Weft.

Mrs. Sul. North.

Sul. South; far as the poles afunder,

Foig. Upon my fhoul, a very pretty fheremony.

Sir Ch. Now, Mr. Sullen, there wants only my fifter's fortune to make us eafy.

Sul. Sir Charles, you love your fifter, and I love her fortune; every one to his fancy.

Arch. Then you won't refund.

Sul.

Sul. Not a ftiver.

Arch. What is her portion?

Sir Ch. Twenty thoufand pounds, Sir.

Arch. I will pay it. My lord, I thank him, has enabled me, and, if the lady pleafes, fhe fhall go hme with me. This night's adventure has proved ftrangely lucky to us all—For Captain Gibbet, in his walk, has made bold, Mr. Sullen, with your ftudy and efcritore, and has taken out all the writings of your eftate, all the articles of marriage with your lady, bills, bonds, leafes, receipts, to an infinite value; I took them from him, and will deliver them to Sir Charles.

[Gives him a parcel of papers and parchments.]

Sul. How, my writings! My head achs confumedly. Well, gentlemen, you fhall have her fortune, but I cannot talk. If you have a mind, Sir Charles, to be merry, and celebrate my fifter's wedding and my divorce, you may command my houfe! But my head achs confumedly—Scrub, bring me a dram.

Arch. 'Twou'd be hard to guefs which of thefe parties is the better pleafed, the couple joined or the couple parted; the one rejoicing in hopes of an untafted happinefs, and the other in their deliverance from an experienced mifery.

> Both happy in their feveral ftates we find;
> Thefe parted by confent, and thofe conjoin'd.
> Confent, if mutual, faves the lawyer's fee;
> Confent is law enough to fet you free.

END of the FIFTH ACT.

J. Roberts del.   Publish'd for Bell's British Theatre June 4.th 1776.   Thornthwaite

M.ʳ FOOTE in the Character of FONDLEWIFE

Speak I say, have you consider'd, what it is
to Cuckold your Husband?

THE OLD BATCHELOR.

A COMEDY,

As written by Mr. CONGREVE,

AND PERFORMED AT THE

Theatre=Royal in Drury=Lane.

Regulated from the Prompt-Book,

By PERMISSION of the MANAGERS,

By Mr. HOPKINS, Prompter.

Quem tulit ad fcenam vetofo gloria curru,
Exanimat lentus fpectator, fedulus inflat. -
Sic leve, fic parvum eft, animum quod laudis avarum
Subruit, aut reficit—— HORAT. Epift. I. Lib. ii.

A NEW EDITION.

LONDON:

Printed for JOHN BELL, near *Exeter-Exchange*, in the *Strand*.

MDCCLXXVIII.

PROLOGUE.

HOW this vile world is chang'd! In former days,
Prologues were serious speeches before plays;
Grave solemn things, as graces are to feasts;
Where poets begg'd a blessing from their guests;
But now, no more like suppliants we come;
A play makes war, and prologue is the drum;
Arm'd with keen satire, and with pointed wit,
We threaten you who do for judges sit,
To save our plays, or else we'll damn your pit.
But for your comfort, it falls out to-day,
We've a young author, and his first-born play;
So, standing only on his good behaviour,
He's very civil, and intreats your favour.
Not but the man has malice, would he shew it,
But, on my conscience, he's a bashful poet:
You think that strange,—no matter, he'll out-grow it.
Well, I'm his advocate—— by me he prays you,
(I don't know whether I shall speak to please you)
He prays—O bless me! what shall I do now?
Hang me if I knows what he prays, or how!
And 'twas the prettiest prologue as he wrote it!
Well, the deuce take me, if I han't forgot it.
O Lord! for Heaven's sake, excuse the play,
Because you know if it be damn'd to-day,
I shall be hang'd for wanting what to say.
For my sake then —— But I'm in such confusion,
I cannot stay to hear your resolution.   [Runs off.

DRAMATIS PERSONÆ.

M E N.

Drury Lane.

Heartwell, a surly old batchelor, pretending to slight women, secretly in love with *Silvia*, } Mr. Burton.

Bellmour, in love with *Belinda*, Mr. Palmer.

Vainlove, capricious in his love, in love with *Araminta*, } Mr. Packer.

Sharper, Mr. Lee.

Sir *Joseph Wittol*, Mr. King.

Captain *Bluff*, Mr. Love.

Fondlewife, a banker, Mr. Yates.

Setter, a pimp, Mr. Baddeley.

Servant to *Fondlewife*.

W O M E N.

Araminta, in love with *Vainlove*, Mrs. Davis.

Belinda, her cousin, an affected lady, in love with *Bellmour*, } Miss Haughton.

Lætitia, wife to *Fondlewife*, Miss Pope.

Silvia, *Vainlove*'s forsaken mistress, Miss Plym.

Lucy, her maid, Mrs. Bennet.

Betty, Miss Mills.

Boy and Footmen.

SCENE, LONDON.

THE

THE
OLD BATCHELOR.

*** The lines diftinguifhed by inverted commas, 'thus,' are omitted in the reprefentation.

ACT I.
SCENE *the Street*.

Bellemour *and* Vainlove, *meeting*.

BELLMOUR.

Vainlove, and abroad fo early! Good morrow. I thought a contemplative lover could no more have parted with his bed in a morning, than he could have flept in't.

Vain. Bellmour, good morrow—Why, the truth on't is, thefe early fallies are not ufual to me; but bufinefs, as you fee, Sir—[*Shewing letters.*] And bufinefs muft be followed, or be loft.

Bell. Bufinefs!—And fo muft t'me, my friend, be clofe purfued or loft. Bufinefs is the rub of life, perverts our aim, cafts us off the bias, and leaves us wide and fhort of the intended mark.

Vain. Pleafure, I guefs, you mean.

Bell. Ay, what elfe has meaning!

Vain. Oh, the wife will tell you——

Bell. More than they believe—or underftand.

Vain. How, how, Ned! a wife man fay more than he underftands?

Bell. Ay, ay, wifdom's nothing but a pretending to know and believe more than we really do. You read of but one wife man, and all that he knew was, that he knew nothing, Come, come, leave bufinefs to idlers, and

A 3

wifdom

wisdom to fools ; they have need of 'em : wit be my faculty, and pleasure my occupation ; and let father Time shake his glass.   Let low and earthly souls grovel 'till they have work'd themselves six feet deep into a grave—Business is not my element—I roll in a higher orb, and dwell—

Vain. In castles i' th' air, of thy own building ; that's thy element, Ned—Well, as high a flier as you are, I have a lure may make you stoop. -   ,   [*Flings a letter.*

Bell. Aye, marry, Sir, I have a hawk's eye at a woman's hand—There's more elegancy in the false spelling of this superscription [*Takes up the letter.*] than in all Cicero—Let me see—How now ! " Dear, perfidious Vainlove."   [*Reads.*

Vain. Hold, hold, 'slife, that's the wrong.

Bell. Nay, let's see the name ; " Silvia !" How can'st thou be ungrateful to that creature ? She's extremely pretty, and loves thee intirely——I have heard her breathe such raptures about thee————

Vain. Ay, or any body that she's about————

Bell. No, faith, Frank, you wrong her ; she has been just to you.

Vain. That's pleasant, by my troth, from thee, who hast had her.

Bell. Never—her affections : 'tis true, by Heav'n, she own'd it to my face ; ' and blushing like the virgin morn, ' when it disclos'd the cheat which that trusty bawd of ' nature, night, had hid,' confess'd her soul was true to you, tho' I by treachery had stol'n the bliss——

Vain. So was true as turtle——in imagination, Ned, ha ? Preach this doctrice to husbands, and the married women will adore thee.

Bell. Why, faith, I think it will do well enough——if the husband be out of the way——for the wife to shew her fondness and impatience of his absence, by chusing a lover as like him as she can, and what is unlike, she may help out with her own fancy.

Vain. But is it not an abuse to the lover to be made a blind of ?

Bell. As you say, the abuse is to the lover, not the husband ; for 'tis an argument of her zeal towards him, that she will enjoy him in effigy.

Vain.

Vain. It muſt be a very ſuperſtitious country, where ſuch zeal paſſes for true devotion. I doubt it will be damn'd by all our proteſtant huſbands for flat idolatry——But if you can make alderman Fondlewife of your perſuaſion, this letter will be needleſs.

Bell. What, the old banker, with the handſome wife?

Vain. Ay.

Bell. Let me ſee Lætitia! Oh! 'tis a delicious morſel. Dear Frank, thou art the trueſt friend in the world.

Vain. Ay, am I not? to be continually ſtarting of hares for you to courſe. We were certainly cut out for one another; for my temper quits an amour, juſt were thine takes it up——But read that, it is an appointment for me, this evening, when Fondlewife will be gone out of town to meet the maſter of a ſhip, about the return of a venture which he's in danger of loſing. Read, read.

Bell. [*Reads.*] Hum, hum——" Out of town this evening, and talks of ſending for Mr. Spintext to keep me company; but I'll take care he ſhall not be at home." Good! Spintext! Oh, the fanatick one-ey'd parſon.!

Vain. Ay.

Bell. [*Reads.*] Hum, hum——" That your converſation will be much more agreeable, if you can counterfeit this habit to blind the ſervants." Very good—Then I muſt be diſguiſed—With all my heart——' It adds a guſto to ' an amour; gives it the greater reſemblance of theft; ' and, among us lewd mortals, the deeper the ſin the ' ſweeter.' Frank, I'm amazed at thy good nature.——

Vain. Faith, I hate love, when 'tis forc'd upon a man, as I do wine——and this buſineſs is none of my ſeeking; I only happened to be once or twice where Lætitia was the handſomeſt woman in company, ſo, conſequently, apply'd myſelf to her—And it ſeems ſhe has taken me at my word——Had you been there, or any body, t'ad been the ſame.

Bell. I wiſh I may ſucceed as the ſame.

Vain. Never doubt it: ' for if the ſpirit of cuckoldom ' be once raiſed up in a woman, the devil can't lay it, 'till ' ſhe has don't.

Bell. Pry'thee what ſort of fellow is Fondlewife?

Vain. A kind of mongrel zealot, ſometimes very preciſe and peeviſh: but I have ſeen him pleaſant enough in

his

his way: much addicted to jealousy, but more to fondness: so that as he's often jealous without a cause, he's as
often satisfied without reason.

Bell. A very even temper, and fit for my purpose. I
must get your man Setter to provide my disguise.

Vain. Ay, you may take him for good and all, if you
will, for you have made him fit for nobody else————
Well————

Bell. You're going to visit in return of Silvia's letter
————Poor rogue! Any hour of the day or night will serve
her————But do you know nothing of a new rival there?

Vain. Yes, Heartwell, that, surly old, pretended woman-hater, thinks her virtuous; that's one reason why I
fail her: I would have her fret herself out of conceit with
me, that she may entertain some thoughts of him. I
know he visits her every day.

Bell. Yet rails on still, and thinks his love unknown to
us; a little time will swell him so, he must be forc'd to
give it birth; and the discovery must needs be very pleasant from himself; to see what pains he will take, and
how he will strain to be delivered of a secret, when he
has miscarried of it already.

Vain. Well, good morrow; let's dine together; I'll
meet at the old place.

Bell. With all my heart; it lies convenient for us to
pay our afternoon services to our mistresses; I find I am
damnably in love, I'm so uneasy for not having seen Belinda yesterday.

Vain. But I saw my Araminta, yet am as impatient.
                                                    [*Exit.*

Bell. Why, what a cormorant in love am I! who not
contented with the slavery of honourable love in one place,
‘ and the pleasure of enjoying some half a score mistresses
‘ of my own acquiring, must yet take Vainlove's business
upon my hands, because it lay too heavy upon his: ‘ so
‘ am not only forc'd to lie with other men's wives for 'em,
‘ but must also undertake the harder task of obliging
‘ their mistresses.————I must take up, or I shall never
hold out; ‘ flesh and blood cannot bear it always.’

Enter Sharper.

Sharp. I'm sorry to see this, Ned: if once a man comes
to his soliloquies, I give him for gone.

Bell.

Bell. Sharper, I'm glad to see thee.

Sharp. What, is Belinda cruel, that you are so thoughtful?

Bell. No, faith, not for that——But there's a business of consequence fall'n out to-day, that requires some consideration.

Sharp. Pr'ythee, what mighty business of consequence can'st thou have ?

Bell. Why, you must know 'tis a piece of work towards the finishing of an alderman ; it seems I must put the last hand to it, and dub him cuckold, that he may be of equal dignity with the rest of his brethren ; so I must beg Belinda's pardon.

Sharp. Faith, e'en give her over for good and all : you can have no hopes of getting her for a mistress ; and she is too proud, too inconstant, too affected, too witty, and too handsome, for a wife.

Bell. But she can't have too much money—There's twelve thousand pounds, Tom.——'Tis true she is excessively foppish and affected : but, in my conscience, I believe the baggage loves me ; for she never speaks well of me herself, nor suffers any body else to rail at me. Then, as I told you, there's twelve thousand pounds—Hum—Why, faith, upon second thoughts, she does not appear to be so very affected neither——Give her her due, I think the woman's a woman, and that's all. As such, I am sure I shall like her ; for the devil take me if I don't love all the sex.

Sharp. And here comes one who swears as heartily he hates all the sex.

Enter Heartwell.

Bell. Who? Heartwell! Ay, but he knows better things——How now, George, where hast thou been snarling odious truths, ' and entertaining company, like ' a physician, with discourses of their diseases and infir- ' mities ? What fine lady hast thou been putting out of ' conceit with herself, and persuading, that the face she ' had been making all the morning, was none of her ' own ;' for I know thou art as unmannerly and as unwelcome to a woman, as a looking-glass after the small-pox.

Heart. I confess I have not been sneering fulsome lies,

2

and

and naufeous flattery, fawning upon a little tawdry whore that will fawn upon me again, and entertain any puppy that comes, like a tumbler, with the fame tricks over and over ; for fuch, I guefs, may have been your late employment.

Bell. Wou'd thou had'ft come a little fooner, Vainlove would have wrought thy converfion, and been a champion for the caufe.

Heart. What, has he been here ? That's one of love's April-fools, is always upon fome errand that's to no purpofe ; ever embarking in adventures, yet never comes to harbour.

' *Sharp.* That's becaufe he always fets out in foul weather, loves to buffet with the winds, meet the tide, and
' fail in the teeth of oppofition.

' *Heart.* What, has he not dropt anchor at Araminta ?

' *Bell.* Truth on't is, fhe fits his temper beft ; is a
' kind of floating ifland ; fometimes feems in reach, then
' vanifhes and keeps him bufied in the fearch.

Sharp. She had need have a good fhare of fenfe to manage fo capricious a lover.'

Bell. Faith, I don't know. He's of a temper the moft eafy to himfelf in the world ; ' he takes as much always
' of an amour as he cares for, and quits it when it grows
' ftale or unpleafant.

' *Sharp.* An argument of very little paffion, very good
' underftanding, and very ill-nature.

' *Heart.* And proves that Vainlove plays the fool with
' difcretion.'

Sharp. You, Bellmour, are bound in gratitude to ftickle for him ; you with pleafure reap that fruit which he takes pains to fow. He does the drudgery in the mine, and you ftamp your image on the gold.

Bell. He's of another opinion, and fays I do the drudgery in the mine. Well, we have each our fhare of fport, and each that which he likes beft ; 'tis his diverfion to fet 'tis mine to cover the partridge.

Heart. And it fhould be mine to let 'em go again.

Sharp. Not till you had mouth'd a little, George ; I think that's all thou art fit for now.

Heart. Good, Mr. young fellow, you're miftaken ;

as able as yourself, and as nimble too, though I mayn't have so much mercury in my limbs. 'Tis true indeed I don't force appetite, but ' wait the natural call of my ' lust, and' think it time enough to be wicked, after I have had the temptation.

Bell. Time enough! ay, too soon, I should rather have expected from a person of your gravity.

Heart. Yet it is oftentimes too late with some of you young, termagant, flashy sinners—you have all the guilt of the intention, and none of the pleasure of the practice —'Tis true you are so eager in pursuit of the temptation, that you save the devil the trouble of leading you into it: nor is out of discretion, that you don't swallow that very hook yourselves have baited, but you are cloy'd with the preparative, and what you mean for a whet, turns the edge of your puny stomach. ' Your love is like your courage, which ' you shew for the first year or ' two upon all occasions; 'till in a little time, being ' disabled or disarmed, you abate of your vigour; and ' that daring blade, which was so often drawn, is bound ' to the peace for ever hereafter.'

Bell. Thou art an old fornicator of a singular good principle indeed! and art for encouraging youth, that they may be as wicked as thou art at thy years.

Heart. I am for having every body be what they pretend to be; ' a whoremaster be a whoremaster;' and not, like Vainlove, kiss a lap-dog, with passion, when it would disgust him from the lady's own lips.

' *Bell.* That only happens sometimes, where the dog ' has the sweeter breath, for the more cleanly convey-' ance.' But, George, you must not quarrel with little gallantries of this nature. Women are often won by 'em. Who would refuse to kiss a lap-dog if it were preliminary to the lips of his lady?

Sharp. Or omit playing with her fan, ' and cooling ' her if she were hot, when it might intitle him to the office of warming her when she should be cold.

Bell. Or what is it to read a play in a rainy day! Though you should be now and then interrupted in a witty scene, and she perhaps preserve her laughter 'till the jest were over; even that may be borne with, considering the reward in prospect.

Heart.

Heart. I confeſs, you that are women's aſſes, bear greater burdens; are forc'd to undergo dreſſing, dancing, ſinging, ſighing, whining, rhyming, flattering, lying, grinning, cringing, and the drudgery of loving to boot.

Bell. O brute! the drudgery of loving!

Heart. Ay, why to come to love through all theſe incumbrances, is like coming to an eſtate over-charg'd with debts; which by the time you have paid, yields no further profit than what the bare tillage and manuring of the land will produce, at the expence of your own ſweat.

Bell. Pr'ythee, how doſt thou love?

Sharp. He! he hates the ſex.

Heart. So I hate phyſic too—yet I may love to take it for my health.

Bell. Well come off, George, if at any time you ſhould be taken ſtraying.

Sharp. He has need of ſuch an excuſe, conſidering the preſent ſtate of his body.

Heart. How d'ye mean?

Sharp. Why, if wenching be phyſic, as you call it, then, I may ſay, marriage is entering into a courſe of phyſic.

Bell. How, George, does the wind blow there!

Heart. It will as ſoon blow north and by ſouth—Marry, quotha! I hope in heaven I have a greater portion of grace; and I think I have baited too many of thoſe traps, to be caught in one myſelf.

Bell. Who the devil would have thee? unleſs 'twere an oyſter-woman, to propogate young fry to Billingſgate ———Thy talent will never recommend thee to any thing of better quality.

Heart. My talent is chiefly that of ſpeaking truth, which I don't expect ſhould ever recommend me to people of quality———I thank heaven, I have very honeſtly purchaſed the hatred of all the great families in town.

Sharp. And you, in return of ſpleen, hate them. But could you hope to be received into the alliance of a noble family?

Heart. No, I hope I ſhall never merit that affliction—to be puniſhed with a wife of birth.———be a ſtag of the firſt head, and bear my horns aloft, like one of the ſup-

porters

porters of my wife's coat. 'Sdeath, I would not be a cuckold to e'er an illustrious whore in England.

Bell. What not to make your family, man, and provide for your children?

Sharp. For her children, you mean.

Heart. Ay, there you've nick'd it——there's the devil upon devil——Oh, the pride and joy of heart 'twould be to me, to have my son and heir resemble such a duke — to have a fleering coxcomb scoff and cry, Mr. your son's mighty like his grace, has just his smile and air of's face. Then replies another——Methinks he has more of the marquis of such a place, about his nose and eyes ; though he has my lord what-d'ye-call's mouth to a tittle—— Then, I, to put it off unconcerned, come chuck the infant under the chin, force a smile, and cry, Ay, the boy takes after his mother's relations——when the devil and she knows, 'tis a little compound of the whole body of nobility.

Bell. and Sharp. Ha, ha, ha.

Bell. Well, but George, I have one question to ask you——

Heart. Pshaw, I have prattled away my time—I hope you are in no haste for an answer——for I shan't stay now.   [*Looking on his watch.*

Bell. Nay, pr'ythee, George——

Heart. No, besides my business, I see a fool coming this way.   Adieu.   [*Exit.*

Bell. What does he mean ? Oh, 'tis Sir Joseph Wittol, with his friend ; but I see he has turned the corner, and goes another way.

Sharp. What, in the name of wonder, is it ?

Bell. Why, a fool.

Sharp. 'Tis a tawdry outside.

Bell. And a very beggarly lining—yet he may be worth your acquaintance—A little of thy chymistry, Tom, may extract gold from that dirt.

Sharp. Say you so ? 'Faith, I am as poor as a chymist, and would be as industrous.   But what was he that followed him ? Is not he a dragon that watches those golden pippins ?

Bell. Hang him, no, he a dragon ! if he be, 'tis a very peaceful one ; I can insure his anger dormant ; or

should

ſhould he ſeem to rouſe, 'tis but well laſhing him, and he will ſleep like a top.

Sharp. Ay, is he of that kidney?

Bell. Yet is adored by that bigot, Sir Joſeph Wittol!, as the image of valour.   He calls him his back, and indeed they are never aſunder—yet laſt night, I know not by what miſchance, the knight was alone, and had fallen into the hands of ſome night-walkers, who, I ſuppoſe, would have pillaged him : but I chanced to come by, and reſcued him ; though I believe he was heartily frightened, for as ſoon as ever he was looſe he ran away, without ſtaying to ſee who had helped him.

Sharp. Is that bully of his in the army?

Bell. No, but is a pretender, and wears the habit of a ſoldier ; ' which now-a-days as often cloaks cowardice ' as a black gown does atheiſm,'——You muſt know he has been abroad—went purely to run away from a campaign, enrich'd himſelf with the plunder of a few oaths, and here vents 'em againſt the general, who ſlighting men of merit, and preferring only thoſe of intereſt, has made him quit the ſervice.

Sharp. Wherein, no doubt, he magnifies his own performance.

Bell. Speaks miracles ; is the drum to his own praiſe —the only implement of a ſoldier he reſembles ; like that, being full of bluſtering noiſe and emptineſs——

Sharp. And, like that, of no uſe but to be beaten.

Bell. Right ; but then the compariſon breaks ; for he will take a drubbing with as little noiſe as a pulpit cuſhion.

Sharp. His name, and I have done.

Bell. Why, that, to paſs it current too, he has gilded with a title : he is called Captain Bluff.

Sharp. Well, I'll endeavour his acquaintance——you ſteer another courſe, are bound

For love's iſland ; I, for the golden coaſt.

May each ſucceed in what he wiſhes moſt.

END of the FIRST ACT.

A C T II.

Sir Joseph Wittoll, Sharper *following.*

SHARPER.

SURE that's he, and alone.

Sir Jo. Um———Ay, this, this is the very damn'd place: the inhuman cannibals, the bloody-minded villa ns, would have butcher'd me laſt night. No doubt, they would have flea'd me alive, have ſold my ſkin, and devoured me.

Sharp. How's this !

Sir Jo. An it hadn't been for a civil gentleman as came by and frighted 'em away——but, agad, I durſt not ſtay to give him thanks.

Sharp. This muſt be Bellmour, he means——Ha ! I have a thought——

Sir Jo. Zooks, would the Captain would come ; the very remembrance makes me quake ; agad, I ſhall never be reconciled to this place heartily.

Sharp. 'Tis but trying, and being where I am at worſt. Now luck !——Curs'd fortune ! this muſt be the place, this damned unlucky place——

Sir Jo. Agad, and ſo 'tis——Why here has been more miſchief done, I perceive.

Sharp. No, 'tis gone, 'tis loſt——ten thouſand devils on that chance which drew me hither ! Ay, here, juſt here ; this ſpot to me is hell ; nothing to be found, but the deſpair of what I have loſt.

[*Looking about as in ſearch.*

Sir Jo. Poor gentleman——by the lord Harry, I'll ſtay no longer, for I have found too——

Sharp. Ha ! who's that has found ? What have you found ? Reſtore it quickly, or by——

Sir Jo. Not I, Sir, not I ; as I've a ſoul to be ſaved, I have found nothing but what has been to my loſs, as I may ſay, and as you were ſaying, Sir.

Sharp. O, your ſervant, Sir, you are ſafe then it ſeems ; tis an ill wind that blows nobody good. Well, you may rejoice over my ill-fortune, ſince it paid the price of your ranſom.

Sir Jo. I rejoice! agad, not I, Sir. I'm very sorry for your loss, with all my heart, blood, and guts, Sir; and if you did but know me, you'd ne'er say I were so ill-natured.

Sharp. Know you! Why can you be so ungrateful, to forget me!

Sir Jo. O, lord, forget him! No, no, Sir, I don't forget you——because I never saw your face before, agad. Ha, ha, ha.

Sharp. How!   [*Angrily.*

Sir Jo. Stay, stay, Sir, let me recollect——he's a damned angry fellow——I believe I had better remember him, till I can get out of his sight; but out o'sight out o'mind, agad.   [*Aside.*

Sharp. Methought the service I did you last night, Sir, in preserving you from those ruffians, might have taken better root in your shallow memory.

Sir Jo. Gads-daggers-belts-blades and scabbards, this is the very gentleman! How shall I make him a return suitable to the greatness of his merit——I had a pretty thing to that purpose, if he han't frighted it out of my memory. Hem! hem!—Sir, I most submissively implore your pardon for my transgression of ingratitude and omission; having my intire dependence, Sir, upon the superfluity of your goodness, which, like an inundation, will, I hope, totally immerge the recollection of my error, and leave me floating in your sight, upon the full-blown bladders of repentance—by the help of which, I shall once more hope to swim into your favour. [*Bows.*

Sharp. So-h, O, Sir, I am easily pacify'd; the acknowledgment of a gentleman ————

Sir Jo. Acknowledgment! Sir, I am all over acknowledgment, and will not stick to shew it in the greatest extremity, by night or by day, in sickness or in health, winter or summer; all seasons and occasions shall testify the reality and gratitude of your superabundant humble servant, Sir Joseph Wittoll, knight. Hem! hem!

Sharp. Sir Joseph Wittol!

Sir Jo. The same, Sir, of Wittoll-Hall, in Comitatu Bucks.

Sharp. Is it possible! Then I am happy to have obli-
                                                    ged

ged the mirror of knighthood and pink of courtefy in the age.   Let me embrace you,

Sir Jo. O lord, Sir!

Sharp. My lofs I efteem as a trifle, repaid with in-tereft, fince it has purchas'd me the friendfhip and ac-quaintance of the perfon in the world whofe character I admire.

Sir Jo. You are only pleafed to fay fo, Sir——But pray, if I may be fo bold, what is that lofs you men-tioned?

Sharp. O, term it no longer fo, Sir. In the fcuffle, laft night, I only dropt a bill of a hundred pound, which I confefs, I came half defpairing to recover ; but thanks to my better fortune——

Sir Jo. You have found it, Sir, then it feems ; I pro-fefs I'm heartily glad.——

Sharp. Sir, your humble fervant—I don't queftion but you are ; that you have fo cheap an opportunity of ex-prefling your gratitude and generofity. Since the paying fo trivial a fum, will wholly acquit you and doubly en-gage me.

Sir Jo. What a dickins does he mean by a trivial fum? [*Afide.*] But han't you found it, Sir?

Sharp. No otherwife, I vow to God, but in my hopes in you, Sir.

Sir Jo. Humh.

Sharp. But that's fufficient——'Twere injuftice to doubt the honour of Sir Jofeph Wittoll.

Sir Jo. O lord, Sir.

Sharp. You are above, I'm fure, a thought fo low, to fuffer me to lofe what was ventured in your fervice, Nay, 'twas in a manner——paid down for your deliverance ; 'twas fo much lent you——and you fcorn, I'll fay that for you——

Sir Jo. Nay, I'll fay that for myfelf, with your leave, Sir, I do fcorn a dirty thing. But, agad, I'm a little out of pocket at prefent.

Sharp. 'Pfhaw, you can't want a hundred pound. Your word is fufficient any where. 'Tis but borrowing fo much dirt, you have large acres, and can foon repay it—Money is but dirt, Sir Jofeph—mere dirt.

B 3

Sir Jo.

Sir Jo. But I profess, 'tis a dirt I have washed my hands of at present; I have laid it all out upon my back.

Sharp. Are you so extravagant in clothes, Sir Joseph?

Sir Jo. Ha, ha, ha, a very good jest, I profess; ha, ha, ha, a very good jest, and I did not know that I had said it, and that's a better jest than t'other. 'Tis a sign you and I ha'n't been long acquainted; you have lost a good jest for want of knowing me——I only mean a friend of mine, whom I call my back, he sticks as close to me, and follows me through all dangers——he is indeed back, breast, and head-piece, as it were, to me—agad, he's a brave fellow—Pauh, I am quite another thing, when I am with him. I don't fear the devil, bless us, almost, if he be by. Ah, had he been with me last night!

Sharp. If he had, Sir, what then? He could have done no more, nor perhaps have suffered so much—Had he a hundred pound to lose?   [*Angrily.*

Sir Jo. O lord, Sir, by no means—but I might have saved a hundred pound. [*Aside.*] I meant innocently, as I hope to be saved. A damned hot fellow. [*Aside.*] Only as I was saying, I let him have all my ready money to redeem his great sword from limbo—But, Sir, I have a letter of credit to alderman Fondlewife, as far as two hundred pounds, and this afternoon you shall see I am a person, such a one as you would wish to have met with——

Sharp. That you are, I'll be sworn. [*Aside.*] Why that's great, and like yourself.

Enter Captain Bluff.

Sir Jo. O, here a' comes——Ay, my Hector of Troy! welcome, my bully, my back; agad my heart has gone a pit-pat for thee.

Bluff. How now, my young knight! Not for fear, I hope; he that knows me, must be a stranger to fear.

Sir Jo. Nay, agad, I hate fear, ever since I had like to have died of a fright——But——

Bluff. But! Look you here, boy, here's your antidote, here's your Jesuit's powder for a shaking fit---But who hast thou got with thee, is he of mettle?

[*Laying his hand upon his sword.*

Sir Jo. Ay, bully, a devilish smart fellow: 'a will fight like a cock.

Bluff.

Bluff. Say you fo? Then I honour him————But has he been abroad? for every cock will fight upon his own dunghill.

Sir Jo. I don't know, but I'll prefent you————

Bluff. I'll recommend myfelf---Sir, I honour you: I underftand you love fighting. I reverence a man that loves fighting. Sir, I kifs your hilts.

Sharp. Sir, your fervant, but you are mifinformed; for unlefs it be to ferve my particular friend, as Sir Jofeph here, my country, or my religion, or in fome very jufti-fiable caufe, I'm not for it.

Bluff. O lord, I beg your pardon, Sir, I find you are not of my palate; you can't relifh a difh of fighting with-out fweet fauce. Now, I think————fighting for fighting fake's fufficient caufe; fighting to me's religion and the laws.

Sir Jo. Ah, well faid, my hero; was not that great, Sir? By the lord Harry, he fays true; fighting is meat, drink, and cloth to him. But, back, this gentleman is one of the beft friends I have in the world, and faved my life laft night————You know I told you.

Bluff. Ay! then I honour him again————Sir, may I crave your name?

Sharp. Ay, Sir, my name's Sharper.

Sir Jo. Pray, Mr. Sharper, embrace my back; very well————by the lord Harry, Mr. Sharper, he's as brave as Cannibal, are not you, Bully-Back?

Sharp. Hannibal, I believe you mean, Sir Jofeph.

Bluff. Undoubtedly he did, Sir; faith, Hannibal was a very pretty fellow; but, Sir Jofeph, comparifons are odious. Hannibal was a very pretty fellow in thofe days, it muft be granted—But, alas, Sir! were he alive now, he would be nothing, nothing in the earth.

Sharp. How, Sir! I make a doubt if there be at this day a greater general breathing.

Bluff. Oh, excufe me, Sir; have you ferved abroad, Sir?

Sharp. Not I, really, Sir.

Bluff. Oh, I thought fo; why then you can know no-thing, Sir; I am afraid you fcarce know the hiftory of the late war in Flanders, with all its particulars.

Sharp.

Sharp. Not I, Sir, no more than public letters or gazettes tell us.

Bluff. Gazettes! why there again, now; why, Sir,
there are not three words of truth, the year round, put
into the Gazette. I'll tell you a strange thing, now, as
to that——You must know, Sir, I was resident in Flanders the last campaign; had a small post there; but no
matter for that. Perhaps, Sir, there was scarce any thing
of moment done, but an humble servant of yours, that
shall be nameless, was an eye-witness of; I won't say had
the greatest share in't: though I might say that too, since
I name nobody, you know. Well, Mr. Sharper, would
you think it? In all this time, as I hope for a truncheon,
this rascally Gazette-writer never so much as once men-
tioned me; not once, by the wars! Took no more notice,
than as if Nol Bluff had not been in the land of the living.

Sharp. Strange!

Sir Jo. Yes, by the Lord Harry, 'tis true, Mr. Sharper; for I went every day to coffee-houses to read the
Gazette myself.

Bluff. Ay, ay, no matter. You see, Mr. Sharper,
after all, I am content to retire, live a private person:
Scipio and others have done it.

Sharp. Impudent rogue!   [*Aside.*

Sir Jo. Ay, this damned modesty of yours——Agad,
if he would put in for't, he might be made general himself yet.

Bluff. O fy, no, Sir Joseph—You know I hate this.

Sir Jo. Let me but tell Mr. Sharper a little, how you
eat fire once out of the mouth of a cannon——agad he
did; those impenetrable whiskers of his have confronted
flames——

Bluff. Death, what do you mean, Sir Joseph?

Sir Jo. Look you now, I tell you he's so modest he'll
own nothing.

Bluff. Pish! you have put me out, I have forgot what
I was about. Pray, hold your tongue, and give me leave.
                                        [*Angrily.*

Sir Jo. I am dumb.

Bluff. This sword, I think, I was telling you of, Mr.
Sharper——This sword, I'll maintain to be the best di-
                                        vine

vine, anatomiſt, lawyer, or caſuiſt in Europe ; it ſhal
decide a controverſy, or ſplit a cauſe——

Sir Jo. Nay, now I muſt ſpeak ; it will ſplit a hair ;
by the lord Harry, I have ſeen it.

Bluff. Zouns, Sir, it's a lie, you have not ſeen it, nor
ſhan't ſee it ; Sir, I ſay you can't ſee ; what d'ye ſay to
that, now ?

Sir Jo. I am blind.

Bluff. Death ! had any other man interrupted me——

Sir Jo. Good Mr. Sharper, ſpeak to him ; I dare not
look that way.

Sharp. Captain, Sir Joſeph's penitent.

Bluff. O I am calm, Sir, calm as a diſcharged culverin
——But 'twas indiſcreet, when you know what will provoke me——Nay, come, Sir Joſeph, you know my
heat's ſoon over.

Sir Jo. Well, I am a fool ſometimes——But I'm
ſorry.

Bluff. Enough.

Sir Jo. Come, we'll go take a glaſs to drown animoſities ; Mr. Sharper, will you partake ?

Sharp. I wait on you, Sir. Nay, pray, Captain——
you are Sir Joſeph's back.   [*Exeunt.*

S C E N E, Araminta's *Apartment.*

Araminta *and* Belinda, Betty *waiting.*

Belin. Ah ! nay, dear——pr'ythee good, dear,
ſweet couſin, no more, Oh, gad! I ſwear you'd make
one ſick to hear you

Aram. Bleſs me ! what have I ſaid to move you thus ?

Belin. O you have raved, talked idly, and all in com-
mendation of that filthy, awkward, two-legg'd creature,
man——you don't know what you've ſaid, your fever
has tranſported you.

Aram. If love be the fever which you mean, kind
Heav'n avert the cure.: let me have oil to feed that flame,
and never let it be extinct, 'till I myſelf am aſhes.

Belin. There was a whine !—O gad, I hate your horrid fancy—this love is the devil ; and ſure to be in love,
is to be poſſeſs'd—'Tis in the head, the heart, the blood,
the——all over——O gad, you are quite ſpoil'd—I
ſhall loath the ſight of mankind for your ſake.

Aram.

Aram. Fie ! this is grofs affectation————A little of Bellmour's company would change the fcene.

Belin. Filthy fellow ! I wonder, coufin————

Aram. I wonder, coufin, you fhould imagine I don't perceive you love him.

Belin. Oh, I love your hideous fancy ! Ha, ha, ha, love a man !

Aram. Love a man ! yes, you would not love a beaft.

Belin. Of all beafts, not an afs—which is fo like your Vainlove—Lard, I have feen an afs look fo chagrin, ha, ha, ha ! (you muft pardon me, I can't help laughing) that an abfolute lover would have concluded the poor creature to have had darts, and flames, and altars, and all that, in his breaft. Araminta, come, I'll talk feriouf-ly to you now ; could you but fee, with my eyes, the buffoonery of one fcene of addrefs, a lover, fet out with all his equipage and appurtenances ; O gad ! fure you would ————But you play the game, and confequently can't fee the mifcarriages obvious to every ftander by.

Aram. Yes, yes, I can fee fomething near it, when you and Bellmour meet. You don't know that you dreamt of Bellmour laft night, and call'd him aloud in your fleep.

Belin. Pifh ! I can't help dreaming of the devil fome-times ; would you from thence infer I love him ?

Aram. But that's not all ; you caught me in your arms when you named him, and prefs'd me to your bofom—Sure, if I had not pinch'd you till you wak'd, you had ftifled me with kiffes.

Belin. O barbarous afperfion !

Aram. No afperfion, coufin, we are alone—Nay I can tell you more,

Belin. I deny it all.

Aram. What, before you hear it ?

Belin. My denial is premediated, like your malice——Lard, coufin, you talk oddly—Whatever the matter is, o' my foul, I'm afraid you'll follow evil courfes.

Aram. Ha, ha, ha ! this is pleafant.

Belin. You may laugh, but——

Aram. Ha, ha, ha!

Belin. You think the malicious grin becomes you—The devil take Bellmour. Why do you tell me of him ?

Aram.

Aram. Oh, is it come out—now you are angry, I am sure you love him.   I'll tell nobody else, cousin—I have not betrayed you yet.

Belin. Pr'ythee, tell it all the world; it's false.

Aram. Come, then, kiss and friends.

Belin. Pish.

Aram. Pr'ythee don't be so peevish.

Belin. Pr'ythee don't be so impertinent—Betty.

Aram. Ha, ha, ha,!

Betty. Did your ladyship call, Madam?

Belin. Get my hoods and tippet, and bid the footman call a chair.   [*Exit* Betty.

Aram. I hope you are not going out in dudgeon, cousin.

Enter Footman.

Foot. Madam, there are—

Belin. Is there a chair?

Foot. No, Madam, there are Mr. Bellmour and Mr. Vainlove, to wait upon your ladyship.

Aram. Are they below?

Foot. No, Madam, they sent before, to know if you were at home.

Belin. The visit's to you, cousin, I suppose I am at my liberty.

Aram. Be ready to shew 'em up.   [*Exit* Footman.

Enter Betty *with hoods and looking-glass.*

I can't tell, cousin, I believe we are equally concerned; but if you continue your humour, it won't be very entertaining—I know she'd fain be persuaded to stay.

[*Aside.*

Belin. I shall oblige you in leaving you to the full and free enjoyment of that conversation you admire. Let me see; hold the glass—Lard, I look wretchedly to-day!

Aram. Betty, why don't you help my cousin?

[*Putting on her hoods.*

Belin. Hold off your fists, and see that he gets a chair with a high roof, or a very low seat—Stay, come back here, you, Mrs. Fidget—you are so ready to go to the footman—Here; take 'em all again, my mind's changed, I won't go.   [*Exit* Betty.

Aram. So, this I expected. You won't oblige me, then, cousin, and let me have all the company to myself.

Belin. No; upon deliberation, I have too much charity

ty to truſt you to yourſelf.   The devil watches all oppor‐
tunities ; and in this favourable diſpoſition of your mind,
heaven knows how far you may be tempted ; I am tender
of your reputation.

Aram. I am obliged to you—But who's malicious now,
Belinda ?

Belin. Not I ; witneſs my heart, I ſtay out of pure
affection.

Aram. In my conſcience I believe you.

Enter Bellmour, Vainlove, *and Footman.*

Bell. So, fortune be praiſed ! To find you both within,
ladies, is—

Aram. No miracle, I hope.

Bell. Not o'your ſide, Madam, I confeſs : but my ty‐
rant, there, and I, are two buckets that can never come
together.

Belin. Nor are ever like. Yet we often meet and claſh.

Bell. How, never like ! Marry, Hymen forbid.   But
this is to run ſo extravagantly in debt ; I have laid out
ſuch a world of love in your ſervice, that you think you
can never be able to pay me all ; ſo ſhun me, for the ſame
reaſon that you would a dun.

Belin. Ay, on my conſcience, and the moſt imperti‐
nent and troubleſome of duns—A dun for money will be
quiet, when he ſees his debtor has not wherewithal—But
a dun for love is an eternal torment, that never reſts——

Bell. 'Till he has created love where there was none,
and then gets it for his pains.   For importunity in love,
like importunity at court, firſt creates its own intereſt,
and then purſues it for the favour.

Aram. Favours that are got by impudence and impor‐
tunity, are like diſcoveries from the rack, when the af‐
flicted perſon, for his eaſe, ſometimes confeſſes ſecrets
his heart knows nothing of.

Vain. I ſhould rather think, favours, ſo gained, to be
due rewards to indefatigable devotion.   For as love is a
deity, he muſt be ſerved by prayer.

Belin. O gad, would you would all pray to love, then,
and let us alone.

Vain. You are the temples of love, and 'tis through
you, our devotion muſt be conveyed.

2

Aram.

Aram. Rather, poor filly idols of your own making, which, upon the leaſt diſpleaſure, you forſake, and ſet up new——Every man, now, changes his miſtreſs and his religion, as his humour varies or his intereſt.

Vain. O Madam——

Aram. Nay, come, I find we are growing ſerious, and then we are in great danger of being dull —— ' If my ' muſick-maſter be not gone, I'll entertàin you with a ' new ſong, which comes pretty near my own opinion of ' love, and your ſex.—Who's there ? Is Mr. Gavot gone ?
[*Calls.*

' *Foot.* Only to the next door, Madam ; I'll call him.
[*Exit.*'

Bell. Why, you won't hear me with patience.

Aram. What's the matter, couſin ?

Bell. Nothing, Madam, only——

Belin. Pr'ythee hold thy tongue——Lard, he has ſo peſter'd me with flames and ſtuff——I think I ſhan't endure the ſight of a fire this twelvemonth.

Bell. Yet all can't melt that cruel, frozen heart.

Belin. ' O gad, I hate your hideous fancy'—you ſaid that once before——If you muſt talk impertinently, for heaven's ſake, let it be with variety ; don't come al- ways, like the devil, wrapt in flames—I'll not hear a ſen- tence more, that begins with an, I burn—or an, I be- ſeech you, Madam ?

Bell. But tell me how you would be ador'd—I am very tractable.

Belin. Then, know, I would be ador'd in ſilence.

Bell. Humph, I thought ſo, that you might have all the talk to yourſelf—You had better let me ſpeak ; for if my thoughts fly to any pitch, I ſhall make villainous ſigns.

Belin. What will you get by that ? to make ſuch ſigns as I won't underſtand.

Bell. Ay, but if I'm tongue-ty'd, I muſt have all my actions free, to—quicken your apprehenſion—and 'egad, let me tell you, my moſt prevailing argument is expreſs'd in dumb-ſhew.

' *Enter* Muſick-maſter.

' *Aram.* O I am glad we ſhall have a ſong to divert ' the diſcourſe——Pray oblige us with the laſt new ſong.

* C   ' SONG.

'SONG.

I.

' Thus to a ripe, confenting maid,
' Poor, old, repenting Delia faid :
' Would you long preferve your lover ?
' Would you ftill his goddefs reign ?
' Never let him all difcover,
' Never let him much obtain.

II.

' Men will admire, adore and die,
' While wifhing at your feet they lie :
' But admitting their embraces,
' Wakes 'em from the golden dream ;
' Nothing new befides our faces,
' Every woman is the fame.

' Aram. So, how d'ye like the fong, gentlemen ?
' Bell. O, very well perform'd—but I don't much
' admire the words.
' Aram. I expected it————there's too much truth in
' 'em: if Mr. Gavot will walk with us in the garden,
' we'll have it once again————you may like it better at
' fecond hearing. You'll bring my coufin.'
* Aram. If you'll walk into the next room, I'll entertain you with a fong, to divert the difcourfe————
You'll bring my coufin.
Bell. Faith, Madam, I dare not fpeak to her ; but I'll
make figns.   [Addreffes Belinda in dumb fhew.
Belin. Oh, foh ! your dumb rhetorick is more ridiculous than your talking impertinence ; ' as an ape is a
' much more troublefome animal than a parrot.
' Aram. Ay, coufin, and 'tis a fign the creatures mi-
' mick nature well ; for there are few men but do more
' filly things than they fay.
' Bell. Well, I find my apifhnefs has paid the ranfom
for my fpeech, and fet it at liberty————tho', I confefs, I

____

* This fpeech is inferted, on account of the fong, &c. being
omitted in the reprefentation.

could

could be well enough pleas'd to drive on a love bargain, in that silent manner---'Twould save a man a world of lying and swearing at the year's end. Besides, I have had a little experience, that brings to mind————.

When wit and reason both have fail'd to move;
Kind looks and actions (from success) do prove,
Ev'n silence may be eloquent in love.

 END of the SECOND ACT.

A C T   III.

S C E N E, *the Street.*

Silvia *and* Lucy.

SILVIA.

WILL he not come, then?

Lucy. Yes, yes, come, I warrant him, if you will go in, and be ready to receive him.

Silv. 'Why did not you tell me?' Whom mean you?

Lucy. Whom you should mean, Heartwell.

Silv. Senseless creature, I meant my Vainlove.

Lucy. You may as soon hope to recover your own maidenhead as his love. Therefore, e'en set your heart at rest, and in the name of opportunity mind your own business. Strike, Heartwell, home, before the bait's worn off the hook. Age will come. He nibbled fairly yesterday; and, no doubt, will be eager enough to-day to swallow the temptation.

Silv. Well, since there's no remedy—Yet tell me—for I wou'd know, though to the anguish of my soul; how did he refuse? Tell me——how did he receive my letter, in anger or in scorn?

Lucy. Neither; but what was ten times worse, with damn'd, senseless indifference. By this light, I could have spit in his face—Receive it! Why he received it as I would one of your lovers that should come empty-handed; as a court lord does his mercer's bill, or a begging dedication——he received it, as if't had been a letter from his wife.

Silv. What! did he not read it?

Lucy.

Lucy. Humm'd it over, gave you his refpects, and faid, he would take time to perufe it, but then he was in hafte.

Silv. Refpects, and perufe it ! He's gone, and Araminta has bewitch'd him from me. Oh, how the name of rival fires my blood ! ' I could curfe 'em both ;' eternal jealoufy attend her love, and difappointment meet his. ' Oh, that I could revenge the torment he has caus'd--- ' Methinks, I feel the woman ftrong within me, and ven- ' geance kindles in the room of love.'

Lucy. I have that in my head may make mifchief.

Silv. How, dear Lucy ?

Lucy. You know Araminta's diffembled coynefs has won, and keeps him hers——

Silv. Could we perfuade him, that fhe loves another.

Lucy. No, you're out ; could we perfuade him, that fhe dotes on him, himfelf——Contrive a kind letter as from her, 'twould difguft his nicety, and take away his ftomach.

Silv. Impoffible ! 'twill never take.

Lucy. Trouble not your head. Let me alone, I will inform myfelf of what paft between 'em to-day, and about it ftraight—Hold, I'm miftaken, or that's Heartwell, who ftands talking at the corner, 'tis he—Go get you in, Madam, receive him pleafantly, drefs up your face in innocence and fmiles, and diffemble the very want of diffimulation——You know what will take him.

Silv. 'Tis as hard to counterfeit love, as it is to conceal it : but I'll do my weak endeavour, though I fear I have no art.

Lucy. Hang art, Madam, and truft to nature for diffembling.

Man, was by nature woman's creature made.
We never are but by ourfelves betray'd.

[Exeunt.

Enter Heartwell, Vainlove *and* Bellmour *following.*

Bell. Hift, hift, is not that Heartwell going to Silvia ?

Vain. He's talking to himfelf, I think ; pr'ythee let's try if we can hear him.

Heart.

Heart. Why, whither, in the devil's name, am I a going now? Hum!—let me think—Is not this Silvia's house, the cave of that enchantress, and which consequently I ought to shun as I would infection? To enter here, is to put on the envenom'd shirt, to run into the embraces of a fever, and in some raving fit, be led to plunge myself into that more consuming fire, a woman's arms. Ha! well recollected, I will recover my reason and be gone.

Bell. Now Venus forbid!

Vain. Hush————

Heart. Well, why do you not move? Feet, do your office—Not one inch; ho, foregad, I'm caught———There stands my north, and thither my needle points.—Now could I curse myself, yet cannot repent. O thou delicious, damn'd, dear, destructive woman! 'Sdeath, how the young fellows will hoot me! I shall be the jest of the town; nay, in two days, I expect to be chronicled in ditty, and sung in woeful ballad, to the tune of the superannuated maiden's comfort, or the batchelor's fall; and upon the third, I shall be hang'd in effigy, pasted up for the exemplary ornament of ' necessary houses and' cobler's stalls—Death, I can't think on't—I'll run into the danger to lose the apprehension.   [*Exit.*

Bell. A very certain remedy, *probatum est*—Ha, ha, ha, poor George, thou art i'th' right, thou hast sold thyself to laughter; the ill-natur'd town will find the jest just where thou hast lost it. Ha, ha, how, a' struggled, like an old lawyer between two fees.

Vain. Or a young wench, between pleasure and reputation.

Bell. Or, as you did to-day, when, half afraid, you snatch'd a kiss from Araminta.

Vain. She has made a quarrel on't.

Bell. Pauh, women are only angry at such offences, to have the pleasure of forgiving 'em.

Vain. And I love to have the pleasure of making my peace————I should not esteem a pardon, if too easily won.

Bell. Thou dost not know what thou would'st be at; whether thou would'st have her angry or pleas'd. Could'st thou be content to marry Araminta?

Vain. Could you be content to go to Heav'n ?

Bell. Hum, not immediately, in my confcience, not heartily ? I'd do a little more good in my generation firft, in order to deferve it.

Vain. Nor I to marry Araminta, 'till I merit her.

Bell. But how the devil doft thou expect to get her, if fhe never yield ?

Vain. That's true ; but I would——

Bell. Marry her without her confent. Thou'rt a riddle beyond woman——

Enter Setter.

Trufty Setter, what tidings ? How goes the project ?

Set. As all wicked projects do, Sir, ' where the devil ' prevents our endearments' with fuccefs.

Bell. A good hearing, Setter.

Vain. Well, I'll leave you with your engineer.

Bell. And haft thou provided neceffaries ?

Set. All, all, Sir. The large fanctified hat, and the little precife band, with a fwinging long fpiritual cloak, to cover carnal knavery—not forgetting the black patch, which Tribulation Spintext wears, as I'm informed, upon one eye, as a penal mourning for the ogling offences of his youth ; and fome fay, with that eye, he firft difcovered the frailty of his wife.

Bell. Well, in this fanatic father's habit, will I confefs Lætitia.

Set. Rather prepare her for confeffion; Sir, by helping her to fin.

Bell. Be at your mafter's lodging in the evening, I fhall ufe the robes.   [*Exeunt* Bell. *and* Vain.

Set. I fhall, Sir——I wonder to which of thefe two gentlemen I do moft properly appertain——the one ufes me as his attendant ; the other, being the better acquainted with my parts, employs me as a pimp. Why, that's much the more honourable employment—by all means— I follow one as my mafter, t'other follows me as his conductor.

Enter Lucy.

Lucy. There's the hang-dog, his man——I had a power over him in the reign of my miftrefs : but he is too true a valet de chambre not to affect his mafter's faults ; and confequently is revolted from his allegiance.

Set.

Set. Undoubtedly, 'tis impoffible to be a pimp and not a man of parts ; that is, without being politic, diligent, fecret, wary and fo forth——And to all this valiant as Hercules—that is, paffively valiant and actively obedient. Ah ! Setter, what a treafure is here loft for want of being known ?

Lucy. Here's fome villainy a-foot, he's fo thoughtful ; may be I may difcover fomething in my mafk—Worthy Sir, a word with you.   [*Puts on her mafk.*

Set. Why, if I were known, I might come to be a great man——

Lucy. Not to interrupt your meditation——

Set. And I fhould not be the firft that has procured his greatnefs by pimping.

Lucy. Now poverty and the pox light upon thee, for a contemplative pimp.

Set. Ha ! what art, who thus malicioufly haft awakened me from my dream of glory ? Speak, thou vile difturber——

Lucy. Of thy moft vile cogitations——thou poor, conceited wretch, how wert thou valuing thyfelf, upon thy mafter's employment? For he's the head pimp to Mr. Bellmour.

Set. Good words, damfel, or I fhall——But how doft thou know my mafter or me ?

Lucy. Yes, I know both mafter and man to be——

Set. To be men perhaps ; nay, 'faith like enough ; I often march in the rear of my mafter, and enter the breaches which he has made.

Lucy. Ay, the breach of faith, which he has begun. Thou traitor to thy lawful princefs.

Set. Why, how now ! pr'ythee who art ? Lay by that worldly face and produce thy natural vizor.

Lucy. No, firrah, I'll keep it on to abufe thee, and leave thee without hopes of revenge.

Set. Oh ! I begin to fmoak ye. Thou art fome forfaken Abigail ; we have dallied with thee heretofore—— and art come to tickle thy imagination with remembrance of iniquity paft.

Lucy. No, thou pitiful flatterer of thy mafter's imperfections ; thou maukin, made up of the fhreds and parings of his fuperfluous fopperies.

I   *Set.*

Set. Thou art thy miftrefs's foul's felf, compofed of her unfullied iniquities and clothing.

Lucy. Hang thee——beggar's cur————Thy mafter is but a mumper in love, lies canting at the gate ; but never dares prefume to enter the houfe.

Set. Thou art the wicket to thy miftrefs's gate, to be opened for all comers. In fine, thou art the high road to thy miftrefs.

Lucy. Beaft, filthy toad, I can hold no longer, look and tremble. [*Unmafks.*

Set. How, Mrs. Lucy !

Lucy. I wonder thou haft the impudence to look me in the face.

Set. Adfbud, who is in fault, miftrefs of mine ? Who flung the firft ftone ? Who undervalued my function ? And who the devil could know you by inftinct ?

Lucy. You could know my office by inftinct, and be hanged, which you have flandered moft abominably. It vexes me not what you faid of my perfon : but that my innocent calling fhould be expofed and fcandaliz'd—— I cannot bear it.

Set. Nay, faith, Lucy, I'm forry, I'll own myfelf to blame, though we were both in fault as to our offices ——Come, I'll make you any reparation.

Lucy. Swear.

Set. I do fwear to the utmoft of my power.

Lucy. To be brief then ; what is the reafon your ma-fter did not appear to-day, according to the fummons I brought him ?

Set. To anfwer you as briefly—He has a caufe to be tried in another court.

Lucy. Come, tell me, in plain terms, how forward he is with Araminta.

Set. Too forward to be turned back——Though he's a little in difgrace at prefent about a kifs which he forced. You and I can kifs, Lucy, without all that.

Lucy. Stand off————He's a precious jewel.

Set. And therefore you'd have him to fet in your lady's locket.

Lucy. Where is he now ?

Set. He'll be in the piazza prefently.

Lucy.

Lucy. Remember to-day's behaviour——Let me fee you with a penitent face.

Set. What no token of amity, Lucy ? You and I don't ufe to part with dry lips.

Lucy. No, no, avaunt——I'll not be flabber'd and kifs'd now, I'm not i'th'. humour.

Set. I'll not quit you fo——I'll follow and put you into the humour.   [*Exeunt.*

Enter Sir Jofeph Wittoll *and* Bluff.

Bluff. And fo out of your unwonted generofity——

Sir Jo. And good-nature, back; I am good-natur'd and I can't help it.

Bluff. You have given him a note upon Fondlewife for a hundred pound.

Sir Jo. Ay, ay, poor fellow, he ventur'd fair for't.

Bluff. You have difobliged me in it—for I have occafion for the money, and if you would look me in the face again and live, go, and force him to re-deliver you the note——go——and bring it me hither. I'll ftay here for you.

Sir Jo. You may ftay 'till the day of judgment then, by the Lord Harry. I know better things than to be run through the guts for a hundred pound. Why, I gave that hundred pound for being faved, and d'ye think, an' there were no danger, I'll be fo ungrateful to take it from the gentleman again ?

Bluff. Well, go to him from me——Tell him, I fay, he muft refund——or bilbo's the word, and flaughter will enfue——if he refufe, tell him——but whifper that ——tell him——I'll pink his foul——but whifper that foftly to him.

Sir Jo. So foftly, that he fhall never hear on't, I warrant you——Why, what a devil's the matter, bully, are you mad ? Or d'ye think I'm mad ? Agad, for my part, I don't love to be the meffenger of ill news; 'tis an ungrateful office——So tell him yourfelf.

Bluff. By thefe hilts, I believe he frightened you into this compofition. I believe you gave it him out of fear, pure paltry fear——Confefs.

Sir Jo. No, no, hang't, I was not afraid, neither— though I confefs he did in a manner fnap me up—yet I

can't

say that it was altogether out of fear, but partly to prevent mischief—for he was a devilish choleric fellow. And if my choler had been up too, agad, there would have been mischief done, that's flat. And yet, I believe, if you had been by, I would as soon have let him a' had a hundred of my teeth. Adshart, if he would come now, just when I'm angry, I'd tell him————Mum.

Enter Bellmour *and* Sharper.

Bell. Thou'rt a lucky rogue; there's your benefactor, you ought to return him thanks, now you have received the favour.

Sharp. Sir Joseph,—your note was accepted, and the money paid at sight. I'm come to return my thanks.

Sir Jo. They won't be accepted so readily as the bill, Sir.

Bell. I doubt the knight repents, Tom—He looks like the knight of the sorrowful face.

Sharp. This is a double generosity————Do me a kindness, and refuse my thanks————But I hope you are not offended, that I offered them, without any offence to you, Sir.

Sir Jo. May be I am, Sir; may be I am not, Sir—may be I am both, Sir.—What then? I hope I may be offended.

Sharp. Hey day! Captain, what's the matter? You can tell.

Bluff. Mr. Sharper, the matter is plain————Sir Joseph has found out your trick, and does not care to be put upon, being a man of honour.

Sharp. Trick, Sir!

Sir Jo. Ay, trick. Sir, and won't be put upon, Sir, being a man of honour, Sir; and so, Sir————

Sharp. Heark'e, Sir Joseph, a word with ye————in consideration of some favours lately received, I would not have you draw yourself into a premunire, by trusting to that sign of a man there————that pop-gun charged with wind.

Sir Jo. O lord, O lord, Captain, come justify yourself————I'll give him the lie, if you'll stand to it.

Sharp. Nay, then I'll be beforehand with you, take that, oafe. [*Cuffs him.*

Sir Jo.

Sir Jo. Captain, will you see this ? Won't you pink his soul ?

Bluff. Hush, 'tis not so convenient now—I shall find a time.

Sharp. What do you mutter about a time, rascal ? You were the incendiary.—There's to put you in mind of your time——A memorandum.   [*Kicks him.*

Bluff. Oh, this is your time, Sir, you had best make use on't.

Sharp. 'Egad, and so I will.   There's again for you.
                                        [*Kicks him.*

Bluff. You are obliging, Sir, but this is too public a place to thank you in : but in your ear——You are to be seen again.

Sharp. Ay, thou inimitable coward, and to be felt—as for example.   [*Kicks him.*

Bell. Ha, ha, ha, pr'ythee come away ; 'tis scandalous to kick this puppy, unless a man were cold, and had no other way to get himself a heat.   [*Exit* Sharper.

Bluff. Very well——very fine——But 'tis no matter————Is not this fine, Sir Joseph ?

Sir Jo. Indifferent, agad, in my opinion very indifferent————I'd rather go plain all my life than wear such finery.

Bluff. Death and hell, to be affronted thus! I'll die before I'll suffer it.   [*Draws.*

Sir Jo. O lord, his anger was not raised before—Nay, dear Captain, don't be in a passion, now he's gone————Put up, put up, dear back, 'tis your Sir Joseph begs. Come, let me kiss thee. So, so, put up, put up.

Bluff. By heav'n, 'tis not to be put up.

Sir Jo. What, bully ?

Bluff. The affront.

Sir Jo. No, agad, no more 'tis, for that's put up already, thy sword I mean.

Bluff. Well, Sir Joseph, at your intreaty—But were not you, my friend, abus'd, and cuff'd, and kick'd ?
                            [*Putting up his sword.*

Sir Jo. Ay, ay, so were you too : no matter, 'tis past.

Bluff. By the immortal thunder of great guns, 'tis false——he sucks not vital air who dares affirm it to this face.
                                        [*Looks big.*
                                        Sir Jo.

Sir Jo. To that face, I grant you, Captain—No, no, I grant you ——Not to that face, by the lord Harry.—— If you had put on your fighting face before, you had done his bufinefs ——he durft as foon have kifs'd you, as kick'd you to your face——But a man can no more help what's done behind his back, than what's faid.—Come, we'll think no more of what's paft.

Bluff. I'll call a council of war within to confider of my revenge to come.   [*Exeunt.*

SCENE, Silvia's Apartment.

Enter Heartwell and Silvia.

S O N G.

As Amoret and Thyrfis lay
Melting the hours in gentle play;
Joining faces, mingling kiffes,
And exchanging harmlefs bliffes.
He trembling cry'd, with eager hafte,
O ler me feed as well as tafte,
I die, if I'm not wholly, wholly bleft.

After the fong, a dance of anticks.

Sil. Indeed, it is very fine————I could look upon 'em all day.

Heart. Well, has this prevail'd for me, and will you look upon me?

Silv. If you could fing and dance fo, I fhould love to look upon you too.

Heart. Why, 'twas I fung and danc'd; I gave mufic to the voice, and life to their meafures—Look you here, Silvia. [*Pulling out a purfe and chinking it.*] Here are fongs and dances, poetry and mufic—hark! how fweetly one guniea rhymes to another—and how they dance to the mu- fic of their own chink. This buys all t'other—and this thou fhalt have; this, and all that I am worth for the purchafe of thy love. Say, is it mine then, ha? Speak, fyren——Oons, why do I look on her! Yet I muft—— Speak, dear angel, devil, faint, witch; do not rack me with fufpenfe.

Silv.

Silv. Nay, don't ſtare at me ſo——You make me bluſh——I cannot look.

Heart. Oh, manhood, where art thou ! What am I come to ? A woman's toy, at theſe years ! Death, a bearded baby for a girl to dandle. ' O dotage, dotage! ' That ever that noble paſſion, luſt, ſhould ebb to this ' degree——No reflux of vigorous blood ; but milky ' love ſupplies the empty channels, and prompts me to ' the ſoftneſs of a child——a mere infant, and would ' ſuck.' Can you love me, Silvia ? Speak.

Silv. I dare not ſpeak 'till I believe you, and indeed I'm afraid to believe you yet.

Heart. Death ! how her innocence torments and pleaſes me ! Lying, child, is indeed the art of love ; and men are generally maſters in it : but I'm ſo newly entered, you cannot diſtruſt me of any ſkill in the treacherous myſtery——Now, by my ſoul, I cannot lie, though it were to ſerve a friend or gain a miſtreſs.

Silv. Muſt you lie then, if you ſay you love me ?

Heart. No, no, dear ignorance, thou beauteous changeling——I tell thee, I do love thee, and tell it for a truth, a naked truth, which I'm aſhamed to diſcover.

Silv. But love, they ſay, is a tender thing, ' that will ' ſmooth frowns, and make calm an angry face ; will ſof- ' ten a rugged temper, and make ill-humoured people ' good.' You look ready to fright one, and talk as if your paſſion were not love, but anger.

Heart. 'Tis both ; for I am angry with myſelf, when I am pleaſed with you—And a pox upon me for loving thee ſo well——' yet I muſt on——'Tis a bearded ar- ' row, and will more eaſily be thruſt forward than drawn ' back.

Silv. Indeed, if I were well aſſur'd you lov'd——but how can I be well aſſur'd ?

Heart. Take the ſymptoms——and aſk all the tyrants of thy ſex, if their fools are not known by this party-coloured livery——I am melancholic when thou art abſent ; look like an aſs when thou art preſent ; wake for thee when I ſhould ſleep ; and even dream of thee when I am awake ; ſigh much, drink little, eat leſs, court ſolitude, am grown very entertaining to myſelf, and, as I am informed, very troubleſome to every body

elſe.

elfe. If this be not love it is madnefs, and then it is pardonable————Nay, yet a more certain fign than all this ; I give thee my money.

Silv. Ay, but that is no fign ; for they fay, gentlemen will give money to any naughty woman to come ' to ' bed' to them—O Gemini, I hope you don't mean fo—for I won't be a whore.

Heart. The more is the pity.   [*Afide.*

Silv. Nay, if you would marry me, you fhould not come to ' bed to' me—' you have fuch a beard, and ' would fo prickle one.' But do you intend to marry me ?

Heart. That a fool fhould afk fuch a malicious queftion !. Death ! I fhall be drawn in, before I know where I am——However, I find I am pretty fure of her confent, if I am put to it. [*Afide.*] Marry you ? No, no, I'll love you.

Silv. Nay, but if. you love me, you muft marry me ; what, don't I know my father lov'd my mother, and was marry'd to her ?

Heart. Ay, ay, in old days people married where they lov'd : but that fafhion is chang'd, child.

' *Silv.* Never tell me that : I know 'tis not chang'd ' by myfelf ; for I love you, and would marry you.

' *Heart.* I'll have my beard fhav'd, it fhan't hurt thee, ' and we'll go to bed.

Silv. No, no, I'm not fuch a fool neither, but I can keep myfelf honeft.—Here, I won't keep any thing that's yours, I hate you now, [*Throws the purfe.*] and I'll never fee you again, 'caufe you'd have me naught.   [*Going.*

Heart. Damn her, let her go, and a good riddance—. Yet fo much tendernefs and beauty, and honefty together, is a jewel —Stay, Silvia——But then to marry—— Why every man plays the fool once in his life : but to marry is playing the fool all one's life long.

Silv. What do you call me for?

Heart. I'll give thee all I have ; and thou fhalt live with me in every thing fo like my wife, the world fhall believe it : nay, thou fhalt think fo thyfelf————only let me not think fo.

Silv. No, I'll die before I'll be your whore————
as well as I love you.

Heart. [*Afide.*] A woman; and ignorant, may be honeft, when 'tis out of obftinacy and contradiction——But,
'fdeath, it is but a may-be, and upon fcurvy terms——
Well, farewel then ————if I can get out of fight, I
may get the better of myfelf.

Silv. Well, good bye.   [*Turns and weeps.*

Heart. Ha! Nay, come, we'll kifs at parting.————
[*Kiffes her.*] By Heav'n her kifs is fweeter than liberty
————I will marry thee————There thou haft don't.
All my refolves melted in that kifs————One more.

Silv. But when!

Heart. I'm impatient 'till it be done; I will not give
myfelf liberty to think, left I fhould cool————I will
about a licence ftraight————In the evening expect
me————One kifs more, to confirm me mad; fo.

[*Exit Heart.*

Silv. Ha, ha, ha, an old fox trapp'd————

Enter Lucy.

Blefs me! you frighted me; I thought he had been come
again, and had heard me.

' *Lucy.* Lord, Madam, I met your lover in as much
hafte, as if he had been going for a midwife.

' *Silv.* He's going for a parfon, girl, the forerunner
' of a midwife, fome nine months hence————Well, I
' find diffembling to our fex is as natural as fwimming to
' a negro. We may depend upon our fkill to fave us at a
' plunge, though till then we never make the experi-
' ment.'——But how haft thou fucceeded?

Lucy. As you would wifh——fince there is no reclaiming
Vainlove; I have found out a pique fhe has taken at him;
and have fram'd a letter that makes her fue for reconciliation firft. I know that will do——walk in, and I'll fhew it
you. Come, Madam, you're like to have a happy time
on't, both your love and anger fatisfied!——All that can
charm our fex confpire to pleafe you.

That woman fure enjoys a bleffed night,
Whom love and vengeance both at once delight.

END of the THIRD ACT.

A C T   IV.

S C E N E, *the Street.*

Enter Bellmour, *in a Fanatick Habit, and* Setter.

BELLMOUR.

'TIS pretty near the hour. [*Looking on his watch.*]
Well, and how, Setter, ha, does my hypocri-
sy fit me, ha? Does it sit easy on me?

Set. O most religiously well, Sir.

' *Bell.* I wonder why all our young fellows should glo-
' ry in an opinion of atheism; when they may be so
' much more conveniently lewd under the coverlet of re-
' ligion.'

Set. 'Sbud, Sir, away quickly, there's Fondlewife just
turn'd the corner, and's coming this way.

Bell. Gad's so, there is, he must not see me.

Enter Fondlewife *and* Barnaby.

Fond. I say, I will tarry at home.

Bar. But, Sir.

Fond. Good lack! I profess the spirit of contradiction
hath possess'd the lad—I say, I will tarry at home, varlet.

Bar. I have done, Sir, then farewel five hundred
pound.

Fond. Ha, how's that? Stay, stay, did you leave
word, say you, with his wife? With Comfort herself.

Bar. I did; and Comfort will send Tribulation hither
as soon as ever he comes home—I could have brought
young Mr. Prig, to have kept my mistress company in
the mean time : but you say——

Fond. How, how, say varlet! I say let him not come
near my doors. I say he is a wanton young Levite, and
pampereth himself up with dainties, that he may look
lovely in the eyes of women ——Sincerely, I am afraid,
he hath already defiled the tabernacle of our sister Comfort ; while her good husband is deluded by his godly appearance——I say, that even lust doth sparkle in his eyes,
and

and glow upon his cheeks, and that I would as soon trust my wife with a lord's high-fed chaplain.

Bar. Sir, the hour draws nigh————and nothing will be done there 'till you come.

Fond. And nothing can be done here 'till I go—So that I'll tarry, d'ye fee.

Bar. And run the hazard to lose your affair, Sir!

Fond. Good lack! good lack————I profess it is a sufficient vexation, for a man to have a handsome wife.

Bar. Never, Sir, but when the man is an insufficient husband. 'Tis then, indeed, like the vanity of taking a fine house; and yet be forc'd to let lodgings, to help to pay the rent.

Fond. I profess, a very apt comparison, varlet. Go, and bid my Cocky come out to me; I will give her some instructions; I will reason with her before I go. [*Exit Bar.*] And in the mean time, I will reason with myself—Tell me, Isaac, why art thee jealous; why art thee distrustful of the wife of thy bosom?—Because she is young and vigorous, and I am old and impotent————Then, why didst thee marry, Isaac?————Because she was beautiful and tempting, and because I was obstinate and doating; ' so that my inclination was, and is still, greater 'than my power.'————And will not that which tempted thee, also tempt others, who will tempt her, Isaac?————I fear it much——But does not thy wife love thee, nay, doat upon thee;————Yes——Why, then! Ay, but to say truth, she's fonder of me, than she has reason to be; and in the way of trade, we still suspect the smoothest dealers of the deepest designs——And that she has some designs deeper than thou canst reach, th'st experimented, Isaac————But mum.

Enter Lætitia.

Læt. I hope my dearest jewel is not going to leave me————are you, Nykin?

Fond. Wife————Have you thoroughly consider'd how detestable, how heinous, and how crying a sin, the sin of adultery is? Have you weigh'd it, I say?

Læt. Bless me! what means my dear!

Fond. [*Aside.*] I profess she has an alluring eye; I am doubtful whether I shall trust her, even with Tribulation

D 3

himself.

himself.——Speak, I say, have you considered what it is to cuckold your husband ?

Læt. [*Aside.*] I'm amazed : sure he has discovered nothing———Who has wrong'd me to my dearest ? I hope my jewel does not think that ever I had any such thing in my head, or ever will have.

Fond. No, no, I tell you I shall have it in my head.

Læt. [*Aside.*] I know not what to think. But I'm resolved to find the meaning of it——Unkind dear ! Was it for this you sent to call me ? Is it not affliction enough that you are to leave me, but you must study to encrease it by unjust suspicions ? [*Crying.*] Well—well——you know my fondness, and you love to tyrannize——Go, on, cruel man, do ; triumph over my poor heart, while it holds, which cannot be long, with this usage of yours——But that's what you want——Well, you will have your ends soon——You will—You will——Yes, it will break to oblige you.   [*Sighs.*

Fond. Verily, I fear I have carried the jest too far.——Nay, look you, now, if she does not weep——'tis the fondest fool—Nay, Cocky, Cocky, nay, dear Cocky, don't cry, I was but in jest, I was not, ifeck.

Læt. O then, all's safe. I was terribly frighted.[*Aside.*]——My affliction is always your jest, barbarous man ! Oh, that I should love to this degree ! yet———

Fond. Nay, Cocky,

Læt. No, no, you are weary of me, that's it——that's all, you would get another wife—another fond fool, to break her heart—Well, be as cruel as you can to me, I'll pray for you ; and when I am dead with grief, may you have one that will love you as well as I have done : I shall be contented to lie at peace in my cold grave——since it will please you.   [*Sighs.*

Fond. Good lack, good-lack, she would melt a heart of oak——I profess I can hold no longer——Nay, dear Cocky,——Ifeck you'll break my heart—Ifeck you will.——See, you have made me weep——made poor Nykin weep——Nay, come kiss, buss poor Nykin, and I won't leave thee———I'll lose all first.

Læt. [*Aside.*] How ! Heaven forbid ! that will carry the jest too far, indeed.

Fond. Won't you kiss Nykin ?

Læt.

Lœt. Go, naughty Nykin, you don't love me.

Fond. Kifs, kifs, ifeck I do.

Lœt. No, you don't,.   [*She kiffes him.*

Fond. What, not love Cocky?

Lœt. No———h.   [*Sighs.*

Fond. I profefs I do love thee better than five hundred pounds—and fo thou fhalt fay, for I'll leave it to ftay with thee.

Lœt. No, you fhan't neglect your bufinefs for me—— No, indeed you fant, Nykin——If you don't go, I'll think you been dealous of me ftill.

Fond. He, he, he, wilt thou, poor fool? Then, I will go; I won't be dealous————Poor Cocky, kifs Nykin, kifs Nykin; 'ee, ee, ee—Here will be the good man anon, to talk to Cocky, and teach her how a wife ought to behave herfelf.

Lœt. I hope to have one that will fhew me how a hufband ought to behave himfelf. [*Afide.*]———I fhall be glad to learn to pleafe my jewe   [*Kifs.*

Fond. That's my good dear————Come, kifs Nykin once more, and then get you in————So——Get you in, get you in. By, by.

Lœt. By, Nykin.

Fond. By, Cocky.

Lœt. By, Nykin.

Fond. By, Cocky, by, by.   [*Exeunt.*

Enter Vainlove *and* Sharper.

Sharp. How! Araminta loft!

Vain. To confirm what I have faid, read this——

              [*Gives a letter.*

Sharp. [*Reads.*] " Hum, hum. And what then appear'd a fault, upon reflection, feems only an effect of too powerful paffion. I'm afraid I give too great a proof of my own at this time—I am in diforder for what I have written. But fomething, I know not what, forc'd me. I only beg a favourable cenfure of this, and am your

                       Araminta."

Sharp. Loft! Pray Heaven thou haft not loft thy wits. Here, here, fhe's thy own, man, fign'd and feal'd too. —To her, man—a delicious melon, pure, and confenting ripe, and only waits thy cutting up———She has

                               been

been breeding love to thee all this while, and just now she's deliver'd of it.

Vain. 'Tis an untimely fruit, and she has miscarried of her love.

Sharp. Never leave this damn'd, ill-natur'd whimsy, Frank? Thou hast a sickly, peevish appetite; only chews love, and cannot digest it.

Vain. Yes, when I feed myself——But I hate to be cramm'd ————By Heav'n, there's not a woman will give a man the pleasure of a chace: ' my sport is always ' baulk'd, or cut short. I stumble over the game I would ' pursue'————'Tis dull and unnatural to have a hare run full in the hound's mouth; and would distaste the keenest hunter————I would have overtaken, not have met my game.

Sharp. However, I hope you don't mean to forsake it; that will be but a kind of mongrel cur's trick. Well, are you for the Mall?

Vain. No, she will be there this evening————Yes, I will go too————and she shall see her error in————

Sharp. In her choice, 'egad————But thou can'st not be so great a brute as to slight her?

Vain. ' I should disappoint her if I did not'———— By her management, 'I should think she expects it.

All naturally fly what does pursue:
'Tis fit men should be coy, when women woo.

SCENE, *a Room in* Fondlewife's *House.*

A Servant *introducing* Bellmour *in a fanatic habit, with a patch upon one eye, and a book in his hand.*

Serv. Here's a chair, Sir, if you please to repose yourself. My mistress is coming, Sir. [*Exit.*

Bell. Secure in my disguise, I have out-fac'd suspicion, and ev'n dared discovery————This cloak my sanctity, and trusty Scarron's novels my prayer-book—Methinks I am the very picture of Montufar, in the Hypocrites—— Oh, she comes.

Enter Lætitia.

So breaks Aurora through the veil of night,
Thus fly the clouds, divided by her light,
And every eye receives a new-born sight,

        }

[*Throwing off his cloak, patch, &c.*

Læt.

Læt. Thus ſtrew'd with bluſhes like————Ah ! Heav'n defend me ! Who's this ?

[Diſcovering him, ſtarts.

Bell. Your lover.

Læt. Vainlove's friend ! I know his face, and he has betray'd me to him. [Aſide.

Bell. You are ſurprized. Did you not expect a lover, Madam ? Thoſe eyes ſhone kindly on my firſt appearance, tho' now they are o'er-caſt.

Læt. I may well be ſurpriz'd at your perſon and impudence ; they are both new to me—You are not what your firſt appearance promiſed : the piety of your habit was welcome, but not the hypocriſy,

Bell. Rather the hypocriſy was welcome, but not the hypocrite.

Læt. Who are you, Sir ? You have miſtaken the houſe, ſure.

Bell. I have directions in my pocket. which agree with every thing but your unkindneſs. [*Pulls out the letter.*

Læt. My letter ! Baſe Vainlove ! Then 'tis too late to diſſemble. [*Aſide.*] 'Tis plain, then you have miſtaken the perſon. [Going.

Bell. If we part ſo, I'm miſtaken————Hold, hold, Madam————I confeſs I have run into an error———— I beg your pardon a thouſand times—What an eternal blockhead am I ! Can you forgive me the diſorder I have put you into ?—But it is a miſtake which any body might have made,

Læt. What can this mean ? 'Tis impoſſible he ſhould be miſtaken, after all this————A handſome fellow, if he had not ſurpriz'd me. Methinks, now I look on him again, I would not have him miſtaken. [*Aſide.*] We are all liable to miſtakes, Sir ; if you own it to be ſo, there needs no farther apology.

Bell. Nay, faith, Madam, 'tis a pleaſant one, and worth your hearing. Expecting a friend, laſt night, at his lodgings, 'till 'twas late ; my intimacy with him gave me the freedom of his bed : he not coming home all night, a letter was deliver'd to me, by a ſervant, in the morning : upon the peruſal, I found the contents ſo charming, that I could think of nothing all day, but put-

ting

ting 'em in practice—————'till juſt now, (the firſt time I ever look'd on the ſuperſcription) I am the moſt ſurpriz'd in the world to find it directed to Mr. Vainlove. Gad, Madam, I aſk you a million of pardons, and will make you any ſatisfaction.

Læt. I am diſcover'd——and either Vainlove is not guilty, or he has handſomely excus'd him.   [*Aſide.*

Bell. You appear concern'd, Madam.

Læt. I hope you are a gentleman—and ſince you are privy to a weak woman's failing, won't turn it to the prejudice of her reputation. You look as if you had more honour.

Bell. And more love ; or my face is a falſe witneſs, and deſerves to be pillory'd—————No, by Heaven, I ſwear—————

Læt. Nay, don't ſwear if you'd have me to believe you ; but promiſe—————

Bell. Well, I promiſe—————A promiſe is ſo cold— give me leave to ſwear—by thoſe eyes, thoſe killing eyes ; by thoſe healing lips—Oh ! preſs the ſoft charm cloſe to mine, and ſeal 'em up for ever.

Læt. Upon that condition.   [*He kiſſes her.*

Bell. Eternity was in that moment—One more, upon any condition.

Læt. Nay, now—I never ſaw any thing ſo agreeably impudent. [*Aſide.*] Won't you cenſure me for this, now ? —————but 'tis to buy your ſilence. [*Kiſs.*] Oh, but what am I doing !

Bell. No tongue can expreſs it—not thy own ; nor any thing, but thy lips. I am faint with the exceſs of bliſs —————Oh, for love's ſake, lead me any whither, where I may lay down ;—quickly, for I am afraid I ſhall have a fit.

Læt. Bleſs me ! What fit ?

Bell. Oh, a convulſion—————I feel the ſymptoms.

Læt. Does it hold you long ? I'm afraid to carry you into my chamber.

Bell. Oh, no : let me lay down upon the bed ;————— the fit will be ſoon over.   [*Exeunt.*

SCENE

SCENE, *St. James's Park.*

Araminta and Belinda meeting.

Bel. Lard, my dear: I am glad I have met you——
I have been at the Exchange since, and am so tir'd——

Aram. Why, what's the matter?

Bell. Oh, the most inhuman barbarous hackney coach!
I am jolted to a jelly——Am not I horridly touz'd?

           [Pulls out a pocket glass.

Aram. Your head's a little out of order.

Bel. A little? O frightful! What a furious phiz I
have! O most rueful! Ha, ha, ha! O gad, I hope nobody will come this way, 'till I have put myself in re-
pair—Ah! my dear————I have seen such unhewn
creatures since————Ha, ha, ha! I can't for my soul
help thinking that I look just like one of 'em————Good
dear, pin this, and I'll tell you——Very well——So,
thank you my dear————But, as I was telling you——
Pish, this is the untoward'st lock————So, as I was
telling you————How d'ye like me now? Hideous, ha?
Frightful still; or how?

Aram. No, no; you're very well as can be.

Bel. And so————But where did I leave off, my
dear? I was telling you————

Aram. You were about to tell me something, child——
but you left off before you began.

Bel. Oh, a most comical sight: a country squire, with
the equipage of a wife and two daughters, came to Mrs.
Snipwell's shop while I was there————But, Oh, gad!
two such unlick'd cubs!

Aram. I warrant, plump, cherry-cheek'd country
girls.

Bel. Ay, o' my conscience, fat as barn-door fowls:
but so bedeck'd, you would have taken 'em for Friezland
hens, with their feathers growing the wrong way————
O, such out-landish creatures: Such Tramontanæ, and
foreigners to the fashion, or any thing in practice! I had
no patience to behold————I undertook the modeling
of one of their fronts, the more modern structure.

Aram. Bless me, cousin; why would you affront any
body so? They might be gentlewomen of a very good
family————

               Bel.

Bel. Of a very ancient one, I dare swear, by their dress——Affront ! Pshaw, how you're mistaken ! The poor creature, I warrant, was as full of curtsies, as if I had been her godmother.   The truth on't is, I did endeavour to make her look like a christian—and she was sensible of it ; for she thank'd me, and gave me two apples, piping hot, out of her under petticoat pocket——Ha, ha, ha ! And t'other did so stare and gape—— I fancied her like the front of her father's hall ; her eyes were the two jut-windows, and her mouth the great door, most hospitably kept open for the entertainment of travelling flies.

Aram. So, then, you have been diverted.   What did they buy ?

Bel. Why, the father bought a powder-horn, and an almanack, and a comb-case ; the mother, a great fruz-tower, and a fat amber necklace ; the daughters, only tore two pair of kid-leather gloves, with trying 'em on. ——————Oh, gad, here comes the fool that din'd at my Lady Freelove's t'other day.

Enter Sir Joseph *and* Bluff.

Aram. May be he may not know us again.

Bel. We'll put on our masks, to secure his ignorance.
[They put on their masks.

Sir Jo. Nay, gad, I'll pick up ; I'm resolv'd to make a night on't——————I'll go to alderman Fondlewife by and by, and get fifty pieces more from him. Adslidikins, bully, we'll wallow in wine and women.   Why, this some Madeira-wine has made me as light as a grashopper. Hist, hist, bully, dost thou see those tearers ;   [*Sings.*]
        Look you what here is,
        Look you what here is ;
                        Toll, loll. *&c.*
Agad, t'other glass of Madeira, and I durst have attack'd 'em in my own proper person, without your help.

Bluff. Come on then, knight——————But d'ye know what to say to 'em ?

Sir Jo. Say : Pooh.   Pox, I've enough to say—never fear it——————that is, if I can but think on't : truth is, I have but a treacherous memory.

Bel. Oh, frightful ! Cousin, what shall we do ? These things come towards us.

Aram.

Aram. No matter——I see Vainlove coming this way —and, to confess my failing, I am willing to give him an opportunity of making his peace with me—and to rid me of these coxcombs, when I seem oppress'd with them, will be a fair one.

Bluff. Ladies, by these hilts, you are well met.

Aram. We are afraid not.

Bluff. What says my pretty little knapsack carrier ?

[*To* Belinda.

Bel. O monstrous filthy fellow ? Good slovenly Captain Huff, Bluff, what is your hideous name ? Begone : you stink of brandy and tobacco, most soldier-like. Foh !

[*Spits.*

Sir Jo. Now am I slap-dash down in the mouth, and have not one word to say ! [*Aside.*

Aram. I hope my fool has not confidence enough to be troublesome. [*Aside.*

Sir Jo. Hem ! Pray, Madam, which way's the wind ?

Aram. A pithy question—Have you sent your wits for a venture, Sir, that you enquire ?

Sir Jo. Nay, now I'm in——I can prattle like a magpie. [*Aside.*

Enter Sharper *and* Vainlove, *at some distance.*

Bel. Dear Araminta, I'm tir'd.

Aram. 'Tis but pulling off our masks, and obliging Vainlove to know us. I'll be rid of my fool by fair means——Well, Sir Joseph, you shall see my face—— But, begone immediately—I see one that will be jealous to find me in discourse with you—Be discreet—No reply ; but away. [*Unmasks.*

Sir Jo. The great fortune, that din'd at my Lady Free-love's ! Sir Joseph, thou art a made man. Agad, I'm in love up to the ears. But I'll be discreet, and husht.

[*Aside.*

Bluff. Nay, by the world, I'll see your face.

Bel. You shall. [*Unmasks.*

Sharp. Ladies, your humble servant. We were afraid you would not have given us leave to know you.

Aram. We thought to have been private—But we find fools have the same advantage over a face in a mask, that

E   a coward

a coward has, while the sword is in the scabbard——
So were forced to draw in our own defence.

Bluff. My blood rises at that fellow : I can't stay where
he is : and I must not draw in the park.   [*To Sir* Joseph.

Sir Jo. I wish I durst stay to let her know my lodging.
[*Exeunt Sir* Jo. *and* Bluff.

Sharp. There is in true beauty, as in courage, somewhat which narrow souls cannot dare to admire—and
see, the owls are fled, as at the break of day.

Bel. Very courtly—I believe Mr. Vainlove has not
rubb'd his eyes since break of day neither, he looks as if
he durst not approach—Nay, come, cousin, be friends
with him——I swear he looks so very simply, ha, ha,
ha! Well, a lover in the state of separation from his
mistress, is like a body without a soul. Mr. Vainlove,
shall I be bound for your good behaviour for the future ?

Vain. Now must I pretend ignorance equal to hers,
of what she knows as well as I. [*Aside.*] Men are apt to
offend, 'tis true, where they find most goodness to forgive——————But, Madam, I hope I shall prove of a
temper not to abuse mercy, by committing new offences.

Aram. So cold !   [*Aside.*]

Bel. I have broke the ice for you, Mr. Vainlove;
and so I leave you. Come, Mr. Sharper, you and I
will take a turn, and laugh at the vulgar—both the great
vulgar and the small——Oh, gad ! I have a great passion for Cowley————Don't you admire him ?

Sharp. Oh, Madam ! He was our English Horace.

Bel. Oh, so fine ! So extremely fine ? So every thing
in the world that I like—O Lord, walk this way—I see
a couple, I'll give you their history.

[*Exeunt* Belinda *and* Sharp.

Vain. I find, Madam, the formality of the law must
be observed, tho' the penalty of it be dispens'd with ; and
an offender must plead to his arraignment, though he
has his pardon in his pocket.

Aram. I'm amaz'd ! This insolence exceeds t'other ;
—whoever has encourag'd you to this assurance——
presuming upon the easiness of my temper, has much deceiv'd you, and so you shall find.

Vain. Hey day ! Which way now ! Here's fine dou-
bling.   [*Aside.*]

3   *Aram.*

Aram. Bafe man! Was it not enough to affront me with your faucy paffion?

Vain. You have given that paffion a much kinder epithet than faucy, in another place.

Aram. Another place! Some villainous defign to blaft my honour—But tho' thou hadft all the treachery and malice of thy fex, thou canft not lay a blemifh on my fame—No, I have not err'd in one favourable thought of mankind——' How time might have deceived me in ' you, I know not; my opinion was but young, and ' your early bafenefs has prevented its growing to a wrong ' belief.'———Unworthy and ungrateful! Begone and never fee me more.

Vain. Did I dream? Or do I dream? Shall I believe my eyes or ears? The vifion is here ftill—Your paffion, Madam, will admit of no farther reafoning—But here's a filent witnefs of your acquaintance———

> [*Takes out a letter, and offers it: fhe fnatches it, and throws it away.*

Aram. There's poifon in every thing you touch—— blifters will follow————

Vain. That tongue which denies what the hands have done————

Aram. Still myftically fenfelefs and impudent—I find I muft leave the place.

Vain. No, Madam, I'm gone—She knows her name's to it, which fhe will be unwilling to expofe to the cenfure of the firft finder.   [*Exit.*

Aram. Woman's obftinacy made me blind, to what woman's curiofity now tempts me to fee.

> [*Takes up the letter, and exit.*

Enter Belinda *and* Sharper.

Belin. Nay, we have fpared nobody, I fwear. Mr. Sharper, you're a pure man; where did you get this excellent talent of railing?

Sharp. Faith, Madam, the talent was born with me. ————I confefs, I have taken care to improve it; to qualify me for the fociety of ladies.

Belin. Nay, fure railing is the beft qualification in a woman's man.

Enter Footman.

Sharp. The fecond beft————indeed, I think.

Belin. How now Pace ? Where's my cousin ?

Foot. She's not very well, Madam, and has sent to know, if your Ladyship would have the coach come again for you.

Belin. O Lord, no ! I'll go along with her. Come, Mr. Sharper.

SCENE, *a Chamber in* Fondlewife's *House.*

Enter Lætitia *and* Bellmour, *his cloak, hat, &c. lying loose about the chamber.*

Bell. Here's nobody, nor no noise——'twas nothing but your fears.

Læt. I durst have sworn I had heard my monster's voice.———I swear I was heartily frightened——Feel how my heart beats.

Bell. 'Tis an alarm to love——Come in again, and let us————

Fond. [*Without.*] Cocky, cocky, where are you, cocky ? I'm come home.

Læt. Ah ! there he is ; make haste, gather up your things !

Fond. Cocky, cocky, open the door.

Bell. Pox choak him, would his horns were in his throat. My patch, my patch.

[*Looking about, and gathering up his things.*]

Læt. My jewel, art thou there ? No matter for your patch——You s'an't tum in, Nykin——Run into my chamber, quickly, quickly. You s'an't tum in.

Fond. Nay, pr'ythee, dear, ifeck I'm in haste.

Læt. Then I'll let you in. [*Opens the door.*]

Enter Fondlewife *and Sir* Joseph.

Fond. Kiss, dear——I met the master of the ship by the way——And I must have my papers of accounts out of your cabinet.

Læt. Oh, I'm undone ! [*Aside.*

Sir Jo. Pray, first let me have fifty pounds, good alderman, for I'm in haste.

Fond. A hundred has already been paid by your order. Fifty ? I have the sum in ready gold, in my closet.

[*Exit* Fond.

Sir Jo. Agad, it's a curious, fine, pretty rogue; I'll speak to her—Pray, Madam, what news do you hear ?

Læt.

Læt. Sir, I feldom ftir abroad.

[*Walks about in diforder.*]

Sir Jo. I wonder at that, Madam, for 'tis moft curious fine weather.

Læt. Methinks, 't has been very ill weather.

Sir Jo. As you fay, Madam, 'tis pretty bad weather, and has been fo a great while.

Enter Fondlewife.

Fond. Here are fifty pieces in this purfe, Sir Jofeph—if you will tarry a moment, 'till I fetch my papers, I'll wait upon you down ftairs.

Læt. Ruin'd, paft redemption! What fhall I do——Ha! this fool may be of ufe. [*Afide.*] *As* Fondlewife *is going into the chamber, fhe runs to Sir* Jofeph, *almoft pufhes him down, and cries out.*] Stand off, rude ruffian! Help me, my dear——O blefs me! Why will you leave me alone with fuch a fatyr?

Fond. Blefs us! What's the matter? What's the matter?

Læt. Your back was no fooner turn'd, but like a lion, he came open-mouth'd upon me, and would have ravifhed a kifs from me by main force.

Sir Jo. Oh, Lord! Oh, terrible! Ha, ha, ha! Is your wife mad, alderman!

Læt. Oh! I'm fick with the fright. Won't you take him out of my fight?

Fond. Oh, traitor! I'm aftonifhed. Oh, bloody-minded traitor!

Sir Jo. Hey-day! Traitor yourfelf——By the lord Harry, I was in moft danger of being ravifh'd, if you go to that.

Fond. Oh, how the blafphemous wretch fwears! Out of my houfe, thou fon of the whore of Babylon; off-fpring of Bell and the dragon——Blefs us! Ravifh my wife! my Dinah! Oh, Shechemite! Begone, I fay.

Sir Jo. Why the devil's in the people, I think. [*Exit.*]

Læt. Oh! won't you follow and fee him out of doors, my dear?

Fond. I'll fhut this door to fecure him from coming back——Give me the key of your cabinet, cocky——Ravifh my wife before my face! I warrant he's a Papift in his heart, at leaft, ' if not a Frenchman.'

E 3

Læt.

Læt. What can I do now ? [*Aside.*] Oh ! my dear, I have been in such a fright, that I forgot to tell you, poor Mr. Spintext has a sad fit of the cholic, and is forced to lie down upon our bed ————You'll disturb him ; I can tread softlier.

Fond. Alack, poor man—No, no—you don't know the papers—I won't disturb him : give me the key.

[*She gives him the key, goes to the chamber door, and speaks aloud.*

Læt. 'Tis nobody but Mr. Fondlewife ; Mr. Spintext, lie still on your stomach ; lying on your stomach will ease you of the cholic.

Fond. Ay, ay, lie still, lie still ; don't let me disturb you. [*Exit* Fond.

Læt. Sure, when he does not see his face, he won't discover him. Dear Fortune, help me but this once, and I'll never run in thy debt again————But this opportunity is the devil.

Fondlewife *returns with papers.*

Fond. Good lack ! good lack !————I profess, the poor man is in great torment, he lies as flat—Dear, you should heat a trencher, or a napkin————Where's Deborah ? Let her clap some warm thing to his stomach, or chafe it with a warm hand rather than fail. What book's this ? [*Sees the book that* Bellmour *forgot.*

Læt. My Spintext's prayer-book, dear————Pray heav'n it be a prayer-book. [*Aside.*

Fond. Good man ! I warrant he dropped it on purpose, that you might take it up, and read some of the pious ejaculations. [*Taking up the book.*] O bless me ; O monstrous ! A prayer book ! Ay, this is the devil's Pater-noster. Hold, let me see, The Innocent Adultery.

Læt. Misfortune ! now all's ruin'd again. [*Aside.*

' *Bell.* [*Peeping.*] Damn'd chance ! If I had gone a
' whoring with the Practice of Piety in my pocket, I had
' never been discovered.'

Fond. Adultery and innocent ! O lord ! Here's doctrine ! Ay, here's discipline !

Læt. Dear husband, I'm amazed————Sure it is a good book, and only tends to the speculation of sin.

Fond.

Fond. Speculation ! No, no ; something went farther than speculation, when I was not to be let in—— Where is this apocryphal elder ? I'll ferret him.

Læt. I'm so distracted I can't think of a lie.   [*Aside.*
                              [*Fondlewife hauls out* Bellmour.

Fond. Come out here, thou Ananias incarnate——— Who, how now ! Who have we here ?

Læt. Ha !   [*Shrieks as surpriz'd.*

Fond. Oh, thou salacious woman ! Am I then brutified ? Ay, I feel it here ! I sprout, I bud, I blossom, I am ripe horn-mad. But who, in the devil's name, are you ? Mercy on me, for swearing. But——

Læt. Oh, goodness keep us ! Who's this ? Who are you ? What are you ?

Bell. Soh !

Læt. In the name of the——Oh ! Good, my dear, don't come near it. I'm afraid 'tis the devil ! indeed it has hoofs, dear.

Fond. Indeed, and I have horns, dear. The devil ! No, I am afraid, 'tis the flesh, thou harlot ! Dear, with the pox. Come, siren, speak, confess who is this reverends rampant pastor ?

Læt. Indeed, and indeed now, my dear Nykin—I never saw this wicked man before.

Fond. Oh, it is a man then, it seems.

Læt. Rather, sure, 'tis a wolf in the cloathing of a sheep.

Fond. Thou art a devil in his proper cloathing, woman's flesh. What, you know nothing of him but his fleece here—You don't love mutton ?———You Magdalen unconverted.

Bell. Well, now, I know my cue——that is, very honourably to excuse her, and very impudently accuse myself.   [*Aside.*

Læt. Why then, I wish I may never enter into the heaven of your embraces again, my dear, if ever I saw his face before.

Fond. O lord ! O strange ! I am in admiration of your impudence. Look at him a little better; he is more modest, I warrant you, than to deny it. Come, were you two never face to face before ? Speak.

Bell.

Bell. Since all artifice is vain——and I think myself oblig'd to speak the truth, in justice to your wife———No.

Fond. Humph!

Læt. No, indeed, dear.

Fond. Nay, I find you are both in a story; that I must confess. But, what——not to be cured of the cholic? Don't you know your patient, Mrs. Quack? Oh, lie upon your stomach; lying upon your stomach will cure you of the cholic. Ah! Answer me, Jezabel!

Læt. Let the wicked man answer for himself? Does he think that I have nothing to do but excuse him; 'tis enough, if I can clear my own innocence to my own dear.

Bell. By my troth, and so t'is————I have been a little too backward, that's the truth on't.

Fond. Come, Sir, who are you, in the first place? And what are you?

Bell. A whore-master.

Fond. Very concise.

Læt. O beastly, impudent creature!

Fond. Well, Sir, and what came you hither for?

Bell. To lie with your wife.

Fond. Good, again————A very civil person this, and, I believe, speaks truth.

Læt. Oh, insupportable impudence!

Fond. Well, Sir,————Pray, be cover'd————and you have————Heh! You have finish'd the matter, heh? And I am, as I should be, a sort of a civil perquisite to a whore-master, called a Cuckold, heh. Is it not so? Come, I'm inclining to believe every word you say.

Bell. Why, faith, I must confess, so I designed you— But you were a little unlucky in coming so soon, and hindred the making of your own fortune.

Fond. Humph. Nay, if you mince the matter once, and go back of your word, you are not the person I took you for. Come, come, go on boldly——What, don't be ashamed of your profession—Confess, confess, I shall love thee the better for't——I shall, i'feck.———— What, dost think I don't know how to behave myself in the employment of a cuckold, and have been three

years

years apprentice to matrimony! Come, come, plain dealing is a jewel.

Bell. Well, since I see thou art a good honest fellow, I'll confess the whole matter to thee.

Fond. Oh, I am a very honest fellow———You never lay with an honester man's wife in your life.

Læt. How, my heark akes! All my comfort lies in his impudence, and, heav'n be prais'd, he has a considerable portion.   [*Aside.*

Bell. In short then, I was informed of the opportunity of your absence, by my spy; for, faith, honest Isaac, I have a long time designed thee this favour: I knew Spintext was to come, by your direction; but I laid a trap for him, and procured his habit, in which I pass'd upon your servants, and was conducted hither. I pretended a fit of the cholic, to excuse my lying down upon your bed; hoping that when she heard of it, her good-nature would bring her to administer remedies for my distemper————You know what might have followed—— But, like an uncivil person, you knock'd at the door, before your wife was come to me.

Fond. Ha! this is apocryphal; I may choose whether I will believe it or no.

Bell. That you may, faith, and I hope you won't believe a word on't———But I can't help telling the truth, for my life.

Fond. How! would not you have me believe you, say you?

Bell. No; for then you must of consequence part with your wife, and there will be some hopes of having her upon the public: then, the encouragement of a separate maintenance————

Fond. No, no; for that matter—when she and I part, she'll carry her separate maintenance about her.

Læt. Ah, cruel dear! how can you be so barbarous? You'll break my heart if you talk of parting.   [*Cries.*

Fond. Ah! dissembling vermin!

Bell. How canst thou be so cruel, Isaac? Thou hast the heart of a mountain-tiger. By the faith of a sincere sinner, she's innocent for me. Go to him, Madam, fling your snowy arms about his stubborn neck. Bathe his relentless face in your salt trickling tears————

[*She*

[*She goes and hangs upon his neck, and kisses him. Bell-*
mour kisses *her hand behind* Fondlewife's *back.*

So, a few soft words, and a kiss, and the good man melts.
See how kind nature works, and boils over in him.

Læt. Indeed, my dear, I was but just come down stairs,
when you knock'd at the door; and the maid told me,
Mr. Spintext was ill of the cholic upon our bed. And
won't you speak to me, cruel Nykin? Indeed, I'll die,
if you don't.

Fond. Ah! No, no, I cannot speak, my heart's so
full————I have been a tender yokefellow; you know
I have————But thou hast been a faithless Dalilah, and
the Philistines————Heh! Art thou not vile and unclean,
heh? Speak. 　　　　　　　　　　　　　　[*Weeping.*

Læt. No——h. 　　　　　　　　　　　　[*Sighing.*

Fond. Oh, that I could believe thee!

Læt. Oh! my heart will break! 　　[*Seeming to faint.*

Fond. Heh! how! No, no, stay, stay, I will believe
thee, I will ————Pray bend her forward, Sir.

Læt. Oh! Oh! Where is my dear?

Fond. Here, here; I do believe thee——I won't believe my own eyes.

Bell. For my part, I am so charm'd with the love of
your turtle to you, that I'll go and solicit matrimony
with all my might and main.

Fond. Well, well, Sir; as long as I believe it, 'tis
well enough. No thanks to you, Sir, for her virtue.
————But, I'll shew you the way out of my house,
if you please. Come, my dear. Nay, I will believe
thee, I do, i'feck.

Bell. See the great blessing of an easy faith; opinion
cannot err.

　　　No husband, by his wife, can be deceiv'd,
　　　She still is virtuous, if she's so believ'd.

　　　　　End of the Fourth Act.

ACT

ACT V.

Enter Bellmour *in a fanatic habit;* Setter, Heartwell, *and* Lucy.

BELLMOUR.

SEtter! well encounter'd.

Set. Joy of your return, Sir. Have you made a good voyage; or have you brought your own lading back?

Bell. No, I have brought nothing but ballaft back—— made a delicious voyage, Setter ; and might have rode at anchor in the port till this time, but the enemy furpriz'd us.'————I would unrig.

Set. I attend you, Sir.

Bell. Ha.! Is not that Heartwell at Silvia's door? Begone quickly, I'll follow you :————I would not be known. Pox take 'em, they ftand juft in my way.

[*Exit* Setter.

Heart. I'm impatient till it be done.

Lucy. That may be, without troubling yourfelf to go again for your brother's chaplain. Don't you fee that talking form of godlinefs ?

Heart. Oh, ay, he's a fanatic.

Lucy. An executioner, qualified to do your bufinefs. He has been lawfully ordained.

Heart. I'll pay him well, if you'll break the matter to him.

Lucy. I warrant you——Do you go and prepare your bride.

[*Exit* Heart.

Bell. Humph, fits the wind there ?————What a lucky rogue am I ! Oh, what fport will be here, if I can perfuade this wench to fecrefy ?

Lucy. Sir ; reverend Sir.

Bell. Madam.   [*Difcovers himfelf.*

Lucy. Now, goodnefs have mercy upon me ! Mr. Bellmour ! is it you ?

Bell. Even I, what doft think !

Lucy. Think ! that I thou'd not believe my eyes, and that you are not what you feem to be,

Bell.

Bell. True. But to convince thee who I am, thou knowſt my old token. [*Kiſſes her.*

Lucy. Nay, Mr. Bellmour: O Lard! I believe you are a parſon in good earneſt, you kiſs ſo devoutly.

Bell. Well, your buſineſs with me, Lucy?

Lucy. I had none, through miſtake.

Bell. Which miſtake you muſt go through with, Lucy——Come, I know the intrigue between Heartwell and your miſtreſs; and you miſtook me for Tribulation Spintext, to marry 'em——Ha! are not matters in this poſture?——Confeſs. Come, I'll be faithful; I will, i'faith.——What, diffide in me, Lucy?

Lucy. Alas-a-day! You and Mr. Vainlove, between you, have ruin'd my poor miſtreſs: you have made a gap in her reputation! and can you blame her, if ſhe make it up with a huſband!

Bell. Well, is it as I ſay?

Lucy. Well, it is then: but you'll be ſecret?

Bell. Phuh, ſecret, ay!—And to be out of thy debt, I'll truſt thee with another ſecret. Your miſtreſs muſt not marry Heartwell, Lucy.

Lucy. How! O Lord!——

Bell. Nay, don't be in a paſſion, Lucy—I'll provide a fitter huſband for her——Come, here's earneſt of my good intentions for thee, too; let this molify.——[*Gives her money.*] Look you, Heartwell is my friend; and though he be blind, I muſt not ſee him fall into the ſnare, and wittingly marry a whore.

Lucy. Whore! I'd have you to know my miſtreſs ſcorns——

Bell. Nay, nay; look you, Lucy; there are whores of as good quality——But to the purpoſe, if you will give me leave to acquaint you with it—Do you carry on the miſtake of me: I'll marry 'em——Nay, don't pauſe!——If you do, I'll ſpoil all.——I have ſome private reaſons for what I do, which I'll tell you within.——In the mean time, I promiſe,——and rely upon me—to help your miſtreſs to a huſband: nay, and thee too, Lucy——Here's my hand, I will, with a freſh aſſurance. [*Gives her more money.*

Lucy. Ah, the devil is not ſo cunning——You know my eaſy nature——Well, for once I'll venture
to

to ferve you; but if you do deceive me, the curfe of all kind, tender-hearted women light upon you.

Bell. That's as much as to fay, the pox take me.——Well, lead on.   [*Exeunt.*

Enter Vainlove, Sharper, *and* Setter.

Sharp. Juft now, fay you, gone in with Lucy?

Set. I faw him, and ftood at the corner where you found me, and overheard all they faid: Mr. Bellmour is to marry 'em.

Sharp. Ha, ha! 'twill be a pleafant cheat.——I'll plague Heartwell, when I fee him. Pr'ythee, Frank, let's teaze him; make him fret, till he foam at the mouth, and difgorge his matrimonial oath with intereft——Come, thou'rt mufty——

Set. [*To* Sharper.] Sir, a word with you.

[*Whifpers him.*

Vain. Sharper fwears fhe has forfworn the letter——I'm fure he tells me truth;——but I am not fure fhe told him truth—Yet fhe was unaffectedly concern'd, he fays; and often blufh'd with anger and furprize;——And fo I remember in the Park——She had reafon, if I wrong her——I begin to doubt.

Sharp. Say'ft thou fo!

Set. This afternoon, Sir, about an hour before my mafter receiv'd the letter.

Sharp. In my confcience, like enough.

Set. Ay, I know her, Sir: at leaft I'm fure I can fifh it out of her: fhe's the very fluice to her lady's fecrets. 'Tis but feting her mill a going, and I can drain her of 'em all.

Sharp. Here, Frank, your blood-hound has made out the fault. This letter, that fo fticks in thy maw, is counterfeit; only a trick of Silvia, in revenge, contriv'd by Lucy.

Vain. Ha! It has a colour——But how do you know it, firrah?

Set. I do fufpect as much;——becaufe why, Sir,——She was pumping me about how your worfhip's affairs ftood towards Madam Araminta; as, when you had feen her laft; when you were to fee her next; and, where you were to be found at that time; and fuch like.

F

Vain.

Vain. And where did you tell her?

Set. In the Piazza.

Vain. There I receiv'd the letter——It muft be fo——
——And why did you not find me out, to tell me this
before, fot?

Set. Sir, I was employed for Mr. Bellmour.

Sharp. You were well employ'd——I think there is no
objection to the excufe.

Vain. Pox o'my faucy credulity——If I have loft her,
I deferve it. But if confeffion and repentance be of force,
I'll win her or weary her into a forgivenefs.   [*Exit.*

Sharp. Methinks I long to fee Bellmour come forth.

Enter Bellmour.

Set. Talk of the devil——See, where he comes.

Sharp. Hugging himfelf in his profperous mifchief——
No real fanatic can look better pleas'd, after a fuccefsful
fermon of fedition.

Bell. Sharper, fortify thy fpleen: fuch a jeft! Speak
when thou art ready.

Sharp. Now, were I ill-natur'd, would I utterly dif-
appoint thy mirth : ' hear thee tell thy mighty jeft,
' with as much gravity as a bifhop hears venereal caufes in
' the fpiritual court :' not fo much as wrinkle my face
with one fmile, but let thee look fimply, and laugh by
thyfelf.

Bell. Pfhaw, no: I have a better opinion of thy wit
——————Gad, I defy thee.——————

Sharp. Were it not lofs of time, you fhould make the
experiment. But honeft Setter, here, overheard you
with Lucy, and has told me all.

Bell. Nay, then, I thank thee for not putting me out
of countenance. But, to tell you fomething you don't
know——I got an opportunity, after I had married 'em,
of difcovering the cheat to Silvia. She took it, at firft,
as another woman wou'd the like difappointment ; but
my promife to make her amends quickly with another
hufband, fomewhat pacified her.

Sharp. But how the devil do you think to acquit yourfelf of your promife? Will you marry her yourfelf?

Bell. I have no fuch intentions at prefent——Pr'ythee,
wilt thou think a little for me? I am fure the ingenious
Mr. Setter will affift.

Set. O Lord, Sir!

Bell.

Bell. I'll leave him with you, and go shift my habit.

                                            [Exit.

Enter Sir Joseph, *and* Bluff.

Sharp. Heh ! Sure Fortune has sent this fool hither on purpose. Setter, stand close ; seem not to observe them ; and, heark'e——   *[Whispers.*

Bluff. Fear him not—I am prepar'd for him now ; and he shall find he might have safer rous'd a sleeping lion.

Sir Jo. Hush, hush ; don't you see him ?

Bluff. Shew him to me.——Where is he ?

Sir Jo. Nay, don't speak so loud——I don't jest, as I did a little while ago————Look yonder——Agad, if he should hear the lion roar, he'd cudgel him into an ass, and his primitive braying. Don't you remember the story of Æsop's Fables, bully ? A-gad, there are good morals to be pick'd out of Æsop's Fables, let me tell you that ; and Reynard the Fox, too.

Bluff. Damn your morals.

Sir Jo. Pr'ythee, don't speak so loud.

Bluff. Damn your morals : I must revenge the affront done to my honour.   *[In a low voice.*

Sir Jo. Ay, do, do, Captain, if you think fitting ——You may dispose of your own flesh as you think fitting, d'ye see. but, by the Lord Harry, I'll leave you.

                      [Stealing away upon his tiptoes.

Bluff. Prodigious ! What, will you forsake your friend in extremity ! You can't in honour refuse to carry him a challenge.

        [Almost whispering, and treading softly after him.

Sir Jo. Pr'ythee, what do you see in my face, that looks as if I would carry a challenge ? Honour is your province, Captain ; take it——All the world know me to be a knight and a man of worship.

Set. I warrant you, Sir, I'm instructed.

Sharp. Impossible ! Araminta take a liking to a fool !

                                [Aloud.

Set. Her head runs on nothing else, nor she can talk of nothing else.

Sharp. I know she commended him all the while we were in the Park, but thought it had been only to make Vainlove jealous.

F 2   *Sir Jo.*

Sir Jo. How's this! Good bully, hold your breath, and let's hearken. • A-gad, this muſt be I.

Sharp. Death, it can't be.——An oaf, an ideot, a wittal.

Sir Jo. Ay, now it's out ; 'tis I, my own individual perſon.

Sharp. A wretch, that has flown for ſhelter to the loweſt ſhrub of mankind, and ſeeks protection from a blaſted coward.

Sir Jo. That's you, bully back.

[Bluff *frowns upon Sir* Joſeph.

Sharp. She has given Vainlove her promiſe to marry him before to-morrow morning.——Has ſhe not ?

[*To* Setter.

Set. She has, Sir——And I have it in charge to attend her all this evening, in order to conduct her to the place appointed.

Sharp. Well, I'll go and inform your maſter ; and do you preſs her to make all the haſte imaginable.   [*Exit.*

Set. Were I a rogue, now, what a noble prize could I diſpoſe of! A good pinnace, richly laden, and to launch forth under my auſpicious convoy.. Twelve thouſand pounds, and all her rigging : beſides what lies conceal'd under hatches——Ha ! all this committed to my care ! ——Avaunt, temptation—Setter, ſhew thyſelf a perſon of worth ; be true to thy truſt, and be reputed honeſt. Reputed honeſt ! Hum ; is that all ? Ay ; for to be honeſt is nothing ; the reputation of it is all. Reputation ! what have ſuch poor rogues as I to do with reputation ? 'tis above us ; and for men of quality, they are above it ; ſo that reputation is e'en as fooliſh a thing as honeſty. And for my part, if I meet Sir Joſeph, with a purſe of gold in his hand, I'll diſpoſe of mine to the beſt advantage.

Sir Jo. Heh, heh, heh : here 'tis for you, i'faith, Mr. Setter. Nay, I'll take you at your word.

[*Chinking a purſe.*

Set. Sir Joſeph ! and the Captain too ! Undone, undone ! I'm undone, my maſter's undone, my lady's undone, and all the buſineſs is undone.

Sir Jo.

Sir Jo. No, no, never fear, man, the lady's bufinefs shall be done. What——Come, Mr. Setter, I have over-heard all, and to fpeak is but lofs of time ; but, if there be occafion, let thefe worthy gentlemen intercede for me.   [*Gives him gold.*

Set. O Lord, Sir ! what d'ye mean ? Corrupt my honefty——They have, indeed very perfuading faces. But——

Sir Jo. 'Tis too little ; there's more, man. There, take all ——Now——

Set. Well, Sir Jofeph, you have fuch a winning way with you——

Sir Jo. And how, and how, good Setter, did the little rogue look, when fhe talk'd of Sir Jofeph ? Did not her eyes twinkle and her mouth water ? ' Did not fhe pull up ' her little bubbies ? And—Agad, I'm fo overjoy'd—— ' And ftroke down her belly ; and then ftep afide to tie ' her garter,' when fhe was thinking of her love ? Heh, Setter !

Set. O yes, Sir.

Sir Jo. How now, bully ? What, melancholy, becaufe I'm in the lady's favour ?——No matter, I'll make your peace——I know they were a little fmart upon you—But, I warrant I'll bring you into the lady's good graces.

Bluff. Pfhaw ! I have petitions to fhew from otherguefs toys than fhe. Look here ; thefe were fent me this morning—There, read, [*Shews letters.*] That—— that's a fcrawl of quality. Here, here's from a countefs, too. Hum——No, hold——that's from a knight's wife, fhe fent it me by her hufband——But here, both thefe are from perfons of great quality.

Sir Jo. They are either from perfons of great quality, or no quality at all, 'tis fuch a damn'd ugly hand.

[*While Sir* Jofeph *reads,* Bluff *whifpers* Setter.

Set. Captain, I would do any thing to ferve you ; but this is fo difficult——

Bluff. Not at all. Don't I know him ?

Set. You'll remember the conditions ;——

Bluff. I'll giv't you under my hand——In the mean time, here's earneft. [*Gives him money.*] Come, knight——I'm capitulating with Mr. Setter, for you.

F 3

Sir Jo.

Sir Jo. Ah, honest Setter——Sirrah, I'll give thee any thing, ' but a night's lodging.'   [*Exeunt.*

Enter Sharper, *tugging in* Heartwell.

Sharp. Nay, pr'ythee leave railing, and come along with me, may be she mayn't be within. 'Tis but to yond' corner-house.

Heart. Whither? Whither? Which corner-house?

Sharp. Why, there; the two white posts.

Heart. And who would you visit there, say you? (Oons, how my heart akes.)

Sharp. Pshaw! thou'rt so troublesome and inquisitive ——Why, I'll tell you; 'tis a young creature that Vainlove debauched, and has forsaken. Did you never hear Bellmour chide him about Silvia?

Heart. Death, and hell, and marriage! my wife.

                              [*Aside.*

Sharp. Why, thou art as musty as a new-married man, that had found his wife knowing the first night.

Heart. Hell and the devil! Does he know it? But, hold——If he should not, I were a fool to discover it ———I'll dissemble, and try him: [*Aside.*] Ha, ha, ha! Why, Tom, is that such an occasion of melancholy? Is it such an uncommon mischief?

Sharp. No, faith; I believe not.——Few women, but have their probation, before they are cloister'd in the narrow joys of wedlock. But, pr'ythee come along with me, or I'll go and have the lady to myself. B'w'ye, George.   [*Going.*

Heart. O torture! How he racks and tears me!—— Death! Shall I own my shame, or wittingly let him go and whore my wife? No, that's insupportable——Oh, Sharper!

Sharp. How, now?

Heart. Oh, I am——marry'd.

Sharp. Now, hold spleen. [*Aside.*] Marry'd!

Heart. Certainly, irrecoverably marry'd.

Sharp. Heav'n forbid, man!—How long?

Heart. Oh, an age, an age! I have been marry'd these two hours.

Sharp. My old batchelor marry'd! That were a jest. Ha, ha, ha!

                              Heart.

Heart. Death! d'ye mock me? Heark ye, if either
you esteem my friendship, or your own safety—come not
near that house—that corner house——that hot brothel.
Ask no questions.

Sharp. Mad, by this light.   [*Exit* Heart.
Thus grief still treads upon the heels of pleasure.
Marry'd in haste, we may repent at leisure.

Enter Setter.

Set. Some by experience find those words misplac'd:
At leisure marry'd, they repent in haste,
As I suppose my master Heartwell.

Sharp. Here again, my Mercury!

Set. Sublimate, if you please, Sir: I think my at-
chievements do deserve the epithet——Mercury was a
pimp too; but though I blush to own it at this time, I
must confess, I am somewhat fallen from the dignity of
my function, and do condescend to be scandalously employ'd in the promotion of vulgar matrimony.

Sharp. As how, dear, dexterous pimp?

Set. Why, to be brief, for I have weighty affairs de-
pending———Our stratagem succeeded as you intended;
Bluff turns arrant traitor; bribes me to make private conveyance of the lady to him, and put a sham-settlement
upon Sir Joseph.

Sharp. O rogue! Well, but I hope.———

Set. No, no: never fear me, Sir———I privately informed the knight of the treachery; who has agreed,
seemingly to be cheated, that the Captain may be so in
reality.

Sharp. Where's the bride?

Set. Shifting clothes for the purpose, at a friend's
house of mine. Here's company coming; if you'll walk
this way, Sir, I'll tell you.   [*Exeunt.*

Enter Bellmour, Belinda, Araminta, *and* Vainlove.

Vain. Oh, 'twas frenzy all: cannot you forgive it?——
Men in madness have a title to your pity. [*To* Araminta.

Aram.——Which they forfeit, when they are resto-
red to their senses.

Vain. I am not presuming beyond a pardon.

Aram.

Aram. You, who cou'd reproach me with one counterfeit, how infolent would a real pardon make you? But there's no need to forgive what is not worth my anger.

Belin. O' my confcience, I cou'd find in my heart to marry thee, purely to be rid of thee——At leaft, thou art fo troublefome a lover, there's hopes thou'lt make a more than ordinary quiet-hufband.   [*To Bellmour.*

Bell. Say you fo———— Is that a maxim among ye?

' *Belin.* Yes: you fluttering men of the mode have
' made marriage a mere French difh.

' *Bell.* I hope there's no French fauce.   [*Afide.*

' *Belin.* You are fo curious in the preparation, that is,
' your courtfhip, one wou'd think you meant a noble
' entertainment——But when we come to feed, 'tis all
' froth and poor, but in fhow: Nay, often, only re
' mains, which have been I know not how many times
' times warm'd for other company, and at laft ferv'd up
' cold to the wife.

' *Bell.* That were a miferable wretch indeed, who
' could not afford one warm difh for the wife of his bo
' fom—But you, timorous virgins, form a dreadful chi
' mera of a hufband, as of a creature contrary to that
' foft, humble, pliant, eafy thing, a lover; fo guefs at
' plagues in matrimony, in oppofition to the pleafures of
' courtfhip. Alas! courtfhip to marriage, is but as the
' mufic in the play-houfe, 'till the curtain's drawn; but
' that once up, then opens the fcene of pleafure.

' *Belin.* Oh, foh—no: rather, courtfhip to marriage,
' as a very witty prologue to a very dull play.

Enter Sharper.

Sharp. Hift,—— Bellmour: if you'll bring the ladies, make hafte to Silvia's lodgings, before Heartwell has fretted himfelf out of breath.————.

Bell. You have an opportunity now, Madam, to revenge yourfelf upon Heartwell, for affronting your fquirrel.   [*To Belinda.*

Belin. Oh, the filthy rude beaft.

Aram. 'Tis a lafting quarrel: I think he has never been at our houfe fince.

Bell. But give yourfelves the trouble to walk to that corner-houfe, and I'll tell you by the way what may divert and furprize you.   [*Exeunt.*

SCENE,

SCENE, Silvia's *Lodgings.*

Enter Heartwell *and Boy.*

Heart. Gone forth, say you, with her maid?

Boy. There was a man too that fetch'd 'em out—Setter, I think they call him.

Heart. Soh——That precious pimp too——Damn'd, damn'd strumpet! Cou'd she not contain herself on her wedding day! Not hold out 'till night! O cursed state! How wide we err, when apprehensive of the load of life,

——————We hope to find }
That help which nature meant in womankind, }
To man that suplemental self design'd; }
But proves a burning caustic when apply'd, }
And, Adam, sure, cou'd with more ease abide }
The bone when broken, than when made a bride. }

Enter Bellmour, Belinda, Vainlove *and* Araminta.

Bell. Now, George, what rhyming? I thought the chimes of verse were past, when once the doleful marriage knell was rung.

Heart. Shame and confusion! I am expos'd.

[*Vainlove and* Araminta *talk apart.*

Belin. Joy, joy, Mr. Bridegroom: I give you joy, Sir.

Heart. 'Tis not in thy nature to give me joy —— A woman can as soon give immortality.

Belin. Ha, ha, ha! O gad, men grow such clowns when they are marry'd.

Bell. That they are fit for no company but their wives.

Belin. Nor for them neither, in a little time—I swear, at the month's end, you shall hardly find a marry'd man that will do a civil thing to his wife, or say a civil thing to any body else. How he looks already? Ha, ha, ha!

Bell. Ha, ha, ha!

Heart. Death! am I made your laughing stock? For you, Sir, I shall find a time; but take off your wasp here, or the clown may grow boisterous: I have a fly-flap.

Belin. You have occasion for't, your wife has been blown upon.

Bell. That's home.

Heart.

Heart. Not friends or furies could have added to my vexation, or any thing else, but another woman—You've rack'd my patience ; begone, or by————

Bell. Hold, hold! What the devil, thou wilt not draw upon a woman?

Vain. What's the matter?

Aram. Bless me! What have you done to him!

Belin. Only touch'd a gall'd beast 'till he winc'd.

Vain. Bellmour, give it over ; you vex him too much : 'tis all serious to him.

Belin. Nay, I swear, I begin to pity him myself.

Heart. Damn your pity—But let me be calm a little—How have I deserv'd this of you, any of ye? Sir, have I impaired the honour of your house, promis'd your sister marriage and seduc'd her? Wherein have I injur'd you? Did I bring a physician to your father when he lay expiring, and endeavour to prolong his life, and you one and twenty? Madam, have I had an opportunity with you and baulk'd it? Did you ever offer me the favour and I refus'd it? Or————

Belin. Oh, foh! What does the filthy fellow mean? Lard, let me begone.

Aram. Hang me, if I pity you ; you are right enough serv'd.

' *Bell.* This is a little scurrilous, tho'.

Vain. ' Nay, 'tis a sore of your own scratching——' Well, George————

Heart. You are the principal cause of all my present ills. If Silvia had not been your mistress, my wife might have been honest.

Vain. And if Silvia had not been your wife, my mistress might have been just—There we are even——but have a good heart, I heard of your misfortune, and am come to your relief.

Heart. When execution's over, you offer a reprieve.

Vain. What would you give?

Heart. Oh! any thing, every thing, a leg, or two, or an arm : ' nay, I would be divorc'd from my virility, ' to be divorc'd from my wife.'

Enter Sharper.

Vain. Don't offer so much, for here's one can sell you freedom cheaper.

Sharp.

Sharp. Vainlove, I have been a kind of a god-father, to you, yonder. I have promis'd and vow'd some things in your name, which I think you are bound to perform.

Vain. No signing to a blank, friend.

Sharp. No; I'll deal fairly with you————'Tis a full and free discharge to Sir Joseph Wittol and Captain Bluff; for all injuries whatsoever, done unto you, by them, until the present date hereof—How say you?

Vain. Agreed.

Sharp. Then, let me beg these ladies to wear their masks a moment. Come in, gentlemen and ladies. —

Heart. What the devil's all this to me!

Vain. Patience.

Enter Sir Joseph, Bluff, Silvia, Lucy, *and* Setter.

Bluff. All injuries whatsoever, Mr. Sharper.

Sir Jo. Ay, ay, whatsoever, Captain, stick to that; whatsoever.

Sharp. 'Tis done, these gentlemen are witnesses to the general release.

Vain. Ay, ay, to this instant moment—I have pass'd an act of oblivion.

Bluff. 'Tis very generous, Sir, since I needs must own————

Sir Jo. No, no, Captain, you need not own; heh, heh, heh, 'tis I must own————

Bluff. That you are over-reach'd too, ha, ha, ha! only a little art military used—only undermined, or so, as shall appear by the fair Araminta, my wife's permission. [Lucy *unmasks.*] Oh, the devil, cheated at last!

Sir Jo. Only a little art-military trick, Captain, only countermin'd, or so————Mr. Vainlove, I suppose you know whom I have got————now; but all's forgiven.

Vain. I know whom you have not got. Pray, ladies, convince him. [Aram. *and* Belin. *unmask.*

Sir Jo. Ah! O lord, my heart akes—Ah, Setter, a rogue of all sides.

Sharp. Sir Joseph, you had better have pre-engaged this gentleman's pardon : for though Vainlove be so generous to forgive the loss of his mistress, I know not how Heartwell may take the loss of his wife. [Silvia *unmasks.*

Heart.

Heart. My wife ! By this light 'tis she, the very cock-
atri   harper ! Let me embrace thee——But art
th ce—Oh, S really marry'd to him ?
ou sure she is d lawfully marry'd, I am witness.

Sharp. Bellmour will unriddle to you.

[*Heartwell goes to* Bellmour.

Sir Jo. Pray, Madam, who are you ? For I find, you
and I are like to better acquainted.

Silv. The worst of me is, that I am your wife——

Sharp. Come, Sir Joseph, your fortune is not so bad
as your fear——A fine lady, and a lady of very
good quality.

Sir Jo. Thanks to my knighthood, she's a lady——

Vain.——That deserves a fool with a better title—
Pray use her as my relation, or you shall hear on't.

Bluff. What, are you a woman of quality too spouse ?

Set. And my relation ; pray let her be respected accordingly——Well, honest Lucy, fare thee well—I think
you and I have been play-fellows, off and on, any time
this seven years.

Lucy. Hold your prating—I'm thinking what vocation
I shall follow while my spouse is planting laurels in the
wars.

Bluff. No more wars, spouse, no more wars—While
I plant laurels for my head abroad, I may find the branches
sprout at home.

Heart. Bellmour, I approve thy mirth, and thank
thee—And I cannot in gratitude, for I see which way
thou art going, see thee fall into the same snare out of
which thou hast delivered me.

Bell. I thank thee, George, for thy good intention—
But there is a fatality in marriage————for I find I'm resolute.

Heart. Then good counsel will be thrown away upon
you————For my part, I have once escaped——And
when I wed again, may she be——ugly as an old bawd.

Vain. Ill-natur'd as an old maid————

Bell. Wanton as a young widow————

Sharp. And jealous as a barren wife.

Heart. Agreed.

Bell. Well ; 'midst of these dreadful denunciations,
and

and notwithstanding the warning and example before me,
I commit myself to lasting durance.

Belin. Prisoner, make much of your fetters.

[*Giving her hand.*

Bell. Frank, will you keep us in countenance ?

Vain. May I presume to hope so great a blessing ?

Aram. We had better take the advantage of a little of
our friends' experience first.

Bell. O' my conscience she dare not consent, for fear
he shou'd recant. [*Aside.*] Well, we shall have your company to church in the morning————May be it may
get you an appetite to see us fall on before you, ' Setter,
' did not you tell me————

' *Set.* They're at the door ; I'll call 'em in.

[' *A Dance.*

Bell. Not set me forward on a journey for life—Come,
take your fellow travellers. Old George, I'm sorry to see
thee still plod on alone.

Heart. With gaudy plumes, and gingling bells made
  proud,
The youthful beast sets forth, and neighs aloud.
A morning-sun his tinsell'd harness gilds,
And the first stage a down-hill green-swerd yields.
But, Oh !
What rugged ways attend the noon of life !
Our sun declines, and with what anxious strife;
What pain we tug that galling load, a wife.
All coursers the first heat with vigour run ;
But 'tis with whip and spur the race is won.

[*Exeunt Omnes.*

END of the FIFTH ACT.

G

E P I-

EPILOGUE.

As a rash girl, who will all hazards run,
*   Will be enjoy'd, tho' sure to be undone;*
Soon as her curiosity is over,
Would give the world she could her toy recover:
So fares it with our poet; and I'm sent
To tell you, he already does repent.
Would you were all as forward to keep Lent.
Now the deed's done, the giddy thing has leisure
To think o'th' sting, that's in the tail of pleasure.
Methinks, I hear him in consideration:
What will the world say? Where's my reputation?
Now that's at stake——No, fool, 'tis out o' fashion.
If loss of that should follow want of wit,
How many undone men were in the pit!
Why, that's some comfort to an author's fears,
If he's an ass, he will be try'd by's peers.
But hold——I am exceeding my commission;
My business here, was humbly to petition.
But we're so us'd to rail on these occasions,
I could not help one trial of your patience:
For 'tis our way, you know, for fear o'th' worst,
To be beforehand still, and try fool first.
How say you, sparks? How do you stand affected?
I swear, young Bayes within, is so dejected,
'Twould grieve your hearts to see him; shall I call him?
But then you cruel critics would so maul him!
Yet, may be, you'll encourage a beginner;
But how?——Just as the devil does a sinner.
Women and wits are us'd e'en much at one,
You gain your end, and damn 'em when you've done.

Mr MOODY in the Character of TEAGUE.
A poor Irishman & Christ save me, & save you,
Iprythee give me Sixpence good Masters.

THE
COMMITTEE.

A COMEDY,

As written by the Hon. Sir R. HOWARD.

DISTINGUISHING ALSO THE

VARIATIONS OF THE THEATRE,

AS PERFORMED AT THE

Theatre-Royal in Drury-Lane.

Regulated from the Prompt-Book,

By PERMISSION of the MANAGERS,

By Mr. HOPKINS, Prompter.

LONDON:

Printed for JOHN BELL, near *Exeter-Exchange,* in the *Strand,*

MDCCLXXVII.

PROLOGUE.

TO cheat the most judicious eyes, there be
    Ways in all trades, but this of poetry:
Your tradesman shews his ware by some false light,
To hide the faults and slightness from your sight:
Nay, though 'tis full of bracks, he'll boldly swear
'Tis excellent, and so help off his ware.
He'll rule your judgment by his confidence,
Which in a poet you'd call impudence;
Nay, if the world afford the like again,
He swears he'll give it you for nothing, then.
Those are words too a poet dares not say;
Let it be good or bad, you're sure to pay.
—Wou'd 'twere a penn'worth; ——but in this you are
Abler to judge, than he that made the ware.
However, his design was well enough,
He try'd to shew some newer fashion'd-stuff.
Not that the name Committee can be new,
That has been too well known to most of you:
    But you may smile, for you have past your doom;
    The poet dares not, his is still to come.

 DRA-

DRAMATIS PERSONÆ.

MEN.

Drury-Lane.

Colonel *Careless*	Mr. Brereton.
Colonel *Blunt*	Mr. Aickin.
Lieutenant *Story*	Mr. Fawcet.
Nehemiah Catch	Mr. Waldron.
Joseph Blemish	
Jonathan Headstrong	Committee-men.
Ezekiel Scrape	
Mr. *Day*, the Chairman to the Committee	Mr. Baddeley.
Abel, Son to Mr. *Day*	Mr. Burton.
Obadiah, Clerk to the Committee	Mr. Parsons.
Teague	Mr. Moody.
Tavern Boy	Mr. Everard.
Bailiff	Mr. Griffith.
Soldier	Mr. Blanchard.
Two Chairmen	Mr. Heath, &c.
Gaol-keeper	Mr. Kear.
A Servant to Mr. *Day*	
A Stage Coachman	
Bookseller	Mr. Carpenter.
Porter	Mr. Wrighten.

WOMEN.

Mrs. *Ruth*	Miss Pope.
Mrs. *Day*	Mrs. Bradshaw.
Mrs. *Arbella*	Miss Jarrat.
Mrs. *Chat*	Mrs. Cartwright.

SCENE, *LONDON.*

THE

THE COMMITTEE.

ACT I.

Enter Mrs. Day, *brushing her hoods and scarfs, Mrs. Arbella,* Mrs. Ruth, Col. Blunt, *and a Stage-Coachman.*

Mrs. DAY.

NOW, out upon't, how dusty 'tis! All things considered, 'tis better to travel in the winter; especially for us of the better sort, that ride in coaches. And yet, to say truth, warm weather is both pleasant and comfortable; 'tis a thousand pities that fair weather should do any hurt.—Well said, honest coachman, thou hast done thy part! My son, Abel, paid for my place at Reading, did he not?

Coach. Yes, an't please you.

Mrs. D. Well, there's something extraordinary, to make thee drink.

Coach. By my whip, 'tis a groat of more than ordinary thinness.—Plague on this new gentry, how liberal they are. [*Aside.*] Farewel, young mistress; farewel, gentlemen. Pray when you come by Reading, let Toby carry you.   [*Exit Coachman.*

Mrs. D. Why how now, Mrs. Arbella! What, sad! Why, what's the matter?

Arbel. I am not very sad.

A 3

Mrs. D.

Mrs. D. Nay, by my honour, you need not, if you knew as much as I. Well——I'll tell you one thing; you are well enough; you need not fear, whoever does; say I told you so—if you do not hurt yourself; for as cunning as he is, and let him be as cunning as he will, I can see with half an eye that my son Abel means to take care of you in your compofition, and will needs have you his gueft. Ruth and you fhall be bedfellows. I warrant, that fame Abel many and many a time will wifh his fifter's place; or elfe his father ne'er got him. Though I say it that fhou'd not fay it, yet I do fay it———'tis a notable fellow———

Arbel. I am fallen into ftrange hands, if they prove as bufy as her tongue——— [*Afide.*

Mrs. D. And now you talk of this fame Abel, I tell you but one thing: I wonder that neither he nor my hufband's honour's chief clerk, Obadiah, is not here ready to attend me. I dare warrant my fon Abel as been here two hours before us; 'Tis the verieft Princox; he will ever be galloping, and yet he is not full one and twenty, for all his appearances. He never ftole this trick of galloping; his father was juft fuch another before him, and wou'd gallop with the beft of 'em: he and Mrs. Bufie's hufband, were counted the beft horfemen in Reading, ay, and Berkfhire to boot. I have iode formerly behind Mr. Bufie, but in truth I cannot now endure to travel but in a coach; my own is at prefent in diforder, and fo I was fain to fhift in this; but I warrant you, if his honour, Mr. Day, chairman of the honourable committee of fcqueftrations, fhou'd know that his wife rode in a ftage-coach, he wou'd make the houfe too hot for fome.——Why how is't with you, Sir? What weary of your journey?

[To the Colonel.

Blunt. Her tongue will never tire. [*Afide*]—So many, Miftrefs, riding in the coach, has a little diftemper'd me with heat.

Mrs. D. So many, Sir! Why there were but fix— What wou'd you fay if I fhould tell you, that I was one of the eleven that travell'd at one time in one coach?

Blunt. O, the devil! I have given her a new theme—

[Afide.

Mrs. D. Why, I'll tell you—Can you guefs how 'twas?

Blunt.

Blunt. Not I, truly. But 'tis no matter, I do believe it.

Mrs. D. Look you, thus it was; there was, in the first place, myself, and my husband I shou'd have said first, but his honour wou'd have pardon'd me, if he had heard me: Mr. Busie that I told you of, and his wife; the mayor of Reading and his wife; and this Ruth that you see there, in one of our laps——But now, where do you think the rest were?

Blunt. A top o'th' coach, sure.

Mrs. D. Nay, I durst swear you wou'd never guess—why—wou'd you think it; I had two growing in my belly, Mrs. Busie one in hers, and Mrs. Mayoress of Reading a chopping boy, as it proved afterwards, in hers, as like the father as if it had been spit out of his mouth; and if he had come out of his mouth, he had come out of as honest a man's mouth as any in forty miles of the head of him: for, wou'd you think it? at the very same time when this same Ruth was sick, it being the first time the girl was ever coach'd; the good man, Mr. Mayor, I mean, that I spoke of, held his hat for the girl to ease her stomach in.————

Enter Abel, *and* Obadiah:

—Oh, are you come? Long look'd for come at last. ' What—you have a slow set pace, as well as your hasty ' scribble, sometimes.' Did you not think it fit, that I shou'd have found attendance ready for me when I alighted?

Oba. I ask your honour's pardon; for I do profess unto your ladyship, I had attended sooner, but that his young honour, Mr. Abel, demurr'd me by his delays.

Mrs. D. Well, son Abel, you must be obey'd, and I partly, if not quite, guess your business; providing for the entertainment of one I have in my eye. Read her and take her: Ah, is't not so?

' *Abel.* I have not been deficient in my care, forsooth.

Mrs. D. Will you never leave your forsooths? Art thou not asham'd to let the clerk carry himself better, and shew more breeding, than his master's son.

Abel. If it please your honour, I have some business for your more private ear.

Mrs. D. Very well.

Ruth.

Ruth. What a lamentable condition has that gentleman been in! faith I pity him.

Arbel. Are you so apt to pity men?

Ruth. Yes, men that are humoursome, as I would children that are froward; I wou'd not make them cry on purpose.

Arbel. Well, I like his humour, I dare swear he's plain and honest.

Ruth. Plain enough of all conscience; faith I'll speak to him.

Arbel. Nay, pr'ythee don't; he'll think thee rude.

Ruth. Why then I'll think him an ass.——How is't after your journey, Sir?

Blunt. Why, I am worse after it.

Ruth. Do you love riding in a coach, Sir?

Blunt. No, forsooth, nor talking after riding in a coach.

Ruth. I shou'd be loth to interrupt your meditations, Sir: we may have the fruits hereafter.

Blunt. If you have, they shall break loose spite of my teeth.——This spawn is as bad as the great pike. [*Aside.*

Arbel. Pr'ythee, peace!——Sir, we wish you all happiness.

Blunt. And quiet, good sweet ladies——I like her well enough.——Now wou'd not I have her say any more, for fear she should jeer too, and spoil my good opinion. If, 'twere possible, I wou'd think well of one woman.

Mrs. D. Come, Mrs. Arbella, 'tis as I told you, Abel has done it; say no more. Take her by the hand, Abel. I profess, she may venture to take thee for better, for worse. Come, Mrs. the honourable committee will sit suddenly. Come, let's along. Farewel, Sir.

[*Ex. all but* Blunt.

Blunt. How! the committee ready to sit! Plague on their honours; for so my honour'd lady, that was one of the eleven, was pleas'd to call 'em. I had like to have come a day after the fair. 'Tis pretty, that such as I have been must compound for their having been rascals. Well, I must go seek a lodging, and a solicitor: I'll find the arrantest rogue I can, too: for according to the old saying, set a thief to catch a thief.

Enter

Enter Col. Careless, *and Lieutenant.*

Car. Dear Blunt, well met ; when came you, man ?

Blunt. Dear Careless, I did not think to have met thee
fo fuddenly. Lieutenant, your fervant. I am landed
juft now, man.

Car. Thou fpeak'ft as if thou had'ft been at fea

Blunt. It's pretty well guefs'd ; I have been in a ftorm.

' *Car.* What bufinefs brought thee ?

' *Blunt.* May be the fame with yours ; I am come to
' compound with their honours.

' *Car.* That's my bufinefs too. Why, the commit-
' tee fits fuddenly.

' *Blunt.* Yes, I know it ; I heard fo in the ftorm I
told thee of.'

Car. What ftorm, man ?

Blunt. Why, a tempeft, as high as ever blew from
woman's breath. I have rode in a ftage-coach, wedged in
with half a dozen ; one of them was a committee-man's
wife ; his name is Day ; and fhe accordingly will be call'd,
your honour, and your ladyfhip ; ' with a tongue that
' wags as much fafter than all other women's, as in the
' feveral motions of a watch, the hand of the minute
' moves fafter than that of the hour.' There was her
daughter, too ; but a baftard, without queftion : for fhe had
no refemblance to the reft of the notch'd rafcals, and very
pretty, and had wit enough to jeer a man in profperity to
death.——There was another gentlewoman, and fhe was
handfome ; nay, very handfome : but I kept her from being as bad as the reft.

Car. Pr'ythee, how, man ?

Blunt. Why, fhe began with two or three good words,
and I defired her fhe would be quiet while fhe was well.

Car. Thou wert not fo mad ?

Blunt. I had been mad if I had not—But when we came
to our journey's end, there met us two fuch formal and
ftately rafcals, that yet pretended religion and open rebel-
lion ever painted : they were the hopes and guide of the
honourable family, viz. The eldeft fon, and the chiefeft
clerk, rogues—and hereby hangs a tale.——This gentlewoman, I told thee I kept civil, by defiring her to fay nothing, is a rich heirefs of one that died in the king's fervice, and left his eftate under fequeftration. This young
chick-

chicken has this kite snatch'd up, and designs her for this
her eldest rascal.

Car. What a dull fellow wert thou, not to make love
and rescue her.

Blunt. I'll wooe no woman.

Car. Wou'd'st thou have them court thee? A Soldier
and not love a siege! ——How now, who art thou?

Enter Teague.

Tea. A poor Irishman, Heav'n save me, and save all
your three faces; give me a thirteen.

Car. I see thou would'st not lose any thing for want of
asking.

Tea. I can't afford it.

Car. Here, I am pretty near; there's sixpence for thy
confidence.

Tea. By my troth it is too little; give me another six-
pence-halfpenny, and I'll drink your healths.

Car. How long hast thou been in England?

Tea. Ever since I came here, and longer too, faith.

Car. What hast thou done since thou cam'st into England?

Tea. Serv'd Heaven, and St. Patrick, and my good
sweet king, and my good sweet master; yes, indeed.

Car. And what dost thou do now?

Tea. Cry for them every day, upon my soul.

Car. Why, where's thy master?

Tea. He's dead, mastero, and left poor Teague. Upon my soul he never serv'd poor Teague so before in all
his life.

Car. Who was thy master,?

Tea. E'en the good Colonel Danger.

Car. He was my dear and noble friend.

Tea. Yes, that he was, and poor Teague's too.

Car. What dost thou mean to do?

Tea. I will get a good master, if any good master
wou'd get me; I cannot tell what to do else, by my soul;
for I went to one Lilly's; he lives at that house, at the
end of an other house, by the may-pole house, and tells
every body by one star, and t'other star, what good look
they shall have, but he cou'd not tell nothing for poor
Teague.

Car. Why, man?

Tea.

Tea. Why, 'tis done by the stars and the planters; and he told me there was no stars for Irishmen. I told him there was as many stars in Ireland as in England, and more too; and if a good master cannot get me, I will run into Ireland, and see if the stars be not there still; and if they be, I will come back, and beat his pate, if he will not then tell me some good look, and some stars.

Car. Poor fellow! I pity him; I fancy he's simply honest.——Hast thou any trade?

Tea. Bo, bub bub bo! a trade, a trade! an Irishman with a trade! an Irishman scorns a trade; his blood is too thick for a trade. I will run for thee forty miles; but I scorn to have a trade.

Bl. Alas, poor simple fellow!

Car. I pity him; nor can I endure to see any man miserable that can weep for my prince and friend. Well, Teague, what sayst thou, if I will take thee?

Tea. Why, I say you cou'd not do a better thing.

Car. Thy master was my dear friend; wert thou with him when he was kill'd?

Tea. Yes, upon my soul, that I was; and I did howl over him, and I ask'd over him why he died, but the devil burn the word he said to me; and i'faith I staid kissing his sweet face, 'till the rogues came upon me, and took all away from me, and left me nothing but this mantle; I have never any victuals, neither, but a little snuff.

Car. Come, thou shalt live with me; love me as thou didst thy master.

Tea. That I will, if you will be good to poor Teague.

Car. Now, to our business; for I came but last night myself; and the lieutenant and I were just going to seek a solicitor.

Blunt. One may serve us all; what say you, lieutenant, can you furnish us?

Lieu. Yes, I think I can help you to plough with a heifer of their own.

Car. Now I think on't, Blunt, why didst not thou begin with the committee-man's cow?

Blunt. Plague on her, she lowbell'd me so, that I thought of nothing, but stood shrinking like a dar'd lark.

Lieu. But, hark you, gentlemen, there's an illustrating dose to be swallow'd first; there's a covenant to be taken.

Tea.

Tea. Well, what is that covenant ? By my f
take it for my new mafter.

Car. Thank thee, Teague—A covenant, fay

Tea. Well, where is that covenant ?

Car. We'll not fwear, lieutenant.

Lieu. You muft have no land, then

Blunt. Then, farewel acres, and may the dirt c

Car. 'Tis but being reduc'd to Teague's e
'twas a lucky thing to have a fellow that can t
this cheap diet of fnuff.

Tea. Oh, you fhall have your belly full of it

Lieu. Come, gentlemen, we muft lofe no m
I'll carry you to my poor houfe, where you fh
for, know, I am married to a moft illuftrious pe
had a kindnefs for me.

Car. Pry'thee, how didft thou light upon
fortune ?

Lieu. Why, you fee there are ftars in Eng
none in Ireland. Come, gentlemen, time calls
fhall have my ftory hereafter. [*Ex.* Blunt *and L*

Car. Come, Teague ; however, I have a fuit
for thee ; thou fhalt lay by thy blanket for f
It may be, thee and I may be reduced toget
country fafhion.

Tea. Upon my foul, joy, I will carry thee to
eftate in Ireland.

Car. Haft thou got an eftate?

Tea. By my foul, and I have ; but the land
a nature, that if you had it for nothing, you wo
make your money of it.

Car. Why, there's the worft on't ; the beft wi
felf.

Enter Mr. Day, *and Mrs.* Day.

Mr. Day. Welcome, fweet duck ; I profefs
brought home good company, indeed ; money
ney's worth : if we can but now make fure of th
Mrs. Arbella, for our fon Abel.

Mrs. Day. If we can ! you are ever at your i
afraid of your own fhadow ; I can tell you one
that is, *if* I did not bear you up, your heart
down in your breeches at every turn. Well, i
gone—there's another *if* for you.

Mr. Day. I profefs thou fayeft true ; I fhould

what to do, indeed. I am beholden to thy good counsel for many a good thing; I had ne'er got Ruth, nor her estate, into my fingers elfe.

Mrs. Day. Nay, in that bufinefs, too, you were at your *ifs.* Now, you fee fhe goes currently for our own daughter; and this Arbella fhall be our daughter too, or fhe fhall have no eftate.

Mr. Day. If we cou'd but do that, wife!

Mrs. Day. Yet again at your *ifs*

Mr. Day. I have done, I have done; to your counfel, good duck; you know I depend upon that.

Mrs. Day. You may, well enough; you find the fweet on't; and, to fay truth, 'tis known too well, that you rely upon it. In truth they are ready to call me the committee-man; they well perceive the weight that lies upon me, hufband.

Mrs. Day. Nay, good duck, no chiding now, but to your counfel.

Mrs. Day. In the firft place, (obferve how I lay a defign in politicks) d'ye mark? counterfeit me a letter from the king, where he fhall offer you great matters, to ferve him and his intereft under-hand. Very good; and in it let him remember his kind love and fervice to me. This will make them look about 'em, and think you fomebody. Then promife them, if they'll be true friends to you, to live and die with them, and refufe all great offers; then, whilft 'tis warm, get the compofition of Arbella's eftate into your own power, upon your defign of marrying her to Abel.

Mr. Day. Excellent.

Mrs. Day. Mark the luck on't too, their names found alike; Abel and Arbella, they are the fame to a trifle, it feemeth a providence.

Mr. Day. Thou obferveft right, duck; thou canft fee as far into a mill-ftone as another.

Mrs. Day. Pifh! do not interrupt me.

Mrs. Day. I do not, good duck, I do not.

Mrs. Day. You do not, and yet you do; you put me off from the concatenation of my difcourfe. Then, as I was faying, you may intimate to your honourable fellows, that one good turn deferves another. That language is underftood amongft you, I take it, ha?

Mr. Day. Yes, yes, we use those items often.

Mrs. Day. Well, interrupt me not.

Mr. Day. I do not, good wife.

Mrs. Day. You do not, and yet you do. By this means get her composition put wholly into your hands; and then, no Abel, no land—But, in the mean time, I would have Abel do his part, too.

Mr. Day. Ay, ay, there's a want; I found it.

Mrs. Day. Yes, when I told you so before.

Mr. Day. Why, that's true, duck, he is too backward; if I were in his place, and as young as I have been.

Mrs. Day. Oh, you'd do wonders! But, now I think on't, there may be some use made of Ruth; 'tis a notable witty harlotry.

Mrs. Day. Aye, and so she is, duck; I always thought so.

Mr. Day. You thought so, when I told you I had thought on't first.——Let me see——It shall be so; we'll set her to instruct Abel, in the first place; and then to incline Arbella; they are hand and glove; and women can do much with one another.

Mr. Day. Thou hast hit upon my own thoughts.

Mrs. Day. Pray, call her in; you thought of that, too, did you not?

Mr. Day. I will, duck. Ruth! why, Ruth!

Enter Ruth.

Ruth. Your pleasure, Sir?

Mr. Day. Nay, 'tis my wife's desire, that——

Mrs. Day. Well, if it be your wife's, she can best tell it herself, I suppose. Dy'e hear, Ruth; you may do a business that may not be the worse for you. You know I use but few words.

Ruth. What does she call a few?   [*Aside*

Mrs. Day. Look you, now, as I said, to be short, and to the matter; my husband and I do design this Mrs Arbella for our son Abel, and the young fellow is not forward enough. You conceive? Pry'thee give him a little instructions how to demean himself, and in what manner to speak, which we call address, to her; ' for ' women best know what will please women.' Then work on Arbella, on the other side; work, I say, my good girl; no more, but so. You know my custom is

to ufe but few words. Much may be faid in a little ; you
fhan't repent it ;

Mr. Day. And I fay fomething too, Ruth,

Mrs. Day. What need you ? Don't you fee it all faid
already to your hand ; what fayeft thou, girl ?

Ruth. I fhall do my beft—I would not lofe the fport
for more than I'll fpeak of.   [*Afide.*

Mrs. Day. Go, call Abel, good girl. [*Exit* Ruth.]
By bringing this to pafs, hufband, we fhall fecure ourfelves, if the king fhould come ; you'll be hanged elfe.

Mr. Day. Oh, good wife, let's fecure ourfelves by
all means. There's a wife faying : 'Tis good to have a
fhelter againft every ftorm. I remember that.

Mrs. Day. You may well, when you have heard me
fay it fo often.

Enter Ruth *with* Abel.

Mr. Day. O, fon Abel, d'ye hear——

Mrs. Day. Pray, hold your peace, and give every body
leave to tell their own tale—D'ye hear, fon Abel, I
have formerly told you that Arbella would be a good
wife for you : a word's enough to the wife ; fome endeavours muft be ufed, and you muft not be deficient.
I have fpoken to your fifter Ruth, to inftruct you what
to fay, and how to carry yourfelf ; obferve her directions, as you'll anfwer the contrary ; be confident, and
put home. Ha, boy, hadft thou but thy mother's pate.
Well, 'tis but a folly to talk of that that cannot be ! Be
fure you follow your fifter's directions.

Mr. Day. Be fure, boy.—well faid, duck, I fay.

[*Exeunt Mr. and Mrs.* Day.

Ruth. Now, brother Abel.

Abel. Now, fifter Ruth.

Ruth. Hitherto he obferves me punctually.   [*Afide.*]
Have you a month's mind to this gentlewoman, Mrs.
Arbella ?

Abel. I have not known her a week yet.

Ruth. O, cry you mercy, good brother Abel. Well,
to begin then, you muft alter your pofture, ' and by
' your grave and high demeanour, make yourfelf appear
' a hole above Obadiah ; left your miftrefs fhould take
' you for fuch another fcribble-fcrabble as he is ;' and
always hold up your head, as if it were bolfter'd up with
high matters ; your hands join'd flat together, projecting

B 2

a lit-

a little beyond the rest of your body, as ready to separate when you begin to open.

Abel. Must I go apace, or softly ?

Ruth. O, gravely, by all means, as if you were
loaded with weighty considerations—so—Very well.
Now, to apply our prescription. Suppose, now, that
I were your mistress, Arbella, and met you by accident
—Keep your posture—so—and when you come just to
me, start like a horse that has spy'd something on one
side of him, and give a little gird out of the way, decla-
ring that you did not see her before, by reason of your
deep contemplations. Then you must speak. Let's
hear.

Abel. Save you, mistress.

Ruth. O, fie, man ! you shou'd begin thus : Pardon,
Mistress, my profound contemplations, in which I was
so buried that I did not see you :——and then, as she
answers, proceed, I know what she'll say, I am so used
to her.

Abel. This will do well, if I forget it not.

Ruth. Well, try once.

Abel. Pardon, Mistress, my profound contemplations,
in which I was so hid that you could not see me.

Ruth. Better sport than I expected. [*Aside*] Very well
done, you're perfect. Then she will answer, Sir, I suppose you are so busied with state affairs, that it may well
hinder you from taking notice of any thing below
them.

Abel. No, forsooth, I have some profound contemplations, but no state-affairs.

Ruth. O, fie, man ! you must confess that the weighty
affairs of state lie heavy upon you ; but tis a burthen
you must bear ; and then shrug your shoulders.

Abel. Must I say so ? I am afraid my mother will
be angry, for she takes all the state-matters upon herself.

Ruth. Pish ! Did she not charge you to be ruled by
me ? Why, man, Arbella will never have you, if she
be not made believe you can do great matters with parliament-men and committee-men ; how should she hope
for any good by you else in her composition ?

Abel. I apprehend you now ? I shall observe.

Ruth.

Ruth. 'Tis well; at this time I'll say no more; put yourself in your posture——so——Now go look your mistress; I'll warrant you the town's our own.

Abel. I go.   [*Exit* Abel.

Ruth. Now I have fixed him, not to go off till he discharges on his mistress. I could burst with laughing.

Enter Arbella.

Arb. What dost thou laugh at, Ruth?

Ruth. Didst thou meet my brother Abel?

Arb. No.

Ruth. If thou hadst met him right, he had played at hard head with thee.

Arb. What dost thou mean?

Ruth. Why, I have been teaching him to wooe, by command of my superiors; and have instructed him to hold up his head so high, that of necessity he must run against every thing that comes in his way.

Arb. Who is he to wooe?

Ruth. Even thy own sweet self.

Arb. Out upon him!

Ruth. Nay, thou wilt be rarely courted; I'll not spoil the sport by telling thee any thing before-hand. They have sent to Lilly; and his learning being built upon knowing what most people would have him say, he has told them for a certain, that Abel shall have a rich heiress; and that must be you.

Arb. Must be?

Ruth. Yes, committee-men can compel, more than stars.

Arb. I fear this too late. You are their daughter, Ruth.

Ruth. I deny that.

Arb. How!

Ruth. Wonder not that I begin thus freely with you; 'tis to invite your confidence in me.

Arb. You amaze me.

Ruth. Pray, do not wonder, nor suspect——When my father, Sir Basil Thoroughgood, died, I was very young ' not above two years old:' 'tis too long to tell you how this rascal, being a trustee, catch'd me and my estate, ' being the sole heiress unto my father, into his gripes;'

and now for some years has confirmed his unjuft power by the unlawful power of the times. I fear they have defigns as bad as this on you. You fee I have no ref-ferve, and endeavour to be thought worthy of your friendfhip.

Arb. I embrace it with as much clearnefs. Let us love and affift one another.——Would they marry me to this their firft-born puppy?

Ruth. No doubt, or keep your compofition from you.

Arb. 'Twas my ill fortune to fall into fuch hands, foolifhly enticed by fair words and large promifes of affift-ance.

Ruth. Peace!

Enter Obadiah.

Obad. Mrs. Ruth, my mafter is demanding your com-pany, together, and not fingly, with Mrs. Arbella; you will find them in the parlour. The committee being rea-dy to fit, calls upon my care and circumfpection to fet in order the weighty matters of ftate, for their wife and honourable infpection. [*Exit.*

Ruth. We come. Come, dear Arbella, never be per-plexed; chearfuxjl fpirits are the beft bladders to fwim with: if thou art fad, the weight will fink thee. Be fe-cret, and ftill know me for no other than what I feem to be, their daughter. Another time thou fhalt know all particulars of my ftrange ftory.

Arb. Come, wench, they cannot bring us to compound for our humours; they fhall be free ftill. [*Exeunt.*

END of the FIRST ACT.

———————————

A C T II.

Enter Teague.

TEAGUE.

I 'Faith, my fweet mafter has fent me to a rafcal; I have a great mind to go back and tell him fo. He afked me, why he could not fend one that cou'd fpeak En-glifh. Upon my foul, I was going to give him an Irifh

knock,

knock. The devil's in them all, they will not talk with me. I will go near to knock this man's pate, and that man Lilly's pate too——that I will: I will teach them prate to me. [*One cries* Books *within.*] How now, what noises are that ?——

Enter Bookseller.

Book. New books, new books ! A desperate plot and engagement of the bloody cavaliers ! Mr. Saltmarsh's larum to the nation, after having been three days dead ; Mercurius Britannicus, &c.

Tea. How's that ? They cannot live in Ireland after they are dead three days !

Book. Mercurius Britannicus, or the Weekly Post ; or The Solemn League and Covenant.

Tea. What is that you say ? Is it the covenant you have ?

Book. Yes ; what then, Sir ?

Tea. Which is that covenant ?

Book. Why, this is the covenant.

Tea. Well, I must take that covenant.

Book. You take my commodities ?

Tea. I must take that covenant, upon my soul, now.

Book. Stand off, Sir, or I'll set you further.

Tea. Well, upon my soul now, I will take that covenant for my master.

Book. Your master must pay me for't then ?

Tea. I must take it first, and my master will pay you afterwards.

Book. You must pay me now——

Tea. Oh, that I will—[*Knocks him down.*] Now your'e paid, you thief o' the world. Here's covenants enough to poison the whole nation. [*Exit.*

Book. What a devil ails this fellow ? [*Crying.*] He did not come to rob me certainly, for he has not taken above two pennyworth of lamentable ware away ! But I feel the rascal's fingers. I may light upon my wild Irishman again, and if I do, I will fix him with some catchpoles that shall be worse than his own country bogs. [*Exit.*

Enter Col. Careless, *Col.* Blunt, *and Lieut.* Story.

Lieu. And what say you, noble colonels ? How, and how d'ye like my lady ? I gave her the title of Illustrious,

ous, from thofe illuftrious commodities which
in, hot water and tobacco.

Car. Pr'ythee, how cam'ft thou to think of m

Lieu. Why, that which hinders other m
' thofe venereal conditions,' prompted me to m
hunger and cold, colonel.

' *Car.* Which you deftroyed with a fat woma
' water, and ftinking tobacco.

' *Lieu.* No, faith, the woman conduced b
' but the reft cou'd not be purchafed without.

' *Car.* She's beholden to you.

' *Lieu.* For all your mocking, fhe had been
' it had not been for me.

' *Car.* Pr'ythee, make but that good.

' *Lieu.* With eafe, Sir,——Why, look you,
' know fhe was always a moft violent cavalier,
' moft ready and large faith; abundance of ra
' found her foft place, and perpetually wou'd b
' news, news of all prices; they would tell
' from half a crown, to a gill of hot water, or
' the worft mundungus. I have obferved th
' rates; they wou'd borrow half a crown upo
' of five thoufand men up in the north; a fhill
' a town's revolting; fix-pence upon a fmall ca
' confume hot water and tobacco, whilft they
' ling news of arms conveyed into feveral parts,
' munition hid in cellars; that at laft, if I had
' ried, and blown off thefe flies, fhe had been at
' confumed.

' *Car.* Well, Lieutenant, we are beholden to
' thefe hints; we may be reduced to as bad.' S
Teague comes. Goodnefs, how he fmiles.
merry, Teague?

Enter Teague, *fmiling.*

Tea. I have done a thing for you indeed.

Car. What haft thou done, man?

Tea. Guefs.

Car. I can't.

Tea. Why, then, guefs again—I have taken tl
nant.

Car. How came you by it?

Tea. Very honeſtly ; I knocked a fellow down in the ſtreet, and took it from him.

Car. Was there ever ſuch a fancy ? Why, didſt thou think this was the way to take the covenant ?

Tea. I am ſure it is the ſhorteſt, and the cheapeſt way to take it.

Blunt. I am pleaſed yet with the poor fellow's miſtaken kindneſs ; I dare warrant him honeſt, to the beſt of his underſtanding.

Car. This fellow, I propheſy, will bring me into many troubles by his miſtakes : I muſt ſend him on no errand but, How d'ye: and to ſuch as I wou'd have no anſwer from again.——Yet his ſimple honeſty prevails with me, I cannot part with him.

Lieu. Come, gentlemen, time calls—How now, who's this ?

Enter Obadiah, *and four perſons more, with papers.*

Car. I am a rogue if I have not ſeen a picture in hangings walk as faſt.

Blunt. 'Slife, man, this is that good man of the committee family that I told thee of, the very clerk ; how the rogue's loaded with papers !--Thoſe are the winding-ſheets to many a poor gentleman's eſtate. 'Twere a good deed to burn them all.

Car. Why, thou art not mad ?—Well met, Sir ; pray do not you belong to the committee of ſequeſtrations ?

Obad. I do belong to that honourable committee, who are now ready to ſit for the bringing on the work.

Blunt. Oh, plague ! what work, raſ——

Car. Pr'ythee be quiet, man—Are they to ſit preſently ?

Obad. As ſoon as I can get ready, my preſence being material. [*Exit.*

Car. What, wert thou mad ? Wouldſt thou have beaten the clerk, when thou wert going to compound with the raſcals his maſters ?

Blunt. The ſight of any of the villains ſtirs me.

Lieu. Come, colonels, there's no trifling, let's make haſte, and prepare your buſineſs ; let's not loſe this ſitting. Come along, Teague. [*Exeunt.*

Enter

Enter Arbella *at one Door,* Abel *at another, as if he saw her not, and starts when he comes to her, as* Ruth *had taught him.*

Arb. What's the meaning of this? I'll try to steal by him.

Abel. Pardon, Miſtreſs, my profound contemplations, in which I was ſo hid that you could not ſee me.

Arb. This is a ſet form——they allow it in every thing, but their prayers.   [*Aſide.*

Abel. Now you ſhould ſpeak, forſooth.

' *Arb.* Ruth, I have found you ; but I'll ſpoil the dia-
' logue.' [*Aſide.*]——What ſhould I ſay, Sir ?

Abel. What you pleaſe, forſooth.

Arb. Why, truly, Sir, 'tis as you ſay ; I did not ſee you.

Enter Ruth, *as over-bearing them, and peeps.*

Ruth. This is lucky.

Abel. No, forſooth, 'tis I that was not to ſee you.

Arb. Why, Sir, wou'd your mother be angry if you ſhou'd ?

Abel. No, no, quite contrary——I'll tell you that preſently ; but firſt I muſt ſay, that the weighty affairs lie heavy upon my neck and ſhoulders.   [*Shrugs.*

Arb. Wou'd he were tied neck and heels.——This is a notable wench ; look where the raſcal peeps too ; if I ſhou'd beckon to her ſhe'd take no notice ; ſhe is reſolved not to relieve me.   [*Aſide.*

Abel. Something I can do, and that with ſomebody ; that is, with thoſe that are ſomebodies.

Arb. Whiſt, whiſt, [*Beckons to* Ruth, *and ſhe ſhakes her head.*] Pr'ythee, have ſome pity. Oh, unmerciful girl !

Abel. I know parliament-men, and ſequeſtrators ; I know committee-men, and committee-men know me.

Arb. You have great acquaintance, Sir ?

Abel. Yes, they aſk my opinion ſometimes——

Arb. What weather 'twill be. Have you any ſkill, Sir ?

Abel. When the weather is not good, we hold a faſt.

Arb. And then it alters ?

Abel. Aſſuredly.

Arb. In good time——No mercy, wench ?

Abel. Our profound contemplations are cauſed by the
con-

consternation of our spirits for the nation's good; we are in labour.

Arb. And I want a deliverance.—Hark ye, Ruth, take off your dog, or I'll turn bear indeed.

Ruth. I dare not; my mother will be angry.

Arb. Oh, hang you!

Abel. You shall perceive that I have some power, if you please to——

Arb. Oh, I am pleased, Sir, that you shou'd have power! I must look out my hoods and scarfs, Sir; 'tis almost time to go.

Abel. If it were not for the weighty matters of state which lie upon my shoulders, myself wou'd look them.

Arb. Oh, by no means, Sir; 'tis below your greatness——Some luck yet; she never came seasonably before.

Enter Mrs. Day.

Mrs. Day. Why, how now, Abel? Got so close to Mrs. Arbella; so close indeed! Nay, then I smell something. Well, Mr. Abel, you have been so us'd to secrecy in counsel and weighty matters, that you have it at your fingers ends. Nay, look ye, mistress, look ye, look ye; mark Abel's eyes; ah, there he looks. Ruth, thou art a good girl; I find Abel has got ground.

Ruth. I forbore to come in, till I saw your honour first enter; but I have o'er-heard all.

Mrs. Day. And how has Abel behaved himself, wench, ha?

Ruth. Oh, beyond expectation! ' If it were lawful, ' I'd undertake he'd make nothing to get as many wo- ' men's good-wills as he speaks to;' he'll not need much teaching; you may turn him loose.

Arb. Oh, this plaguy wench!

Mrs. Day. Say'st thou so, girl? It shall be something in thy way; a new gown, or so; it may be a better penny. Well said, Abel, I say; I did think thou wouldst come out with a piece of thy mother's at last;——But I had forgot, the committee are near upon sitting. Ha, Mrs. you are crafty; you have made your composition before-hand. Ah, this Abel's as bad as a whole com- mittee: take that item from me. Come, make haste, call the coach, Abel. Well said, Abel, I say.

[*Exeunt. Mrs.* Day *and* Abel.
' *Arb.*

‘ *Arb.* We’ll fetch our things and follow you. Now,
‘ wench, canſt thou ever hope to be forgiven ?

‘ *Ruth.* Why, what’s the matter ?

‘ *Arb.* The matter ! couldſt thou be ſo unmerciful,
‘ to ſee me practiſed on, and pelted at, by a blunderbuſs
‘ charged with nothing but proofs, weighty affairs, ſpi-
‘ rit, profound contemplation, and ſuch like ?

‘ *Ruth.* Why, I was afraid to interrupt you ; I thought
‘ it convenient to give you what time I could, to make
‘ his young honour your friend.

‘ *Arb.* I am beholden to you : I may cry quittance.

‘ *Ruth.* But did you mark Abel’s eyes ? Ah, there
‘ were looks !

‘ *Arb.* Nay, pr’ythee give off ; my hour’s approach-
‘ ing, and I can’t be heartily merry till it be paſt. Come,
‘ let’s fetch our things ; her Ladyſhip’s honour will ſtay
‘ for us.

‘ *Ruth.* I’ll warrant ye, my brother Abel is not in or-
‘ der yet ; he’s bruſhing a hat almoſt a quarter of an
‘ hour, and as long a driving the lint from his black
‘ clothes, with his wet thumb.

‘ *Arb.* Come, pr’ythee hold thy peace, I ſhall laugh
‘ in’s face elſe, when I ſee him come along. Now for
‘ an old ſhoe.’　　　　　　　　　　　　　[*Exeunt.*

A Table ſet out.

The Committee, and Obadiah *ordering books and papers.*

Obad. Shall I read your honours laſt order, and give
you the account of what you laſt debated ?

Mr. Day. I firſt crave your favours, to communicate
an important matter to this honourable board, in which
I ſhall diſcover unto you my own ſincerity, and zeal to
the good cauſe.

1 *Com.* Proceed, Sir.

Mr. Day. The buſineſs is contained in this letter : ’tis
from no leſs a man than the king ; and ’tis to me, as ſimple as I ſit here. Is it your pleaſures that our clerk
ſhould read it.

2 *Com.* Yes, pray give it him.

Obad. [*Reads.*] “ Mr. Day, we have received good
intelligence of your great worth and ability, eſpecially in

3

ſtate-

ſtate-matters ; and therefore thought fit to offer you any preferment, or honour, that you ſhall deſire, if you will become my intire friend. Pray remember my love and ſervice to your diſcreet wife, and acquaint her with this ; whoſe wiſdom, I hear, is great. So recommending this to her and your wiſe conſideration, I remain,

Your friend, C. K."

2 Com. C. K.!

Mr. Day. Ay, that's for the king.

2 Com. I ſuſpect. [*Aſide.*] Who brought you this let-ter ?

Mr. Day. Oh, fie upon't ! my wife forgot that parti-cular. [*Aſide.*] Why, a fellow left it for me, and ſhrunk away when he had done. I warrant you, he was afraid I ſhould have laid hold on him. You, ſee, brethren, what I reject ; but I doubt not but to receive my re-ward ; and I have now a buſineſs to offer, which in ſome meaſure may afford you an occaſion.

2 Com. This letter was counterfeited certainly.

[*Aſide.*

Mr. Day But firſt be pleaſed to read your laſt order.

2 Com. What does he mean ? That concerns me.

[*Aſide.*

Obad. The order is, that the compoſition ariſing out of Mr. Laſhley's eſtate be and hereby is inveſted and allowed to the honourable Mr. Nathaniel Catch, for and in re-ſpect of his ſufferings and good ſervice.

Mr. Day. It is meet, very meet ; we are bound in du-ty to ſtrengthen ourſelves againſt the day of trouble, when the common enemy ſhall endeavour to raiſe com-motions in the land, and diſturb our new-built Zion.

' *2 Com.* Then I'll ſay nothing, but cloſe with him ;
' we muſt wink at one another. I receive your ſenſe of
' my ſervices with a zealous kindneſs. Now, Mr. Day,
' I pray you propoſe your buſineſs.'

Mr. Day. I deſire this honourable board to underſtand, that my wife being at Reading, and to come up in the ſtage-coach ; it happened that one Mrs. Arbella, a rich heireſs of one of the cavalier party, came up alſo in the ſame coach. Her father being newly dead, and her eſtate before being under ſequeſtration, my wife, who has

C

a no-

a notable pate of her own (you all know her)
caſt about to get her for my ſon Abel ; and ac
invited her to my houſe ; where, though time
ſhort, yet my ſon Abel made uſe of it.   They ;
out, ' as I ſuppoſe : but before we call them ii
' let us handle ſuch other matters as are before

' 1 *Com.* Let us hear then what eſtates beſid
' fore us, that we may ſee how large a field w
' walk in.

' 2 *Com.* Read.

' *Obad.* One of your laſt debates was upon
' of an infant, whoſe eſtate is under ſequeſtrati

' *Mr. Day.* And fit to be kept ſo till he come
' and may anſwer for himſelf ; that he may i
' poſſeſſion of the land till he can promiſe he
' turn to the enemy.

' *Obad.* Here is another of almoſt the like
' an eſtate before your honours under ſequ
' The plea is, that the party died without an
' taking up arms ; but in his opinion, he wa
' king.   He has left his widow with child, whi
' the heir ; and his truſtees complain of wr
' claim the eſtate.

' 2 *Com.* Well, the father, in his opinion, wa
' lier ?

' *Obad.* So it is given in.

' 2 *Com.* Nay, 'twas ſo, I warrant you ; and
' young cavalier in his widow's belly ; I warran
' too ; for the perverſe generation encreaſeth.
' therefore, that their two eſtates may rema
' hands of our brethren here, and fellow-labou
' Joſeph Blemiſh, and Mr. Jonathan Headſt
' Mr. Ezekiel Scrape, and they to be accountab
' pleaſures ; whereby they may have a godly op
' of doing good for themſelves.

' *Mr. Day.* Order it, order it.

' 3 *Com.* Since it is your pleaſures, we are c
' take the burthen upon us, and be ſtewards t
' tion.

' 2 *Com.* Now verily it ſeemeth to me that
' goeth forward, when brethren hold together i

'*Mr. Day.* Well, if we have now finiſhed, give me
leave to tell you my wife is without,' together with
he gentlewoman that is to compound. She will needs
have a finger in the pie.

'*3 Com.* I profeſs we are to blame to let Mrs. Day
wait ſo long.

Mr. Day. We may not neglect the public for private
reſpects. I hope, brethren, that you will pleaſe to caſt
the favour of your countenances upon Abel.

2, 3 Com. You wrong us to doubt it, brother Day.
Call in the compounders.

Obad. Call in the compounders.

Por. Come in, the compounders.

Enter Mrs. Day, Abel, Arbella, Ruth; *and after them
the Colonels, and* Teague; *they give the door-keeper ſomething, who ſeems to ſcrape.*

Mr. Day. Come, duck, I have told the honourable
committee that you are one that will needs endeavour to
do good for this gentlewoman.

2 Com. We are glad, Mrs. Day, that any occaſion
brings you hither.

Mrs. Day. I thank your honours. I am deſirous of
doing good, which I know is always acceptable in your
eyes.

Mr. Day. Come on, ſon Abel, what have you to ſay?

Abel. I come unto your honours, full of profound
contemplations for this gentlewoman.

Arbel. 'Slife, he's at's leſſon, wench. [*Aſide to* Ruth.

Ruth. Peace—Which whelp opens next? Oh, the
wolf is going to bark. [*Aſide.*

Mrs. Day. May it pleaſe your honours, I ſhall preſume to inform you, that my ſon Abel has ſettled his affections on this gentlewoman, and deſires your honours
favour to be ſhewn unto him in her compoſition.

2 Com. Say you ſo, Mrs Day? Why the committee
have taken it into their ſerious and pious conſideration;
together with Mr. Day's good ſervice, upon ſome knowledge that is not fit to communicate.

Mrs. Day. That was the letter I invented [*Aſide.*

2 Com. And the compoſition of this gentlewoman is
conſigned to Mr. Day; that is, I ſuppoſe, to Mr. Abel,

C 2

and

and fo, confequently, to the gentlewoman. You may be thankful, miftrefs, for fuch good fortune; your eftate's di'charged; Mr. Day fhall have the difcharge.

Bl. Oh, damn the vultures!   [*Afide.*

Car. Peace, man.   [*Afide.*

Arb. I am willing to be thankful when I underftand the benefit. I have no reafon to compound for what's my own; but if I muft, if a woman can be a delin-quent, I defire to know my public cenfure, not to be left in private hands.

2 *Com.* Be contented, gentlewoman; the committee does this in favour of you. We underftand how eafily you can fatisfy Mr. Abel; you may if you pleafe be Mrs. Day.

Ruth. And then, good night to all.   [*Afide.*

Arb. How, gentlemen! are you private marriage-job-bers? D'ye make markets for one another?

2 *Com.* How's this, gentlewoman?

Bl. A brave noble creature!   [*Afide.*

Car. Thou art fmitten, Bluut; that other female too, methinks, fhoots fire this way.   [*Afide.*

Tea. Take care fhe don't burn your wig.

Mrs. Day. I defire your honours to pardon her incef-fant words; perhaps fhe doth not imagine the good that is intended her.

2 *Com.* Gentlewoman, the committee, for Mrs. Day's fake, paffes by your expreffions; ' you may fpare your ' pains, you have the committee's refolution;' you may be your own enemy, if you will.

Arb. My own enemy!

Ruth. Pr'ythee peace, 'tis to no purpofe to wrangle here; we muft ufe other ways.   [*Afide.*

2 *Com.* Come on, gentlemen! What's your cafe?
                          [*To the Colonels.*

Ruth. Arbella, there's the downright cavalier that came up in the coach with us——On my life there's a fprightly gentleman with him.
          [*While they fpeak, the Colonels pull the papers out,
             and deliver 'em.*

Car. Our bufinefs is to compound for our eftates; of which here are the particulars, which will agree with your own furvey.

                                             Tea.

Tea. And here's the particulars of Teague's estate, forty cows, and the devil a bull amongst them.

Obad. The particulars are right.

Mr. Day. Well, gentlemen, the rule is two years purchase; the first payment down, the other at six months end, and the estate to secure it.

Car. Can you afford it no cheaper?

2 Com. 'Tis our rule.

Car. Very well; 'tis but selling the rest to pay this, and our more lawful debts.

2 Com. But, gentlemen, before you are admitted, you are to take the covenant. You have not taken it yet, have you?

Car. No.

Tea. Upon my shoul, but he has now: I took it for him, and he has taken it from me, ' that he has.

' *Ruth.* What sport are we now like to have?'

2 Com. What fellow's that?

Car. A poor simple fellow, that serves me. Peace, Teague.

Tea. Why, did not I knock the fellow down?

2 Com. Well, gentlemen, it remains, whether you'll take the covenant?

Tea. Why he has taken it.

Car. This is strange, and differs from your own principle, to impose on other men's consciences.

Mr. Day. Pish, we are not here to dispute; we act according to our instructions, and we cannot admit any to compound without taking it; therefore your answer.

Tea. Was it for nothing I took the————

Car. Hold your tongue. No; we will not take it. Much good may it do them that have swallows large enough; 'twill work one day in their stomachs.

Bl. The day may come, when those that suffer for their consciences and honour may be rewarded.

Mr. Day. Ay, ay, you make an idol of that honour.

Bl. Our worships then are different; you make that your idol which brings you interest, we can obey that which bids us lose it.

Arb. Brave gentlemen!   [*Aside.*

Ruth. I stare at them till my eyes ake; [*Aside.*

2 Com. Gentlemen, you are men of dangerous spirits. Know, we muſt keep our rules and inſtructions, leſt we loſe what providence hath put into our hands.

Car. Providence! ſuch as thieves rob by.

2 Com. What's that, Sir? Sir, you are too bold.

Car. Why in good ſooth you may give loſers leave to ſpeak; I hope your honours, out of your bowels of compaſſion, will permit us to talk over our departing acres.

Mr. Day. It is well you are ſo merry,

Car. O, ever whilſt you live, clear ſouls make light hearts: faith would I might aſk one queſtion?

2 Com. Swear not then.

Car. Thou ſhalt not covet thy neighbour's goods, there's a Rowland for your Oliver.

Tea. There's an Oliver for your Rowland, take that till the pot boils.

Car. My queſtion is only, which of all you is to have our eſtates: or will you make traitors of them, draw. 'em, and quarter 'em?

2 Com. You grow abuſive.

Bl. No, no, 'tis only to intreat the honourable perſons that will be pleaſed to be our houſe-keepers, to keep them in good reparations; we may take poſſeſſion again, without the help of the covenant.

2 Com. You'll think better on't, and take this covenant.

Car. We will be as rotten firſt as their hearts that invented it.

Ruth. 'Slife, Arbella, we'll have theſe two men; there are not two ſuch again to be had for love nor money.

Mr. Day. Well, gentlemen, your follies light upon your own heads; we have no more to ſay.

Car. Why then hoiſt ſails for a new world—

Tea. Ay, for old Ireland.

Car. D'ye hear, Blunt, what gentlewoman is that?

Bl. 'Tis their witty daughter I told thee of.

Car. I'll go ſpeak to 'em; I'd fain convert that pretty covenanter.

Bl. Nay, pr'ythee let's go.

Car.

Car. Lady, I hope you'll have that good fortune, not to be troubled with the covenant.

Arb. If they do, I'll not take it.

Bl. Brave lady! I must love her against my will——

Car. For you, pretty one, I hope your portion will be enlarged by our misfortunes. Remember your benefactors.

Ruth. If I had all your estates, I could afford you as good a thing.

Car. Without taking the covenant?

Ruth. Yes, but I would invent another oath.

Car. Upon your lips?

Ruth. Nay, I am not bound to discover.

Bl. Pr'ythee come! Is this a time to spend in fooling?

Car. Now have I forgot every thing.

Bl. Come, let's go.

2 Com. Gentlemen, void the room.

Car. Sure, 'tis impossible that kite should get that pretty merlin.

Blunt. Come, pr'ythee let's go; these muck-worms will have earth enough to stop their mouths with, one day.

Car. Pray use our estates husband-like; and so, our most honourable bailiffs, farewel.   [*Exeunt.*

Tea. Ay, bum-baily rascals——

Mr. Day. You are rude. Door-keeper, put 'em forth there.

Por. Come forth, ye there; this is not a place for such as you.

Tea. Devil burn me, but ye are a rascal, that you are.

Por. And please your honours, this profane Irishman swore an oath at the door, even now, when I would have put him out.

2 Com. Let him pay for't.

Por. Here, you must pay, or lie by the heels.

Tea. What must I pay by the heels? I will not pay by the heels. Master, ubbub boo!

Enter Careless.

Car. What's the matter?

Tea. This gander-fac'd gag says, I must pay by the heels.

Car. What have you done?

Tea.

Tea. Only fwore a bit of an oath.

Car. Here's a fhilling, pay for't, and come along.

[*Exit.*

Tea. Well, I have not curs'd, how much had that been?

Por. That had been but fix-pence.

Tea. Och, if I had but one fix-pence-half-penny in the world, but I would give it for a curfe to eafe my ftomach on you. My money is like a wild colt, I am obliged to drive it up in a corner to catch it. I have hold of it by the fcruff of the neck. Here, Mifter, there's the fhilling for the oath. And there's the fixpence-half-penny for you, for the curfe, before-hand; and now, my curfe and the curfe of Cromwell, light upon you all, you thieves, you. [*Knocks down the Porter and exit.*

' *Ruth.* Hark ye, Arbella; 'twere a fin not to love thefe men.

' *Arbel.* I am not guilty, Ruth.

Mrs. Day. Has this honourable board any other commands?

2 *Com.* Nothing farther, good Mrs. Day.—Gentlewoman, you have nothing to care for, but be grateful and kind to Mr. Abel.

Arbel. I defire to know what I muft directly truft to, or I will complain.

Mrs. Day. The gentlewoman needeth no doubt, fhe fhall fuddenly perceive the good that is intended her, if fhe does not interpofe in her own light.

Mr. Day. I pray withdraw; the committee has pafs'd their order, and they muft now be private.

Com. Nay, pray, Miftrefs, withdraw. [*Exeunt all but the committee.*] ' So, brethren, we have finifhed this ' day's work; and let us always keep the bonds of ' unity unbroken, walking hand in hand, and fcattering ' the enemy.

' *Mr. Day.* You may perceive they have fpirits never ' to be reconcil'd; they walk according to nature, and ' are full of inward darknefs.

' 2 *Com.* It is well truly for the good people, that they ' are fo obftinate, whereby their eftates may of right fall ' into the hands of the chofen, which truly is a mercy.

Mr.

Mr. Day. I think there remaineth nothing farther, but to adjourn till Monday. ' Take up the papers there, ' and bring home to me their honours' order for Mrs. ' Arbella's estate. So, brethren, we separate ourselves ' to our particular endeavours, 'till we join in public on ' Monday, two of the clock ;' and so peace remain with you. *[Exeunt.*

END of the SECOND ACT.

A C T III.

Enter Col. Careless, *Col.* Blunt, *and Lieutenant* Story.

LIEUTENANT.

BY my faith, a sad story. I did apprehend this covenant would be the trap.

Car. Never did any rebels fish with such cormorants ; no stoppage about their throats ; the rascals are all swallow.

' *Blunt.* Now am I ready for any plot ; I'll go find some ' of these adjutants, and fill up a blank commission with ' my name. And if I can but find two or three gather'd ' together, they are sure of me ; I will please myself, ' however, with endeavouring to cut their throats.

' *Car.* Or do something to make them hang us, that ' we may but part on any terms.'

Enter Teague.

How now, Teague ! what says the learned——

Tea. Well then, upon my shoul, the man in the great cloak, with the long sleeves, is mad, that he is.

Car. Mad, Teague !

Tea. Yes i'faith is he ; he said, I was sent to make game of him.

Car. Why, what didst thou say to him ?

Tea. I asked him if he would take any counsel.

Car. 'Slife, he might well enough think thou mock'st him. Why, thou shouldest have asked him when we might have come for counsel.

Tea. Well, that is all one, is it not ? If we would take any counsel, or you would take any counsel, is not that all one then?

Car.

Car. Was there ever such a mistake?

Blunt. Pr'ythee never be troubled at this; we are past counsel. If we had but a friend amongst them, that could but slide us by this covenant.

Car. Nothing anger'd me so, as that my old kitchen-stuff acquaintance, turned her head another way, and seemed not to know me.

Blunt. How! kitchen-stuff acquaintace?

Car. Mrs. Day, that commanded the party in the stage coach, was my father's kitchen maid, and in days of yore was called Gillian.

Lieu. Hark ye, Colonel; what if you did visit this translated kitchen-maid?

Tea. Well, how is that? a kitchen-maid! where is she now?

Blunt. The Lieutenant advises well.

Car. Nay, stay, stay; in the first place, I'll send Teague to her, to tell her I have a little business with her, and desire to know when I may have leave to wait on her.

Blunt. We shall have Teague mistake again.

Tea. I will not mistake the kitchen-maid. Whither must I go now, to mistake that kitchen-maid?

Car. But do you hear, Teague? you must take no notice of that, upon thy life; but, on the contrary, at every word you must say, your ladyship, and your honour. As for example, when you have made a leg, you must begin thus; My master presents his service to your ladyship, and having some business with your honour, desires to know when he may have leave to wait upon your ladyship. [Teague *turns his back on the Col.*] Blockhead, you must not turn your back.

Tea. Oh, no, Sir, I always turn my face to a lady— But was she your father's kitchen-maid?

Car. Why, what then?

Tea. Upon my shoul, I shall laugh upon her face, for all I would not have a mind to do it.

Car. Not for a hundred pounds, Teague; you must be sure to set your countenance, and look very soberly, before you begin.

Tea. If I should think then of any kettles, or spits, or

any

any thing that will put a mind into my head of a kitchen, I should laugh then, should I not?

Car. Not for a thousand pounds, Teague; thou mayest undo us all.

Tea. Well, I will hope I will not laugh then : I will keep my mouth if I can, that I will, from running to one side, and t'other side. Well now, where does this Mrs. Tay live.

Lieu. Come, Teague, I'll walk along with thee, and shew thee the house, that thou mayest not mistake that. however.

Tea. Shew me the door and I'll find the house myself.

Car. Pr'ythee do, Lieutenant.

Tea. O, Sir, what is Mrs. Tay's name?

' *Car.* Have a care, Teague ; thou shalt find us in the
' Temple.' [*Exeunt Lieutenant and* Teague.] Now,
' Blunt, have I another design.

' *Blunt.* What further design canst thou have?

' *Car.* Why, by this means I may chance to see these
' women again, and get into their acquaintance.

' *Blunt.* With both, man?

' *Car.* 'Slife, thou art jealous ; dost love either of 'em?

' *Blunt.* Nay, I can't tell ; all is not as 'twas.

' *Car.* Like a man that is not well, and yet knows not
' what ails him.

' *Blunt.* Thou art something near the matter ; but I'll
' cure myself with considering, that no woman can ever
' care for me.

' *Car.* And why, pr'ythee?

' *Blunt.* Because I can say nothing to them.

' *Car.* The less thou canst say, they'll like thee better ;
' she'll think 'tis love that has ham-string'd thy tongue.
' Besides, man, a woman can't abide any thing in the
' house should talk, but she and her parrot. What, is it
' the cavalier girl thou lik'st?

' *Blunt.* Canst thou love any of the other breed?

' *Car.* Not honestly—yet I confess that ill begotten,
' pretty rascal never look'd towards me, but she scatter'd
' sparks as fast as kindling charcoal ; thine's grown alrea-
' dy to an honest flame. Come, Blunt, when Teague
' comes we will resolve on something.

' [*Exeunt.*
Enter

' *Enter* Arbella *and* Ruth.

' *Arb.* Come, now, a word of our own matters.
' How doft thou hope to get thy eftate again ?

' *Ruth.* You fhall drink firft ; I was juft going to afk you
' how you would get yours again. You are as faft, as
' if you were under covert-baron.

' *Arb.* But I have more hopes than thou haft.

' *Ruth.* Not a fcruple more, if there were but fcales
' that could weigh hopes ; for thefe rafcals muft be hang-
' ed, before either of us fhall get our own. You may eat
' and drink out of yours, as I do, and be a fojourner
' with Abel.

' *Arb.* I am hamper'd ; but I'll not entangle myfelf
' with Mr. Abel's conjugal cords—Nay, I am more
' hamper'd than thou thinkeft ; for if thou art in as bad
' cafe as I, (you underftand me) hold up thy finger.

' *Ruth.* Behold ! Nay, I'll ne'er forfake thee. [Ruth
' *holds up her finger.*] If I were not fmitten, I would per-
' fuade myfelf to be in love, if 'twere but to bear thee
' company.

' *Arb.* Dear girl ! Hark ye, Ruth, the compofition
' day made an end of all ; all's gone.

' *Ruth.* Nay, that fatal day put me in the condition of
' a compounder too ; there was my heart brought under
' fequeftration.

' *Arb.* That day, wench !

' *Ruth.* Yes, that very day, with two or three forcible
' looks, 'twas driven an inch, at leaft, out of its old place.
' Senfe or reafon can't find the way to't now.

' *Arb.* That day, that very day ! If you and I fhould
' like the fame man ?

' *Ruth.* Fie upon't ! as I live thou makeft me ftart.
' Now dare not I afk which thou likeft.

' *Arb.* Would they were now to come in, that we
' might watch one anothers eyes, and difcover by figns.
' I am not able to afk thee, neither.

' *Ruth.* Nor I to tell thee. Shall we go afk Lilly
' which it is ?

' *Arb.* Out upon him ! Nay, there's no need of ftars ;
' we know ourfelves, if we durft fpeak.

' *Ruth.* Pifh ! I'll fpeak ; if it be the fame, we'll draw
' cuts.

' Arb.

' *Arb.* No; hark ye, Ruth, do you act them both,
' for you faw their feveral humours, and then watch my
' my eyes where I appear moft concern'd. I can't dif-
' femble, for my heart.

' *Ruth.* I dare fwear that will hinder thee to diffemble,
' indeed—Come, have at you, then; I'll fpeak as if I
' were before the honourable rafcals. And firft, for my
' brave, blunt colonel, who, hating to take the oath,.
' cry'd out, with a brave fcorn (fuch as made thee in love
' I hope) hang yourfelves, rafcals ; the time will come,
' when thofe that dare be honeft, will be rewarded.
' Don't I act him bravely ? Don't I act him bravely ?

' *Arb.* Oh, admirably well! Dear wench, do it once
' more.

' *Ruth.* Nay, nay, I muft do the other now.

' *Arb.* No, no ; this once more, dear girl, and I'll
' act the other for thee.

' *Ruth.* No, forfooth, I'll fpare your pains ; we are
' right ; no need of cuts ; fend thee good luck with him
' I acted ; and wifh me well with my merry colonel,.
' that fhall act his own part.

' *Arb.* And a thoufand good lucks attend thee. We
' have fav'd our blufhes admirably well, and reliev'd our
' hearts from hard duty—But mum, fee where the mo-
' ther comes, and with her, her fon, a true exemplifi-
' cation or duplicate of the original Day. Now for a
' charge.'

Enter Mrs. Day *and* Abel.

' *Ruth.* Stand fair ; the enemy draws up.'

Mrs. Day. Well, Mrs. Arbella, I hope you have confider'd enough by this time ; you need not ufe fo much
confideration for your own good ; you may have your
eftate, and you may have Abel, and you may be worfe
offer'd—Abel, tell her your mind ; ne'er ftand, fhilly,
fhally—Ruth, does fhe incline, or is fhe wilful ?

Ruth. I was juft about the point, when your honour
interrupted us. One word in your Ladyfhip's ear.

Abel. You fee, forfooth, that I am fomebody, though
you make nobody of me ; you fee I can prevail ; therefore, pray, fay what I fhall truft to ; for I muft not ftand
fhilly. fhally.

Arb. You are hafty, Sir.

<table>
<tr><td>D</td><td align="right">*Ab. l.*</td></tr>
</table>

Abel. I am called upon by important affairs ; and therefore I muſt be bold, in a fair way, to tell you, that it lies upon my ſpirit exceedingly.

Arb. Saffron-poſſet-drink is very good againſt the heavineſs of the ſpirit.

Abel. Nay, forſooth, you do not underſtand my meaning.

Arb. You do, I hope, Sir ; and 'tis no matter, Sir, if one of us know it.

Enter Teague.

Tea. Well, now, who are all you ?

Arb. What's here, an Iriſh elder come to examine us all ?

Tea. Well, now, what is your names, every one ?

Ruth. Arbella, this is a ſervant to one of the colonels ; upon my life, 'tis the Iriſhman that took the covenant the right way.

Arb. Peace, what ſhould it mean ?

Tea. Well, cannnot ſome of you all ſay nothing, without ſpeaking ?

Mrs. Day. Why, how now, ſaucebox ! what wou'd you have ? What, have you left your manners without ? Go out, and fetch 'em in.

Tea. What ſhould I fetch now ?

Mrs. Day. D'you know who you ſpeak to, ſirrah ?

Tea. Yes, I do ; and it is little, my own mother thought I ſhou'd ſpeak to the like of you.

Abel. You muſt not be ſaucy to her Honour.

Tea. Well, I will knock you down, if you be ſaucy, with my hammer.

Ruth. This is miraculous !

Tea. Is there none of you that I muſt ſpeak to, now ?

Arb. Now, wench, if he ſhould be ſent to us ! [*Aſide.*

Tea. Well, I wou'd have one Mrs. Tay ſpeak unto me ?

Mrs. Day. Well, ſirrah, I am ſhe ; what's your buſineſs ?

Tea. O, are you there ? With yourſelf, Mrs. Tay— Well, I will look well firſt, and I will ſet my face, and tell her my meſſage.   [*Aſide.*

Ruth. How the fellow begins to mould himſelf !

Arb.

' *Arb.* And tempers his chops, like a hound that has
' lapp'd before his meat was cold enough.

' *Ruth.* He looks as if he had some gifts to pour forth ;
' those are Mr. Day's own white eyes, before he begins
' to say grace. Now for a speech rattling in his kecher,
' if his words stumbled in their way.

Tea. ' Well, now I will tell thee, i'faith.' My maſter, the good colonel Careleſs, bid me aſk thy good Ladyſhip —— Upon my ſoul, now, the laugh will come upon
my mouth, in ſpite of me.

[*He laughs always when he ſays Ladyſhip or Honour.*

Mrs. Day. Sirrah, ſirrah ! What were you ſent to
abuſe me ?

Ruth. As ſure as can be.   [*Aſide.*

Tea. I do not abuſe thy good honour—I cannot help
my laugh now. I will try again, now ; I will not think
of a kitchen, nor a dripping-pan, nor a muſtard-pot—
My maſter would know of your ladyſhip——

Mrs. Day. Did your maſter ſend you to abuſe me, you
raſcal ? By my honour, ſirrah——

Tea. Why do you abuſe yourſelf, now, joy ?

Mrs. Day. How, ſirrah ! Do I mock myſelf ? This is
ſome Iriſh traitor.

Tea. I am no traitor, that I am not ; I am an Iriſh rebel. You are cozen'd now.

Mrs. Day. Sirrah, ſirrah, I will make you know who
I am—An impudent Iriſh raſcal !

Abel. He ſeemeth a dangerous fellow, and of a bold,
ſeditious ſpirit.

Mrs. Day. You are a bloody raſcal, I warrant ye.

Tea. You are a fooliſh, brabble-bribble woman, that
you are.

Abel. Sirrah, we, that are at the head of affairs, muſt
puniſh your ſauⅽineſs.

Tea. And we that are at the tail of affairs, will puniſh
your ſauⅽineſs.

Mrs. Day. Ye raſcally varlet, get out of my doors.

Tea. Will not I give you my meſſage, then ?

Mrs. Day. Get you out, raſcal.

Tea. I pr'ythee let me tell my meſſage.

Mrs. Day. Get you out, I ſay.

D 2

Tea.

' *Tea.* The devil burn your ladyship, and honourship,
and kitchenship.   [*Exit.*

' *Arb.* Was there ever such a scene ? 'Tis impossible
' to guess any thing.

' *Ruth.* Our colonels have don't, as sure as thou livest,
' to make themselves sport ; being all the revenge that
' is in their power. Look, look, how her honour trots
' about, like a beast stung with flies.'

Mrs. Day. How the villain has distemper'd me ! Out
upon't too, that I have let the rascal go unpunish'd. And
you [*To Abel.*] can stand by, like a sheep ; run after him,
then, and stop him. I'll have him laid by the heels, and
make him confess who sent him to abuse me. Call help,
as you go. Make haste, I say.   [*Exit* Abel.

Ruth. 'Slid, Arbella, run after him, and save the poor
fellow for sake's sake ; stop Abel, by any means, that he
may 'scape.

Arb. Keep his dam off, and let me alone with the
puppy.   [*Exit.*

Ruth. Fear not.

Mrs. Day. 'Uds my life, the rascal has heated me !—
Now I think on't, I'll go myself, and see it done——A
saucy villain !

Ruth. But I must needs acquaint your honour with one
thing first, concerning Mrs. Arbella.

Mrs. Day. As soon as ever I have done. Is't good
news, wench ?

Ruth. Most excellent ! If you go out, you may spoil
all. Such a discovery I have made, that you will bless
the accident that angered you.

Mrs. Day. Quickly then, girl.

Ruth. When you sent Abel after the Irishman, Mrs.
Arbella's colour came and went in her face ; and at last,
not able to stay, she slunk away after him, for fear the
Irishman should hurt him ; she stole away, and blushed
the prettiest.

Mrs. Day. I protest he may be hurt, indeed. I'll run
myself, too.

Ruth. By no means, forsooth, ' nor is there any need
' on't, for she resolved to stop him before he could get
' near the Irishman. She has done it, upon my life ;
                                          ' and

' and if you should go out, you might spoil the kindest
' encounter that the loving Abel is ever like to have.

' *Mrs. Day.* Art sure of this?'

Ruth. If you do not find she has stopt him, let me
ever have your hatred. Pray, credit me.

' *Mrs. Day.* I do, I do believe thee. Come, we'll go
' in, where I use to read; there thou shalt tell me all
' the particulars, and the manner of it. I warrant 'twas
' pretty to observe.

' *Ruth.* Oh, 'twas a thousand pities you did not see it:
' when Abel walk'd away so bravely, and foolishly, after,
' this wild Irishman, she stole such kind looks from her
' own eyes; and having robbed herself, sent them after
' her own Abel; and then——'

Mrs. Day. Come, good wench; I'll go in, and hear
all at large. It shall be the best tale thou hast told these
two days. Come, come, I long to hear all. Abel, for
his part, needs no help by this time. Come, good wench.
[*Exit.*

' *Ruth.* So far I am right. Fortune, take care for fu-
' ture things.' [*Exit.*

Enter Colonel Blunt, *as taken by bailiffs.*

Blunt. At whose suit, rascals?

1 *Bail.* You shall know that time enough.

Blunt. Time enough, dogs! Must I wait your leisures?

1 *Bail.* Oh, you are a dangerous man! 'Tis such traitors as you that disturb the peace of the nation.

Blunt. Take that, rascal. [*Kicking him.*] If I had any
thing at liberty, besides my foot, I would bestow it on
you.

1 *Bail.* You shall pay dearly for this kick, before you
are let loose, and give good special bail. Mark that, my
surly companion; we have you fast.

Blunt. 'Tis well, rogues, you caught me conveniently;
had I been aware, I should have made some of your scur-
vy souls my special bail.

' 1 *Bail.* Oh, 'tis a bloody-minded man! I'll warrant
' ye, this vile cavalier has eat many a child.

' *Blunt.* I could gnaw a piece or two of you, rascals.'

Enter Colonel Careless.

Car. How is this! Blunt in hold! You catchpole,
let go your prey, or——
[*Car.*

[*Car. draws, and* Blunt, *in the scuffle, throws up one of their heels, gets a sword, and helps to drive them off.*

1 *Bail.* Murder, murder!

Blunt. Faith, Careless, this was worth thanks. I was fairly going.

Car. What was the matter, man?

Blunt. Why, an action or two for free quarter, now made trover and conversion. Nay, I believe we shall be sued with an action of trespass, for every field we have marched over; and be indicted for riots, for going at unseasonable hours, above two in a company.

Enter Teague, *running.*

Car. Well, come, let's away.

Tea. Now, upon my shoul, run as I do; the men in red coats are running too, and they cry, murder, murder! I never heard such a noise in Ireland in all my life.

Car. 'Slife, we must shift several ways. Farewel. If we 'scape, we meet at night; I shall take heed now.

Tea. Shall I tell Mrs. Tay's message.

Car. Oh, good Teague, no time for messages.

[*Exeunt several ways.*

A noise within. Enter bailiffs and soldiers.

1 *Bail.* This way, this way! Oh, villains! My neighbour Swash, is hurt dangerously. Come, good soldiers, follow, follow.

Enter Careless *and* Teague *again.*

Car. I am quite out of breath, and the blood-hounds are in a full cry upon a burning scent: plague on 'em, what a noise the kennels make! What door's this, that graciously stands a little open? What an ass am I to ask? Teague, scout abroad; if any thing happens extraordinary, observe this door, there you shall find me. Now, by your favour, landlord, as unknown.

[*Exeunt severally.*

Enter Mrs. Day, *and* Obadiah.

Mrs. Day. It was well observed, Obadiah, to bring the parties to me, first. 'Tis your master's will that I shou'd, as I may say, prepare matters for him. In truth, in truth, I have too great a burthen upon me; yet for the public good, I am content to undergo it.

Obad. I shall, with sincere care, present unto your honour, from time to time, such negotiations as I may

discreetly

difcreetly prefume may be material for your honour's infpection.

Mrs. Day. It will become you fo to do. You have the prefent that came laft ?

Obad. Yes, and pleafe your honour, the gentlewoman, concerning her brother's releafe, hath alfo fent in a piece of plate.

Mrs. Day. It's very well.

Obad. But the man without, about a bargain of the king's land, is come empty.

Mrs. Day. Bid him begone ; I'll not fpeak with him. He does not underftand himfelf.

Obad. I fhall intimate fo much to him.

[*As* Obadiah *goes out C.* Carelefs *meets him, and tumbles him back.*]

Mrs. Day. Why, how now ? What rude companion's this ? What wou'd you have ? What's your bufinefs; What's the matter ? Who fent you ? Who d'you belong to ? Who————

Car. Hold, hold, if you mean to be anfwer'd to all thefe interrogatories. You fee I refolve to be your companion. I am a man ; there's no great matter : nobody fent me ; nor I belong to nobody. I think I have anfwer'd to the chief heads.

Mrs. Day. Thou haft committed murder, for ought I know. How is't Obadiah ?

Car. Ha ! What luck have I, to fall into the territories of my old kitchen acquaintance. I'll proceed upon the ftrenghth of Teague's meffage, tho' I had no anfwer.

[*Afide.*

Obad. Truly he came forceably upon me, and I fear has bruifed fome intellectuals within my ftomach.

Mrs. Day. Go in, and take fome Irifh flat, by way of prevention, and keep yourfelf warm. [*Ex.* Obad. Now, Sir, have you any bufinefs, that you came in fo rudely, as if you did not know who you came to ? How came you in, Sir Royfter ? Was not the porter at the gate ?

Car. No, truly ; the gate kept itfelf, and ftood gaping, as if it had a mind to fpeak, and fay, I pray, come in.

Mrs. Day. Did it fo, Sir ? And what have you to fay ?

Car. Ay, there's the point. Either fhe does not, or

will

will not know me.   What shou'd I say ?   How dull am
I !   Pox on't, this wit is like a common friend, when
one has need of him, he won't come near one.   [*Aside.*

Mrs. Day. Sir, are you studying for an invention ?
For ought I know, you have done some mischief, and
'twere fit to secure you.

Car. So, that's well ; 'twas pretty to fall into the head
quarters of the enemy.   [*Aside.*

Mrs. Day. Nay, 'tis e'en so ; I'll fetch those that
shall examine you.

Car. Stay, thou mighty states-woman ; I did but give
you time to see if your memory would but be so honest,
as to tell you who I am.

Mrs. Day. What do you mean, sauce-box ?

Car. There's a word yet of thy former employments :
that sauce.   You and I have been acquainted.

Mrs. Day. I do not use to have acquaintance with
cavaliers.

Car. Nor I with committee-men's utensils ; ‘ but in
‘ *diebus illis*, you were not honourable, nor I malignant.’
Lord, Lord, you are horridly forgetful.   ‘ Pride comes
‘ with godliness, and good cloaths.’   What, you think I
should not know you, because you are disguised with
curled hair, and white gloves ?   Alas !   I know you as
well as if you were in your sabbath-day's cinnamon waist-
coat, ‘ with a silver edging round the skirt,’

Mrs. Day. How, sirrah !

Car. And with your fair hands bath'd in lather ; or,
with your fragrant breath driving the fleeting ambergrease
off from the waving kitchen-stuff.

Mrs. Day. Oh, you are an impudent cavalier !   I remember you now, indeed ; but I'll——

Car. Nay, but hark you, the now honourable, *non
obstante* past conditions ; did I not send my footman, an
Irishman, with a civil message to you ?   Why all this
strangeness, then ?

Mrs. Day. How, how, how's this !   Was't you that
sent that rascal to abuse me, was't so ?

Car. How now !   What, matters grow worse, and
worse !

Mrs. Day. I'll teach you to abuse those that are in
authority.   Within there, who's within ?

Car.

Car. 'Slife I'll stop your mouth, if you raise an alarm.

[*She cries out, he stops her mouth.*

Mrs. Day. Stop my mouth, sirrah! whoo, whoo, ho!

Car. Yes, stop your mouth. What, are you good at a who-bub, ha?

Enter Ruth.

Ruth. What's the matter, forsooth?

Mrs. Day. The matter! Why here's a rude cavalier has broke into my house; 'twas he too, that sent the Irish rascal to abuse me, too, within my own walls. Call your father, that he may grant an order to secure him. 'Tis a dangerous fellow.

Car. Nay, good, pretty gentlewoman, spare your motion.—What must become of me? Teague has made some strange mistake. [*Aside.*

Ruth. 'Tis he! What shall I do? Now, invention, be equal to my love. [*Aside.*] Why, your ladyship will spoil all. I sent for this gentleman, and enjoin'd him secrecy, even to you yourself, till I had made his way. Oh, fie upon't, I am to blame; but, in truth, I did not think he would have come these two hours.

Car. I dare swear she did not; I might very probably not have come at all.

Ruth. How came you to come so soon, Sir? 'Twas three hours before you appointed.

Car. Hey-day! I shall be made believe I came hither on purpose, presently. [*Aside.*

Ruth. 'Twas upon a message of his to me, and please your honour, to make his desires known to your lady-ship, that he had consider'd on't, and was resolv'd to take the covenant, and give you five hundred pounds, to make his peace, and bring his business about again, that he may be admitted in his first condition.

Car. What's this?—D'ye hear pretty gentlewoman?

Ruth. Well, well, I know your mind; I have done your business.

Mrs. Day. Oh, his stomach's come down.

Ruth. Sweeten him again, and leave him to me; I warrant the five hundred pounds, and—— [*Whispers.*

Car. Now I have found it; this pretty wench has a mind to be left alone with me, at her peril. [*Aside.*

Mrs.

Mrs. Day. I underſtand thee—Well, Sir, I can paſs by rudeneſs, when I am inform'd there was no intention of it. I leave you and my daughter to beget a right underſtanding.   [*Ex. Mrs.* Day.

Car. We ſhould beget ſons and daughters ſooner. What does all this mean?   [*Aſide.*

Ruth. I am ſorry, Sir, that your love for me ſhou'd make you thus raſh.

Car. That's more than you know; but you had a mind to be left alone with me, that's certain.

Ruth. 'Tis too plain, Sir; you'd ne'er have run your-ſelf into this danger elſe.

Car. Nay, now you're out; the danger run after me.

Ruth. You may diſſemble.

Car. Why, 'tis the proper buſineſs here; but we loſe time; you and I are left to beget a right underſtanding. Come, which way?

Ruth. Whither;

Car. To your chamber or cloſet.

Ruth. But I'm engaged you ſhall take the covenant.

Car. No, I never ſwear when I am bid.

Ruth. But you wou'd do as bad.

Car. That's not againſt my principles.

Ruth. Thank you for your fair opinion, good Signor Principle. There lies your way, Sir. However, I will own ſo much kindneſs for you, that I repent not the civility I have done, to free you from the trouble you were like to fall into. Make me a leg, if you pleaſe, and cry, thank you. And ſo the gentlewoman that de-ſired to be left alone with you, deſires to be left alone with herſelf, ſhe being taught a right underſtanding of you.

Car. No: I am rivetted; nor ſhall you march off thus with flying colours. My pretty commander in chief, let us parley a little farther, and but lay down ingenu-ouſly the true ſtate of our treaty. The buſineſs in ſhort is this: we differ ſeemingly upon two evils, and mine the leaſt; and therefore to be choſen. You had better take me, than I take the covenant.

Ruth. We'll excuſe one another.

Car. You would not have me take the covenant then?

Ruth. No; I did but try you. I forgive your idle
                                                  looſe-

loosenefs, for that firm virtue.   Be conftant to your fair principles, in fpite of fortune.

Car. What's this got into petticoats!—' But, d'ye
' hear: I'll not excufe you from my propofition, not-
' withftanding my releafe.   Come, we are half way to a
' right underftanding——Nay, I do love thee.

' *Ruth.* Love virtue: you have but here and there a
' patch of it; y'are ragged ftill.

' *Car.* Are you not the committee Day's daughter?'

Ruth. Yes. What then?

Car. Then am I thankful.   I had no defence againft thee and matrimony, but thy own father and mother, which are a perfect committee to my own nature.

' *Ruth.* Why, are you fure I would have matched
' with a malignant, not a compounder neither?

' *Car.* Nay, I have made thee a jointure againft my
' will. Methinks it were but as reafonable, that I fhould
' do fomething for my jointure; but by the way of ma-
' trimony, honeftly to encreafe your generation, this,
' to tell you truth, is againft my confcience.

' *Ruth.* Yet you would beget right underftandings.

' *Car.* Yes, I would have them all baftards.

' *Ruth.* And me a whore.

' *Car.* That's a coarfe name; but 'tis not fit a com-
' mittee-man's daughter fhould be too honeft, to the re-
' proach of her father and mother.'

Ruth. When the quarrel of the nation is reconciled, you and I fhall agree: 'till when, Sir——

Enter Teague.

Tea. Are you here then? Upon my fhoul, the good colonel Blunt is over-taken again now, and carried to the devil, ' that he is, i'faith now.'

Car. How, taken and carried to the devil!

Tea. He defired to go to the devil; I wonder of my fhoul he was not afraid.

Car. I underftand it now.   What mifchief's this?

Ruth. You feem troubled, Sir.

Car. I have but a life to lofe, that I am weary of. Come, Teague.

Ruth. Hold, you fhan't go before I know the bufinefs. What d'ye talk of?

Car. My friend, my deareft friend, is caught up by

I   rafcally rascally bailiffs, and carried to the Devil-tavern. Pray let me go.

Ruth. Stay but a minute, if you have any kindness for me.

Car. Yes, I do love you.

Ruth. Perhaps I may serve your friend.

Enter Arbella.

O Arbella, I was going to seek you.

Arb. What's the matter?

Ruth. The Colonel which thou likest, is taken by bailiffs; there's his friend too, almost distracted. You know the mercy of these times.

Arb. What dost thou tell me? I am ready to sink down!

Ruth. Compose yourself, and help him nobly; you have no way, but to smile upon Abel, and get him to bail him.

Enter Abel *and* Obadiah.

Arb. Look, where he and Obadiah come; sent hither by Providence——Oh, Mr. Abel, where have you been this long time? Can you find of your heart to keep thus out of my sight?

Abel. Assuredly some important affairs constrained my absence, as Obadiah can testify, *bona fide.*

Tea. The devil brake your bones a Friday.

Obad. I can do so, verily, myself being a material party.

Car. Pox on 'em, how slow they speak.

Tea. Speak faster.

Arb. Well, well, you shall go no more out of my sight; I'll not be satisfied with you *bona fide*'s. I have some occasions that call me to go a little way? you shall e'en go with me, and good Obadiah too. You shall not deny me any thing.

Abel. It is not meet I should. I am exceedingly exalted. Obadiah, thou shalt have the best bargain of all my tenants.

Obad. I am thankful.

' *Car.* What may this mean?'   [*Aside.*

Arb. Ruth, how shall we do, to keep thy swift mother from pursuing us?

Ruth. Let me alone: as I go by the parlour, where

the

she fits, big with expectation, I'll give her a whisper, that
we are going to fetch the very five hundred pounds.

Arb. How can that be?

Ruth. No question now. Will you march, Sir?

Car. Whither?

Ruth. Lord, how dull these men in love are!—Why,
to your friend. No more words.

' *Car.* I will stare upon thee, though.'

- END of the THIRD ACT.

ACT IV.

'*Colonel* Blunt *brought in by Bailiffs.*

1 BAILIFF.

AY, ay, we thought how well you'd get bail.

Blunt. Why, you unconscionable rascal, are you
angry that I am unlucky, or do you want some fees? I'll
perish in a dungeon, before I'll give you a farthing.

1 *Bail.* Chuse, chuse. Come, along with him.

Blunt. I'll not go your pace neither, rascals; I'll go
softly, if it be but to hinder you from taking up some
other honest gentleman.

' 1 *Bail.* Very well, surly Sir; we will carry you
' where you shall not be troubled what pace to walk;
' you'll find a large bill. Blood is dear.

' *Blunt.* Not yours, is it?—A farthing a pint were
' very dear for the best blood you have.'

Enter Arbella, Ruth, Abel, *Col.* Careless *and* Obadiah .

1 *Bail.* How now! are these any of your friends?

Blunt. Never. if you see women; that's a rule.

Arb. [*To* Abel.] Nay, you need have no scruple, 'tis
a near kinsman of mine. You do not think, I hope,
that I would let you suffer——You—that must be nearer
than a kinsman to me.

Abel. But my mother doth not know it.

Arb. If that be all, leave it to me and Ruth; we'll save
you harmless: besides, I cannot marry, if my kinsman be
in prison; he must convey my estate, as you appoint; for
'tis all in him. We must please him.

E

Abel.

Abel. The confideration of that doth convince me, Obadiah, 'tis neceffary for us to fet at liberty this gentleman, being at ruftee for Mrs. Arbella's eftate. Tell 'em therefore, that you and I will bail this gentleman—and—d'ye hear, tell them who I am.

Obad. I fhall.—Gentlemen, this is the honourable Mr. Abel Day, the firft-born of the honourable Mr. Day, chairman of the committee of fequeftrations; and I myfelf, by name Obadiah, and clerk to the faid honourable committee.

1 *Bail.* Well, Sir, we know Mr. Day, and Mr. Abel.

Abel. Yes that's I; and I will bail this gentleman. I believe you dare not except againft the bail: nay, you fhall have Obadiah's too, one that the ftate trufts.

1 *Bail.* With all our hearts, Sir.——But there are charges to be paid.

Arb. Here, Obadiah, take this purfe and difcharge them, and give the bailiffs twenty fhillings to drink.

Car. This is miraculous!

1 *Bail.* A brave Lady!—I'faith, miftrefs, we'll drink your health.

Abel. She's to be my wife, as fure as you are here: what fay you to that now?

1 *Bail.* [*Afide.*] That's impoffible: here's fomething more in this.—Honourable Mr. Abel, the fheriff's deputy is hard by in another room, if you pleafe to go thither, and give your bail, Sir.

Abel. Well, fhew us the way, and let him know who I am.   [*Exeunt* Abel, Obadiah, *and Bailiffs.*

Car. Hark ye, pretty Mrs. Ruth, if you were not a committee-man's daughter, and fo confequently againft monarchy, two princes fhould have you and that gentlewoman.

Ruth. No, no, you'll ferve my turn; I am not ambitious.

Car. Do but fwear then that thou art not the iffue of Mr. Day; and, though I know 'tis a lie, I'll be content to be cozened, and believe.

Ruth. Fie, fie; you can't abide taking of oaths. Look, look, how your friend and mine take aim at one another. Is he fmitten?

Car. Cupid has not fuch another wounded fubject;
nay,

nay, and is vex'd he is in love too. Troth, 'tis partly my own cafe.

Ruth. Peace! fhe begins, as need requires.

Arb. You are free, Sir,

Bl. Not fo free as you think.

Arb. What hinders it?

Bl. Nothing, that I'll tell you.

Arb. Why, Sir?

Bl. You'll laugh at me.

Arb. Have you perceived me apt to commit fuch a rudenefs? Pray let me know it.

Bl. Upon two conditions you fhall know it.

Arb. Well, make your own laws.

Bl. Firft, I thank ye, y'have freed me nobly: pray believe it; you have this acknowledgement from an honeft heart, one that would crack a ftring for you; that's one thing.

Arb. Well, the other.

Bl. The other is only, that I may ftand fo ready, that I may be gone juft as I have told it you; together with your promife not to call me back: and upon thefe terms, I give you leave to laugh when I am gone. Carelefs, come, ftand ready, that, at the fign given, we may vanifh together.

Ruth. If you pleafe, Sir, when you are ready to ftart, I'll cry one, two, three, and away.

Bl. Be pleafed to forbear, good fmart gentlewoman: you have leave to jeer when I am gone, and I am juft going; by your fpleen's leave, a little patience.

Arb. Pr'ythee, peace.

Ruth. I fhall contain, Sir.

Bl. That's much for a woman to do.

Arb. Now, Sir, perform your promife.

Bl. Carelefs, have you done with your woman?

Car. Madam——

Bl. Nay, I have thanked her already; pr'ythee no more of that dull way of gratitude. Stand ready, man; yet nearer the door. So, now my misfortune that I promifed to difcover, is, that I love you above my fenfe or reafon. So farewel, and laugh. Come, Carelefs.

E 2

Car.

Car. Ladies, our lives are yours; ' be but so kind
' as to believe it, till you have something to command.'

[*Exeunt.*

Ruth. Was there ever such humour?

Arb. As I live his confession shews nobly.

Ruth. It shews madly, I am sure. An ill-bred fellow!
not indure a woman to laugh at him!

Arb. He's honest, I dare swear.

Ruth. That's more than I dare swear for my colonel.

Arb. Out upon him.

Ruth. Nay, 'tis but want of a good example; I'll
make him so.

Arb. But d'ye hear, Ruth, we were horribly to blame
that we did not enquire where they lodged, under pretence of sending to them about their own business.

Ruth. ' Why, thy whimsical colonel discharged him-
' self off like a gun: there was no time between the
' flashing in the pan and the going off, to ask a question.
' But hark ye,' I have an invention upon the old account
of the five hundred pounds, which shall make Abel send
Obadiah, to look 'em.

Arb. Excellent! the trout Abel will bite immediately
at that bait. ' The message shall be as from his master,
' Day, senior, to come and speak with him; they'll
' think presently, 'tis about their composition, and come
' certainly. In the mean time, we'll prepare them
' with counter expectations.'

Enter Abel *and* Obadiah.

Ruth. Peace! see where Abel and the gentle squire of
low degree, Obadiah, approach, having newly entered
themselves into bonds.

Arb. Which I'll be sure to tell his mother, if he be
ever more troublesome.

Ruth. And that he's turned an arrant cavalier, by
bailing one of the brood.

Abel. I have, according to your desires, given freedom
to your kinsman and trustee. I suppose he doth perceive
that you may have power in right of me.

Arb. Good, Mr. Abel, I am sincerely beholden to
you, and your authority.

Ruth. O, fie upon't, brother, I did forget to acquaint
you with a business before the gentlemen went. O me,

what

what a sieve-like memory have I! 'Twas an important affair too.

Abel. If you discover it to me, I shall render you my opinion upon the whole.

Ruth. The two gentlemen have repented of their obstinacy, and would now present five hundred pounds to your good honourable mother, to stand their friend, that they may be permitted to take the covenant; and we, negligent we, have let them go before we knew where to send to them.

Abel. That was the want of being us'd to important affairs. It is ill to neglect the accepting of their conversion, together with their money.

Ruth. Well, there is but one way; ' do you send ' Obadiah, in your father's name, to desire them both ' to come to his house about some business that will be ' for their good, but no more, for then they'll take it ' ill: for they enjoin'd us secrecy; and when they come ' let us alone:' Obadiah may enquire them out.

Obad. The bailiffs did say they were gone to the Devil.

Abel. Hasten thither, good Obadiah, as if you had met my honourable father, and desire them to come unto his house, about an important affair, that is for their good.

Obad. I shall use expedition. [*Exit.*

Abel. And we will hasten ' home, lest the gentlemen ' should be before us, and not know how to address their ' offers; and then we will hasten' our being united in the bonds of matrimony.

Arb. Soft and fair goes far. [*Exeunt.*

Enter the two Colonels, and Teague, as at the Tavern.

Car. Did ever man get away so craftily from the thing he lik'd? Terrible business! afraid to tell a woman what she desired to hear. ' I pray heartily that the boys do ' not come to the knowledge of thy famous retreat: we ' shall be followed by those small birds, as you have seen ' an owl pursued.

' *Bl.* I shall break some of their wings then.'

Car. To leave a handsome woman; a woman that came to be bound body for body for thee, one that does that which no woman will hardly do again.

E 3

BA

Bl. What's that?

Car. Love thee, and thy blunt humour; a meer chance, man. Come, Teague, give us a song.

Tea. I am a cup too low.

Car. Here then.   [*Gives him a Glass.*

Tea. I should like to wet t'other eye.

Car. Here.

SONG *by* Teague.

Last Patrick-mass night 'bove all days in the year,
I set out for London before I got there :
But when I took leave of my own natural shore.
O, whilil-a-lu, I did screech, bawl, and roar.

I did wake in the morning, while yet it was night,
And could not see one bit of land but was quite out of
       sight ;
So, with tumbling and tossing, and jolting poor Teague,
My stomach was sea-sick in less than a league.

At Chester, to shew my high birth and great mind,
I took a place in the coach, but walk'd in it behind ;
The seas they did roar, and the winds were uncivil,
And, upon my soul, I thought we were all blown to the
       devil.

At Coventry next, where you see Peeping Tom,
Who was killed for a look at the Duchess's bum ;
But when her grace rid on her saddle all bare,
Devil burn me, no wonder that old Snob did stare.

' *Bl.* You practise your wit to no purpose ; I am not
' to be persuaded to lie still, like a jack-a-lent, to be cast
' at ; I had rather be a wisp hung up for a woman to
' scold at, than a fix'd lover for 'em to point at. Your
' squib began to hiss.'

Enter Obadiah.

Car. Peace, man, here's Jupiter's Mercury. Is his message to us, trow ?

Obad. Gentlemen, you are opportunely over-taken, and found out.

Bl. How's this ?

Obad. I come unto you in the name of the honoura-
          ble

ble Mr. Day, who defires to fpeak with you both about fome important affair, which is conducing for your good.

Bl. What train is this?

Car. Peace, let us not be rafh.————Teague.

Tea. Eh!

Car. Were it not poffible that you could entertain this fellow in the next room, till he were pretty drunk? [*Afide.*

Tea. I warrant you, I will make him and myfelf too drunk, for thy fweet fake.

Car. Be fure, Teague.————Some bufinefs, that will take us up a very little time to finifh, makes us defire your patience till we difpatch it. In the mean time, Sir, do us the favour to call for a glafs of fack, in the next room; Teague fhall wait upon you, and drink your mafter's health.

Obad. It needeth not; nor do I ufe to drink healths.

Car. None but your mafter's, Sir; and that by way of remembrance.

Obad. We that have the affairs of ftate under our tuition cannot long delay; my prefence may be required for carrying on the work.

Car. Nay, Sir, it fhall not exceed above a quarter of an hour; perhaps we'll wait upon you to Mr. Day prefently. Pray, Sir, drink but one glafs or two; we would wait upon you ourfelves, but that would hinder us from going with you.

Obad. Upon that confideration I fhall attend a little.

Car. Go, wait upon him————Now, Teague, or never.

Tea. I will make him fo drunk as can be, upon my fhoul. [*Exeunt* Teague *and* Obadiah.

Bl. What a devil fhould this meffage mean?

Car. 'Tis too plain; this cream of committee rafcals, who has better intelligence than a ftate-fecretary, has heard of his fon Abel's being hamper'd in the caufe of the wicked, and in revenge would intice us to perdition.

Bl. If Teague could be fo fortunate as to make him drunk, we might know all.

' *Car.* If the clofe-hearted rogue will not be open-
' mouth'd, we'll leave him pawned for all our fcores,
' and ftuff his pockets with blank commiffions.

' *Blunt.* Only fill up one with his mafter's name.

' *Car.*

'*Car.* And another with his wife's name for adjutant
' general, together with a bill of ammunition hid under
' Day's house, and make it be digged down, with scan-
' dal of delinquency.   A rascal, to think to invite us in-
' to Newgate !

' *Blunt.* Well, we must resolve what to do.

' *Car.* I have a fancy come into my head, that may
' produce an admirable scene.

' *Blunt.* Come, let's hear.

' *Car.* 'Tis upon supposition, that Teague makes him
' drunk ; and, by the way, 'tis a good omen that we
' have no sober apparition in that wavering posture of
' frailty ; we'll send him home in a sedan, and cause him
' to be delivered in that good-natured condition, to the
' ill-natured rascal his master.

' *Blunt.* It will be excellent.   How I pray for Teague
' to be victorious !'

Enter Musician.

Muf. Gentleman, will you have any musick ?
Blunt. Pr'ythee no, we are out of tune.
Car. Pish, we will never be out humour.

Enter Teague *and* Obadiah *drunk.*

' See and rejoice where Teague with laurel comes.'

Blunt. And the vanquished Obadiah, with nothing fixed about him but his eyes.

Tea. Well now, upon my shoul, Mr. Obadiah sings
as well as the man now.   Come then, will you sing an
Irish song after me ;

Obad. I will sing Irish for the king now.

Tea. I will sing for the king, as well as you.   Hark
you now !   [*He sings an Irish song, and Obadiah tries.*

S. O. N. G.

Oh, Teady-foley, you are my darling,
You are my looking-glass, both night and morning ;
I had rather have you without a farthing,
Than Bryan Gaulichar, with his house and garden.

La, ral, lidy.

O No-

O Norah, agra, I do not doubt you,
And for that reason I kifs and mouth you;
And if there was ten and twenty about you,
Devil burn me, if I would go without you.

                               La, ral, lidy.

Obad. That is too hard stuff; I cannot do these and these material matters.

Tea. Here, now, we will take some snuff for the king——So, there, lay it upon your hand; put one, of your noses to it now; so, snuff now. Upon my shoul, Mr. Obad. Commit. will make a brave Irishman. Put this in your other nose.

Obad. I will snuff for the king no more. Good Mr. Teague, give me some more sack, and sing English, for my money.

Tea. I will tell you that Irish is as good and better too. Come, now, we will dance. Can you play an Irish tune?   [*Dance, Obadiah tumbles down.*

Tea. Obid, Obid! upon my soul I believe he's dead.

Car. Dead!

Tea. Dead drunk. Poor Obid is sick, and I will mull him some wine—I will put some spice in't. [*Puts some snuff into the funnell.*] Now I will howl over him as they do in Ireland: oh, oh, oh.

Car. Peace, Teague, you'll alarm the enemy. Here's a shilling, call a chair, and let them carry him in this condition to his kind master. If you meet the ladies, say, we would speak with them at the Lieutenant's.

Tea. Give me the thirteen, and I will give him an Irish sedan.

Col. How's that?

Tea. This way. [*Takes him by the heels, and draws him off.*   [*Exeunt.*

        Enter Mr. Day *and Mrs.* Day.

Mrs. Day. Dispatch quickly I say, and say I said it; many things fall between the lip and the cup.

Mr. Day. Nay, duck, let thee alone for counsel. Ah, if thou hadst been a man!

Mrs. Day. Why then you would have wanted a woman, and a helper too.

                               Mr.

Mr. Day. I profess so I should, and a notable one too, though I say it before thy face, and that's no ill one.

Mrs. Day. Come, come, you are wand'ring from the matter; dispatch the marriage, I say, whilst she is thus taken with our Abel. Women are uncertain.

Mr. Day. How if she should be coy?

Mrs. Day. You are at your *ifs* again; if she be foolish, tell her plainly what she must trust to: no Abel, no land. Plain-dealing's a jewell. Have you the writings drawn, as I advised you, which she must sign?

Mr. Day. Ay, I warrant you, duck; here, here they be. Oh, she has a brave estate!

Mrs. Day. What news you have!

Mr. Day. Look you, wife——————

            [Day *pulls out writings, and lays out his keys.*

Mrs. Day. Pish, teach your grannum to spin; let me see.

Enter a Servant.

Serv. May it please your honour, your good neighbour Zachariah is departing this troublesome life: he has made your honour his executor, but cannot depart till he has seen your honours.

Mr. Day. Alas! alas! a good man will leave us.—— Come, good duck, let us hasten. Where is Obadiah, to usher you?

Mrs. Day. Why, Obadiah!—A varlet, to be out of the way at such a time; truly he moveth my wrath. Come, husband, along; I'll take Abel in his place.

                                    [*Exeunt.*

Enter Ruth *and* Arbella.

Ruth. What's the meaning of this alarm? There's some carrion discover'd; the crows are all gone upon a sudden.

Arbel. The she Day call'd most fiercely for Obadiah. Look here, Ruth, what have they left behind?

Ruth. As I live, it is the Day's bunch of keys, which he always keeps so closely:——well————if thou hast any mettle now's the time.

Arbel. To do what?

Ruth. To fly out of Egypt.

Enter

Enter Abel.

Arbel. Peace, we are betray'd elfe ; as fure as can be, wench, he's come back for the keys.

Ruth. We'll forfwear 'em in confident words, and no lefs confident countenances.

Abel. An important affair hath call'd my honourable father and mother forth, and in the abfence of Obadiah, I am enforced to attend their honours ; ' and therefore, ' I conceived it right and meet to acquaint you with it ; ' left in my abfence you might have apprehended that ' fome mifchance had befallen my perfon : therefore I de- ' fire you to receive confolation :' and fo I bid you hear- tily farewel. [*Exit.*

Arbel. Given from his mouth, this tenth of April— He put me in a cruel fright

' *Ruth.* As I live I'm all over in fuch a dew as hangs ' about a ftill, when 'tis firft fet a going ; but this is bet- ' ter and better : there never was fuch an opportunity to ' break prifon. I know the very places, the holes in ' his clofet, where the compofition of your eftate lies, ' and where the deeds of my own eftate lie. I have caft ' my eye upon them often, when I have gone up to him ' on errands, and to call him to dinner.'—If I mifs, hang me.

Arbel. But whither fhall we go?

Ruth. To a friend of mine, and of my father's, that lives near the Temple, and will harbour us, fear not ; and fo fet up for ourfelves, and get our colonels.

Arbel. Nay, the mifchief that I have done, and the condition we are in, makes me as ready as thou art. Come, let's about it.

Ruth. Stay ; do you ftand centinel here. That's the clofet-window ; I'll call for thee, if I need thee ; and be fure to give notice of any news of the enemy. [*Exit.*

Arbel. I warrant thee—' May but this departing bro- ' ther have fo much ftring of life left him, as may tie ' this expecting Day to his bedfide, till we have com- ' mitted this honeft robbery'——Hark ! what's that—— this apprehenfion can make a noife when there is none.

Ruth. I have 'em, I have 'em ; nay the whole covey, and his feal at arms bearing a dog's leg. [*Above.*

Arbel. Come, make hafte then.

' *Ruth.*

' *Ruth.* As I live, here's a letter counterfeited, from
' the king, to the rascal his rebellious subject Day ; with
' a remembrance to his discreet wife. Nay, what dost
' thou think these are ? I'll but cast my eye upon these
' papers, that were schismatical, and lay in separation :
' what do'st thou think they are ?

' *Arbel.* I can't tell.   Nay, pr'ythee come away.

' *Ruth.* Out upon the precise baboon ! they are letters
' from two wenches ; one for an encrease of salary to
' maintain his unlawful issue ; another from a wench
' that had more conscience than he, and refus'd to take
' the physic that he prescrib'd to take away a natural
' tympany.

' *Arbel.* Nay, pr'ythee dispatch.

' *Ruth.* Here be abundance more.   Come, run up,
' and help me carry 'em.   We'll take the whole index of
' his rogueries : we shall be furnish'd with such arms,
' offensive and defensive, that we shall never need sue to
' him for a league.   Come, make haste.

' *Arbel.* I come.

Enter Teague, *with* Obadiah *on his back.*

Tea. Long life to you, Madam ; my master is at Lieutenant Story's and wants to speak to you, and that dear
creature too.

Arbel. and Ruth. Conduct us to him.

Tea. Oh, that I will—Come along and I will follow
you.   [*Exeunt all but* Obadiah.

Obad. Some small beer, good Mr. Teague.

Enter as return'd, Mr. Day, Mrs. Day, *and* Abel.

Mr. Day. He made a good end, and departed as unto
sleep.

Mrs. Day. I'll assure you his wife took on grievously ;
I do not believe she'll marry this half year.

Mr. Day. He died full of exhortation. Ha, duck,
thou'dst be sorry to lose me ?

Mrs. Day. Lose you ! I warrant you you'll live as
long as a better thing——Ah, Lord ! what's that ?
                                        [Obadiah *sings.*

Mr. Day. How now ! what's this ?—How ! Obadiah—
and in a drunken distemper assuredly !

Mrs. Day. O fie upon't, who wou'd have believ'd that

we should have liv'd to have seen Obadiah overcome with the creature ?—Where have you been, sirrah ?

Obad. D—d—drinking the ki—ki—king's health.

Mr. Day. O terrible ! some disgrace put upon us, and shame brought within our walls. I'll go lock up my neighbour's will, and come down and shew him a reproof.——How——how——I cannot feel my keys——nor—— [*He feels in his pockets, and leaps up.*] hear 'em gingle.—Didst thou see my keys, duck ?

Mrs. Day. Duck me no ducks. I see your keys ! see a fool's head of your own ! Had I kept them, I warrant they had been forth-coming. You are so flappish, you throw 'em up and down at your tail. Why don't you go look if you have not left them in the door ?

Mr. Day. I go, I go, duck. [*Exit.*

Mrs. Day. Here, Abel, take up this fallen creature, who has left his uprightness ; carry him to a bed, and when he is return'd to himself, I will exhort him.

Abel. He is exceedingly overwhelmed.

[*He goes to lift him up.*

Obad. Stand away, I say, and give me some more sack, that I may drink a health to the king. [Obadiah *sings Teady Foley.*] Where's Mr. Teague ?

Enter Mr. Day.

Mr. Day. Undone, undone ! robb'd, robb'd ! the doors left open, and all my writings and papers stolen ! Undone, undone !—Ruth, Ruth !

Mrs. Day. Why, Ruth, I say ! Thieves, thieves !

Enter Servant.

Serv. What's the matter, forsooth ! Here has been no thieves : I have not been a minute out of the house.

Mrs. Day. Where's Ruth, and Mrs. Arbella ?

Serv. I have not seen them a pretty while.

Mr. Day. 'Tis they have robb'd me, and taken away the writings of both their estates. Undone, undone !

Mrs. Day. This came with staying for you, [*To Abel.*] coxcomb, we had come back sooner else : you flow drone, we must be undone for your dullness.

Obad. Be not in wrath.

Mrs. Day. I'll wrath you, ye rascal you. I'll teach you, you drunken rascal, and you, sober dull man.

F

Obad.

2

Obad. Your feet are swift and violent; their motion will make them fume.

Mrs. Day. D'you lie too, ye drunken rascal?

Mr. Day. Nay, patience, good duck, and let's lay out for these women; they are the thieves.

Mrs. Day. 'Twas you that left your keys upon the table to tempt them: ye need cry, good duck, be patient. Bring in the drunken rascal, ye booby: when he is sober, he may discover something. Come, take him up; I'll have 'em hunted.   [*Exeunt Mr.* Day *and Mrs.* Day.

Abel. I rejoice yet, in the midst of my sufferings, that my mistress saw not my rebukes. Come, Obadiah, I pray, raise yourself upon your feet, and walk.

Obad. Have you taken the covenant? That's the question.

Abel. Yea.

Obad. And will you drink a health to the king? That's t'other question.

Abel. Make not thyself a scorn.

Obad. Scorn in my face! Void, young Satan.

Abel. I pray you, walk in, I shall be assisting.

Obad. Stand off, and you shall perceive, by my steadfast going, that I am not drunk. Look ye now—so, softly, softly; gently, good Obadiah, gently and steadily, for fear it should be said that thou art in drink. So, gently and uprightly, Obadiah.

                    [*He moves his legs, but stands still.*

Abel. You do not move.

Obad. Then do I stand still, as fast as you go.

                    Enter Mrs. Day.

Mrs. Day. What, stay all day! There's for you, Sir; [*To* Abel.] you are a sweet youth to leave in trust. Along, you drunken rascal; [*To* Obadiah.] I'll set you both forward.

Obad. The Philistines are upon us, and Day has broke loose from darkness; high keeping has made her fierce.

                    [*She beats them off.*

Mrs. Day. Out, you drunken rascal! I'll make you move, you beast.   [*Exeunt.*

END of the FOURTH ACT.

                              A C T

A C T   V.

' Enter Bookseller and Bailiffs, having laid hold on
' Teague.

' BOOKSELLER.

' COME along, Sir; I'll teach you to take covenants.
    ' *Tea.* Will you teach me then? Did not I take
' it then? Why will you teach me now?
    ' *Book.* You shall pay dearly for the blows you struck
' me, my wild Irish; by St. Patrick, you shall.
    ' *Tea.* What have you now to do with St. Patrick? he
' will scorn your covenant.
    ' *Book.* I'll put you, Sir, where you shall have
' worse liquour than your bonny-clabber.
    ' *Tea.* Bonny-clabber! By my gossip's hand now, you
' are a rascal if you do not love bonny-clabber; and I
' will break your pate if you will not let me go to my
' master.
    ' *Book.* O, you are an impudent rascal. Come,
' away with him.
                ' *Enter Colonel* Careless.
    ' *Car.* How now!—hold, my friend; whither do
' you carry my servant?
    ' *Book.* I have arrested him, Sir, for striking me,
' and taking away my books.
    ' *Car.* What has he taken away?
    ' *Book.* Nay, the value of the thing is not much;
' 'twas the covenant, Sir.
    ' *Tea.* Well, I did take the covenant, and my master
' took it from me; and we have taken the covenant then,
' have we not?
    ' *Car.* Here, honest fellow, here's more than thy co-
' venant's worth; here, bailiffs, here's for you to drink.
    ' *Book.* Well, Sir, you seem an honest gentleman;
' for your sake, and in hopes of your custom, I release
' him.
    ' 1 *Bail.* Thank ye, noble Sir.
                  ' [*Exeunt Book. and Bail.*
'*Car.* Farewel, my noble friend;——so——d'ye hear,
' Teague, pray take no more covenants.'—Have you
paid the money I sent you with?

                                  Tea.

Tea. Yes, but I will carry no more, look you there now.

Car. Why, Teague?

Tea. God fa' my fhoul now, I fhall run away with it.

Car. Pifh, thou art too honeft.

Tea. That I am too, upon my fhoul now; but the devil is not honeft, that he is not; he would not let me alone when I was going; but he made me go to this little long place; and t'other little long place; and, upon my fhoul, was carrying me into Ireland, for he made me go by a dirty place like a lough now; and therefore I know now it was the way to Ireland. Then I would ftay ftill, and then he would make me go on; and then I would go to one fide, and he would make me go to t'other fide; and then I got a little farther, and did run then; and upon my fhoul the devil could not catch me; and then I did pay the money: but I will carry no money, that I will not.

Car. But thou fha't, Teague, when I have more to fend; thou art proof now againft temptation.

Tea. Well then, if you fend me with money again, and if I do not come to thee upon the time, the devil will make me begone then with the money. Here's a paper for thee, 'tis a quit way indeed.

Car. That's well faid, Teague——   [*Reads.*

Enter Mr. Day, Obadiah, *and Soldiers.*

Obad. See, Sir, Providence hath directed us; there is one of them that cloathed me with fhame, and the moft malignant among the wicked.

Mr. Day. Soldiers, feize him. I charge him with treafon! Here's a warrant to the keeper, as I told you.

' 1 *Sold.* Nay, no refiftance now.'

Car. What's the matter, rafcals?

Mr. Day. You fhall know that, to your coft, hereafter. Away with him.

Car. Teague, tell 'em I fhall not come home to-night, I am engaged.

Tea. I pr'ythee, be not engaged.

Car. Gentlemen, I am guilty of nothing, that I know of.

Mr. Day. That will appear, Sir.—Away with him.

Tea. What will you do with my mafter, now.

Mr.

Mr. Day. Be quiet, Sir, or you shall go with him.

Tea. That I will, for all you, you old fool.

Car. Teague, come hither.

Tea. Sir?

Car. Here, take this key, open my bureau, and burn all the papers you find there; and here, burn this letter.

Tea. Pray, give me that pretty, clean letter, to send to my mother.

Car. No, no; be sure to do as I tell you.

Mr. Day. Away with him. We will be avenged on the scorner; and I'll go home, and tell my duck this part of my good fortune. [*Exeunt.*

' *Enter Chairmen with sedans,* Ruth *and Arbella come out.*

' *Ruth.* So far we are right.—Now, honest fellow,
' step over, and tell the two gentlemen, that we two
' women desire to speak with them.

Enter Col. Blunt, *and Lieutenant.*

' *Chair.* See, mistress, here's one of them.

Ruth. That's thy colonel, Arbella; catch him quickly, or he'll fly again.

Arb. What should I do?

' *Ruth.* Put forth some good words, ' as they use to
' shake oats, when they go to catch a skittish jade.'
Advance.

Arb. Sir.

Blunt. Lady?————'Tis she.

Arb. I wish, Sir, that my friend and I had some conveniency of speaking to you; we now want the assistance of some noble friend.

Blunt. Then I am happy: bring me but to do something for you. I would have my actions talk, not I. My friend will be here immediately; I dare speak for him too—Pardon my last confusion; but what I told you was as true as if I had staid—

Ruth. To make affidavit of it.

Blunt. Good, overcharged gentlewoman, spare me but a little.

Arb. Pr'ythee, peace. Can'st thou be merry, and we in this condition? —Sir, I do believe you noble, truly worthy. If we might withdraw any whither out of sight, I would acquaint you with the business.

F 3

Lieu.

Lieu. My houſe, ladies, is at that door, where both the colonels lodge. Pray, command it. Colonel Care-leſs will immediately be here.

Enter Teague.

Tea. He will not come: that commit rogue Day has got him with men in red coats, and he is gone to priſon here below this ſtreet. He would not let me go with him, i'faith, but made me come tell thee now.

Ruth. O, my heart!—Tears, by your leave, a while.—[*Wipes her Eyes.*] D'ye hear, Arbella, here, take all the trinkets, only the bait that I'll uſe, ' accept of this ' gentleman's houſe, there let me find thee, I'll try my ' ſkill—Nay, talk not.   [*Exit.*

Blunt. Careleſs in priſon! Pardon me, Madam; I muſt leave you for a little while; pray be confident; ' this honeſt friend of mine will uſe you with all reſpects ' till I return.'

Arb. What do you mean to do, Sir?

Blunt. I cannot tell; yet I muſt attempt ſomething. You ſhall have a ſudden account of all things. You ſay you dare believe; pray be as good as your word; and whatever accident befals me, know I love you dearly. ' Why do you weep?

' *Arb.* Do not run yourſelf into a needleſs danger.

' *Blunt.* How! D'ye weep for me? Pray let me ſee, ' Never woman did ſo before, that I know of. I am ' raviſh'd with it. The round gaping earth ne'er ſuck'd ' ſhowers ſo greedily as my heart drinks theſe. Pray, if ' you love me, be but ſo good and kind as to confeſs it.

' *Arb.* Do not aſk what you may tell yourſelf.

' *Blunt.* I muſt go; honour and friendſhip call me. ' Here, dear lieutenant, I never had a jewel but this; ' uſe it as right ones ſhould be uſed; do not breathe up- ' on it, but gaze as I do—Hold—one word more. The ' ſoldier that you often talk'd of to me, is ſtill honeſt?

' *Lieu.* Moſt perfectly.

' *Blunt.* And I may truſt him?

' *Lieu.* With your life.

' *Blunt.* Enough—Pray let me leave my laſt looks ' fix'd upon you——So; I love you, and am honeſt. ' Be careful, good lieutenant, of this treaſure—ſhe ' weeps ſtill—I cannot go, and yet I muſt.'   [*Exit.*

Lieu.

Lieu. Madam, pray let my houſe be honour'd with you. Be confident of all reſpect and faith.

' *Arb.* What uncertainties purſue my love and for-
' tune!' [*Exit.*

Enter Ruth *with a Soldier.*

Ruth. Come, give me the bundle; ſo, now the habit. 'Tis well; there's for your pains. Be ſecret, and wait where I appointed you.

Sold. If I fail, may I die in a ditch. [*Exit.*

Ruth. Now, for my wild colonel. ' Firſt, here's a
' note, with my Lady Day's ſeal to it, for his releaſe;
' if that fails, (as he that ſhoots at theſe raſcals muſt
' have two ſtrings to his bow) then here's my red-
' coat's ſkin to diſguiſe him, and a ſtring to draw up a
' ladder of cords, which I have prepar'd againſt it grows
' dark. One of them will hit ſure. I muſt have him
' out; and I muſt have him, when he is out. I have
' no patience to expect.' Within there—ho!—

Enter Keeper.

Ruth. Have not you a priſoner, Sir, in your cuſtody, one Colonel Careleſs?

Keep. Yes, Miſtreſs; and committed by your father, Mr. Day.

' *Ruth.* I know it; but there was a miſtake in it.
' Here's a warrant for his delivery, under his hand and
' ſeal.

' *Keep.* I wou'd willingly obey it, Miſtreſs; but
' there's a general order come from above, that all the
' king's party ſhou'd be kept cloſe, and none releas'd,
' but by the ſtates order.

' *Ruth.* This goes ill.'—May I ſpeak with him, Sir?

Keep. Very freely, Miſtreſs; there's no order to for-bid any to come to him. To ſay truth, 'tis the moſt pleaſant'ſt gentleman—I'll call him forth. [*Exit.*

Ruth. O' my conſcience. every thing muſt be in love with him. Now for my laſt hopes; if this fail, I'll uſe the ropes myſelf.

Enter Keeper and Careleſs.

Car. Mr. Day's daughter ſpeak with me?

Keep. Ay, Sir, there ſhe is. [*Exit.*

Ruth. Oh, Sir, does the name of Mr. Day's daughter
trouble

trouble you? You love the gentlewoman, but hate his daughter.

Car. Yes, I do love the gentlewoman you speak of, most exceedingly.

Ruth. And the gentlewoman loves you. But what luck this is, that Day's daughter should ever be with her, to spoil all!

Car. Not a whit, one way; I have a pretty room within, dark, and convenient.

Ruth. For what?

Car. For you and I to give counter-security for our kindness to one another.

Ruth. But Mr. Day's daughter will be there, too.

Car. 'Tis dark; we'll ne'er see her.

Ruth. You care not who you are wicked with. Methinks a prison shou'd tame you.

' *Car.* Why, d'ye think a prison takes away blood
' and sight? As long as I am so qualified, I am touch-
' wood; and whenever you bring fire, I shall fall a burn-
' ing.

' *Ruth.* And you wou'd quench it.

' *Car.* And you shall kindle it again.

' *Ruth.* No, you will be burnt out at last, burnt to a
' coal, black as dishonest love.'

Car. Is this your business? Did you come to disturb my contemplations with a sermon? Is this all?

Ruth. One thing more—I love you, it's true; but I love you honestly. If you know how to love me virtuously, I'll free you from prison, and run all fortunes with you.

Car. Yes, I cou'd love thee all manner of ways: ' if
' I cou'd not, freedom were no bait; were it from death,
' I shou'd despise your offer, to bargain for a·lie—'
But——

' *Ruth.* Oh noble!'—But what?

Car. The name of that rascal that got thee. Yet I lie too; he ne'er got a limb of thee. Pox on't! Thy mother was as unlucky to bear thee. But how shall we salve that? Take off but these incumbrances, and I'll purchase thee in thy smock; but to have such a flaw in my title——

Ruth. Can I help nature?

Car.

Car. Or I honour? Why, hark you now; do but
fwear me into a pretence; do but betray me with an
oath, that thou were not begot on the body of Gillian,
my father's kitchen-maid.

Ruth. Who's that;

Car. Why, the honourable Mrs. Day, that now is.

Ruth. Will you believe me if I fwear?

Car. Ay, that I will, though I know all the while
'tis not true.

Ruth. I fwear, then, by all that's good, I am not
their daughter.

Car. Poor, kind, perjur'd, pretty one, I am beholden to thee. Wou'dft damn thyfelf for me?

Ruth. You are miftaken. I have try'd you fully.
' You are noble, and I hope you love me. Be ever
' firm to virtuous principles.' My name is not fo godly a
one as Ruth, but plain Anne, daughter to Sir Bafil
Thorowgood; ' one, perhaps, that you have heard of,
' fince in the world he has ftill had fo loud and fair a cha-
' racter.' 'Tis too long to tell you how this Day got me,
an infant, and my eftate, into his power, and made me
pafs for his own daughter, ' my father dying when I was
' but two years old. This I knew but lately, by an un-
' expected meeting of an ancient fervant of my father's.'
But two hours fince, Arbella and I found an opportunity
of ftealing away all the writings that belong'd to my
eftate, and her compofition. In our flight we met your
friend, with whom I left her, as foon as I had intelligence
of your misfortune, to try to get your liberty ; which if
I can do, you have your eftate, for I have mine.

Car. Thou more than——

Ruth. No, no, no raptures at this time. Here's your
difguife, purchas'd from a true-hearted red-coat. ' Here
' is a bundle.' Let this line down when 'tis almoft dark,
and you fhall draw up a ladder of ropes. ' If the ladder of
' ropes be done fooner, I'll fend it by a foldier that I
' dare truft, and you may. Your window's large enough.'
As foon as you receive it, come down; ' if not, when
' 'tis dark, let down your line,' and at the bottom of the
window you fhall find yours, more than her own, not
Ruth, but Anne.

Car. I'll leap into thy arms——

Ruth.

Ruth. So you may break your neck. If you do, I'll jump too. But time steals on our words—Obferve all I told you. So, farewel.

Car. Nay, as the good fellows ufe to fay, let us not part with dry lips——One kifs.

Ruth. Not a bit of me, 'till I am all yours.

Car. Your hand, then, to fhew I am grown reafonable. A poor compounder.

Ruth. Pifh! there's a dirty glove upon't.——

' *Car.* Give me but any naked part, and I'll kifs it as
' a fnail creeps, and leave fign where my lips flid
' along——

' *Ruth.* Good fnail, get out of your hole firft; think
' think of your bufinefs. So, fare——'

Car. Nay, pr'ythee be not afhamed that thou are loth to leave me. 'Slid, I am a man; but I am as arrant a rogue as thy quondam father, Day, if I could not cry, to leave you a brace of minutes.

Ruth. Away! we grow foolifh—farewel—yet, be careful——Nay, go in.

Car. Do you go firft.

Ruth. Nay, fie, go in.

Car. We'll fairly, then, divide the victory, and draw off together.—So—I will have the laft look.

[Exeunt feverally, looking at one another.
Enter Col. Blunt, *and Soldier.*

Blunt. No more words. I do believe, nay, I know thou art honeft. I may live to thank thee better.

Sol. I fcorn any encouragement to love my king, or thofe that ferve him; I took pay under thefe people, with a defign to do him fervice. The lieutenant knows it.

Blunt. He has told me fo. No more words. Thou art a noble fellow. Thou art fure his window's large enough?

Sol. Fear it not.

Blunt. Here, then, carry him this ladder of ropes. So; now, give me the coat. Say' not a word to him, but bid him difpatch, when he fees the coaft clear. He fhall be waited for, at the bottom of his window. Give him thy fword, too, if he defires it.

Sol. I'll difpatch it inftantly; therefore get to your place. *[Exit.*
Blunt.

Blunt. I warrant ye.

Enter Teague.

Tea. Have you done every thing, then ? By my ſhoul, now, yonder is the man with the hard name; that man, now, that I made drunk for thee; Mr. Tay's raſcal. He is coming along there behind ; now, upon my ſhoul, that he is.

Blunt. The raſcal comes for ſome miſchief. Teague, now or never play the man.

Tea. How ſhould I be a man, then ?

Blunt. Thy maſter is never to be got out, if this rogue gets hither ; meet him therefore, Teague, in the moſt winning manner thou canſt, and make him once more drunk, and it ſhall be called the Second Edition of Obadiah, put forth with Iriſh notes upon him ; and if he will not go drink with thee——

Tea. I will carry him on my back, if he will not go ; and if he will not be drunk, I will cut his throat then, that I will, for my ſweet maſter now, that I will.

Blunt. Diſpatch, good Teague ; and diſpatch him too, if he will not be conformable ; and if thou canſt but once more be victorious, bring him in triumph to Lieutenant Story's, there ſhall be the general rendezvous. Now, or never, Teague.

Tea. I warrant you, I will get drink into his pate, or I will break it for him, that I will, I warrant you. He ſhall not come after you now. [*Exit.*

‘ *Blunt.* Good luck go with thee ! [*Exit* Teague.]
‘ The fellow's faithful and ſtout ; that fear's over. Now
‘ to my ſtation. [*Exit.*
‘ *Col.* Careleſs, *as in priſon.*
‘ *Car.* The time's almoſt come : how ſlow it flutters.
‘ My deſires are better winged. How I long to counter-
‘ feit a faintneſs when I come to the bottom, and ſink into
‘ the arms of this dear witty fair !——Ha, who's this ?
‘ *Enter Soldier.*
‘ *Sol.* Here, Sir, here's a ladder of ropes ; faſten it to
‘ your window, and deſcend : you ſhall be waited for.
‘ *Car.* The careful creature has ſent it—but, d'ye hear,
‘ Sir, could you not ſpare that implement by your ſide ?
‘ it might ſerve to keep off ſmall curs.

‘ *Sol.*

' *Sol.* You'll have no need on't, but there it is; make
' haste, the coast is clear.   [*Exit.*

' *Car.* O this pretty she captain general over my soul
' and body; the thought of her musters every faculty
' I have: she has sent the ropes, and stays for me; no
' dancer of the ropes ever slid down with that swiftness,
' or desire of haste, that I will make to thee.   [*Exit.*

' *Enter* Blunt *in his Soldier's Coat.*

' *Blunt.* All's quiet, and the coast clear; so far it goes
' well; that is the window; in this nook I'll stand, 'till
' I see him coming down.   [*Steps in.*

' *Col.* Careless *above, in his soldier's habit, lets down the*
' *ladder of ropes, and speaks.*

' *Car.* I cannot see my north star that I must sail by;
' 'tis clouded: perhaps she stands close in some corner;
' I'll not trifle time; all's clear. Fortune, forbear thy
' tricks, but for this small occasion.'

Enter Blunt *and* Careless.

Blunt. What's this? a soldier in the place of Careless?
I am betrayed, but I'll end this rascal's duty.

Car. How, a soldier!—Betray'd! this rascal shan't
laugh at me.   [*Both draw.*

Blunt. Dog.

Car. How, Blunt!

Blunt. Careless!

Car. You guess shrewdly. Plague, what contrivance
hath set you and I a tilting at one another?

Blunt. How the devil got you a soldier's habit?

Car. The same friend, for ought I know, that furnish'd
you—This kind gentlewoman is Ruth still. Ha, here
she is! I was just ready to be suspicious.

Enter Ruth.

Ruth. Who's there?

Car. Two notable charging red-coats.

Ruth. As I live, my heart is at my mouth.

Car. Pr'ythee, let it come to thy lips, that I may kiss
it. ' What have you in your lap?'

' *Ruth.* The ladder of ropes: ' how in the name
of wonder got you hither?

Car.

Car. Why, I had the ladder of ropes, and came down by it.

Blunt. Then the miſtake is plainer: 'twas I that ſent the ſoldier with the ropes.

Ruth. What an eſcape was this! Come, let's loſe no time; here's no place to explain matters in.

Car. I will ſtay to tell thee, I ſhall never deſerve thee.

Ruth. Tell me ſo when you have had me a little while. Come, follow me; ' put on your plaineſt garb; not ' like a dancing maſter, with your toes out. Come along. ' [Ruth *pulls their hats over their eyes.*] Hang down your ' head, as if you wanted pay.—So.   [*Exeunt.*

Enter Mr. Day, *Mrs.* Day, *and Mrs.* Chat.

Mrs. Day. Are you ſure of this, neighbour Chat?

Mrs. Ch. I'm as ſure of it, as I am that I have a noſe to my face.

Mrs. Day. Is my——

Mr. Day. Ay! is my——

Mrs. Day. You may give one leave, methinks, to aſk out one queſtion. Is my daughter Ruth with her?

Mrs. Ch. She was not, when I ſaw Mrs. Arbella laſt. I have not been ſo often at your honour's houſe, but that I know Mrs. Arbella, the rich heireſs, that Mr. Abel was to have had, good gentleman, if he has his due. They never ſuſpected me; for I uſed to buy things of my neighbour Story, before ſhe married the lieutenant; and ſtepping in to ſee Mrs. Story that now is, my neighbour Wiſh-well that was, I ſaw, as I told you, this very Mrs. Arbella; and I warrant Mrs. Ruth is not far off.

Mrs. Day. Let me adviſe then, huſband.

Mr. Day. Do, good duck; I'll warrant 'em——

Mrs. Day. You'll warrant, when I have done the buſineſs.

Mr. Day. I mean ſo, duck.

Mrs. Day. Well, pray ſpare your meaning too. Firſt then, we'll go ourſelves in perſon to this Story's houſe, in the mean time ſend Abel for ſoldiers; and when he has brought the ſoldiers, let them ſtay at the door, and come up himſelf; and then, if fair means will not do, foul ſhall.

Mr. Day. Excellent well adviſed, ſweet duck. Ah! et thee alone. Begone, Abel, and obſerve thy mo-
                          G   ther's

ther's direction. Remember the place. We'll be re-veng'd for robbing us, and for all their tricks.

Abel. I shall perform it.

Mrs. Day. Come along, neighbour, and shew us the best way; ' and by and by we shall have news from Oba-
' diah, who is gone to give the other colonel's gaoler
' a double charge, to keep the wild youth close. Come,
' husband, let's hasten.' Mrs. Chat, the state shall know what good service you have done.

Mrs. Chat. I thank your honour. [*Exeunt.*

Enter Arbella *and Lieutenant.*

Lieu. Pray, Madam, weep no more! spare your tears till you know they have miscarried.

' *Arb.* 'Tis a woman, Sir, that weeps: we want men's
' reasons, and their courage to practise with.

' *Lieu.* Look up, Madam, and meet your unexpected
' joys!'

Enter Ruth, Careless, *and* Blunt.

Arb. Oh, my dear friend! My dear, dear Ruth!

Car. Pray, none of these phlegmatic hugs. There, take your colonel; my captain and I can hug afresh every minute.

Ruth. When did we hug last, good soldier?

Car. I have done nothing but hug thee in fancy, ever since you Ruth turned Annice.

Arb. You are welcome, Sir: I cannot deny I shar'd in all your danger.

' *Lieu.* If she had deny'd it, colonel, I would have
' betrayed her.'

Blunt. I know not what to say, nor how to tell, how dearly, how well—I love you.

' *Arb.* Now can't I say I love him; yet I have a great
' mind to tell him too.

' *Ruth.* Keep't in and choak yourself, or get the
' rising of the lights.

' *Arb.* What shall I say?

' *Ruth.* Say something, or he'll vanish.

' *Blunt.* D'ye not believe I love you? Or can't you
' love me? Not a word.—Cou'd you——but'——

Arb. No more; I'll save you the labour of courtship, which should be too tedious to all plain and honest na-tures. It is enough; I know you love me.

Blunt.

Blunt. Or may I perish, whilst I am swearing it.
Enter Prentice.

Lieu. How now, Jack?

Boy. Oh, master, undone! Here's Mr. Day the committee-man, and his fierce wife, come into the shop. Mrs. Chat brought them in, and they say they will come up; they know that Mrs. Arbella, and their daughter Ruth, are here. Deny 'em if you dare, they say.

Lieu. Go down, boy, and tell 'em I'm coming to 'em. [*Exit Boy.*] ' This pure jade, my neighbour Chat, ' has betray'd us. What shall I do? I warrant the ras-' cal has soldiers at his heels. I think I could help the ' colonels out at a back door.

' *Blunt.* I'd die rather by my Arbella. Now you ' shall see I love you.

' *Car.* Nor will I Charles forsake you, Annice.'

Ruth. Come, be chearful; I'll defend you all against the assaults of captain Day, and major-general Day, his new drawn-up wife. Give me my ammunition, [*To Arbella.*] the papers, woman. So, if I do not rout 'em, fall on; let's all die together, and make no more graves but one.

Blunt. 'Slife, I love her now, for all she has jeer'd me so.

Ruth. ' Go fetch 'em in, lieutenant. [*Exit lieute-' nant.*]' Stand you all drawn up as my reserve—so—I for the forlorn hope.

' *Car.* That we had Teague here!' to quarrel with ' the female triumphing Day, whilst I threw the male ' Day out of the window. Hark, I hear the troop march-' ing; I know the she Day's stamp, among the tramples ' of a regiment.'

Arb. They come, wench; charge 'em bravely; I'll second thee with a volley.

Ruth. They'll not stand the first charge, fear not; now the Day breaks.

Car. Wou'd 'twere his neck were broke.
Enter Mr. Day, and Mrs. Day.

Mrs. Day. Ah, ha! My fine run-aways, have I found you? What, you think my husband's honour lives without intelligence. Marry, come up.

Mr.

Mr. Day. My duck tells you how.'tis—We—

Mrs. Day. Why then let your duck tell 'em how 'tis; yet, as I was saying, you shall perceive we abound in intelligence: else 'twere not for us to go about to keep the nation quiet; but if you, Mrs. Arbella, will deliver up what you have stolen, and submit, and return with us, and this ungracious Ruth——

Ruth. Anne, if you please.

Mrs. Day. Who gave you that name, pray?

Ruth. My god-fathers and god-mothers;——on, forsooth, I can answer a leaf farther.

Mr. Day. Duck, good duck, a word: I do not like this name Annice.

Mrs. Day. You are ever in a fright, with a shrivell'd heart of your own.—Well, gentlewoman, you are merry.

Arb. As newly come out of our wardships. I hope Mr. Abel is well.

Mrs. Day. Yes, he is well; you shall see him presently; yes, you shall see him.

Car. That is, with mirmidons. Come, good Anne, no more delay, fall on.

Ruth. Then, before the furious Abel approaches with his red-coats, who perhaps are now marching under the conduct of that expert captain in weighty matters, know the articles of our treaty are only these: this Arbella' will keep her estate and not marry Abel, but this gentleman; and I Anne, daughter to Sir Basil Thorowgood, and not Ruth, as has been thought, have taken my own estate, together with this gentleman, for better for worse. We were modest, though thieves, only plundered our own.

Mrs. Day. Yes, gentlewoman, you took something else, and that my husband can prove; it may cost you your necks, if you do not submit.

Ruth. Truth on't is, we did take something else.

Mrs. Day. Oh, did you so?

Ruth. Pray give me leave to speak one word in private with my father Day?

Mrs. Day. Do so, do so; are you going to compound? Oh, 'tis father Day, now!

Ruth. D'ye hear, Sir; how long is't since you have practis'd physic?　　　　　　　　　　*[Takes him aside.*

Mrs.

Mr. Day. Phyfic! What d'ye mean?

Ruth I mean phyfic. Look ye, here's a fmall pre-
fcription of yours. D'ye know this hand-writing?

Mr. Day. I am undone.

Ruth. Here's another upon the fame fubject. This
young one, I believe, came into this wicked world for
want of your preventing dofe; it will not be taken now
neither. It feems your wenches are wilful: nay, I do
not wonder to fee 'em have more confcience than you
have.

Mr. Day. Peace, good Mrs. Anne! I am undone, if
you betray me.

Enter Abel, *goes to his father.*

Abel. The foldiers are come.

Mr. Day. Go and fend 'em away, Abel; here's no
need, no need, now.

Mrs. Day. Are the foldiers come, Abel?

Abel. Yes, but my father biddeth me fend them away.

Mr. Day. No, not without your opinion, duck; but
fince they have but their own, I think, duck, if we were
all friends————

Mrs. Day. Oh, are you at your *ifs* again? D'you
think they fhall make a fool of me, though they make an
afs of you? Call 'em up, Abel, if they will not fubmit;
call up the foldiers, Abel.

Ruth. Why, your fierce honour fhall know the bufinefs that makes the wife Mr. Day, inclinable to friendfhip.

Mr. Day. Nay, good fweet-heart, come, I pray let
us be friends.

Mrs. Day. How's this! What, am I not fit to be
trufted now? Have you built your credit and reputation
upon my counfel and labours, and am I not fit now to
be trufted?

Mr. Day. Nay, good fweet duck, I confefs I owe all
to thy wifdom. Good gentlemen, perfuade my duck,
that we may be all friends.

Car. Hark you, good Gillian Day, be not fo fierce
upon the hufband of thy bofom; 'twas but a fmall ftart
of frailty: fay it were a wench, or fo?

Ruth. As I live, he has hit upon't by chance. Now
we fhall have fport. [*Afide.*

Mrs.

Mrs. Day. How, a wench, a wench! Out upon the hypocrite. A wench! Was not I fufficient? A wench! I'll be revengd, let him be afhamed if he will; call the foldiers, Abel.

' *Car.* Stay, good Abel; march not off fo haftily.'

Arb. Soft, gentle Abel, or I'll difcover, you are in bonds; you fhall never be releas'd, if you move a ftep.

Ruth. D'ye hear, Mrs. Day, be not fo furious, hold your peace: you may divulge your hufband's fhame, if you are fo fimple, and caft him out of authority; nay and have him try'd for his life: read this. Remember too, I know of your bribery and cheating, and fome-thing elfe: you guefs. Be friends, and forgive one another. Here's a letter counterfeited from the king, to beftow preferment upon Mr. Day, if he would turn honeft; by which means, I fuppofe, you cozen'd your brother cheats; in which he was to remember his fer-vice to you. I believe 'twas your indicting. You are the committee-man. 'Tis your beft way, (nay, never demur) to kifs and be friends.' Now, if you can con-trive handfomely to cozen thofe that cozen all the world, and get thefe gentlemen to come by their eftates eafily, and without taking the covenant, the old fum of five hundred pounds, that I ufed to talk of, fhall be yours yet.

Mrs. Day. We will endeavour.

Ruth. Come, Mrs. Arbella, pray let's all be friends.

Arb. With all my heart.

Ruth. Brother Abel, the bird is flown; but you fhall be releafed from your bonds.

Abel. I bear my afflictions as I may.

Enter Teague, *leading* Obadiah *in a halter, and a Mufician.*

Tea. What is this now? Who are you? Well, are not you Mrs. Tay? Well, I will tell her what I fhould fay now! Shall I then? I will try if I cannot laugh too, as I did, or think of the muftard pot.

Car. No, good Teague, there's no need of thy mef-fage now: but why doft thou lead Obadiah thus?

Tea. Well, I will hang him prefently, that I will. Look you here, Mrs. Tay, here's your man Obadiah,

do

do you see? he would not let me make him drunk, so I did take him in this string, and I am going to choak him by the throat.

Blunt. Honest Teague, thy master is beholden to thee, in some measure, for his liberty.

Car. Teague, I shall requite thy honesty.

Tea. Well, shall I hang him then? It is a rogue now, who wou'd not be drunk for the king.

Obad. I do beseech you, gentlemen, let me not be brought unto death.

Tea. You shall be brought to the gallows, you thief o'the world.

Car. No, poor Teague, 'tis enough; we are all friends. Come, let him go.

Tea. Are you all friends? Then here, little Obid, take the string, and go and hang yourself.

' *Car.* D'ye hear my friend,   [*To the Musician.*]
' is any of your companions with you?

' *Muf.* Yes, Sir.

' *Car.* As I live, we'll all dance; it shall be the cele-
' bration of our weddings. Nay, Mr. Day, as we hope
' to continue friends, you and your duck shall trip it too.

' *Tea.* Ay, by my shoul will we; Obadiah shall be
' my woman too, and you shall dance for the king, that
' you shall.

' *Car.* Go, and strike up then.—No chiding now, Mrs.
' Day. Come, you must not be refractory for once. '

Mrs. Day. Well, husband, since these gentlemen will
' have it so, and that they may perceive we are friends,
' dance.

' *Blunt.* Now, Mr. Day, to your business; get it
' done as soon as you will, the five hundred pounds shall
' be ready.

Car. ' So, friends;' thanks, honest Teague; thou shalt flourish in a new livery for this. Now, Mrs. An-nice, I hope you and I may agree about kissing, and compound every way. Now, Mr. Day,

If you will have good luck in every thing,
Turn cavalier, and cry, God bless the king.

        [*Exeunt.*

END OF THE FIFTH ACT.

EPI-

E P I L O G U E.

BUT now the greatest thing is left to do,
    More just Committee, to compound with you;
For, till your equal censures shall be known,
The poet's under sequestration:
He has no title to his small estate
Of wit, unless you please to set the rate.
Accept this half year's purchase of his wit,
For in the compass of that time 'twas writ:
Not that this is enough; he'll pay you more,
If you yourselves believe him not too poor:
For 'tis your judgments give him wealth: in this,
He's just as rich as you believe he is.
    Wou'd all Committees cou'd have done like you,
    Made men more rich, and by their payments too.

www.ingramcontent.com/pod-product-compliance
Lightning Source LLC
Chambersburg PA
CBHW021528110726
47902CB00004B/792